THE
LAND OF OUR DREAMS

THE
LAND OF OUR DREAMS

Nancy Livingston

St. Martin's Press
New York

All characters in this publication are fictitious and
any resemblance to real persons, living or dead,
is purely coincidental.

THE LAND OF OUR DREAMS. Copyright © 1988 by Nancy Livingston. All rights
reserved. Printed in the United States of America. No part of this book may be
used or reproduced in any manner whatsoever without written permission except
in the case of brief quotations embodied in critical articles or reviews. For information, address St. Martin's Press, 175 Fifth Avenue, New York, N.Y. 10010.

Library of Congress Cataloging-in-Publication Data

Livingston, Nancy.
    The land of our dreams / Nancy Livingston
        p.   cm.
    ISBN 0-312-03374-5
    I. Title.
PR6062.I915L36   1989
823′.914—dc20
                                      89-34833
                                      CIP

First published in Great Britain by Macdonald & Co. (Publishers) Ltd.

BOMC offers recordings and compact discs, cassettes
and records. For information and catalog write to
BOMR, Camp Hill, PA 17012.

*To the memory of Harry Woolsey,
scholar, eccentric and loving father,
with deep affection.*

Acknowledgments

My grateful thanks once again to:
Mrs. C. Copeland, Senior Assistant, Darlington Reference
Library and to Miss Anita Ward, Darlington Reference
Library.

I would also like to thank Mrs Jean Baillis for the loan of her
grandfather's privately printed memoir 'A Stretcher Bearer's
Diary' by J.H. Newton. His experiences together with others
on public record written by men who served with field
ambulances rather than fight during World War I, formed
the basis of part of this fictional book. I honour the memory
of brave men.

McKie Family Tree

Alex McKie m Jeannie in 1869

John McKie (born 1870) m Mary Hamilton (1876-1918)

One stillborn son

Luke (1895)

Beatrice (dec'd) sister to Adelaide Armitage

(no issue)

Joseph Forrest m Jane
(both dec'd)

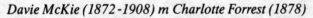

Davie McKie (1872 - 1908) m Charlotte Forrest (1878)

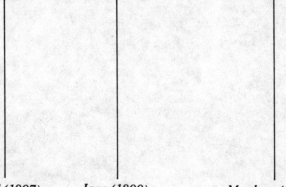

Ted (1897)   *Jane (1899)*   *Matthew (1901)*

Contents

CHAPTER ONE

The Return

The tall dark-haired youth hurried across the cobbled yard, past the stables and in through the back door. 'Hallo? It's me, I'm back.' He didn't really expect to find anyone; commercial travellers lurked in this part of the Emporium during the evenings. Nevertheless his disappointment increased. First the empty station platform, now this. After his first term away at Newcastle University, Luke McKie had been hoping for a warmer welcome.

He'd developed a nervous habit of twitching at his sleeves to hide the bony wrists. He did so now before tapping on the frosted glass door. 'Father . . .?' The office was empty. Familiar smells were a comfort, though. Luke was glad these hadn't changed. The old roll-top desk stacked with samples, catalogues on the shelves, every item had a familiar odour — he could have found his way blindfold. The most unmistakable smell of all wafted up as he stood there; polished linoleum. He remembered that from the day he first learned to crawl.

There was one change. Looking for the old rag rug, he saw the stove had disappeared. In its place was a gas fire. Profits must be improving — or was it Mother? Luke grinned and the adult veneer he'd tried so hard to cultivate disappeared, leaving him idiotically happy. Fancy Mother bullying Father into an extravagance — unbelievable!

Suddenly he couldn't bear the loneliness any longer. He raced along the passage. The lift with his mother's chair was at the bottom of the shaft. Luke tugged the doors shut, hauled on the ropes and shot up like a rocket into the kitchen above.

13

Emily Beal screamed. Her mother dropped a ladle.

'Help!'

'It's all right, Mrs Beal, it's only me —'

'Gawd, I thought you were too old for that trick nowadays!' Mrs Beal clutched the roll of fat that concealed her heart. 'Eee, but I'm glad to see you, pet. Where's your mother?' Luke gazed at her blankly. 'Don't say you missed them at the station? Your dad will be upset. They were meeting your aunt as well, you see.'

'Ah!'

'She was coming back from Harrogate.'

'Maybe her train was late?'

'Go downstairs,' Mrs Beal ordered, 'Mrs Armitage can give you a cup of tea while we send word to tell them what's happened. Emily — find our Billy. He's to go to the station at once —'

'He's out delivering, Ma.'

'So he is, drat it!' Mrs Beal, who had come to 'help out' temporarily seventeen years previously, soon became hot and bothered.

'Don't worry,' Luke soothed, 'I'm home and they'll be back. Let's enjoy the peace before Ted arrives. I don't suppose he's changed?'

'Go and see Mrs Armitage,' Mrs Beal begged. 'You've got to have someone welcome you.'

'You already have, splendidly.' To Mrs Beal's astonishment, Luke hugged her, pinny and all. 'It's good to be home!' Despite her agitation, she blinked. My word, he'd grown handsome! A good job he didn't kiss Emily as well — she could act real daffy sometimes. All the same, Master Luke was far too thin.

'Emily, find that seed-cake. Mrs Armitage only nibbles little scones with her tea. This young man needs fattening up.'

With three hefty slices, Luke went to Mrs Armitage via the shop. The Emporium was busy with Christmas so near. Luke threaded his way through crowds of females buying unsuitable neckwear for their husbands and brothers in Gentlemens' Sundries. The Ladies' department was full of similarly disposed young gentlemen attempting to

14

describe undergarments. Haberdashery, Notions and Household Linens were, by comparison, fairly quiet.

Luke acknowledged greetings shyly. Like his father he found the social aspect of shop-keeping a trial but nervousness faded as he looked about; everywhere paintwork was fresh, glass, brass and mahogany shone. No hint of scrimping here. There was even a new colour scheme: rich paisley shades of red and blue that brought a glow to the December afternoon. 'Nothing but the Best' was the maxim by which John McKie conducted his life and his business.

Luke's own prospects depended so much on McKie Bros.' success. He hadn't yet decided which branch of medicine to follow — it was all too new and exciting — but whatever it turned out to be he would need money.

Destined for medicine since the day he was born, the choice of career and name had been bestowed by John as he held the baby in his arms. Mary McKie had repeated the story so often, her son sometimes fancied he could remember the actual words being spoken: 'Your father said you were to be a doctor and your name was Luke.'

Oddly enough, Luke hadn't needed further persuasion, perhaps because he'd heard of John's thwarted ambitions with equal frequency. Born on one of the poorest of crofts in Western Argyll, John and Davie McKie had been well educated thanks to their father's heroic efforts yet neither had been to university. 'There wasn't enough money . . .' It was a refrain which haunted Luke.

Today gold, silver and banknotes flowed along overhead wires to the cage where two lady cashiers emptied the small leather buckets. As he watched, Luke became conscious of whispers — 'That's Mr McKie's son back from medical school,' — and tried not to quicken his pace. He'd come this way deliberately to see how things were.

He reached the holy of holies, the delicate pink and blue *Salon de Thé* where Darlington ladies sat on elegant gold chairs, gravely contemplating further extravagance. Acknowledging salutes from one or two, Luke went through the pass-door into Mrs Armitage's apartment.

Submitting to her tearful kisses and cries of delight it occurred to him that theirs was an eccentric family composed of few relatives but many more whose lives had simply come together.

Mrs Armitage, stout, Victorian, was aunt to Charlotte, Davie McKie's widow, and 'great-aunt' to everyone else by virtue of affection. Certainly she smothered them equally with love. One mottled hand clutched the jet-embroidered *front* she always wore. Even as he returned her embrace Luke found himself noticing the age freckles on her skin as well as her breathlessness. How old was Mrs Armitage? Over seventy at least. He'd have to ask Father.

She hadn't changed in one particular. As soon as her eyes lighted on the seed-cake, she cried joyfully, 'Oh, how kind of Mrs Beal! Bertha, two more plates.' And that was another member of his 'family'. Tall and buxom, Manageress of the Salon as well as companion to the old lady, Bertha had taken time off this afternoon to welcome him home.

Luke stretched out indolently in front of the fire. It was so pleasant to let them spoil him! 'I managed to miss everyone at the station. They were too busy meeting Aunt Charlotte.'

Appalled by his disappointment, Mrs Armitage heaped more jam on his scones and Bertha topped up his tea. Luke protested, but only feebly. After the cold comfort of student lodgings a little luxury was most acceptable.

Their chatter rose and fell making him drowsy. Bertha piled on more coals and pushed the cushions behind his head. Yesterday, chilled to the bone, Luke had managed to stay awake because he'd been fascinated by anatomy. Today, overcome by cake, jam and affection, his eyelids drooped.

'We'll let him sleep,' Mrs Armitage whispered, 'His brain must be tired after all that exertion. Remind me to order a jar of beef tea next time we're out, Bertha, to build up his strength.'

Young Ted McKie never entered a room, he erupted, demolishing peace and quiet. He hurled himself at Luke, carroty hair ablaze, 'What happened to you? We looked everywhere! Have you cut anyone's leg off? Mama was so angry we'd missed you, she complained to the Station Master —'

Jane followed, close on her brother's heels, 'Luke? Oh, there you are! I'm so glad you're back!' Behind, in more stately fashion came their mother, Charlotte, who never hurried.

'Aunt Armitage . . . how are you?'

'Dear, dear Charlotte — how splendid to have you home again. And all the children!' Mrs Armitage was easily overwhelmed.

'How are you, Luke?' Charlotte had raised her veil so that he could kiss her cheek. Luke ducked under the enormous brim; one had to be extremely careful with Charlotte McKie's hats. Close to she examined him critically. 'You have grown, Luke, but you're very pale. Are you quite sure you're well?'

'Very, thank you, Aunt. Will you excuse me? I must find Mother, I haven't seen her yet.'

'I think she went to speak to Mrs Beal. Ted, Jane, come back at once —' but they'd disappeared like puppies after their master leaving only Matthew, who'd sidled in on his own. The youngest of Charlotte and Davie McKie's children, Matthew spotted the one remaining scone and helped himself without being invited. Bertha stared, so that he should know she'd seen him. Mrs Armitage strove to keep warmth in her smile because she believed all children should be loved. His mother ignored him altogether.

Mary was eager to see her son but she held back. Too many people and Mrs Armitage would need recourse to smelling salts. She forced herself to stay where she was, in the kitchen. Noisy chatter made her look up. 'Luke?'

He embraced her eagerly, 'Yes, I'm home. Three whole weeks — think of that!'

'You're taller!' She couldn't keep the surprise out of her voice.

'I know! It's dreadful so late in life. Makes a fellow feel stupid to find his trousers are all too short.'

Ted flung himself on the floor, yanking at the serge, 'I'll help. Undo your braces!' Jane grabbed her brother's arm.

'Let him go, let go at once!'

Luke raised his voice above the babel. 'Where's Father?'

17

'Waiting downstairs,' Mary shouted back. 'I'm sorry we missed you.'

The fledgling medical man remembered she'd been standing in the damp December cold and led her to a chair. She limped heavily but that was often worse in winter, too. 'I won't be long. Mrs Beal, see she doesn't stir if you please and I'd suggest hot tea.'

Turning, he almost tripped over the wrestlers on the floor; Jane was trying to save her plaits. '*Edward . . .!*'

Ted looked up open-mouthed. 'No-one calls me that!'

'*I* shall in future if you cannot behave. Gentlemen do not interfere with ladies' coiffures.' He offered Jane a hand and pulled her upright. She looked extremely pink.

'Luke, I've missed you ever so!'

'And I've missed you.' He printed a kiss on the palm and wrapped her fingers round it. 'That's on account, 'til I get back. Father must be wondering what's happened.'

He left and Mrs Beal took charge. 'Ted, Jane — outside. Go and bother someone else.' Mary made as if to move. 'No, stay where you are, Mrs McKie. Do what Master Luke tells you for a change. After all, he should know what he's talking about.'

John McKie fidgeted. Thank God things were a little easier. This Christmas they were almost clear of debt — maybe in another twelve-month . . .? But he wouldn't trouble Luke with that, not today. The boy had completed his first term at university. It was a moment John had been anticipating for years.

He tried to interest himself with the pile of charity appeals, more than ever this year because of the slump. It wasn't surprising when wholesale prices had risen astronomically during 1912. John began pencilling in the amounts he would send and did not hear the click of the door.

How like Father not to switch on the light, thought Luke. If there was a way of saving money he would find it, but it was straining his eyes to work in the gloom. He pressed the switch.

The light showed naked love in John's eyes. For a moment Luke wondered if his father had been expecting Mary rather than himself? Then the bakelite shade 'popped' with the heat and broke the tension.

'Now *that's* something I've missed. I never noticed it before but it tells me I'm home. How are you, Father?' Luke exhibited the same shy hesitancy he'd learned from John.

'Luke . . .!' The handshake developed into a hug, 'Never mind me, what about you?'

His voice would never be completely English because of the Gaelic rhythms; with a spare figure and slightly gaunt face with neat mousy hair, John McKie was only forty-two but life had printed more years on him than that.

Luke recovered first. 'Well, Father, according to received opinion, I've grown, I'm thin and, worst of all, Aunt Charlotte declares I'm too pale. No doubt she's even now soaking senna pods to dose me with tomorrow!'

'Do what we all do, flush them away,' said John firmly, 'Now, tell me, how d'you find Newcastle? Is it up to expectation?'

'Oh, yes!' Luke laughed again, at his own enthusiasm. 'I haven't dismembered anyone, much to Ted's disappointment, but Father — that infirmary . . . what they manage to do with such sick people. If only their stamina were greater, even more could be cured!'

John McKie drank it all in. If it was vicarious, Luke would forgive. All those dreams! This time there'd be no mistake: nothing would prevent *his* son becoming a doctor. He listened as Luke talked himself hoarse. The quiet reserve had disappeared and the grey eyes were animated. Outside, the winter dusk grew thick but neither of them noticed. The supper gong took both by surprise.

'Good heavens — that late? Be extremely careful what you say in front of Charlotte, my boy. She might be offended by medical talk, especially anything "unsuitable".'

'I shall be discretion itself, never fear. How's business? I thought everywhere looked particularly spick and span this afternoon. The Christmas rush has obviously begun.' Reading between the cautious phrases of his father's answer, Luke knew the signs were good.

Upstairs, every seat at the large oval dining table was occupied. When they had first begun in business, the McKie

19

brothers declared they would provide all their employees with three meals a day. For John it was a matter of principle. *His* apprentices wouldn't be grey-faced and faint at the end of twelve hours having dined on nothing but bread and butter. It was even more satisfying, after all these years, to realize how many had chosen to stay in his employ.

Tonight, Charlotte was back in her usual place, facing John at the head of the table. She'd never been challenged for that seat, Mary McKie preferring to stay in the kitchen from where she could supervise the food. On either side of Charlotte were her children and beyond, facing one another across the board, the male and female counter-hands. John had Luke beside him.

When everyone was ready, Charlotte's gaze lighted on Ted. 'You may say grace.' He did not dare refuse. Jane held her breath. With Matthew home from boarding school and inclined to pinch, Ted might come a cropper.

'For - what - we - are - about - to - receive - may - the - Lord - make - us - truly - thankful - Amen.' It made a tidal wave across his soup. His mother frowned but lifted her spoon to signify everyone should begin.

Luke was weary. Yesterday, he had been alone in Jesmond; today, the centre of attention, face tight with constant smiling, he could almost wish himself back in Newcastle. Sensitive to his mood, John switched attention away from their end of the table.

'May I compliment you, Charlotte. We can all see that Harrogate has conferred its healthful benefits once more.'

'Thank you, Mr McKie,' She was never less than formal when assistants were present, 'I'm gratified to find myself completely refreshed.'

'And the hats, Mrs Davie? How were they in Harrogate this season?' It wasn't an idle question; fashion was a serious business. Charlotte began to describe headgear to a rapt audience. John relaxed; he and Luke could converse in peace.

Jane watched dreamily. To have Luke home! So grown-up these days, not a bit like Ted. Would he consent to accompany her to the Creswells' party or — horrors! — would he consider it beneath his dignity? Mama considered Ted a suitable partner; Jane disagreed. Ted frequently humiliated his sister in front of her friends. He never danced if he could avoid it, preferring instead to pick fights with other boys. Jane had suggested, daringly, that they might have a party of their own this Christmas but Mama had frowned and said it was far too soon, which made Jane feel rotten. Four years was long enough to wait when you were thirteen.

In her room after supper, she examined her collection of Christmas presents. Threepence a week didn't stretch very far. Fortunately she'd managed to appliqué felt kettle-holders for Emily and Mrs Beal, make an apron for Bertha and embroider handkerchieves. The hemming wasn't all it might be — it was amazing how fingermarks appeared out of nowhere. Oh, bother! She hadn't noticed the spots of blood. That handkerchief would have to go to great-aunt Armitage who could be relied on not to notice. Jane sighed massively. It had to be admitted, the only sewing she really enjoyed was attaching ribbons to new ballet shoes.

She would tie the packages in tinsel and decorate them with gold and silver bells — Father had once shown her how. Jane bit her lip; no more tears, not this time. She cried every year on his birthday and on that other, terrible anniversary. Luke understood. He brought her tea when it was time to wash her face and come downstairs. Well, Luke wouldn't always be there: one term at university had taught her that much.

She lifted the tissue from the last, most precious gift. Her brothers were to have mufflers but Luke's present was extra special: evening gloves of soft creamy kid. Mr Hart, Uncle John's deputy in the Emporium, had executed her order personally. Even the jap silk lining smelled luxurious; Jane took a great glorious sniff at it. Mr Hart had confided there were few Englishmen who possessed gloves like these, apart from King George. Queen Mary gave him a pair every Christmas. Father had always given mother beautiful gloves, to show how much he loved her. Would Luke understand the significance?

Four shillings and eightpence! Jane had raided her dancing lesson money. She was suddenly filled with fore-boding; suppose Luke didn't like the gloves? They could

21

turn out to be the most expensive mistake she'd ever made!

'There's an interesting debate tonight, I wondered if you'd care to come as my guest?'

The implication couldn't be ignored: to attend the Debating Society was to participate in the intellectual life of Darlington but all Luke yearned for was to crawl into a warm bed. He swallowed a yawn.

'Thanks very much, Father. I'd be honoured. What's the subject this evening?'

'The Irish question.'

Oh, lord! How could a chap be expected to stay awake through that?

'If Gladstone is to be believed, it could mean civil war. Do you ever discuss the possibility at university?'

'I'm afraid not, no.' He could see John was disappointed. 'There is one chap in his second year, called Kessel. He's older than the rest of us. I've heard him discussing religious intolerance. His father was from an Austrian Lutheran family originally, his mother's a catholic. I think it helps Kessel see both points of view. Otherwise, I'm afraid most of us don't concern ourselves with politics.'

'It's not a popular subject.' John was grave, 'Poor Mr Kessel. How unfortunate to have parents of mixed faith but from what I read, the situation in Ireland is so serious we may soon become involved whether we wish it or not.'

The evening stretched inexorably ahead. On their way out Luke slipped into the kitchen to bid his mother goodnight. Mary pushed a paper bag into his hand. 'Here . . .'

'Peppermints?'

'Very strong ones. Charlotte confiscated them from Ted. I thought they might help you stay awake. Try, for your father's sake. He's so proud to be taking you tonight.'

'I know. Thanks for the stimulant. I'll buy Ted some bull's-eyes to make up.' He kissed her. 'Don't wait up, we'll probably be late.'

'Nonsense! When you're only home for two weeks?' *And how often will I see you once you're qualified*, Luke read in her eyes.

'All right,' he said awkwardly, 'I'll see you when we get back.'

Despite the December rain, Luke modified his stride to suit John's pace. He'd got into the habit of walking briskly; that way he was always warm by the time he reached his lodgings. With his coat on and a blanket over his knees, the first few hours of study were almost tolerable.

As he followed his father into the brightly-lit institute, Luke found himself thinking about Kessel. *He'd* probably enjoy the discussion this evening, even understand the Irish question. Luke popped the first sweet into his mouth. Concentrate and he might learn something himself.

They joined a throng divesting themselves of their coats and the sight cheered John immensely. 'The chairman will have his work cut out. Everyone wants to join in tonight. I've prepared one or two apposite remarks myself. Should the opportunity arise, I may use them . . .' Luke transferred the rest of the peppermints to his jacket pocket.

Charlotte McKie was restless. After so much excitement Mrs Armitage had retired to her bed. Bertha was attending the Dorcas Society and Charlotte was left with no other prospect than a book. Without Davie to read aloud and bring it to life, it failed to satisfy.

Tonight she'd seen John's arm round Mary's shoulders. No-one would ever comfort her as tenderly. Charlotte sat straighter in her chair. Appearances were what mattered; to exhibit weakness even in private was in her opinion an insult to her husband's memory.

She shut the book — it wasn't nearly as promising as the cover suggested — and went in search of Mary to alleviate her ennui. 'Surely Luke's linen can wait until morning?'

'The bag-wash has to be ready early, Charlotte, because of Christmas.'

'At this time of an evening you really must stop working — for the sake of your health.'

Oh dear, thought Mary, she's bored already. 'Would you like Emily to make us some tea?'

'Ask her to bring it to my parlour.'

It was the most elegant of all the family rooms. Mary sat obediently on an upholstered armchair with its matching footstool.

'That's much better,' Charlotte was complacent, having achieved her objective, 'Upstairs I noticed the dark patches under your eyes. Too much stooping over Luke's box.'

'Yes, dear.'

Charlotte adjusted the new high-waisted gown. Skirts were so much narrower this season, there was an ever-present danger one's ankles might show. 'A Grecian look has returned, had you noticed?'

'Not for me.'

Charlotte frowned. 'It is up to both of us to set an example, Mary. We cannot afford to ignore modern styles if we are to be an advertisement. We must be Darlington's leaders of fashion.'

How like Charlotte to justify her fondness for clothes! Mary hid a smile. 'You, perhaps. Or Jane. She has grown most attractive, I have heard several customers remark on it. Will you permit her to put up her hair this season?'

'Goodness, no!' Her mother's reaction was swift, 'She's far too young.' There was a pause. 'It's too bad . . . Luke disappearing on my first evening. I wanted to hear about medical school.'

'Tomorrow morning,' Mary promised, 'At breakfast, Luke can give you a full report.'

'It's awfully dull, after Harrogate. Evenings at the Old Swan were much more agreeable.'

Mary replied swiftly without thinking. 'For me this is the most perfect part of the day. Everything done, everyone fed and the rest of the evening to do just as I please.'

Charlotte was shocked. 'But how monotonous! You must have more variety, Mary. I shall speak to Mr McKie the moment he returns.'

'Please, Charlotte, I'm perfectly satisfied with the way things are. I like to be alone with my thoughts, occasionally.'

Charlotte remained suspicious. 'Why should John always be the one to go out and enjoy himself?' Another thought occurred to her. 'Mary,' she burst out tactlessly, 'John hasn't found — Another? Not like Miss Crowther?'

'Certainly not.' Shaken, Mary managed to keep her temper, 'Pray don't excite yourself, Charlotte. Nothing like that happened while you've been away, nor will it. Now, you stay here and I'll find out what's happened to our tea.'

'I'll come with you.' Complete boredom for Charlotte meant being alone with nothing but her thoughts to distract her.

The wind was even colder and the rain had turned to sleet as father and son trudged back. Luke hung his coat on the usual peg by the kitchen range. He was aching for a bath and bed but there was a tray on the table. He lifted the cover: a great wedge of meat pie! Saliva filled his mouth.

'Ah, you're back,' Mary hurried in, 'I've just told John to change his shoes — see that you do the same.'

'Yes, Mother.' He nearly laughed. No-one had bullied him about wet shoes for weeks!

'Take your tray downstairs and join him.'

'All right.' He was reluctant, preferring to stay in the warm.

'I lit the gas fire earlier,' she smiled.

Were his thoughts so transparent? When I'm qualified, Luke promised himself, I'm going to have a fine house with a boiler: no draughts, and steaming hot baths full to the brim whenever I want them. Stumbling with tiredness he carried his tray into the lift.

The office was as cosy as she'd promised. Not only that, his father was pouring two drams of whisky. *My word!* thought Luke.

'Your uncle once persuaded me this would help me relax. I've kept up the habit — one tot, at bedtime. I wondered if you'd care to join me?'

'Thank you very much . . .' First the debate, now this; he was part of Man's Estate tonight all right! 'Would you like a piece of this pie? Mother's given me an enormous helping.'

'No, no. You eat it.' John watched it disappear with no trouble at all. 'First thing tomorrow, you must call on Dr Cullen. He asked most particularly that you should.'

'Mother's already promised me to Aunt Charlotte.'

25

'Hang your aunt! Cullen will be looking for a partner one of these days.'

'Oh, Father!'

'Think ahead, that's always been my motto.'

'Yes, but . . .' Luke knew very well what his father and Cullen were hoping for but he was tired. 'It's a little early to decide about general practice.'

'I know. Old men's dreams, Luke. Cullen and I . . . Well, you know how we've talked of it as a possibility.'

'You're not old! And I will go and see him,' Luke promised, 'before Aunt Charlotte gets up. There are lots of things I want to discuss.'

'That talk tonight, of a possible Irish rebellion . . . it's been colouring my thoughts,' John said slowly, 'Making me anxious for all of you.'

'Has Ted had any ideas for a career yet?'

John looked stern. 'None. We've heard no more about joining the Army, thank heavens. For a while he wanted to be a professional boxer, then it was an engineer.'

Luke sipped reflectively. 'That might not be such a bad idea. Ted's good with mechanical things.'

'Yes, but I want him in the Emporium to keep an eye on Matthew!' Luke sighed; the thorn in everyone's flesh. He changed the subject.

'What of Jane? Has Aunt Charlotte relented?'

John shook his head. 'Your aunt is adamant Jane cannot become a dancer. She wants her to stay at home and declares she cannot manage without her.'

'Oh, what rubbish! Forgive me for being rude, but it is, Father. A complete waste of a life.'

'I know.' John was quiet. Luke disturbed him occasionally, with these sudden flashes of authority.

'When Jane is ready, we must simply tell Aunt Charlotte not to be so selfish.'

'Quite,' John agreed drily. And who would bell the cat? It would take more than a dram of whisky to give *him* sufficient courage.

CHAPTER TWO

Sweet and Bitter

It had been freezing during the night. Jane's eiderdown was pulled tight under her chin. Frost flowers were so thick inside her window that each pane now had an individual panel of icy lace through which the street lamp shone dimly. Under the blankets it was warm but once she threw back the covers? Jane shivered. Please, dear Lord Jesus, don't let me have chilblains, not before the concert!

She heard Aunt Mary go downstairs. Katriona was next, with one of the apprentices. Familiar sounds began: someone raking out the kitchen range, the clank of the iron doors as pans of porridge were lifted out of the oven.

Jane was eager to hear other footsteps. When they went past, she bounded out of bed and grabbed her dressing-gown. It was short and the sleeves had been patched but what didn't show didn't matter. She pulled the cord tight, shivering as she pushed her feet into slippers. Brushing her hair fiercely, she hurried downstairs after Luke.

He'd already shaved and was eating his breakfast. Jane tried to slip unnoticed onto a stool opposite. She ignored Aunt Mary's raised eyebrows and perched, quiet as a mouse.

'Good morning,' said Luke, 'You're up early, aren't you?' Jane stared at the table top. Why wouldn't Aunt Mary go away!

Luke looked questioningly but his mother shrugged and went on with preparing fourteen breakfasts. Billy Beal came in to ask for another whitening stone. He saw Luke and shuffled across, grinning all over his face, 'You're back!' It was half-way to a shout.

27

Years ago when an anxious Mrs Beal confessed she had a son who was good with animals but 'wanting', John had offered a situation; the boy could care for the pony and live over the stable. Billy, with his large head set deep between his shoulders and his over-long arms, with his slow understanding and difficult speech, had repaid the kindness. Two objects made up his universe: Blackie whom he tended and Mary whom he adored.

Mary's son was kind and never ridiculed; Billy therefore extended his adoration to Luke. He swayed on his feet as he repeated with delight, 'You're back . . .'

'I am and I'm glad to see you, Billy. How's Blackie?'

'Nicely.' He hadn't many words but this was one of his favourites.

'Is this what you want, Billy?'

Billy took the whitening stone from Mary and went happily away. She shook her head. 'He gets through two of those a week!'

'Yes, but look at the result. The Emporium steps are positively luminous.'

'I know. I mustn't grumble.'

Emily Beal, carrying food between kitchen and dining room stopped short at the sight of Jane. 'What are you doing up? It's not six o'clock!' Jane twisted her fingers; it was too bad! Everyone wandering in and out when she wanted to speak to Luke privately.

'Would you like a cup of tea?' Mary slid the cup and sugar bowl across.

Jane waited until her aunt had moved back to turn slices of bacon. 'Luke!' she hissed.

'Hallo?'

Jane kept her eyes on Mary's back. 'Are you coming to the concert tomorrow?'

'Wouldn't miss it for anything,' he assured her loudly.

Mary turned, smiling. 'Is that what's worrying you? I told Luke in my letters. Your uncle has tickets for all of us safe in his desk. Now, why not go back to bed for an hour?'

Jane blushed. Luke reached for her hand. 'I'm off to see Dr Cullen. I'll be back by the time Aunt Charlotte gets up.'

But Jane couldn't possibly ask her special favour in front of her mother, it would have to be now. 'There's a party tomorrow after the concert. Will you take me? If you don't — I'll have to go with Ted!' The dark eyes were big with despair. 'He's awful at parties, Luke, he ruins everything. Dorothy Creswell — it's at her house — she doesn't want him to go. There'll be dancing, I expect. Mr Creswell bought a gramophone last week, with rosewood needles — and *three* records!'

Mary moved over to the table. She'd heard enough to know what this was about. 'Jane, dear, Luke doesn't want to spend his entire holiday squiring you to other girls' parties —'

Luke stopped her. 'Where do the Creswells live? I don't think I know them?'

'They have a large house set back from the green at Haughton. Mrs Creswell has an account and Jane knows Dorothy through her dancing class.'

'The Creswells are jolly rich but Dorothy can't dance.' Jane described her best friend without compunction, 'She's got a fat *derrière* and she's no idea of rhythm.'

'Pride goeth before a fall,' Mary shook a warning finger, 'Don't let your mother hear you say things like that.'

'No, I won't.' She was solemn. 'Mama's trying to stop me dancing altogether. She's told Uncle John she thinks the classes are a waste of money.'

'Now, listen . . .' Luke steered her away from dangerous ground. 'I'll take you to one party, Jane, and that's all. I must spend some of my holiday with Mother and Father, I haven't seen them for ages.'

Jane's eyes were shining as she whirled round the table, the mass of hair swinging about her face. 'At the concert, you'll see me dance a princess . . . a sad Spanish princess . . .' and she shot out of the kitchen back to her cold bed, as happy as a lark.

'A princess?' Luke reached for his coat and scarf, 'That should please Aunt Charlotte for once.'

Mary handed him his hat. 'I doubt it. She'll find something to criticize.'

'Thanks for letting down the turn-ups last night. You must've been up til all hours?'

She smiled. 'Well my dear, I could hardly let my professional son display his socks to half of Darlington. Was it a good debate?'

Luke reddened. 'I'm not sure. I nodded off.'

'Oh, Luke!' and she laughed. 'Despite the peppermints? Promise you won't tell your father. And remind Dr Cullen he's spending Christmas night here — not that I think he'll have forgotten. And go carefully! Billy Beal says the flagstones are slippery this morning.'

It was a day for moving quickly, provided one could stay upright. On the corner of Tubwell Row Luke paused to watch a cab driver whip his unfortunate horse. The animal had fallen and a shaft had snapped. To Luke it looked as if one of the horse's forelegs was broken. Certainly there were plenty gathering to watch the struggle and give the driver advice.

The street sweepers had done their best: steam rose from piles of dung in the gutters, ready for the carts that would take it away. The air was heavy. Smoke hung in leaden clouds below the chimneys, blotting out the sky. Luke walked over the bridge. The Skerne mirrored the dull grey smoke. He leaned on the parapet, staring at the water and his own frozen breath. He could taste the grimy air as well as smell it. It stuck to the back of his throat, making him cough.

Dr Cullen lived modestly in St John's Crescent. He'd moved twice in the time Luke had known him but always in the same area of Darlington. From habit, Luke went round to the back rather than ring the surgery bell. Ada was in the scullery. William Cullen had enticed her away from the McKies to act as his general factotum because, as he admitted to Mary, Ada had been well-trained. There was another girl to do the 'rough' but however hard she tried, she couldn't reach Ada's standards. This morning Ada was on her hands and knees scrubbing the floor a second time as Luke opened the door.

'Oh, it's you — wipe your feet if you're coming in, pet.' She eased her aching back with chapped hands. 'He was hoping he'd see you but he's been called out. Potter's Yard, back of Bondgate. He said you were to go, to give a hand, like. He'll need it. A woman's scalded herself.'

30

It was back the way Luke had come. The streets were busier now with horse trams bringing families from villages and farms to do Christmas shopping. What a lot more motor-cars there were in Darlington! Father said there was a slump but it didn't show. He stopped to count them and a hand tugged at his sleeve, a hand that stretched out pleadingly. He looked at the woman's face, the infant crooked in her arm and another child clinging to her skirt. 'Please . . .' He couldn't hear the word but saw her lips frame it. She looked about nervously to see if she'd been spotted.

'Here you are . . . I haven't got much, I'm afraid.' He pushed some pennies into her hand and she darted back down an alley-way.

Another vehicle to dodge and Luke was across Park Gate. There were children here pushing home-made wooden barrows filled with coke from the gas-works. 'Sixpence a bag, mister, delivered to ya door!'

'I haven't got a door.'

'Go on, gi' us sixpence then!'

I've scarcely much more than that left, he thought ruefully. His next allowance was due on Christmas Day, and as he couldn't bear to ask John for an advance, he'd just have to go carefully. Perhaps mother could lend him a florin to see him through? He wanted to give Jane flowers at the concert tomorrow, the way her father used to.

Luke eased his way past the stalls set up alongside the covered market. Naptha flares burned through the gloom, turning glossy holly leaves black. Stall-holders shouted cheerfully. Forget talk about a slump, it was Christmas; best time of year for trade.

A scalding . . . burns were dreadfully painful. They had a special room in the infirmary, far away from the wards. He'd seen a child in there once, who'd been in his night-shirt when he reached to touch an oil lamp because the flame was so pretty. A child who screamed until he died.

Luke had to ask the way because the yards were alike, narrow mean courtyards with slippery frozen sets and houses that faced each other. Flat-fronted houses, so difficult to keep clean, with children playing on the doorstep because there wasn't a place for them inside. Dozens of pairs of eyes sized

31

him up because Luke didn't belong. They knew which house he wanted, though. Everyone here knew Dr Cullen.

The woman was in the kitchen. Luke pushed past frightened children and a man who kept saying, 'She were at' tub, an' she leaned over —'

'Yes, I know, Ah, Luke, good to see you. There's carbolic by the basin over there — quick as you can.' Dr Cullen's authority was as impressive as his girth. He turned back to the husband. 'Take the children next door while I attend to your wife, Mr Griffiths. And find a neighbour who can make us some tea.'

The tub steamed away, soaking wet clothes scattered beside it. Hunched in her chair, the woman's eyes were tightly shut. She'd bitten her lip in an effort to stay silent and still.

'This young man is going to assist, Mrs Griffiths.' Luke finished towelling and moved to where Dr Cullen indicated. 'Be very careful, Mr McKie . . . Mrs Griffiths is extremely brave but she's in a lot of pain.' Luke held the woman's arms gently. 'I'll try not to hurt you, my dear. Make a fist for me.'

He inserted the syringe and pushed the plunger home. From where he stood, Luke could see how the woman had torn at her blouse in her agony. Fabric hung in tatters over her breasts; scalding had turned the skin livid and one of her nipples had burst.

'I use morphia sparingly,' William Cullen muttered. 'We'll try twenty drops of laudanum afterwards . . . If the pain's too bad, she can have spirit of chloroform instead . . . There she goes.' The struggles became weaker, then stopped. Luke supported the dead weight while the doctor cleansed the wound.

'Common enough accident in these houses, Luke . . . They do the washing near the fire — less distance to carry hot water — always balance the tub on a stool . . . The washing soda's kept on the shelf above where the children can't get at it. But there's the rub; children, crawling about too near the tub. One eye on them, she reaches for the soda, trips and there you are: face down in boiling water. This one was lucky if you like, she kept her face clear. Breast fell in instead. She's full of milk, blast it! Like most of 'em round here . . . Doesn't matter what you say — "Oh

I can't stop my man, doctor, not on Sat'day nights when he's had his beer . . ."

'So, having cleaned it thoroughly, we apply a dressing. I always use chlorate of potassium whatever they teach you nowadays. Then we bandage.' Dr Cullen was already criss-crossing, lifting each breast tenderly into its white crêpe cradle.

'Shouldn't she be in hospital?'

'Of course, but Mrs Griffiths has four little ones. Who would look after them?'

'Her husband?'

William Cullen looked up incredulously. 'Women's work? At Christmas? Have a bit of sense, Luke. Griffiths wouldn't "demean"' himself. Such are the rules of social behaviour in Potter's Yard — yes?' An anxious face looked round the back door.

'Did you want tea, doctor?'

'Yes, come in, come in.'

'There's probably another family in the second bedroom of that house, to help make ends meet,' Dr Cullen told him as they walked back into Bondgate. 'That's a further reason why Mrs Griffiths would worry herself silly if we took her off to hospital. I'll call this evening to see how she's responding. Provided that wound doesn't turn gangrenous, she should survive.

'Got another patient nearby . . .' He shook his head over it. 'An unwanted soul on its way into this world, fathered by a man who . . .' The doctor changed his mind and didn't finish the sentence. 'It's difficult for them, Luke. Very, very difficult. Thank God some women manage to avoid falling pregnant. All we can do is patch their bodies as best we can. Ah . . . beautiful day! Makes me thirsty.'

In the Raby Hotel, a jug of porter and two glasses appeared without the doctor saying a word. 'They know me in here.' The first jug was emptied without Luke's help. A second appeared but he shook his head.

'I'm due back for breakfast with Aunt Charlotte.'

'Ah . . . mustn't lead you astray, then. So how's my old university? And about the other matter you wrote of, you

33

and I must allow ourselves time for discussion. I want to know if that acquaintance you mentioned has succumbed to delirium tremens?'

The reference made Luke redden. 'That first day was such a disappointment but I'm sorry I wrote so impetuously.'

'The letter certainly contained more than a drop of self-pity.'

Luke's colour increased. 'Have you the time to hear about it now?'

'Why not?' The doctor signalled for more ale. 'Ada knows my habits. She'll find me if I'm needed.'

'At the lodgings in Jesmond, other students began asking questions as soon as I arrived. Whether I'd been to public school, if my father were a physician, that kind of thing?' William Cullen nodded impassively. 'When I said I'd attended a grammar school in Darlington, they hooted.'

'And you admitted your father wasn't even a gentleman but a shop-keeper?'

'Worse than that, I told them he was a Highlander.'

'Dear me, Luke, what were you thinking of?'

Luke managed a grin. 'I realized my mistake when Bennet-Reeves referred to him as a "Scottish emigré".'

'Is that the sophisticate who drinks himself senseless on claret? I hope he has the decency to bequeath his liver to medicine, it should provide an interesting autopsy. So, Luke . . .? Have you come down in favour of John McKie or do you yearn for your true parent? Who knows, *he* might prove superior to Bennet-Reeves' own?' Dr Cullen ignored Luke's confusion and topped up his beer. 'I should have thought hard work and conscientious love worth more than snobbery? Those traits you've inherited from Mary, they must count for something, too? The choice is yours, my boy. You can either apply yourself to medicine or waste John's hard-earned guineas fawning after the scions of the middle-class.'

Luke's voice was low. 'I didn't realize you knew so much?'

'Dear lad, Mary was three months pregnant when your father first met her. It meant the workhouse or more likely, a dead woman lifted out of the Skerne. He realized that.' The doctor took a long meditative swig. 'No, I doubt whether I'll ever meet a finer gentleman than John McKie.'

34

'I have been most fortunate.' It sounded stilted. Fortunately William Cullen appeared not to notice.

'Don't misunderstand me, Luke. I don't despise the wealthy when they have the sense to consult *me*. Their guineas pay for those less fortunate. And on that subject, see to it that the word "guinea" trips unhesitatingly off your tongue. Had you been John's true son I shouldn't need to advise you. His instinct for gauging precisely what a customer can afford is finely tuned.'

'At Newcastle my background has meant ostracism,' Luke said painfully, 'Fortunately there is a chap called Kessel. He and I attend lectures together.'

'Glad to learn there's one decent specimen. The rest sound nauseating. It was very different in my day . . .' The doctor wagged his jowls and took out his watch. 'Didn't you mention breakfast with Mrs Davie?'

'Oh, heavens, she'll be furious!' Luke was on his feet, reaching for his hat, 'Before I forget, you're due for supper on Christmas night.'

'But I shall see you at the concert first. Luke, while you're on holiday, d'you fancy acting as my assistant?'

'I should like it very much indeed!'

'Of course the visits won't all be as *glamorous* as Potter's Yard,' William Cullen stared into the depths of the jug, 'But I wouldn't be surprised if you didn't learn a little . . . about what it means to be a doctor.'

Mrs Beal urged Ted and Matthew outside as soon as they'd finished breakfast. 'We're far too busy to have you two under our feet. Put your scarves on and get back in time for your dinners, that's all I ask. You can give our Billy a hand cleaning out the stable if you like.'

Ted was half-inclined but Matthew dissuaded him. 'Where's the fun in doing that? Mama will only make us wash, you know what she's like.'

They wandered into the Emporium. There was a crush of good-natured customers. John McKie, standing halfway up the staircase, directed shop assistants who ran to keep up with his orders. In Gents Outfitting, Mr Hart's aitches succumbed to the strain. 'More silk socks, Mr 'enry, h'at

35

the double if you please,' he bawled. 'Shan't keep you a moment, Madam. And two dozen white cambric, best quality while you're h'at it!'

Ted wanted to escape but Matthew stood a moment longer, watching the leather buckets and the cashiers thumbing banknotes. 'You needn't think you can steal any of that,' Ted said hotly, 'I heard Uncle John tell Mr Hart you weren't to be allowed anywhere near —'

'I don't take money nowadays,' Matthew interrupted calmly. It was his way of saying he didn't take it if he thought he might be caught, certainly not from the Emporium where they kept a sharp watch.

'Mrs Beal says once a thief, always a thief.'

Matthew smiled; his intelligent pale blue cats-eyes weren't upset. 'She's stupid. There wouldn't be enough up there to make it worth my while.'

'Not enough!' Ted was incredulous, 'There's hundreds of pounds, I expect. Maybe five hundred — or seven!' Red hair quivered with indignation and loyalty. 'There'll be more money taken in McKie's than in the rest of Darlington.'

'Yes, but Uncle John pays such big wages, I've heard other people say so, and doesn't keep enough for himself.'

'He's always fair . . . even if he is a bit strict.'

Matthew was alert. 'Wasn't your report any good this term?'

'I was top at games!'

'I was top at maths.'

Ted stared with loathing. The discussion with his uncle hadn't been pleasant. 'You're a toad! I got a "B" for geometry but the trouble is . . .' He kicked the nearest wall. 'Uncle John says "B"s aren't worth having.'

Matthew was thoughtful. 'Did he really?' His own interview was scheduled for later that afternoon.

'Yes, why?' Ted's gaze narrowed, 'Were you telling fibs or did you really get an "A"?'

'Of course. More than one as a matter of fact.' Matthew's smile masked his thoughts and he did not tell Ted what the other "A" was for. 'I think Uncle's right. What's the point in coming second?'

'Hark at you!' muttered Ted.

If I come top of everything, Matthew's inner voice whispered passionately, Mama's bound to be impressed: then she'll have to love me more than Ted and Jane . . .

'Come on,' Ted urged, 'Let's go to Feethams. Somebody might have a football, you never know.'

Ted's leather ball, confiscated regularly by Charlotte, was at present under lock and key until the holidays were over. 'I hit one of the houses in Victoria Embankment,' he boasted as they strolled along, 'I was in the middle of the road when I kicked it — and boom! Smashed a window.'

'Did you get the cane?'

'Of course!'

The sun wasn't up but the town was fully alive. They stood at the North End of High Row, hands in their pockets, monarchs of all they surveyed. Drays and carts were thickly packed, facing the pavement in a line that stretched as far as Edward Pease's monument. Cabs pushed their way through a sea of bowler-hatted businessmen. Ted caught a whiff of hot spicy potato cakes from one of the market stalls. 'Got any money?' His need was urgent.

'No.'

'Bet you have!'

'You can borrow if you pay me interest.'

'What's that?'

Matthew explained and Ted was stunned. 'You mean, pay you back more than you give me?'

'For the loan, yes. For the use of my money. It's what you do in business.'

'Hang it, no!' Hot and succulent, the potato cakes' fragrance was even more enticing. Ted thumped the railings in frustration, 'I haven't got more than a penny in my box!'

'You've got those marbles.'

Even though his mouth watered, Ted hesitated. 'You can have the blue one,' he offered, 'that's worth more than a ha'penny.' His alleys had been swopped and saved for over a year; it was a fine collection.

'The stripey red one.'

'That's my best! It's the biggest!'

'Please yourself.' Matthew turned away, thin shoulders nonchalant.

37

'Oh, hang it all!' Ted took the money and pushed his way through to the stall. Behind him, Matthew followed discreetly.

'Three for a penny! With drippin' an' salt on, three a penny!'

As he shoved the second one in his mouth, Ted saw Matthew half-hidden behind the open market door, nibbling at a single potato cake. 'I thought you hadn't got any more money?'

Matthew popped the last piece into his mouth and licked his fingers fastidiously. 'I didn't pay. I'm not stupid.'

It was the dress rehearsal. Backstage there was a frenzy of mothers, fluffing up petticoats and combing their darlings' hair. Jane rehearsed arm movements in front of a mirror. Beside her, Katriona knitted placidly. Chaperoning Jane gave her the rare opportunity to sit for an hour or two.

On the rail amid massed white tulle, Jane's dress was dramatic: vivid red and black. She'd found a picture by Velázquez and Mrs Hart had offered to make it up. Great-aunt Armitage provided a black lace fan. 'I know I can rely on you to take great care of it, Jane. It was a present from my dear husband.' Everyone was eager to help her succeed — everyone except Charlotte.

Arms above her head, Jane thought of her Mama as she gazed at the mirror. She'd been permitted to attend classes because of a promise once extracted by father but as for a career . . .? No matter how well she performed Mama refused to be persuaded. 'Well-bred girls do not flaunt their bodies on stage, Jane.'

'Perhaps she'll change her mind?' Jane whispered to her reflection, 'When she sees me dance a Princess?'

As a child, when solos had been as a sprite or a bird — revealing her legs — her mother's anger had baffled Jane. 'People need to see them to know how well I'm dancing, Mama!' At thirteen, slender and increasingly shapely, understanding had finally come. When her mother demanded, 'I trust you will be wearing a skirt this time?' Jane was ready with her answer.

'Yes, Mama, very long. Down to here.' She sketched a hemline just above her ankles.

'With petticoats?'

'Yes, lots.'

'What about the bodice?' Charlotte looked severely at Mrs Hart who'd brought the garment for a fitting.

'It is cut quite high across the er, chest, as you can see, Mrs Davie. With a fichu. Most respectable and fully lined.'

'And her legs?'

'Oh, white stockings, Mrs Davie. Thick cotton, not lisle.'

The orchestra conductor made his way round the group, collecting scores. As well as the inevitable Tchaikovsky and Chopin he was handed Jane's music; 'Ravel? You're being very modern?'

'Yes, please.'

'Oh, it's Miss McKie.' He smiled in recognition, 'An *infanta*, this time? And a very popular piece. Made Mr Ravel quite famous. I daresay you know precisely what tempo you require?' Jane nodded shyly. 'Like to show me?'

He watched her take on the character of the dance, elegant and dignified, and slid the weight up the metronome pendulum to match her beat. Other mothers waited impatiently but this was the only girl worth bothering about. 'Got that, thank you, Miss McKie.' Jane became a schoolgirl again although a much more charming one this year. How sensible of her mother to send that Scottish dragon to guard her!

Up in their attic under the Emporium roof, the apprentices preferred to soak their feet in mustard and water during their supper hour. 'Gawd, I ache!'

'Just think, after tomorrow . . . two whole days!'

'An' a fowl, if we're lucky. Your ma going down the market?'

'After ten o'clock . . . She says that's the time to get a real bargain. After ten and before midnight. Hope she manages it. We only had brisket last year.'

Luke and Mary were parcelling the last of the orders in the storeroom. Luke's fingers were chafed and sore. He tore another piece from a roll of brown paper. 'It's good of you to help,' said his mother for the umpteenth time.

'Nonsense! Only two more and we're finished.' He watched her fold and crease the paper. 'I'm glad there's something I *can* do. You've never stopped the live-long day. I don't think Father's come down from that staircase once. He can hardly speak. Glycerine and honey for him tonight.'

'I'll make sure he takes it. Knot.' He pressed down firmly. 'Thanks.' Scissors and a knife hung from a chain on her belt and the string was in her apron pocket. 'I miss Jane today but it's the same every year,' Mary said tiredly, 'With the matinée on Christmas Eve, the final rehearsal has to be the day before.'

'You don't begrudge —?'

'Of course not, dear! It's the one thing Jane's set her heart on. Although whether Charlotte will ever relent and let her take it up as a career, I doubt it very much indeed. It wouldn't be *respectable*, which is what concerns her most. Charlotte wants Jane to stay at home — make calls, leave cards and so on — because that is the way conventional daughters behave.'

'Not any more, Mother!' Luke was amazed to find her so hidebound. 'Young women leave home and have proper careers nowadays.'

'As — dancers?' He was silent for a moment.

'If that is where Jane's talent lies,' he said finally.

'Luke, do you think any young man would consider a wife who'd been on the stage? Or more important, any young man's *mother*?'

Luke flushed. 'It's far too soon to talk of marriage. Jane's still a child.' Mary said carefully, 'You realize she's very fond of *you*?' Even as she spoke, Mary wondered if it was wise. She didn't want to make Luke self-conscious or put thoughts into his head but it disconcerted her when he laughed.

'Oh, Mother, Jane looks on me as an elder brother just as she leans on Father since Uncle Davie died.' And he smiled with all the worldly wisdom of seventeen.

What fools men are, thought Mary, however clever they became.

In his bedroom, Matthew considered the presents he'd accumulated. He hadn't bothered with anyone not important to his life; that would be a wasted effort.

He hadn't stolen any money for ages. It didn't make sense to be caned for a shilling or expelled for half-a-crown. Gifts were different. Matthew resented using *his* money to purchase them. It gave him a deep physical pain to part with cash.

He gazed at the bowl of pot-pourri he'd acquired for his mother; surely that would earn her affection?

What would she give him? A new ten-shilling note with strict instructions to make it last until Easter? Uncle John could be relied on for a pound but Mrs Armitage was the best bet. Matthew had already shown her his exercise book. She understood book-keeping — she'd spotted the mistakes but when she came across the remark 'Continues to improve', she'd kissed him. Matthew sensed this was from a desire to treat him equally rather than true affection. No-one had cuddled him spontaneously for years. It never occurred to him that they were waiting for some sign of reciprocal love.

He hoped his uncle would appreciate the shoe-horn. That had cost money because the shop assistant had spotted his hand at a crucial moment. Surely *paying* for a gift added to its value? What a nuisance he couldn't explain.

The school books were ready for inspection, meticulously labelled. Matthew took pleasure in neatness. Uncle John would say as he always did, 'You take after my mother, Matthew. She had beautiful writing even though she never went to school.'

Sitting on the bed, Matthew had a sudden, brilliant idea: this year he wouldn't ask for money at all, he'd ask for a different present altogether! He wrapped thin arms round his chest; it was exactly the sort of thing to please Uncle John. How clever to think of it! But then he'd always known he was more intelligent than Ted or Luke.

CHAPTER THREE

Contrasts

Luke was deeply asleep when Mary whispered, 'Luke, there's a boy come for you . . .'

'Mmm?'

'Sent by Dr Cullen.' He was awake. 'A woman's started her labour, apparently.'

'Oh, yes. Right.' Luke swung his feet out of bed, wincing at the chilly oilcloth, 'I'll be down in five minutes.'

'You'll eat something hot before you go,' she whispered. 'It's bitter out tonight.'

The boy in his huge greasy cap was wan and thin. He clutched a bowl of soup with both hands but managed to hang on to the hunk of bread Mary had given him.

'This'll keep you going.' She filled another bowl for Luke, 'The lad says he's from behind Potter's Yard?'

'That's right.' Luke was tugging at his laces so he didn't see Mary's expression.

'What I meant was . . . does the mother need anything? For herself or the baby?'

'If it's like the place where we were yesterday, I'd say anything would be welcome.'

'I'll be back in a minute.'

On his own, Luke found nothing to say. The steady chomping as the boy shoved in every morsel inhibited conversation. Eventually he asked, 'Is it your mother who's having the baby?'

'Nah . . . me sister. D'you want that?'

Luke pushed across his slice of bread. 'Is it her first baby?'

'Her last. Da's swore she'n the bastard could go on the parish.'

Mary came hurrying back. 'Here you are, blankets, sheets and I found an old shawl. It'll keep the baby warm.' She tied the corners of the bundle together, 'Can you manage?'

'Yes, thanks.' All of a sudden, Luke found it difficult to look his mother in the face. 'Come on,' he said abruptly to the boy, 'We'd best hurry.'

A hard frost crackled under their feet. The world was dark with silvery moonlight and for once the air smelled clean. Luke felt the cold fill his lungs. The skinny child whimpered, 'It were nice back theer, nice and warm!' but Luke's thoughts were of the confinement; he'd never attended one before.

'Is there a midwife?'

The boy stared at him. 'Theer's doctor and theer's thee.'

Frost couldn't obliterate the odours of Potters Yard, for there was too much humanity packed into too small a space, but it had turned slates black and paving stones silver-white. The windows were dark-eyed, full of secrets.

The boy led him past fetid earth closets, through a door and up a stair. There was the glimmer of a candle at the top.

'Ah, Luke . . .' Was Dr Cullen more subdued than usual or was it Luke's imagination? On the bed, a girl moaned and arched her back. Luke averted his eyes.

'Mother sent these —'

'I'll take them.' A woman, half-hidden behind Dr Cullen, reached out to snatch the bundle but the doctor grabbed her arm.

'No, you don't. These are for that poor wench. Now, get downstairs and keep the fire alight. I'll shout when we need hot water.'

'She's got to go. The minute it's born, the pair of them. They're goin' to the workhouse —'

'That's as maybe. Now, get out!'

The woman pushed past, muttering defiance. In the corner of the room, the boy with the cap crouched, trying to make himself invisible. Dr Cullen said quietly, 'You as well.'

'It's cold outside!'

'Find a corner where she can't see you.'

'She 'ates me as well as our Elsie.' He went reluctantly down the stair.

'Here . . .' Dr Cullen handed Luke two more candle stubs. 'Stand 'em where we can see the bed.'

The girl screamed as a contraction took hold and Luke busied himself with the matches. 'I haven't attended an *accouchement* before.'

'Then you'll discover the wonder of one of nature's mysteries. That's better.'

More light revealed more dirt. Everything about the room was filthy; walls, floor, bedding. Yesterday there had only been poverty; this was different.

The girl lay under a single blanket, her hair pale against the soiled mattress. Dr Cullen spoke quietly. 'Elsie, we're going to make you comfortable . . . make a proper bed for the baby to be born. Luke, slip those newspapers under her when I give the word — one, two, three . . .'

Luke pushed the papers beneath the girl, averting his eyes from the aperture between her legs. Through there a child would be born — the skimpy shift didn't even cover her, he thought distractedly — a new life, delivered onto smudged newsprint.

'Now, my dear, I want to see how that baby of yours is progressing.' The girl moaned, then shrieked as another spasm swept over her. When he'd finished, Dr Cullen drew Luke away from the bed.

'She shouldn't be having a child with that narrow brim —'

'I don't want it!' Her cry made them turn round.

Dr Cullen said quickly, 'Luke, go and chase that slut. I want hot water up here at once.'

At breakfast, Jane asked where he was.

'Out helping Dr Cullen.'

'When will he be back?'

'I couldn't say, dear.' Mary was preoccupied. Not only that, Charlotte forbade all reference to procreation, especially at Christmas, because she judged it unsuitable.

'But if he doesn't get back — he might miss the Concert!'

'Oh, I shouldn't worry. It won't take that long.' Mary glanced at the clock and revised her opinion. 'If he does, you could dance for him another time.'

'It wouldn't be the same!' All the disappointed agony of thirteen was in Jane's voice, but Mary had a full day ahead of her.

'I'm sorry, Jane, I have work to do. Don't upset yourself. There's every chance Luke will be back in time.'

In John's office, the interview was progressing as Matthew had calculated. He savoured the pleasure in his uncle's voice. 'This is a very creditable school report, Matthew. A great improvement on last term. Your mother will be pleased, as indeed am I.'

'I wasn't expecting an A for chemistry, Uncle.'

'Very well done indeed. There remains the question of your Christmas gift, my boy.'

'I want to learn about accountancy, Uncle. Will you give me lessons?'

John was startled. 'Not so fast. Simple double-entry book-keeping comes first.'

'But I already understand that, or nearly. I want to learn the proper way to run a business.'

If only Ted would make the same request! John polished his pince-nez. 'If that genuinely interests you?'

'Yes, please!' Matthew's smile was guileless.

'And — for Christmas?'

'That's it, the lessons. Perhaps I could have a new exercise book but I don't need anything else, honestly. Can we begin tomorrow, Uncle?'

John continued to sit after the door had closed. How very odd that he found the prospect disquieting.

Goods poured into the stockroom in a never-ending stream. Jane and the youngest apprentice, Gertie, struggled tearfully with paper and string. 'I hate everybody!' Jane cried desperately. 'If they keep on buying, we'll never finish!'

'Yes we will, Miss. We've got to. Every order's got to go out tonight so no-one's disappointed Christmas morning. Mr McKie's orders.'

'But the Concert! I've got to be at the theatre by half-past two!'

'Oh, they'll let you off.' Gertie wasn't much older than Jane but her prospects weren't encouraging, 'I shall have to stay. Maybe Ivy can give a hand when you've gone. If they're not too busy upstairs, that is.'

'I'm sorry . . .' And Jane was for a fleeting instant, but she still fretted. 'Luke's not back yet, either!'

'I shouldn't worry, Miss . . . theatre's going to be full from what I heard. Tickets have sold out in the Salon.' But that wasn't what Jane meant.

Daylight; a dull yellow gleam through the pall of smoke that refused to lift because the air was so still. Fog added another layer, hiding the middens below.

A grey-haired woman had arrived but she wasn't a qualified midwife. Dr Cullen explained. 'Carrie will be here when you and I leave, Luke. She's the only nurse they have in Potters Yard. She understands enough about birth and death. Now, I must return to the surgery.' He checked his watch. 'Unless Carrie thinks it's urgent, I'll be back in a couple of hours.'

Carrie made the room more habitable; Mary's shawl now lined a box, ready to take the baby. Elsie's screams changed to moans but Carrie insisted they must wait. 'This baby's not in any hurry to be born . . . I wouldn't be in his place, neither.'

With the daylight, Luke had discovered how pretty Elsie was. Under the sweaty sheen, the face with its pale gold hair was sweet and gentle. Once, when Carrie had gone to fetch clean water, she'd whispered urgently, 'Don't let it live. You can do that much for me, can't you?'

Luke soothed her because he'd been taught that women in childbirth have strange notions but Elsie turned away in despair.

'Happen we'd better send for him . . .' Carrie was at the bed, one hand on the girl's belly, 'I think summat's wrong.' Luke was beside her immediately, listening for the foetal heartbeat.

46

She went to the door and called downstairs, 'Alfie, go an' fetch t'doctor.' Watching the oval face with its spun-gold frame, Luke saw Elsie's eyes open wide.

'Be brave a little longer, Dr Cullen is on his way.'

'It's dead, isn't it?' Elsie said expressionlessly. 'The baby's died.'

'Hush!' She gave a tired sigh.

'Thank God . . .'

There was a different smell now; disinfectant, sharp and pungent. Dr Cullen stared down at the exhausted girl.

'Your prayers have been answered, my lass.' He glanced at Carrie, 'You did nothing . . .?'

'Cross my heart. Anyway, he were here.'

Dr Cullen reached for bottle and pad and they caught the familiar, sickly aroma of chloroform. 'Breathe deeply for me, Elsie.'

Carrie waited, ready to wrap the dead infant in a scrap of blanket. Dr Cullen picked up the craniotomy forceps.

'God's been merciful for once,' Carrie said quietly.

'Don't bring that kind of talk in here.'

'But he has,' Carrie insisted. 'The way they treat Elsie. I've heard neighbours blaming her.'

'Her good looks are undoubtedly her misfortune.' With careful pressure William Cullen tightened the screw. Carrie took the tiny crushed corpse, observing 'It were a boy, then?' but Dr Cullen made no comment.

He watched Carrie sponge the girl's body and glanced at Luke, 'You haven't guessed why I needed you to watch over her? The baby's father is the same as Elsie's own.'

Once outside, picking his way carefully along the icy street, William Cullen beamed at his companion. 'Wonderful day, Luke. Christmas Eve! Makes you glad to be alive,' but Luke couldn't respond to the familiar change of mood.

In the Sun Inn, he found his voice. 'That girl . . . Elsie.'

'Yes, I know. Tragic but not unique. I must call on one of the Friends, they might know of a position. We must get her away from there as soon as she's recovered her strength.' Dr Cullen took out his pocket-book and unscrewed his pen.

47

'Yes, but . . .' Luke was still shocked.

'"Judge not that ye be not judged", old chap . . .' Dr Cullen scribbled busily. 'Especially if ye be a doctor.' Luke was silent. He watched the pocket-book disappear, then the porter.

'Elsie's father has been attacking women in and around Potter's Yard for years. Most are too frightened to protest. I don't know how long he's been abusing Elsie.'

'How old is she?'

'Fourteen or fifteen, I forget. Carrie told me. If she hadn't and if I hadn't insisted on attending Elsie, the man might have compounded incest with murder. As it is . . .' The doctor paused to drain his jug, 'Carrie was right. God was merciful for once. A wiser child than Elsie might have tried to escape but she stayed to look after her brother. The father beats him when he's drunk.'

'But surely you must expose such a man's wickedness?' Luke was outraged, 'As soon as you discovered what he'd done to Elsie, why did you not denounce him?' William Cullen looked cynical.

'Because he claimed that his daughter had *tempted* him.'

'Oh — God!'

'Ours is a world full of narrow-minded folk, Luke. As you observed, Elsie was too pretty for her own good. Who d'you think magistrates would prefer to believe, eh?'

'Couldn't you . . .?' Luke swallowed and tried again. 'You could've helped her, once you knew.'

'And commit another sin?' The words dropped like pebbles, shattering any pretence. 'That's a slippery slope once you begin to go down it.' Dr Cullen's voice was serious. 'It's a choice you'll have to make some day.'

A pot-boy went past, sprinkling damp sawdust and sweeping the flagstones. Luke's emotions were in chaos.

'You'll find the strength to make the right decision when the time comes, Luke. I try to avoid all condemnation. What does accusation achieve, eh? It brings out the worst in me, I know. Makes me behave like a Methodist.' Dr Cullen gave a disapproving belch. 'Far more important — I try to avoid lice. With most of my patients, that's far from easy. Take my advice and use Orris powder. Good heavens — is that the time! We'll be late for that blessed matinée!'

Luke ran down Raby Street and cut across to Skinnergate. He wanted a bath, he couldn't take Jane to her party feeling itchy. Half cursing Dr Cullen for putting the thought in his mind, he raced in the back way and up the stairs.

Mary called out from the kitchen, 'Katriona has laid out your things.'

'Is there enough hot water —'

'Yes, but be quick. Billy's waiting to take us when you're ready.'

'You go and send him back for me,' Luke shouted, careering down the passage. He wanted to buy Jane flowers. It was when he was in the bath he remembered he hadn't any money — bother!

Perhaps because she guessed at his impecunious state, Mary had left a pile of coins beside his clothes. Billy waited patiently outside the florists. He and Blackie had another much longer journey ahead of them, delivering parcels to Cockerton. The pony was as tired as he was; she'd lost her footing more than once on the frozen cobbles. He hoped it wouldn't be thick ice where the road crossed over Cocker Beck.

'Right, Billy, onward, quick as you like.' Luke tucked the posies under the seat; violets for Jane and three small camellias for Mrs Creswell.

The foyer of the Theatre Royal was empty. He could hear the familiar music as he handed in his coat. Even the scene he could glimpse on stage didn't change: little girls in white dresses watched by an audience of fond parents. It was the same every year.

'Will you wait, please? I'll show you to your seat when this item is finished.'

'Has Miss Jane McKie danced yet?'

The attendant studied the programme. 'She is listed among the ensemble in the next item and has a solo after the interval.'

'Ah, Luke . . .' Dr Cullen's familiar rumble was beside him. 'Sorry I'm late. Another case of varicella when I got

49

back. Sixth this week. Shouldn't be surprised if we're in for a minor epidemic. Have I missed Jane?'

'Her solo's in the second half.'

'Ah. I've left word with Ada — it's highly likely I'll be called out.' He gave the programme-seller his card. 'If anyone asks for me, let me know immediately.'

'Yes, doctor.'

'Can I come with you?' Luke begged.

'Certainly not!' His indignation caused one or two to murmur, Ssh! Dr Cullen waited until the music swelled. 'Jane would never forgive you and neither would I. You're her support. Don't fail her.'

Backstage, Dorothy Creswell attempted to console her friend. 'There's still the interval. It's supposed to be twenty minutes but it always lasts until they've sold the ice-cream. I wish my family *weren't* in the audience,' she said plaintively, 'I know I'm going to fall off my points again!' Blonde hair, blue-eyed and with a delightfully plump little figure, dancing was not her forte. 'Every time I try to count the bars, it comes out differently!'

'I'll whisper them if you like.'

'That's frightfully kind, Jane, but I shall still wobble; I always do.'

'Nymphs! Arms in the first position, if you please.'

They were swansdown, floating across the stage. Mothers, fathers and aunts 'Oooh'd' to see them rise on their toes. At the finish, gloved hands applauded ecstatically. Amid the extravagant praise, Dr Cullen asked Luke, 'Not too much strong medicine, today?' but the interval lights came on before he had time to reply.

In the foyer, Dr Cullen heard his name being called. 'Ted, finish this ice for me. Farewell for the present, all of you. Tell Jane, what I saw of her, she looked charming.'

Ted turned to Matthew. 'Would you like a lick?'

'Thanks.' The pink tongue flickered in and out quickly.

'Isn't it boring!' Ted's yawn threatened to crack his jaw, 'The only good bit was when Dorothy Creswell bashed that other girl.'

50

'You shouldn't have laughed so loud. Mama was cross.'

'When she fell over you could see the other girl's B.t.m. —'

'Ssh!' Matthew gazed round fearfully, 'You'll get the cane if she hears you say that.'

'I hope Jane gives us decent Christmas presents considering what we've endured for her sake,' Ted said darkly. 'Here, you don't think she's knitted any more of those awful scarves?'

Katriona was twisting the mass of dark hair into a chignon. 'He's arrived. I peeped through the hole in the curtain. Large as life and twice as handsome, all right?'

'Oh, good!' Jane was all contentment. 'Do I look like a princess?'

'Stand up.' Katriona smoothed the wide satin skirt, 'Show me with the fan.' Jane flicked it open and struck a pose. 'You'll do.'

'Overture and beginners. Miss McKie on stage, please.'

Music stole over them with its gentle melancholy. On stage the red and black figure moved very slowly at first, weighed down by sadness and tradition. It was strange, thought Luke, he'd known Jane all his life but he couldn't reconcile his memories with this stately puppet.

There was a change of mood. Under the heavy satin, limbs moved restlessly as if to slough off their encumbrance. The girl had changed into a woman, unwilling to accept her fate, begging to be allowed to live. Luke found her sensual awakening disturbing. He wanted to stand up and shout, No! Jane must remain innocent and pure always.

The movements became stiff and regal once more; the fan curved finally, in an arc that embraced her fate as the princess relinquished hope, bowing her head in submissive acceptance of death.

He couldn't applaud. His cheeks were wet not just for Jane but for Elsie and for all the evil that could sully them.

'She wasn't at all bad,' Ted pronounced judiciously. 'In fact, Jane's the best of all of them.'

51

'Look at Mama's face,' Matthew whispered, 'She doesn't like it when everyone claps so much.' They heard Charlotte's irritated remark to Mary.

'No matter how many petticoats Jane has, one is always aware of her *body* beneath.'

Two young faces stared at the mirror in breathless concentration. They were at Dorothy's dressing-table, watching Mam'zelle 'put up' the fair curls. 'Why not let her do yours, dearest?'

'Mama's forbidden it.'

'Your mama isn't coming to the party,' Dorothy pointed out reasonably.

'Someone would tell her,' sighed Jane. 'Someone always does. Anyway, it wouldn't look right with this silly frock.' White organdie, smocked across the chest, had been Charlotte's choice two seasons ago and Jane was expected to make it last. Dorothy gazed complacently at the reflection of her own dress spread out on the bed. It was so beautiful it made her heart beat faster. Jane looked at it, too.

'That's the loveliest thing I ever saw,' she said simply.

'Yes . . . and darling Jack is responsible. You know how mean father can be? When Jack heard I was "coming out", he said I had to have a decent dress. Mother sent to Paris for it.'

'Yes.' Jane had absorbed sufficient fashion lore to know the significance of Paris.

'So . . .' Mam'zelle held the hand-mirror for both girls to see the full effect, 'Does it feel secure, Dorothy?' The blonde head tossed vigorously.

'Yes, thank you.'

'You do look grown-up,' Jane said humbly.

'*Enfin.*' The woman held out the powder-blue gown, Dorothy stepped into it. Even her petticoat is silk, Jane thought disconsolately, *and* she's wearing stays!

Dorothy was enormously satisfied: a tiny waist, silk ruffles which emphasized her pearly shoulders and bosom, and a flat blue bow that restrained the burst of pleats behind. What did it matter if she couldn't stay on her points? 'Why not let Mam'zelle retie your sash at least, dearest?' she suggested kindly, 'She can do it so the creases hardly show.'

At the top of the stairs, the two paused, a little shy of the assembly below. 'I'm so glad Luke came instead of Ted. Isn't he handsome nowadays! Nearly as handsome as Jack. It's so refreshing,' Dorothy confided happily, 'when one's brother turns into a man. They seem to change overnight once they leave home.' Jane was leaning over the bannister rail.

'Who are the people with Jack?'

'His Varsity friends. Aren't they gorgeous? The dark-haired one — he's the richest — is Hugo Wilton.' At fifteen, Dorothy's priorities were clear-cut. 'He's frightfully handsome. His eyes are liquid pools of dark-brown fire,' she added with complete sincerity.

'I can only see the top of his head. It looks as if he's a little bit grey.'

'Silver, Jane, not grey. Prematurely silver. By the time he's thirty, Hugo will look divine, so distinguished! Are you ready?'

Shoulders back, heads high, the two began to descend. They made an interesting contrast, one blonde and dimpling, the other dark and solemn, her black stockings and white dress childish compared to Dorothy's elegance. Below, other females moved forward to catch their first glimpse of the Parisian gown.

Jack Creswell sharpened the rosewood gramophone needles patiently. 'Awfully good of you to come, McKie. Dorothy's parties are a bit of a bore. Think you'd find our New Year "do" more to your taste.'

Luke nodded politely and Hugo Wilton drawled, 'Isn't that Dorothy coming down now, Creswell?'

'Ah, yes ... what a difference, eh?' Jack smiled indulgently. 'You wouldn't think it was the same clumsy nymph of a couple of hours ago.'

'That nymph is flirting disgracefully!' Hugo pretended to be shocked. 'Look how she's fluttering those eyelashes — highly reprehensible, old man.'

'I shall have a word,' her brother promised.

'Who's the solemn little filly with her?'

'McKie's sister, I think?' Jack looked enquiringly.

'Cousin,' Luke corrected. 'Jane and Miss Creswell became acquainted at the dancing academy.'

Hugo wrinkled his brow. 'Miss Jane McKie? Wasn't that the name in the programme? "Pavane for a dead infanta"?'

'That's the one.' Luke felt proud.

'Good heavens, is that the same girl? She's a mere child! Younger than Dorothy?'

'Jane's thirteen. I believe Miss Creswell is fifteen.'

'My withers were wrung, I don't mind admittin',' Hugo told him.

'It felt strange, knowing it was Jane up there on the stage.'

'Well . . . Can't just stand here, neglectin' visitin' royalty, don't you know.'

Hugo Wilton advanced, swept off an imaginary hat and made a lavish bow before going down on one knee in front of Jane. Dorothy fluttered her eyelashes even faster but it was Jane's hand he seized and kissed. 'May a broken-hearted supplicant beg a boon, your highness?'

Jane said nervously, 'I do not believe we have been introduced?'

'Hugo Wilton, your highness, a mere commoner who ventures to be bold. Is your card full, for such is my boon?'

Dorothy's tasselled pencil was ready but, to her credit, her smile didn't falter. She nudged her friend. 'He wants a dance!' she hissed.

'Oh, goodness!' Thoroughly confused, Jane found her programme in her pocket, 'Here you are.'

'Number three, perhaps? The waltz?' The 'pools of fire' were gently quizzical.

'Not the waltz, no,' Jane replied quickly, 'I want to keep that for Luke.'

'Ah, the parfait gentil knight?' Hugo smiled, scribbled his name and returned her card, 'I claim the right to take you in to supper, Miss McKie. After all you *were* responsible for breaking my heart this afternoon. Miss Creswell, you look delightful but then I think you know that already.' He bowed but that was all.

Dorothy said huffily, 'How silly! You could've kept any old dance for Luke.'

'He might ask me for the waltz.'

54

'But Hugo's gorgeous and he has fifteen thousand a year!'

Jane was full of remorse. 'Oh, Dorothy, you look so beautiful, I can't think why Mr Wilton didn't ask you instead!'

Friendship was restored. Dorothy felt magnanimous. 'Let's have some lemonade. They're only grown-up boys. Once upon a time they were probably all as horrid as Ted.'

Jack Creswell began marshalling the troops in their stiff eton collars, skulking in a corner. 'Come on you chaps,' he cajoled, 'time for the supreme sacrifice.'

'Do we *have* to dance with them, sir?'

'Yes, you jolly well do. See how delightful your sisters look tonight, all for your benefit.'

'No it's not,' the rebel muttered, 'they dress up 'cause they want to show off.'

'Look, Tommy old man, I've only got three records. Three dances then supper, all right? That's not much to ask, surely?' Jack Creswell clapped his hands and called out, 'Ladies and gentlemen, take your partners for a mazurka.'

It had been heavenly! She had danced every dance even if Luke *had* chosen Dorothy for the waltz. Jack Creswell had made a fuss of her and Hugo had presented her with the rose from his buttonhole. She would press it in her 'Kind Thoughts' book plus the violets Luke had given her.

And now she was on her way home, not in a pumpkin but a tram, beside a silent Luke. Jane twisted the strings of her shoe-bag. 'Are you glad you went?' she asked, 'I don't think you really wanted to.'

'I enjoyed myself very much. Thanks for inviting me to partner you.'

'Dorothy suggested it,' Jane admitted candidly, 'She can't bear Ted. Didn't she look beautiful tonight?'

'Very pretty,' replied Luke absently, twisting the knife in the wound. 'Why was your solo so sad? I've alternated between joy and tragedy all day. This morning a baby died, then your Pavane. Thank heavens the party was a cheerful affair!' Jane sniffed at her violets.

'Perhaps the mother will have another baby?' When Luke didn't reply she said softly, 'I was dancing all my sadness away for ever and ever.'

'What sadness?'

'Over Father. When someone dies the sadness grows big inside. I was dancing mine away.'

'I see.' He smiled, not at her explanation but at her serious face. 'All gone, is it?'

'Not quite but I feel much better.'

'Good!' The mood was broken and Jane grinned. Luke was suddenly struck by how pretty she was. He had a sudden, anxious need to protect her. 'I know you think Dorothy Creswell is the bee's knees but you needn't follow her slavishly.'

'What d'you mean?'

'She's far too vivacious for one thing.'

How very strange, thought Jane. When he'd been dancing with Dorothy, Luke had laughed at her jokes like anything. Men were odd.

CHAPTER FOUR

Christmas

Ted was wide awake as soon as he opened his eyes. He flung back the bedclothes, seized his stocking and prodded it. Mama had declared they were all too old for such nonsense. Neither he nor Jane said a word but they were very relieved when Aunt Mary insisted it wouldn't be Christmas if she wasn't allowed to fill the stockings. What on earth had she put in Luke's this morning — surely not sugar mice!

Despite his hardy nature it was too cold to stay out of bed. Ted scrambled back under the blankets. He could feel the familiar shapes in the dark: he knew what they were. First there was the apple followed by an orange, both wrapped in silver paper; a bag of nuts, then something strange. He peeled off the paper and used his fingers — a yo-yo! He hoped it was bright red. He'd swopped a red one for an alley — the alley Matthew had enticed from him — and regretted it ever since. Never one to bear a grudge, Ted shoved that memory out of his mind.

Stiff paper came next, a cone-shaped bag. Gob-stoppers! The bag would be blue, like a sugar bag, because these were from the corner-shop in Post-House Wynd; Ted was a connoisseur when it came to Darlington sweet-shops.

He lay, sucking contentedly, watching the light increase through the gap in the curtains. Perhaps snow was on the way? It looked like it. If there was enough, maybe he could escape washing up and take his sled to Fleethams, provided Mama gave permission? In the dark, Ted groaned. It was amazing how many reasons Mama could devise as to why a chap shouldn't go out on Christmas Day, apart from church of course. They'd all be going to morning service. It had been different when Papa was alive . . . then they'd go out and run and shout; everything then had been so — vivid. The sweet was a manageable size now. He slid it from cheek to cheek. He didn't think about Papa very often nowadays. Life was so interesting Ted hadn't got time to sit and mope.

He fingered the stocking toe gingerly; yes, there was the mouse. He'd save it for this afternoon. After goose, Christmas pudding and mince pies, Ted always ate his sugar mouse. When he'd been younger, he'd been sick but not now. He could go on eating long after everyone else had finished. Mrs Beal said he'd end up bigger than his father. The retired army sergeant who taught physical training warned him about it: 'Watch your weight, McKie. Get too fat and you'll slow down.'

Slow down! Wasn't he the fastest and bestest boxer in the school? Of course he was. Without thinking, Ted clasped his hands behind his head and swung into his exercise routine: trunk up, down, up, down . . . there was a harsh rending sound, ever so familiar, 'Oh, no!'

'Hey, you awake?' Jane peeped round the door, her teeth chattering, 'Merry Christmas, can I come in?'

'Yes!' She snuggled up under the eiderdown. 'Careful of the sheet . . . it just tore.'

'Oh, Ted!'

'I couldn't help it! Can you mend it for me? Please! Mama said she'd cane me if it happened again. I can't have the cane on Christmas Day!'

'I don't see why not . . . you have it almost every other day. What's extra in your stocking?'

'Gob-stoppers and a yo-yo. What did you get?'

'I think it's a sash. I didn't put the light on — oh dear!' The sheet had ripped another inch or two. 'Ted, I don't think I can manage such a big tear. It'll need a proper patch.'

'Oh, no!'

'I'll talk to Katriona if you like.'

'Mrs Beal,' he decided, 'Katriona might tell on me. Have a gob-stopper?'

'Thanks.'

'Wonder what Matthew's got?' Jane could only chew, not speculate. 'Did you know he's asked Uncle John

for lessons? He says he wants to be an *accountant*!'
This was said in disbelief that anyone could be so
stuffy.

With her mouth still full, Jane answered, 'Mmm.'

'*I* think he's trying to be Uncle John's favourite,' said Ted
with contempt.

'No ... don't think so.' Jane's cheek bulged. 'It was
great-aunt Armitage's idea, remember? When Matthew first
went to this school. She knew how much he likes doing sums
about money.'

'He's stupid!'

Luke could barely make out the familiar room, it was
still too dark. His feet discovered a shape at the end
of the bed — surely not? He reached down and felt
it. Oh, really! Mother must've crept in when he was
asleep. He'd speak to her privately; his *amour-propre*
was too fragile to admit to receiving a Christmas stocking!

All the same, his fingers explored just as Ted's had
done; they found the apple, orange and bag of nuts.
The sugar mouse made him salivate as well as smile.
So much for maturity! There were two small surprises;
the first felt like a packet of collar studs. How typical that
she'd noticed he hadn't many left ... and the second? In
the dark Luke fumbled with the wrapping and twisted off the
lid. Burying his head beneath the bedclothes, he sniffed; Oh,
heavens! Boot-black!

He jumped out of bed and switched on the light. The
snowy top sheet was covered with smears! Could he
persuade someone — anyone — to scrub it clean before
Mother discovered what had happened?

Luke pulled on his dressing gown. If he nipped down now,
before she was awake? Bundling the sheet under his arm, he
sped along to the kitchen.

Mary rose quietly so as not to disturb John. She put on the
old gown she wore every morning — there was much to be
done before she could risk her good dress — and slipped her
club-foot into the built-up shoe.

She could see a crack of light under the kitchen door. What on earth was going on? She flung the door wide, making them jump. 'What *are* you doing!' Sheets billowed all over the floor. At the sink, Luke had soap and a scrubbing brush; Jane had hers spread over the table.

'Oh, morning Aunt Mary.' Ted attempted aplomb. 'Just a little accident. Jane's putting it right. It'll be as good as new when she's finished.'

'What sort of "little accident"?' He showed her reluctantly. 'Oh, Ted!'

'I couldn't help it, honest! I was doing my exercises, like this.' And far too quickly, Ted was on the floor, moving vigorously. As he swung his body upright, he caught his head a smart blow on the corner of the table. 'Ouch!' Blood gushed copiously.

Jane screamed, 'Ted, watch the sheet!' She grabbed the white folds.

'Here, let me see.' Luke rushed across, caught his feet in the sheet and the tear widened ominously. Behind him, his own sodden sheet slithered to the floor. 'I say, I'm awfully sorry, Mother . . .'

'Merry Christmas,' Mary murmured faintly.

Each of them had one important task on Christmas day. Jane's was to decorate the table. This year, because of her Spanish dress, she'd decided on a theme of red and gold. It was a secret because that was part of the excitement. When John walked into the dining room, the colour reminded him of his wedding breakfast in Coburg Street, set on red tissue paper which was all they could afford seventeen years ago. Today, red linen runners were laid on white damask; in the centre of each carefully-folded napkin nestled a polished apple. Wine glasses stood on circles of gold foil to reflect the ruby glints. A centre-piece of red and gold feathers rose like a crest. Scattered about the table were dishes of shiny red berries decorated with gold spangles. As she heard their cries of delight, Jane hugged herself; it had been worth it. Not from Mama of course. Charlotte considered praise bad for the character. She managed to find one dirty fork to send back to the kitchen.

It was odd not to have a single employee, just the family, with Mrs Armitage and Bertha, Mrs Beal, Emily and Billy in place of the shop assistants. Billy's task was to carry in the goose, his face grim with concentration as everyone shouted warnings not to trip over holes in the carpet. Behind him, Ted and Matthew marched with the gravy and vegetables.

After he'd carved the first slice, John broke with tradition; 'Luke, how about exercising your surgical skills?' There were cheers then sniggers as the knife slid off the breastbone. Ted clutched his chest and rolled his eyes until Charlotte cuffed him.

By four o'clock, even Ted declared he couldn't eat another scrap. He lolled, replete, the fire at his back. If he could just shut his eyes and have a little snooze . . . but he didn't get the chance. In a twinkling he was back in the kitchen, a towel round his waist, helping Katriona at the sink: Mama had declared it was time to clear away.

'It's no use complaining,' Katriona told him, 'If you do, *she* won't let you have the present that's under the tree,' which was beastly unfair! Bursting with indignation, Ted grabbed the first slippery plate.

Having delegated everyone to her satisfaction, Charlotte settled on the *chaise longue* beside her aunt. 'I always say, many hands make light work.' Down below they heard a knock at the street door.

'It's too early for the choir,' said John.

'I'll go, Father.' Luke ran downstairs, past the empty shrouded counters and opened the door. It was the ostler from the stables. 'Mr McKie? Dr Cullen sends his compliments . . . wants to know if you'll be accompanying him? Trap's outside, sir.' He shook his head, 'No rest for some, not even on Christmas Day.'

'I'll get my coat.'

Upstairs, Luke asked, 'You don't mind, do you Mother?'

'It's very kind that he should give you the experience. Don't forget to bring him back with you.'

'I won't. I don't know when that might be.'

'Luke! Be back in time for the presents!' Jane implored. He blew her a kiss and was gone.

William Cullen was wiping his face as he opened the door. 'Ah, Luke . . . gave me time to finish my pudding, sending for you.'

'Is it an emergency?'

'Highly unlikely,' he laughed. 'Here, Tom, give me a hand.' Ada passed up the leather bag. 'I shall be at the Enderbys if I'm needed.'

'Yes, doctor.'

'We're off to visit a *malade imaginaire* with enough money to support her folly.'

'On Christmas Day?'

'It might be serious, one can never tell. Northgate, if you please Tom.'

'Right, doctor.' After a moment or two, William Cullen roused himself.

'This should prove invaluable experience provided you exercise a bit of charm. Unknit that threatening brow, Luke. Mrs Enderby is that *rara avis*, a rich patient. Her guineas pay for the others in Potters Yard — we can't afford to lose 'em.'

'Mary . . . are you there?'

She turned away from her dressing-table mirror. 'I'll be down in a moment, John . . .' but he came into the bedroom and shut the door. Mary stopped tidying her hair. 'Nothing's wrong?'

'Everything's peaceful.' John took the brush. 'I simply wanted a few minutes alone with my wife.'

'Goodness me!'

'You know, it's a terrible thing when one has to creep away without the children noticing.'

'Now, why's that?' Her mouth twitched and John protested, 'You're not making it easy.' He brushed the curtain of hair aside and began kissing her throat.

'Later,' Mary said firmly.

'It wouldn't take long,' he pleaded.

'My darling, the carol singers are due any minute.' Still trying not to laugh she twisted her hair into a coil.

'Heigh-ho!' John sighed in mock deprivation. 'Here . . .' he pushed the parcel into her hand. 'There's something

62

under the tree but I wanted to give you this myself. Merry Christmas, my dear love.'

The chemise was finely embroidered with a pearl drop on a thin gold chain pinned to the lace edging. Mary turned away from the mirror and held out her arms: the choir was usually late.

At the Enderby's opulent house, the butler greeted them with relief. 'Thank God you've arrived, doctor.'

'Season's greetings, Tomkins. Hope my patient's still lusty. Don't like it when they go quiet. This is my assistant, Mr McKie.' Tomkins bowed. 'So . . . what appears to be the problem?'

'We think it may have been a game pie, doctor.'

'Strange dish for Christmas?'

'No, sir. A sort of fill-in this afternoon, before tea.'

'Ah . . .'

'Luncheon was the usual festive meal. Soup, a little brill followed by a salmi of black game with lark pie and croquettes of turkey. Served with vegetables, of course.'

'Naturally.'

'Afterwards there was woodcock with a very nice salad, almond pudding and chocolate souffle.'

'Did that complete the menu?'

'Apart from plum pudding served with mince pies and a soupçon of brandy butter, yes sir. Plus an ice. A water ice, nothing rich.'

'This — game pie?'

For the first time, Tomkins appeared uneasy. 'It had been — around, as you might say. The mistress remembered it and feeling peckish, rang the bell. An hour later, she was h'in agony. If you would follow me, gentlemen?'

Silently, the three of them mounted the vast staircase. At the top, an anxious female hovered.

'Ah, Simmons, how is your mistress now?'

'I attempted to administer lime water and milk, as per your usual instructions, doctor.'

'Mrs Enderby refused?'

'She claimed it wasn't to her taste.' Dr Cullen tut-tutted. 'You know what she can be like, doctor? She's properly constipated this time — says it's acidity but you should smell her breath!'

'No doubt that pleasure is to come. Open Sesame!' Simmons flung wide the panelled door and William Cullen swept inside. 'Ah, dear lady, how sad that you should be taken ill today of all days!'

The invalid clutched her distended stomach fretfully. 'I am in pain, Dr Cullen! Why did you not come sooner?'

William Cullen seized the wrist, found the pulse and, before she could protest, thrust a thermometer into her mouth. 'This is my assistant, Mr McKie, at present studying medicine at my old university.'

He withdrew the thermometer and dropped his voice. 'Thank God you sent for me in time!'

In a rush of potent breath, the invalid gasped, 'You mean — it's serious!'

'Dear Mrs Enderby . . .' William Cullen tapped firmly on the vulnerable area.

'Ah!'

'Exactly. Mr McKie, take my bag through to the dressing-room if you please.'

Luke watched him mix liquorice powder with a lavish hand. 'I say,' he muttered.

Sotto voce came the reply, 'Desperate situations call for drastic remedies, Luke, but you and I won't be here when she needs the commode, thank God.' The doctor bore the wine glass back into the bedroom as though it contained the elixir of life eternal. 'Now, dear lady . . . A glass of this three times a day and for nourishment, nothing but fresh figs, oatmeal porridge and Friedrichshalle water.'

'Porridge!'

'If you do not adhere strictly to the regime, I fear I cannot guarantee another Christmas . . .'

'Ooh!'

Back in the trap Dr Cullen was disgruntled. 'She won't stick to it. A week at the most, that's all.'

'All those figs will surely do the trick?' He shrugged. 'They won't do her any harm. Thank God she has a sound constitution.' He tapped Luke on the knee. 'I guess what

64

you're thinking but I depend on the likes of Mrs Enderby for my income. Don't forget, my puritan, a doctor has bills just like everyone else.'

'Does she know you're a sixpenny doctor?'

William Cullen chortled.

'I told her once but she refused to believe it! I came across her in the street in a state of collapse. Heartburn due to indigestion. I prescribed a purge and Mrs Enderby insisted I was her saviour. Who am I to turn my back on Dame Fortune?'

'Where to, doctor?'

'The Emporium. I'm still invited, I take it?'

'Yes, of course.'

Ted and Matthew were fidgety and bored. It was threatening to turn into a rotten Christmas. For some reason when Uncle John and Aunt Mary came down looking happy, Mama was most put out. She snapped open her watch. 'We've waited long enough for Luke,' she announced. 'We'll open our presents now. He can have his later. Jane, sit up straight. I had far better deportment at your age, without the expense of dancing lessons. You can begin, Matthew.'

It was the same every year. As the youngest, Matthew had always had this task, walking to and fro across the warm carpet announcing each package in turn. 'First today, a long thin one . . . "For Jane with dearest love from Great-Aunt and Uncle".'

Close to the fire, Mrs Armitage said a little shakily, 'I decided to give each of you a momento of dear Mr A, this year. One can so easily forget the past. . . .'

Jane rushed to hug her. 'I know what mine is, I can feel it through the paper — it's the fan! You've given me your beautiful fan!'

Mrs Armitage looked on fondly as the wrapping was stripped off. 'It was a Christmas when Armitages was clear of debt for the first time. My dear husband wanted to celebrate.' Jane posed as she had done on stage, the fan in her outstretched hand.

'That's enough,' said Charlotte, 'Christmas is not a time for showing off. Thank your aunt properly and have done, Jane.'

65

Ted held his breath when he saw the old-fashioned gold watch. There was a special knob which when pressed told the time with a tiny tinkling chime. It had been a favourite treat as a child to visit the grocer's sickroom and listen to the silvery sound.

He opened the lid: the white enamel face with gold numerals shone brightly. 'I've had it cleaned,' said Mrs Armitage. 'It keeps perfect time, dear. Great-uncle Armitage always said it would.'

'Thanks very much . . . it's my best present ever!'

'Give Aunt Armitage a kiss, and be very careful!' Mary rescued him.

'The mantelpiece would be a safe place.'

'Thanks.' He'd keep it beside his bed. It more than made up for the loss of his marble. Ted pressed his face against the wrinkled cheek. 'It's what I liked the most of all his things.'

'Yes. I remember how you used to gaze at it when you were a little boy. It was the only time you actually sat still. I think you truly believed the watch was magical.'

'I say . . .' In his corner, Matthew had opened his package. 'A bank-book . . . a proper one.' A shiny stiff cover, with his name in copperplate. He traced the letters: *Matthew David McKie.*

John was about to say the boy was too young when Mrs Armitage urged, 'Open it, Matthew.' They saw his eyes widen.

'I say!' He looked across at the old lady, 'You *are* kind.' Firelight shone on his golden hair and strange blue cat-like eyes. He kissed Mrs Armitage without being bidden. It irritated Charlotte that this child was the most handsome, yet she could not love him.

'I shall make the money grow,' Matthew promised.

'That's what I hoped, dear. It's your nest-egg for the future.'

'How much?' asked Ted, out of curiosity rather than jealousy.

'Fifty pounds,' Matthew stroked the bank-book with a finger.

'Good heavens!' John couldn't stop himself.

'I know it's an enormous sum —'

'Aunt, it's ridiculous!'

'Please don't scold, Charlotte. Matthew won't waste a penny of it, will you dear?' Mrs Armitage put an arm round the thin shoulders. 'With Mr McKie's help, he'll learn to be a good businessman. I have left each of the children exactly the same amount in my Will but I wanted Matthew to have his share now so that he could *learn* to be responsible, just as his father was.'

The old eyes pleaded for understanding but Charlotte was too angry to be kind. 'Give that bank-book to your uncle, Matthew. He will lock it away safely. You are too young for such a responsibility.' This was heavily emphasized so that her aunt should know she'd offended.

But I want Matthew to have a fresh start, thought Mrs Armitage. If he can put the past behind him, why should I not be allowed to help? Her niece steadfastly refused to meet her eyes.

The rest of the gifts were an anti-climax and greeted with mute enthusiasm. When Mary took the children with her to make the tea, Mrs Armitage reached for Charlotte's hand.

'I want Matthew to feel — wanted. He's such a lonely little boy.'

'That is entirely his own fault,' said his mother severely.

'Yes, but he's trying so hard to please you now.'

'He should have tried to please his father when he was alive. Then I might have felt affection for him.' After that there was nothing more to be said.

On their way back, Dr Cullen suddenly recalled several patients who'd asked him to make a social visit. At each house, jugs of porter were waiting and it gradually dawned on Luke that these visits were part of a well-established Christmas ritual. The trap was dismissed and they finished the journey, slightly unsteadily, on foot. As they entered, the doctor enquired a shade too loudly if they'd managed to miss the damn carol singers. Luke hurried him into the kitchen and made him coffee.

William Cullen drank it and burped. 'There's one other thing you can do for me, Luke. If your father offers me a glass or two of port, as I sincerely hope he will, I may not

67

be as capable later on. I'd be obliged if you'd see me to the lift and have Billy Beal convey me home. Once a year I over-indulge myself, d'you see. Ah, Jane! See here, I have my own piece of mistletoe and I'm waiting for a kiss!'

He got more than one for Jane could be lavish. Much to Luke's astonishment, the doctor then went in search of Charlotte, embracing her firmly before bending to salute Mrs Armitage.

Mary caught Luke by the arm. He was surprised how happy she looked after such a busy day. 'Did you notice Billy's present?'

'No?'

'Come back to the kitchen. I've put it on the dresser. He's surpassed himself this year.'

Billy had managed to combine both the objects of his affection: a framed portrait of Blackie, given to Mary.

'But — this was taken in a photographer's studio! How on earth did Billy manage it?'

'When I asked, all he could tell me was "oats". Don't you dare make fun of it!'

'I was picturing Billy laying a trail and Blackie following obediently up the stairs!'

'The studio was on the ground floor, thank goodness.' Luke shook with laughter at the background of velvet curtains and aspidistra.

'I'm astonished the photographer agreed!'

'He made Billy pay double and promise to clean up any mess. Poor Billy! I told him it was the most amazing gift I've ever had and I meant it. No-one is to make fun of him or the photograph. Promise?'

Mary felt a twinge of guilt. She'd only given Billy a pair of curry-combs; there had been little effort in that.

'Would you like your presents now, Luke? We've had ours.'

'How remiss of us,' John apologized. 'Fetch them please, Matthew.'

'Please will you open that one first,' Jane begged.

They gathered round to watch. Luke tustled with the string and asked, 'What did you get?'

68

'A sash from Aunt Mary . . . and the beautiful fan from Aunt Armitage!' Jane sprang to her feet, fan in her hand, the fringed shot silk reflecting the light as she spun round. 'Isn't it gorgeous?!' She stopped spinning, 'And a book on etiquette from Mama.'

'What about Ted?'

'Great-uncle Armitage's watch.'

'The chiming one? I say . . .' — Luke had discovered the gloves — 'Look at these!' He glanced at his mother but she shook her head. As he searched for the card, Charlotte reached across and fingered them curiously.

'You've been very extravagant, Aunt.'

'Those are not my gift, Luke. I gave you slippers.'

'From Jane?' Luke read, astonished. 'My dear girl, these are far too splendid for a mere medical student.'

'You can't refuse them, Luke. I chose them specially!'

'But I've only bought you handkerchieves.' Those had been more than he could afford, but now they seemed paltry.

'Jane needs hankies,' said Ted darkly. 'She's always the first to blub because she's a soppy girl. Ouch!' Charlotte had clipped him on the ear.

'Apologise to your sister, otherwise no supper.'

'I'm sorry, Jane!'

The doctor asked quietly, 'May I be permitted . . .?' Luke handed them over and he felt the fine, soft leather. 'My word! Fit for a king.'

'That's what Mr Hart said.'

'And who better to receive them in this household?' Luke reddened. So he should, thought William Cullen a mite savagely. Yet the boy wasn't to blame; devotion could be tiresome. There'd be broken hearts before Luke found a partner but he must learn to be kind with this tender plant.

'Perhaps you'd like to search my pockets, Miss? Not you, Ted,' he added quickly. 'Your present's in my ulster on the hall-stand. You're so rough, you'd wreck my old jacket.'

It was his custom with their Christmas presents since his first invitation years ago. Bless the child, she knew why he'd suggested it. As Jane smiled gratefully through dewy lashes, William Cullen found himself feeling old. They'd grown up all of a sudden and he hadn't noticed.

69

She opened the heart-shaped box, 'Aren't they beautiful, Mama!' The seed-pearls shone against her skin as Katriona fastened them round her neck.

'My children are dreadfully spoilt,' said Charlotte crossly, 'Jane, you must keep that necklace for special occasions. Dr Cullen, you are too generous.'

'Dear Mrs Davie . . .' he smiled disarmingly, 'How could I do less for a little girl who's turned into a princess?'

Later, in the privacy of their room, John wondered aloud about the money. 'Fifty pounds is more than a year's salary for one of our apprentices.'

'Mrs Armitage understands clearly how much Matthew lacks affection.'

'I treat all the children equally,' John said quickly. 'Perhaps I favour Luke but I try to be fair.'

'That's not what I meant. No one *loves* Matthew, least of all Charlotte.'

'You can't force people to love or buy affection, and Matthew's only a child.'

'Maybe, but Mrs Armitage has demonstrated her faith in him.'

'Charlotte looked furious.'

Mary chuckled. 'Fortunately the old lady was not to be shaken. I even heard her tell Charlotte it was none of her business.'

'Good heavens!'

'It had the desired effect. Charlotte hasn't uttered a word since.'

'I give Matthew his first lesson in accountancy tomorrow.'

'Have the boys decided what they want for their Christmas treat?'

John sighed. 'Another trip to Middlesborough to ride on the Transporter bridge, what else?'

Mary laughed again. 'It's Ted's idea of heaven.'

'I shall use the opportunity to enquire about Jane's future.'

The principal of the dancing academy offered John tea. 'It's a most difficult question, Mr McKie. Jane has talent, we've always known that. She's benefitted most from her classes in Freedom of Expression.' John was baffled. 'Isadora Duncan's methods, Mr McKie. My assistant once studied with the great Isadora.'

'Indeed?' Was this why he'd been asked to pay an additional three-and-sixpence? 'My problem, Miss Robson, lies in persuading Jane's mother to allow her daughter to take it up professionally. Before I can do that, I must be reassured as to Jane's competence. It is a serious business, arranging for a girl to study in London.' His heart quailed at the prospect of trying to convince Charlotte.

'I fear I cannot help with your decision. The responsibility is too great.'

'Nevertheless . . .?'

'Mr McKie, in another year or so, Jane will have learned all we can teach and need more experienced guidance. At present her technique is still weak. If she could practise more regularly, that would be to her advantage.'

John thought he understood. 'She needs to practise after school rather than work in the Emporium?'

'Dancers must exercise constantly if they are to improve.'

'Then Jane must have the opportunity.' He was prepared to argue with Charlotte for that.

After the first five lessons in accountancy, John said, 'You've done very well, Matthew. I don't think I got there much faster and I was older when I began the subject.'

'Thank you, Uncle. And thank you for keeping my bank-book safe. I'd hate to think it might be stolen!'

Which might be one way of teaching you a valuable lesson, thought John wryly.

Towards the end of the week, Luke received his invitation. 'Jack Creswell mentioned a ball but I didn't think he'd remember. Should I accept, d'you think?'

'Of course, dear,' Mary looked genuinely pleased. 'I'm delighted for you. Dr Cullen's been working you hard. How kind of the Creswells. A New Year's Eve Ball?' She turned the card over in her hand, 'It sounds very grand.'

'This note from Jack suggests I stay overnight.'

'And thoughtful. I hope you enjoy yourself.'

71

Luke fingered the envelope awkwardly. 'I feel I've neglected you this holiday, Mother. I didn't mean to.'

'Bless you, of course you haven't, my dear. You're a young man now, ready to leave home and make new friends. It happens to everyone, Luke.'

'Yes, but. . .' He was bashful at trying to express what he felt.

Mary squeezed his hand. 'Just remember to keep coming back to us, Luke. For John's sake as well as mine. That's what matters most to me.'

'You can't go!' Jane wailed when she discovered his plans. 'Not on New Year's Eve!'

It brought a flash of temper. 'Oh for heavens' sake, Jane! A fellow has a right to enjoy himself. I can't be forever trailing after you.'

She went pale as though he'd slapped her. 'Will you be back to let in the New Year?' she whispered.

'No.'

'I expect Dorothy will be allowed to stay up!' The mighty injustice could not be contained. 'She's been at grown-up parties all Christmas!'

'Well, she behaves like a grown-up person not a silly little girl!'

When Luke arrived and was shown to his room, he found a deep, hot bath had been drawn for him. Jack Creswell's valet laid out his clothes. As he fumbled with his tie, Luke revelled in the luxury of a dressing-room. Would he ever be able to afford such a comfortable home, full of books and flowers?

A sixpenny doctor would inevitably mean modest circumstances. To aim higher meant closing his eyes to all he'd seen this holiday. Would his conscience remain quiescent? Worse still, could he face John McKie if he opted for an easier life?

'Mr Creswell's compliments.' The valet was offering one perfect gardenia on a salver. 'May I, sir?' He pinned it in place and took a brush to Luke's shoulders. Instinctively, Luke straightened his back. The man looked him over critically. 'Might I suggest . . .?' and knelt to flick a duster over Luke's shoes.

Dash it, Luke grumbled to himself, a chap is entitled to some of life's rewards.

'Gloves, sir?' Luke produced these with great confidence and slid a hand into the silk-lined kid. It should have reminded him of Jane but, alas, it did not.

Luke walked down the staircase, Jack Creswell beside him. In the hall, the womenfolk waited; elegant women in beautiful dresses, women who spent their lives in easy luxury. Luke could hear an orchestra playing in the ballroom.

A butler approached. 'Champagne, sir?'

There were no schoolgirls tonight. Graceful white necks inclined towards him as cards were proffered and he claimed his share of the dances.

'Mr McKie, I believe this is ours?' It was his hostess in glittering satin with an aigrette of jewels in her hair. A parure of rubies emphasized her husband's success in ship-building; it would have paid for the whole of Potters Yard to be rebuilt with proper sanitation and Luke frowned that such a thought should enter his mind. Mrs Creswell misunderstood. 'You look very handsome in evening clothes, Mr McKie. Jack felt just as embarrassed the first time I insisted he wear them. Shall we go in?'

Champagne, wonderful golden nectar evaporated in his glass. He was suddenly a wag; women laughed at whatever he said. They hung on his arm and he danced with so many of them. Soft skin, milk white under candle-lit sconces, and perfume, rich and heady, stealing his senses away.

'Happy New Year!'

In the Emporium, John raised a glass and kissed Mary's cheek and the pearl pendant nestling in her bosom. 'Here's to Father up on the croft and a prosperous 1913, my dearest.'

CHAPTER FIVE

Admirers

When he returned to the lodgings in Jesmond, it felt to Luke as if he'd been away months rather than weeks. He caught the same train as Kessel who was returning from a holiday abroad. As it steamed into Darlington station, the cheerful tubby figure waved vigorously.

'In here, McKie . . . Happy New Year!'

'Greetings, old fellow. Take care of these will you.' Luke passed up an assortment of bags and kissed Mary hastily.

'I'll write. It's not long till Easter.'

'Pleased to meet you, Mrs McKie.' Kessel raised his cap. 'Hop in old chap, there goes the whistle.'

Acrid smoke blotted her from view and Luke sank back in his seat. 'So, how was Germany?'

Kessel pulled a face. 'So-so . . . Lots of boring politicians making rude speeches. One of my cousins wanted to drag me along but father and I went to *Die Fledermaus* instead.'

'Sounds more fun.'

'It was . . .' Kessel blew a kiss at remembered enchantment. 'After Christmas we had a few days at the family chalet near Halle — now that was wonderful, nothing but deep snow and pine forests. How about you?'

'I spent most of the time with Dr Cullen on his rounds.'

'Did you, by Jove!' Kessel gazed at him enviously. 'Kill any patients?'

'Not more than a couple. That chalet of yours, has it a corner where a friend could seek refuge? Occasionally, my family swamp me with too much affection.'

Kessel nodded sympathetically. 'You're ready to fly the nest. I know the feeling. Why don't you come with me next summer? It's splendid walking country. I'd love to show it to you and there's a lake where we swim.'

Luke grinned at the portly figure opposite. 'Would the beer do as much for me as it has for you?'

'Indubitably!'

In Jesmond, other students had stoked up a blazing fire. There was sufficient seasonal goodwill for them to make room for the newcomers. A muffin man had called and one young gentleman wielded the toasting fork, another the butter-knife as plates were handed round. The leader, Bennet-Reeves, was describing his holiday. 'My father suggested I spend time in his pharmacy. Naturally I didn't object, because of Queenie.'

'Oh-ho!'

'Dashed pretty nurse, Queenie.' He lit a second gasper from his first. 'Taught me all she knew, what.'

'I say!'

'Even learned a thing or two about potions and pills!'

Amid the shocked laughter Luke helped himself to a muffin. 'Are you planning to join your father eventually?' he asked.

'It's not a bad little practice,' Bennett-Reeves admitted. 'Cheltenham's full of widows sufferin' from the vapours, which ain't exactly taxin'. There's decent shootin' and golf. The pater and I ride to hounds regularly — one could do a lot worse. Of course I shan't breathe a word to the surgical tutor — I rely on you fellows to stay mum.'

'Rather!' Another, whose father was in general practice, was equally fervent, 'If Matheson were to hear, you and I would never see inside his operating theatre again!'

'I think that's so much affectation,' said Luke quietly.

'What is?' asked Kessel.

'Mr Matheson's habit of proclaiming general practitioners a sub species. Also his attitude toward any patient who has the temerity to die under his knife. When he walks away from the table there is often little chance of survival.'

'Hang it all, McKie ...' He'd made them uneasy. 'Matheson's a brilliant surgeon and a pioneer in his field. It's not his fault if the occasional patient fails to respond —

75

Look how well his papers are received,' said Bennet-Reeves.

'Nevertheless, I believe an ordinary physician practising among the working class can benefit humanity
more.'

'The working class! Good God, McKie!' Bennet-Reeves
threw his cigarette away in disgust. 'You're not suggesting
Matheson should waste his skill on *them*? Their hospital
tickets entitle them to adequate treatment, what more do
they need? Those who are sober enough to stay in employment have fresh air and exercise to keep them healthy.
Many never consult a doctor in their lives.'

'But that's my point, Bennet-Reeves. Many Poor Law
hospitals are at best, merely "adequate". Most are far worse
and the mortality rates too high.'

'You're not implying a surgeon of the calibre of Cosmo
Matheson should condescend to operate in one? He
wouldn't let you kiss the hem of his garment if he knew you
harboured such thoughts.'

'Surely a surgeon's skills should be available to all?'

''Pon my soul, McKie, you speak like some damned
proselyte who's discovered a vocation to heal the sick!'
Bennet-Reeves sneered. 'You wouldn't dare suggest it to
Matheson's face.'

Luke ignored the challenge. 'Pass me the butter, would
you.'

There was some further muttering which he pretended
not to notice. Kessel murmured, 'Thrown your cap in
the ring with a vengence, McKie?' Luke's knife clattered
against the dish. He obviously wasn't feeling as brave as
his words. To divert the rest, Kessel asked, 'Apart from
the pharmacy, Bennet-Reeves, did you actually assist your
father in his practice?'

'Of course! One of his patients has a pair of deuced pretty
daughters. I practised my bedside manner on them.'

'Meet any "deuced pretty daughters" on your rounds?'
Kessel enquired of Luke.

'Among the working class, yes. One who looked angelic.'

Kessel's eyebrows rose in mock-horror, 'Careful, old
chap. You could be struck off before you're even on
the register.'

76

Later, Kessel tapped on his door. 'May I interrupt?'

'Do.'

He shivered as he came in. 'No fire?'

'I find it makes me sleepy,' said Luke carelessly, 'A rug over my knees is sufficient.'

Hmm, thought Kessel. He handed Luke a photograph. 'Where we'll be staying if you come with me next summer.' It was a winter landscape. He pointed to members of his family standing in front of a picturesque log cabin. 'My cousins Frieda and Lila . . . this is Hans. They'll all be there.'

'They look very jolly.'

'They are. It should be a marvellous holiday,' Kessel beamed, 'I have written of you many times, of course. Our prize student who never lifts his head from a book.'

I've scarcely mentioned you to my family and you're my friend, thought Luke guiltily.

'Would you like to come to Darlington next Easter? There aren't any pine forests but it's a sight nearer than Halle and my parents would be delighted.'

'I should be honoured.'

In her small stone cottage not far from the schoolhouse and the loch, the retired school mistress re-read John's New Year letter impatiently. 'No, I can't come galloping down to England every time Charlotte proves obdurate,' she told the empty air, 'I'm certainly not spending three days on a train at my time of life. You bring her up here, John McKie, or better still, come by yourself.'

In the bedroom, the girl who cleaned twice a week, heard the rumble. Talking to herself again, was she? Mistress Shields often did that; the girl had become accustomed to it. When she'd finished grumbling, there would be another letter to deliver to the post office. Helen Shields had predictable habits.

'Ena, come in here a minute, will you?' The girl returned to the parlour. 'Have you heard anything of Alex McKie recently? The weather's been too bad for me to visit, I was wondering how he was managing?'

'He spent the New Year with the Hamiltons and hasna returned to his croft, I'm thinking.'

'"Hasn't",' Helen Shields corrected automatically, 'Or better still, "has not". What about his beasts?'

'Oh, he doesn't *have* them any more, Mistress Shields, he's too old.'

Helen bit back the retort that Alex wasn't much older than herself. 'How does he live if he has no beasts to sell?'

'On the money his son sends him. Old Mr McKie doesna — doesn't — spend all of it of course, and the Hamiltons wouldn't take a penny, but it's there if it's needed.'

In this community, although it was widely spread, little was hidden. They knew how their neighbours fared on the Peninsula. A lifetime's habit of scrimping couldn't change for Alex McKie. He wouldn't waste money on comfort. If he'd failed to send his sons to university then his savings would be used to help his grandchildren.

'Before I reply to John,' said Helen thoughtfully, 'I'd like to send a note to his father.'

'If you were to give it to me, I'll hand it to the next Hamilton I see.'

Beside a peat fire, Alex McKie read the English carefully. He was in wee George Hamilton's favourite chair, the wood black with age and the sagging upholstery shaped by generations of Hamilton backsides. Every morning Alex McKie never failed to declare how comfortable it was.

Wee George enjoyed seeing the old man sit there. The Hamiltons were carters. Son and grandson had followed wee George into the business but years ago when they were children, John McKie had spared the time to teach wee George to read, which was why it gave him particular satisfaction now to care for Alex.

It was baking day. Wee George's wife stooped to lift the first batch of bread from the oven.

'The old schoolmistress is scolding me over John,' Alex told her.

'Why?'

'He's having difficulties with Davie's widow, Charlotte.'

'Ah!' Charlotte McKie had only visited the Peninsula once but the impact had been considerable.

78

'He wants Mistress Shields to go to England, to reason with Charlotte about her daughter becoming a dancer.'

'What an idea! As if the schoolmistress would agree to that? And is he forgetting how old she is? Fancy expecting an old woman to go all that way in winter-time!' Ann Hamilton checked her indignation. 'Perhaps they do not have the bad weather in England and John has forgotten? That would likely be the reason?'

Alex pondered. 'John showed me Darlington on the map, one time. He did not mention the weather, only that it was a bigger town than Fort William, with factories and engineering works, all belching out smoke.'

Flushed from bending over the peat fire, Ann Hamilton tried to imagine it. 'It sounds a terrible dirty place and not suitable for Mistress Shields at all.'

'Aye . . . I will try and explain that to John.'

John read the letter and noticed how shaky the writing had become. He must make an effort to visit this year: there might not be many more opportunities. He was scribbling a note to remind himself when Mary tapped at the door.

'Sorry to interrupt, dear. I come to petition you on Ted's behalf.'

'What's he been up to now?'

'Don't frown.' She smiled and ran a finger to flatten the offending line across his forehead. 'Ted wants to join the Boy's Brigade, that's all.'

'No.'

'John, my love, he's the only boy in the Sunday School who isn't a member. He feels it keenly.'

'It has become more of a militant organization lately, Mary. Forgive me if I seem to fuss but should the unrest continue in Ireland, the Brigade could be called to the colours.'

'Surely it's not that serious? And all Ted wants to do, like any schoolboy, is bang a drum or blow a bugle. It's only two nights a week until he leaves school: eighteen months. Once he's at university, he'll no doubt look on it as childish. Charlotte has given her permission provided you agree.'

'University!' John shook his head, 'Mary, my love, that would take a miracle — and you know it. As for Charlotte, her family were never called on to fight, so she doesn't really understand.'

Mary chuckled. 'It's a pity Charlotte couldn't become a warrior. She's more warlike than anyone else I know. She might have taught the Boers a thing or two. John, please consider; we cannot forbid Ted everything. Far better let him work off his exuberance in the church hall than irritate Charlotte and I here? Several Brigades are holding a summer camp near Barnard Castle next July and Ted is wild to go. They will be competing in sports — you know how that brings out the best in him.'

'I'll think about it. Here . . .' He picked up a second letter, 'This came from the church.'

Mary held it at arms' length. 'What does it say?'

'Why will you not wear glasses?'

'For the same reason as Charlotte,' she replied a little crisply, 'Because it would spoil my looks.'

Such vanity from his wife came as a shock but John recovered. 'They are holding a Bazaar to raise funds for Ulster and want to put a booklet together, favourite sayings and quotations, that kind of thing. Would you like to contribute?'

'I don't think so, thank you, John. Why not ask Luke?'

'That's a good idea. I can ask him for some witty medical aphorisms.' Oh, dear! thought Mary, and out of love, she kissed him.

When he heard Luke sigh, Kessel looked up from his coffee. 'Problems?'

'Father wants an "amusing and succinct" contribution for this booklet. It's for a church bazaar. Here, you do it, you're good at jokes.'

Kessel glanced through some of the pages '"Ulster will fight and Ulster will be right"' he read, puzzled, 'Rather belligerent for a religious pamphlet? Ah, the proceeds are for Protestant funds in Northern Ireland . . . Here's one submitted by "Ted McKie"?'

'My cousin. What does it say?'

Kessel read aloud:

The shades of night were falling fast,
As through the streets there sneaking past,
A maid, who grasped as in a vice,
A banner with a weird device: VOTES FOR WOMEN!'

'Oh, lor'!' Luke leaned back in his chair, 'I wonder where Ted got hold of that? Poor Father — that'll open old wounds.' Kessel raised his eyebrows and he explained lightly, 'My father was once smitten by a lady suffragette, a Miss Cecilia Crowther. It was a temporary infatuation and ancient history now. Anything else from my family?'

'"If you cannot skim all the cream off life, do not let disappointment sour the milk," donated by Mrs Adelaide Armitage.'

'Dear great-aunt! Come on, conjure up a few *bon mots* and I can send the wretched thing back.' Kessel wrote then passed the page across.

'"Never, never chew your pills,"' read Luke,

'"Nor leave unpaid your doctor's bills,
But take with grace what'er they send,
And be prepared to meet your end!!" I say, Kessel, you'd better not sign that!'

As they walked through the wrought-iron gates of the medical school, Kessel asked, 'Why is everyone concerned with Ulster all of a sudden? I heard one of the other chaps the other day — he sounded very excited.'

'Father tried to explain at Christmas. The trouble was, I wasn't really interested.'

'This chap carried on just like my cousin in Leipzig. When I asked *him* to explain, he couldn't; he was too emotional. Perhaps your esteemed father can enlighten me on Ireland?'

'Good idea,' said Luke comfortably. 'Let's ask him at Easter,' for he had finally remembered to send word to Mary of their impending visit.

'Uncle John?' John took off the pince-nez.

'What is it?' Jane advanced further into the office.

'It's about Mama.'

'Yes?'

'She's had the mirror taken away from the stock-room, where you said I could practice.'

'But you need it to see whether you're doing the exercises correctly?'

'Mama says it's bad for the character and will make me vain.' John closed his eyes. 'Please will you speak to her?'

'Yes ...' He heard her leave then as he picked up his pen, the door re-opened. 'What is it this time — Oh, it's you, Mary.'

'You're looking harassed.'

'Charlotte is a fool!'

'Yes, dear. Will you tell her or shall I? Anyway, I've more important news. Luke wants to bring his student friend here at Easter.'

'Splendid!' John was transformed. 'You know I've often wondered whether Luke would consider us good enough —'

'Of course we are!' Mary pretended to be indignant but in her heart she was just as nervous. 'Is it all right if I send for Mr Clough?'

'As soon as possible. Which rooms should he redecorate?'

'That depends on whether Mr Kessel is to share with Luke?'

'No, no! He must have his own bedroom, somewhere for his books should he need to study —' but before John could enlarge on his plans Mary said, 'There's another matter we should discuss, particularly as it concerns Charlotte. She has an admirer.'

'He's that tall shiny man who always wears a ribbon to keep his hat from blowing away.'

Ted frowned. 'Lots of customers have those, 'specially this time of year.'

'He's got a big, boomy voice.'

As recognition dawned, Ted bounced off his chair. 'Not the one with the pointy beard who calls me "My little man"?'

Jane nodded glumly, 'Mr Eustace Percival.'

'Are you completely sure?' He was horrified.

'They haven't been introduced but Mr Hart told Miss Attewood in confidence that Mr Percival is always dropping in to buy the odd pair of silk hose and when Mrs Beal asked Katriona if there was any truth in the rumour, she said the trouble was Mama was a good catch and she wouldn't be surprised if Mr Percival hadn't got an eye on the main chance.'

'What does that mean?'

'I don't know, we'll have to ask Matthew.'

'But Mama's old!' Ted said scornfully.

'She's thirty-four and she doesn't wear black any more, have you noticed? Katriona says Mr Percival's about forty. He's a widower.'

'Maybe he poisoned his wife?' Ted was an avid reader of Mrs Beal's Sunday newspaper.

'That's a wicked thing to say!'

'Suppose we tell Mama he did, to put her off?'

Jane looked severe. 'You do that and you'll get more than just the cane!'

Matthew added to their gloom. 'Mama inherited father's share of the business so if she marries someone else, they could ask for a bit of it.'

'You mean he'd own a bit of the Emporium, just by marrying her?' asked Ted angrily.

'Sort of. It's called a Settlement, I think.'

'That's damned unfair!'

'Ted!'

'Well it is. Mr Percival didn't work hard like Papa. Anyway why should Mama want to marry a big boomy fool like him?'

'Katriona says she's lonely,' Jane replied.

'Lonely?' The carroty hair was standing on end, 'How can she be when she's got us three?'

The following Sunday, after exhaustive enquiries, John stared gloomily at the tall, broad back in the fourth pew: he could discover nothing to Mr Percival's discredit.

The man was of unblemished character with a house in Westbrook Villas. There were no children and since his wife

83

died the sorrowing husband had devoted himself to business, apart from his hobby of playing the clarinet. John murmured despairingly to Mary, 'I wonder if he knows Charlotte isn't musical? Perhaps we could drop a hint?'

'Don't be ridiculous!'

Beyond them, Charlotte's three children also stared, breasts full of un-Christian sentiments. Ted pondered dark deeds of murder and mayhem. Thoughts of poison turned quite naturally to thoughts of pummelling the shiny, hearty face to pulp. Or better still, if he waited in a dark alley with a knife, he could plunge it deep into Mr Percival's heart!

'Let us pray . . .'

The very idea of that bold, loud man moving into their lives was sickening. Please God, at the very least make his teeth fall out!

Matthew worried about his inheritance. He'd asked several innocent-sounding questions; the answers hadn't been encouraging. The most disturbing, according to Jane, was that women as old as their mother could still have babies. The prospect of sharing everything with Ted and Jane was bad enough; Matthew didn't want it whittled away even further.

Jane was disturbed by the subtle changes in her mother's appearance, particularly the new hairstyle which was soft and flattering. Did Mama feel attracted to Mr Percival? When Jane had asked, Katriona had pulled a face. 'She is and she isn't, as you might say, pet. Your Mama's got over feeling sad about your Papa. Now that it's spring, she's remembered she's still a young woman.'

Jane thought she understood why Mama was lonely. In the old days Papa had been so attentive. After any absence he came home with flowers but no-one did that now.

Was Mr Percival the sort to give bouquets? Suddenly, Jane had a dreadful vision of him in Mama's bedroom, in a night-shirt!! She was vague as to the exact procedure after gentlemen had removed their clothes — Dorothy claimed to know but refused to tell — but the very idea of Mr Percival in bed with her mother made Jane feel ill. Please, please, dear God!

Charlotte looked along the line of bowed heads: the carroty red, the brunette and lastly Matthew's neatly brushed fair one. The children were so well-behaved this morning, it made her very content.

An acknowledged if unspoken truth between Ted and his uncle was that information had a price, particularly the sort John required. A couple of weeks later, on a Saturday afternoon, two fat paper bags lay on the office desk. The first contained liquorice sherbet, the second the sort of sticky fudge Charlotte insisted was bad for the teeth.

John hovered by the half-open door as Ted sauntered past.

The name of the sweet-shop on the bags was one Ted rated highly. It took but a second for him to spot this and gauge the weight of the contents; he changed direction without uttering a word. His uncle closed the door behind them. 'Help yourself.'

'Thanks very much.' The bag with sherbet disappeared inside his clothing and Ted stuffed two pieces of fudge into his mouth.

John waited until the bulge had diminished. 'Was it an interesting walk this afternoon?'

Ted scowled and chewed. Eventually he said, 'Twice round South Park, until it began to rain.'

'I see she's got you into long 'uns.'

Ted contemplated the new grey flannel trousers. 'Mama *said* it was because I was always pulling up my stockings but what she really wanted was to show me off to that chump.'

Greatly daring, John asked the pertinent question. 'Mr Percival was there, was he? In the park?' He had to wait for two more pieces of fudge to be consumed, one for each question, before Ted deigned to reply.

'Yes, he was.'

'Did they speak to one another?'

Ted looked at him pityingly. 'They haven't been properly introduced, have they?' All Charlotte's children had been schooled in correct social behaviour.

'No more they have,' John agreed humbly.

The bag was nearly empty but Ted surprised him with unexpected generosity. 'He's pretty foul,' he volunteered. 'None of us like him.' He slipped the remaining fudge into his pocket. 'I'd better go and wash — it's nearly time for supper.'

Later, in bed, John said complacently, 'The children don't like him,' and Mary knew who he meant.

As Easter approached the smell of distemper increased. Mary's anxiety meant that Mr Clough was given a free hand. Assistants tripped over dust-sheets and Billy Beal mopped up spilt paint from morning 'til night. Despite the activity it was noticeable how silent Charlotte had become, as well as thoughtful. Her toilette, always immaculate, was now extremely fashionable. Her hats were wide, her skirts narrow, so much so that the mincing step they necessitated made Katriona pull yet another face, but only when Charlotte wasn't looking.

The weather was balmy. On the train, Luke relaxed. The first lambs were in the fields, the clouds above looked as white and fluffy. Through the window the massive cathedral high above the bend of the Wear came into view. 'Have you been to Durham?' he asked Kessel.

'Not yet. It is a "must", I think?'

'It definitely merits a detour,' Luke agreed. 'Perhaps we could all go? We'll have to arrange it so that Mother can sit somewhere while we explore. She'd enjoy an outing.'

Always his mother, thought Kessel. Luke's first concern every time. Was it because he was an only child? The McKie household was large by all accounts. His friend fidgeted now they were almost there. 'Not much of a view I'm afraid, nothing but engineering works this end of town . . . There's the river.'

This term Luke had finally stopped growing and begun to fill out. He and Kessel had joined the university cycling club and the results were beginning to show. Both were fitter and Luke's usually pale skin glowed with health. 'Do you like walking, Kessel? There's a chap I know, Jack Creswell, his family sometimes make up a party. There's wonderful moorland countryside up beyond Stanhope.'

86

'They do not object to strangers?'

'Oh no, they're most hospitable.'

Billy was waiting with Blackie but they sent him ahead with their bags, preferring to walk. 'Darlington's not a very grand sort of place,' Luke said. 'Father says the slump is still affecting trade.'

'In Germany there is much unemployment. According to my cousin, that is why they are building so many new ships.'

'Mr Creswell is in ship-building. You and he will have something to talk about.'

I must remember Luke hasn't travelled thought Kessel as they wandered through what was obviously a small industrial town. Luke's pride in it was touching. It looked busy enough and had one or two fine modern buildings. There was a massive old grey church set in a patch of green bounded by a river and beyond, up a cobbled rise, the covered market. On one corner of that was a distinctive clock-tower.

'Quite a landmark,' said Luke proudly. 'Look, there's the Emporium.'

Kessel stared at the colonnade of windows. He'd been prepared to be kind, remembering shops in London, Paris and Berlin, but was surprised. The building occupied the entire corner site and had at one time presumably been a warehouse. Certainly it was an awkward shape but sparkling white paint gave it a unity and against this, the gold legend MCKIE BROTHERS gleamed.

'Let's walk past the windows,' Luke urged, 'They're Father's pride and joy at this time of year. He and Mr Hart spend ages planning every detail.'

Mr Hart was the first to spot them and raised his eyebrows to the cashier who sent a message along the wire. Miss Attewood handed it to an apprentice who ran upstairs to the kitchen. 'They've arrived, Mrs McKie. They're outside looking at the displays.'

'Thank you, Gertie.'

'Oh my!' Kessel paused in front of the final window. He'd been impressed with what he'd seen so far. The displays weren't extensive but the goods were of excellent quality and well laid out. *The* shade of the season was obviously primrose. In consequence, decor was spring-like and delicate but the final tableau stopped Kessel in his tracks.

A group of elegantly-costumed models sat at a garden table in front of a flowery meadow. It was their repast that had caught his eye. 'See what they're supposed to be eating, Luke? Those are slices of torte!' His eyes were alight. 'I haven't tasted that since I was in Leipzig.'

'They've got different sorts of cake in the Salon. I don't know if any come from Germany.'

'No matter — I desire a cream cake. My body is enraptured at the very idea! Would your parents be greatly offended? May I treat you to such a thing in the Salon?'

'Why not! What a joke — come on, let's pretend to be customers.'

'Not customers, old fellow, dignitaries. Of high rank and extremely foreign.'

'I say!'

Luke followed, trying not to laugh as Kessel strutted, his hat balanced in the crook of his arm, his umbrella swinging as he bowed to right and left. Gutteral German showered shop-assistants and customers alike. He advanced, manifesting pleasure at a young lady trying on a hat, nodding enthusiastically to Miss Attewood and finally bent his knee when Luke whispered that it was his aunt who approached them. It was done as a prank but when Kessel looked up into the cool blue eyes, he found himself feeling foolish.

'This is my friend, Theodore Kessel, Aunt.'

'Mr Kessel who is to be our guest?' Charlotte's clear voice sounded puzzled. Theodore scrambled to his feet and dusted his knees.

'Mrs Davie McKie, I believe? Madam, I am enchanted.' He bent over her hand. 'I have looked forward to making your acquaintance after hearing so much from Luke. May I ask you to join us? The cakes in the window cast a spell. We felt an irresistible urge to visit the Salon.' He extended his arm.

Charlotte smiled. 'I don't think I've ever sat in there as a customer. Shall I lead the way? It's my usual custom to take tea with my Aunt — perhaps, Luke, you could go and explain?'

'By no means. She must join us also. Luke old fellow, round up all your family, let it be a proper tea-party.'

'I'll see how many I can find.'

'Come Mrs Davie.' Kessel swept her along. 'Your nephew's too thin, don't you know. As his medical man, I insist he consume at least six cakes this afternoon. Ah . . .!' They had arrived at the Salon, 'How delightful . . . *c'est beau, n'est ce pas?*' His gaze took in the elegance, the pink, blue and gold, 'I truly hadn't expected this. For you, Mrs Davie, it provides the perfect setting.'

Kessel's frank admiration embarrassed her because it was unexpected. His manners were gallant, but extremely continental she decided. All they knew about the young man was that he was several years older than Luke but where Luke was tall and dark, Theodore Kessel was chubby with a beaming face and a fringe of curly hair. The gap in age left Charlotte uncertain how to treat him. This was no raw student but a mature young man and his personality was a breath of fresh air in the stultified gentility of the Salon. Bertha advanced and Theodore made an exaggerated bow.'The very best and largest table if you please.'

Luke met Mary at the foot of the stairs. 'Luke . . . how lovely to see you looking so fit! But where's Mr Kessel?'

'Busy making sheep's eyes at Aunt Charlotte.'

'Good gracious! Does he want his face slapped?'

'Oh, she's loving every minute,' he assured her. 'Go and join them while I find Father. It's tea and buns for everyone in the Salon.'

Under Kessel's direction, chairs were grouped round a table. He handed Mrs Armitage to a seat with great cere-mony then, much to her surprise, did the same for Bertha. 'Sit, sit,' he ordered, 'It is for us to serve you, today. Ah, the father of Luke, yes? How d'you do, Mr McKie. Your son is a very clever fellow — but I'm sure you knew that already. Off with your coat, my boy, it is our turn to serve today. Mrs McKie, it has been my desire to meet you again after that tantalizing glimpse from the train. Tea for six please, Luke and plenty of cakes. I will attend to the other customers.' He began the circuit of giggling ladies.

'Mesdames, how ravishing you look. I close my eyes lest I be dazzled and will only open them to execute your orders. Yes . . .? Chocolate gateau *immédiatement, mademoiselle.*'

'A quaint way to behave,' said John.

'He's an eccentric.' Charlotte was enjoying herself.

After Kessel had sold every cake and demonstrated the latest surgical technique using two éclairs and a fork, there was standing room only in the Salon. Ladies wiped away their laughter and gentlemen from the 'Smoking' crowded in to watch. Luke rushed about fulfilling orders until Mary took pity and sent a message to Mr Hart asking for the apprentices to give a hand.

It took but a murmur from Charlotte that her aunt looked tired for Kessel to bring his performance to a close. He assisted Mrs Armitage back to her parlour himself and made sure both footstool and rug were in place. 'Forty winks, dear lady and no cheating. We will see you again when you are refreshed.'

Luke waited, leaning against a wall. 'Thanks to you, I'm exhausted.'

'Tut-tut, in one so young that is terrible. Where is your beautiful aunt?'

'Who — Aunt Charlotte?'

'You have more? Show me, I beg!'

'I say . . . steady on!' Luke stiffened, 'She is over thirty, you know.'

Kessel shook his head. 'How very British you are, McKie.' A little put out, Luke led the way to their own rooms. It hadn't struck him before that as well as being older, Kessel was half-foreign. Aunt Charlotte, beautiful?

His friend was quieter at supper. He sat facing Jane and the lady assistants and within earshot of Charlotte. There was laughter but at a discreet level. Jane was delighted because Theodore was so lavish in his praise of Luke. After listening to this for a moment or two, Charlotte asked, 'And which branch of medicine do you intend to pursue, Mr Kessel?'

90

'I hope to specialize in anaesthetics, Mrs Davie. To relieve pain is a reward in itself. It is an interesting science with many possibilities.'

'Where will you go to specialize?'

Kessel spread his arms wide. 'Here, there — anywhere. Am I not fortunate? Thanks to my family I studied in Leipzig before coming to Newcastle. I can go wherever the research is, wherever a hospital will take me.' He pretended to be solemn for a moment. 'I am also fortunate that one Luke McKie has not opted for the same speciality.'

'Why?' Jane was round-eyed, elbows on the table.

'I would be forced to choose something else, Miss McKie, for I cannot abide younger men who are cleverer than me.' They laughed but he protested, 'I assure you that it's true.'

At their end of the table, John asked, 'Does he always play the clown?'

'He's a man of many moods, Father. I've known Kessel moved to tears when describing music. On the way here, we were discussing a possible outing to Durham. D'you think Mother would like that?'

John looked pleased. 'Were you intending to go by train?'

'If there are enough of us, perhaps we could hire a chara-banc? It would make it easier for her,' said Luke, which was all John needed to begin making plans.

'Father usually offers me a tot of whisky before bed, down in the office. Would you care to join us?'

'Most definitely,' said Kessel. With luck, he might be permitted to light his pipe there. He was, and he puffed contentedly as John poured three drams and brought Luke up to date with family gossip.

'With whom does Mrs Davie McKie spend her evenings?' he asked in a pause. 'With Mrs Armitage?'

'I don't think so,' Luke answered, 'The old lady goes to bed quite early. The assistants use the dining-room after we've finished with it. I suppose Aunt Charlotte returns to her parlour, does she, Father? I've never really thought about it.'

'It's a very comfortable room,' John said. 'Charlotte has a fire whenever she wants it and Bertha sometimes joins her

91

after the old lady has retired. Of course Charlotte used to go out nearly every evening when my brother was alive because he was on so many committees.'

Kessel accepted his tot. 'Thank you, sir. *Prosit*!'

'*Slâinte mhath*!'

'Must be a bit lonely for her, by comparison.'

'Yes . . .' From John's expression Theodore guessed he was on delicate ground and didn't pursue the subject.

'Any news of the silent wooer?' Luke demanded with a grin.

John considered this improper in front of a stranger. 'Not as far as I am aware,' he said shortly.

Luke wasn't to be suppressed. 'My aunt has an admirer.'

'Aah . . .' Theodore Kessel felt a twinge of something he couldn't name but raised his glass, 'To the fortunate gentleman.'

'We cannot be sure . . . that is to say, Charlotte has not yet expressed an opinion. As far as I am aware, that is.' John's chagrin was obvious. 'The problem is, it could affect the future of the Emporium quite considerably, Mr Kessel.'

Theodore thought he understood. 'A sad situation for a beautiful woman. To have to deny oneself for the sake of business or one's children.' John considered this was putting it far too high but refused to discuss it.

'It might not come to anything, Father,' Luke consoled him.

'I sincerely hope it doesn't. It might affect the business but also the children, who don't like Percival in the slightest.' John downed the rest of his drink, indicating the subject was closed.

Luke's assessment of his friend had been accurate; Theodore could be impulsive as well as emotional, although acutely aware of both these defects. He copied out precepts, much to Luke's amusement. Whenever Luke came across one, he would give an exaggerated sigh, 'I'm doing my best, old fellow, grant me that. Must try harder!' If Luke had recalled his friend's character when on their way to bed Theodore asked, 'What sort of fellow is this Percival?' he might not have replied so off-handedly.

'The place is humming with talk of romance but I fear it's nothing of the sort. Father's pretty shrewd; he thinks the fellow is after a share in the business. Not much of a compliment to Aunt Charlotte perhaps, but more realistic. I realize she must be lonely — Uncle Davie was a marvellous chap — but Percival is scarcely a substitute. She should turn him down.'

'She must be warned!'

'Oh, one couldn't possibly *say* anything, she can be dreadfully obstinate you know. Maybe Ted will succeed in scuppering any plans,' Luke said cheerfully, 'According to Father, he's taken a positive scunner to him.'

But this was far too haphazard. Theodore Kessel thought Charlotte too delightful to be abandoned to a fortune hunter. In his eyes, her voluptuous figure was continental in its elegance and style. He never thought to find in England a woman who attracted him so much.

Loneliness was a state Theodore understood. Before Luke had arrived at Jesmond, he'd been shunned as an outsider. He'd always yearned to belong to a warm, loving family such as the McKies. Had he not arrived in the nick of time, to protect them? Surely nothing but fate had brought him to Darlington? This beautiful woman had entered his life and must be rescued. Caution was thrust aside. Theodore had a vision of cool blue eyes thanking him, coming closer and closer. . . . He slept.

CHAPTER SIX

Theodore

The day of the outing was bright and clear. A wind scoured the atmosphere, giving them a view for miles and whipping colour into their cheeks. John decreed they should all go and the excitement of travelling in a hired charabanc threatened to choke Ted. Mrs Armitage was so overcome to find they were travelling at twenty miles per hour that she needed smelling-salts. After that, Ted was told to keep any further information to himself.

It had taken several days to organize the expedition, a period which had passed surprisingly quickly. In the mornings Luke and Theodore accompanied Dr Cullen on his rounds; in the afternoons they studied, or walked in the surrounding countryside returning in time for tea. Luke had worried lest Kessel find the evenings dull but his friend declared an interest in cards. A routine was established; after supper, Theodore played bezique with Charlotte or whist if Mrs Armitage and Bertha were present.

Ferocious imaginary sums were wagered and lost. Once however, when Charlotte sounded cross about losing, she and Theo suddenly 'won back' several hundred pounds. Watching, Jane whispered, 'Were you cheating?' and Theo put a finger to his lips.

'Only a little bit,' he whispered back, 'Keep it a secret.'

'All right.' He had a way of peeping over his spectacles which made her giggle. More astonishing was the fact that it had the same effect on Mama; she'd become much more relaxed lately.

They began the final seventy-foot ascent from the river up to the Cathedral. 'Magnificent,' Kessel kept repeating, 'There's no other way to describe it. Colossal and powerful.'

'Are there similar cathedrals in Austria or Germany?' John asked.

'Not that I have seen.' Which pleased them all.

'They had to defend themselves when this place was built,' Luke explained, 'Marauders were constantly attacking: Picts, Danes —'

'Any Goths?'

'Very likely,' he grinned, 'Riff-raff of every description. The Prince-Bishops of Durham dealt with them summarily.'

'Today I come in peace to marvel at the handiwork of man,' said Kessel.

The vehicle stopped by the greensward at the top. With Charlotte and Mrs Armitage on either arm, Kessel led the way beneath the Norman arch into the vastness beyond. The first brilliant sunlight of the year made dazzling white patches on pillars that seemed to stretch to infinity. He stared upwards in disbelief.

Luke read from the guidebook, 'It was begun in the year 1093 and finished in 1133. There's a fine screen, according to this, up by the altar.'

Kessel looked enquiringly at Mrs Armitage.

'You go, my dears. I'll sit here for a moment ... such an overwhelming sensation whenever I come here. It never fails. Will you stay with me, Bertha?' Mary joined them.

Jane wandered quietly up the nave. She stopped occasionally to watch motes of dust dart about in the sunlight. Was it at random or did they conform to a vast design? Ahead, her mother leaned on Theodore's arm and once he touched her hand with his. Were they finding it awesome as well? The idea comforted her.

She stared upwards until she felt dizzy and had to close her eyes. When she opened them she saw Mama and Theo were level with the choir. He was speaking and looked very serious. That always happened in church, she sighed to herself; even jokey people began to behave differently.

She looked round for Luke. He was with Uncle John, translating the Latin text on a tomb. Ted and Matthew were trying to encircle one of the pillars with their arms. Mrs Armitage, Aunt Mary and Bertha were chatting quietly. Jane moved on toward the altar. Her mother and Theo were examining the carved screen.

'If you two would like to explore, I'm perfectly happy sitting here.'

'It's enough for me to sit and absorb the atmosphere,' Mary replied.

'And for me, thank you, madam.' Bertha stared at the figures in the distance. 'Mrs Davie's looking well today. That new straw suits her.'

'Charlotte has always been able to wear hats,' said Mrs Armitage. 'What a happy notion of Luke, to suggest an outing here.'

There was a pool of sunlight below the altar. Jane stood in the warmth and admired the Easter lilies. She could hear snatches of conversation and supposed Theo was explaining something. He did know a lot, he must have read hundreds of books.

Her mother looked as serious as Theo now and very pale, almost as though she were about to cry! Jane was stunned. In the quietness, she heard Theo's voice.

'I do not seek to re-awaken sorrow, Mrs Davie. Your husband must have been a fine man.'

'Please!' It was half-fierce, half-pleading. Jane knew without a doubt she shouldn't be listening. This was private but if she moved they might see her. Theo spoke again in a way she'd never heard before.

'Love so strong cannot die. It has the same strength as this.' His cane described an arc which encompassed the Cathedral.

Why was he talking about father and of love, Jane wondered?

'It can bear one on wings like angels —'

'Mr Kessel, please don't!'

'Don't stifle your heart when it speaks. You build too many defences, Mrs Davie.'

'Because they are necessary!' Mama had lowered her voice. Jane could no longer hear clearly, '. . .not an easy role, being solitary, Mr Kessel . . .' Theo bent forward to catch her words.

Jane's mouth was dry. Dare she creep away? A cloud had blotted out the sun leaving the Cathedral cold and sombre. When Theo next spoke, he sounded desperate.

'Open your heart again. Believe me, it will not betray your memories to do so.'

'You are too young to offer such advice, Mr Kessel.'

'It grieves me you should think so.'

For the first time, Charlotte turned and looked him full in the face. She cried out, 'No!'

'Yes. How very stupid of me to fall in love.'

Oh, let me escape, Jane prayed wildly! I shouldn't have stayed but now I'm stuck! She heard Theo say, 'I may be too young to offer advice but not to fall in love,' when salvation came.

Through a door beyond the choir stalls an elderly man emerged carrying music. He nodded politely to Jane. At his footsteps, the voices fell silent. Jane sped quickly away, down the further aisle toward the West door. The organist climbed the stairs to his loft and Charlotte adjusted her veil. When it concealed her face sufficiently, she left the protection of the screen.

Jane was beside the font with Luke and John, crimson with apprehension. Had Mama seen her? What would happen next? Theo made no attempt to follow. Was all that talk of love a proposal? What about Mr Percival? Amid her chaotic thoughts was the absolute certainty that Theodore would be infinitely preferable to *him*.

Jane found it difficult to breathe or hear what anyone said. When Uncle explained something, she nodded dumbly. Mama was nearly level with them, walking as though she ached. When she spoke, her voice was muffled by the veil. 'The first bright sunlight of the year . . . such a strain on one's winter eyes. I think I'll take a turn outside.' She moved on to where great-aunt was sitting. 'Would you walk with me, Bertha? I'm feeling rather tired.'

It was too big a secret. Jane had to share it — but with whom? At first she decided she couldn't possibly tell Dorothy. Ted, she rejected, Matthew was too young and she was unsure of Luke. He could be stern. He poked fun at Mr Percival, not in front of Mama of course, but he might not take kindly to the idea of Theodore as a replacement.

It was difficult not to let Katriona guess. She asked Jane more than once what was troubling her. Jane evaded the questions and wondered about Aunt Mary but she would only tell Uncle John. Then it would all come out how Jane had stood there listening which could mean frightful retribution. In the end, reluctantly, she compromised.

'Promise you won't say a word?'

'Cross my heart.' Dorothy's eyes were wide because she could see it was tremendously serious.

'Theodore Kessel has asked Mama to marry him, at least I think he did.'

'My dear!' Dorothy's hands flew to her breast, 'What d'you mean, you think? Ooh Jane, were you eavesdropping?'

'I couldn't help it!' and she explained.

At the finish, Dorothy sighed, 'Isn't it heavenly? So romantic!' Then she remembered. 'Oh, goodness! What about Mr Percival?'

'He doesn't know so *he'll* probably go ahead and propose as well,' Jane said despondently. 'I just hope I'm not stuck where I can't help overhearing when he does.'

'It was a pity you couldn't stay a little bit longer . . .?'

'I'm sure Mama refused. She and Theo have scarcely spoken to one another since, except at mealtimes. And he's stopped making jokes or playing cards so it's pretty dull in the evenings.'

'But dearest, you'd rather have Mr Kessel for a step-papa, wouldn't you? He sounds divine compared to Mr Percival.'

'He's not handsome or anything,' Jane insisted. 'He's short and rather fat.' All the same, he hadn't produced the same feeling of revulsion she'd experienced when thinking of Mr Percival. She'd seen Theo in dressing-gown and night-shirt plodding to and from the bathroom. He'd looked homey and cuddly; he would fit into their lives and might be a comfort. Dorothy, however, clung to her illusions.

'What about Mr Kessel's eyes? Are they dark and limpid?'

'Sort of — greyish. He hasn't much hair on top but he has a curly fringe, like a monk.'

'I'm sure he's an improvement on Mr Percival. What does Luke think?'

'I haven't told him.'

'I will, if you like,' Dorothy offered brightly. 'After all we are nearer in age.'

'No.' Jane was adamant. 'I don't think Luke's a good idea. I might discuss it with Ted, though.' Her friend's eyebrows reached new heights.

'Dearest, should you? He's so immature.'

'He's growing up,' Jane said loyally, 'and he's reliable. When we share secrets, he never tells.'

'Neither do I, you can rely on me. Oh, isn't it exciting!' But Jane wasn't sure about that.

Telling Dorothy halved the burden but Jane was still confused. There was a difference of seven years and thirty-four days between Mama and Theo. She knew because Theo had signed the birthday page in her Kind Thoughts book. Ted's view when she told him, was practical.

'That doesn't matter. It'll be useful to have another doctor in the family.' Ted's latest bicycling accident had resulted in a visit to Dr Cullen.

'Theo's already said he might work abroad. If Mama marries him she'll have to go too.'

'We can stay here, Uncle John won't mind,' Ted said with sturdy confidence. 'We can visit her for holidays if they're living somewhere special. Of course, she might not choose to marry anyone. I rather hope she doesn't.'

Jane said slowly, 'She's changed lately hasn't she?'

'Not half!' he agreed happily, 'She forgot to make a fuss when I tore my trousers.' He was bored with speculation. 'It doesn't matter what anyone thinks because Mama will please herself in the end. She always does.'

They saw little of Theo during the remaining days of the holiday. He and Luke continued to accompany Dr Cullen. Their expeditions took them further afield so that they rarely returned before supper. During the meal, Theo added little to the general conversation. If Mary noticed how he avoided speaking directly to Charlotte, she kept her own counsel.

Once, he and Luke joined the Creswells for a ramble over the moors but it wasn't the success Luke had anticipated. The Creswells were friendly but there was no doubting Mr Creswell's cold politeness toward Theodore. On their return, Luke began to apologise. His friend shook his head.

'You must understand, Luke, Mr Creswell is in touch with events. He obviously reads the newspapers.'

'I don't follow . . . all that stuff about Germany building ships?' Luke had barely glanced at the *Northern Echo* during the holiday.

'Mr Creswell is well-informed.'

'But it's to ease the unemployment in Germany, isn't it? I don't know why that should annoy Creswell. I thought he wanted to do the same over here.'

Kessel asked sadly, 'And when you have many more ships, what then?'

'You increase trade,' Luke answered promptly. 'You should hear Father on that subject, he can go on for hours.' It was such an obvious answer he wondered why Kessel needed to ask.

For their final evening, Kessel sprang a complete surprise. He booked a box at the Theatre to be followed by a private supper at the King's Head. Luke broke the news at breakfast. 'It's no use protesting, Father, it's all arranged. Theo got the idea a couple of days ago and swore me to secrecy. He's gone to the hotel this morning to bully the chef about a special menu.'

'Good heavens, the cost!'

'He's not short of cash. His family are pretty wealthy, you know.'

The disruption the invitation caused among Emporium staff caused John even greater concern. Counter-hands were completely occupied with the toilettes of Charlotte, Mrs Armitage and Jane; customers had to wait.

'You've outgrown your white, Jane,' her mother decided, 'it's too tight across the chest. Miss Attewood has a taffeta skirt left from last season. With a lace blouse, that should look quite smart.'

'May I put my hair up?'

'Just this once.'

It hadn't escaped Luke's notice that Theodore Kessel and his aunt avoided one another after the outing to Durham. Occasionally he caught Theo watching Charlotte and wondered about it but hadn't the courage to speak. Neither could he understand the size of the treat this evening; it was a lavish return for simple hospitality.

As he changed into evening clothes, Luke felt relieved the holiday was nearly over. It had begun well but somehow the atmosphere had changed. He did not understand why.

As for Kessel himself, he'd poured his energy into making the evening perfect but would *she* understand? Three weeks ago he'd never set eyes on Charlotte McKie; now she dominated every waking moment. If only he hadn't spoken so precipitately! He tore at his thinning hair each time he thought of it. He'd declared himself that day because of the wretched Percival. If Charlotte could have discovered gradually that *he* wasn't simply a student but a flesh-and-blood man who adored her, what a difference that might have made. Theodore had been bowled over by the sight of her it was true but since then he'd fallen inexorably in love; infatuation had developed into a passion which consumed him.

In church on Sundays, Theodore added his silent curses of Percival to those of the children. There stood the cause of all his anguish — Charlotte must be persuaded to delay her decision. She wasn't yet ready for remarriage, their conversation in the Cathedral proved it. Another fifteen months and he would be qualified but would she be prepared to wait that long?

101

There was a crash as Ted hurtled through Luke's door. 'Have you any pomade? Uncle John says my hair's a disgrace.'

'I don't use the stuff. Try cold water.'

'That's no good. It frizzles up as soon as it's dry. Oh, I say!' He had found Luke's silk hat and scarf. 'You'll look a proper masher in these!'

'Ted, put those down at once!'

'Luke?' Jane peered round the door.

'Yes?'

'Theo said he'd like to see me dance but there's only this evening left.'

Luke had seized Ted and began to brush his hair vigorously. He shouted above the yelps. 'When we come back after supper, would that do? If Billy's about, he can roll back the carpet and Katriona could play the music.'

'Shall I do my Spanish dance?'

'Whatever you like.' Luke was curious. Kessel often visited the ballet and the opera; unlike the rest of them, his opinion would be informed.

Luke joined John in front of the dining-room fire, glad to escape from the female excitement upstairs. 'It's a long time since I've felt so festive,' John said happily. 'Perhaps your mother and I should do this more often?'

'Father, have you noticed how Aunt Charlotte has changed these past few weeks? I was wondering if she's come to a decision over Mr Percival?'

John frowned. 'I can't decide which is better: knowing she's accepted him or remaining in suspense a little longer.'

'She might refuse. I think Kessel's visit has affected each of us in one way or another.' It was a strong enough hint but his father didn't make the connection.

'I hope your friend's been comfortable? This must be very modest compared to what he's used to — Ah, here they come!'

John's heart swelled to see his wife so elegant. Miss Attewood had insisted on choosing her gown, far too expensive in Mary's opinion but she'd been overruled. Soft folds of green concealed her limp and a *décolleté* neckline framed

102

her graceful shoulders. Katriona had used the tongs on her hair. John took her hand and kissed it, blushing scarlet. 'Mr Kessel shan't have it all his way.'

Charlotte swept in and took Luke's breath away. He'd seen her in peg-top skirts before but this was incredibly daring. Not only were black velvet, laced boots revealed but half an inch of calf above! Though the outfit was extremely attractive, Luke scarcely knew where to look. He turned to Jane to hide his embarrassment.

Even she had changed, though at first he couldn't think how. Her skirt was deep red, her high-necked blouse creamy and her hair piled high. She was taller than usual and he realized she wore heels like her mother. Pray Heaven nothing had happened to transform Mrs Armitage!

'Thank you, Bertha; if the train is pinned up until we reach the theatre?' The old lady was dressed in a style suited to her age. Full skirts swept the ground. She had feathers in her hair and a sealskin wrap. Instead of her jet she wore a large gold locket containing, Luke was certain, a photograph of Mr Armitage. At Bertha's request, she revolved slowly, smug as a girl. What had got into everyone this evening?

'Splendid.' John was as nervous as Luke about those legs — suppose someone from the church saw them? 'Shall you not need a cloak, Charlotte?'

'I fancy not, Mr McKie. The barometer remains steady.'

Katriona entered with bouquets and buttonholes. 'Oh, that colour suits you to perfection, Mrs Davie! See, Mr Kessel has sent flowers to match.' She held out the mixture of blues to Charlotte, 'Aren't they lovely? If you're ready, the cabs are waiting.'

There were ices for the children and champagne for everyone else. 'Can I have a sip?' Jane whispered. 'Oh, doesn't it make you want to sneeze!' Luke drank his without tasting it — how could he have been so blind?

Kessel's face when he caught sight of Charlotte tonight, the manner in which he'd taken her hand — Luke couldn't be mistaken. And she? He was uncertain. His aunt looked happier than she had for years; did that mean anything? Even if it did, if was so unsuitable! The thought of Kessel changing from friend to 'uncle' was too ridiculous!

He applauded when urged to by Jane. At the finish he helped with the wraps and travelled to the King's Head in silence. Waiting for them was Dr Cullen. 'Was it an entertaining evening?'

'Spiffing!' Ted told him, 'with acrobats and funny clowns —'

'It was lovely and Theodore gave me these roses!' Jane buried her face in them. Does she remember I once gave her violets, Luke wondered?

'Dinner is served, ladies and gentlemen.'

Luke ate and drank and watched Theodore. The laughter was infectious; even the waiter was included once Kessel discovered he was from Hamburg. At one point Dr Cullen murmured, 'Why the puritan look, old chap?' and Luke forced himself to join in. Mary was gazing at him. He smiled to allay any unease. She must have noticed, she always did. Would she blame him for introducing Charlotte to Theodore?

He'd forgotten about Jane's dance. When they arrived back at the Emporium, she ran ahead calling that she wouldn't be long and they crowded into the dining-room where the big table had been pushed against a wall.

Katriona sat at the pianola. Jane entered and took up her opening pose. Suddenly Luke wanted more than anything for her to impress Kessel. He didn't know why — it hadn't mattered before. Was it because his friend could now influence Aunt Charlotte? Whatever the reason, as the music began and Jane failed to move him, Luke felt incredibly sad: the magic had disappeared. He looked for Kessel's face but it was in shadow.

At the finish they applauded louder than they'd done all evening. Jane seemed perfectly happy. Mary hugged her but Luke knew this was because Charlotte did not. As for Kessel, his praise was *too* generous, which confirmed Luke's fears.

On the train the following day he asked, 'Jane hasn't sufficient talent to become a professional dancer, has she?' It

104

was the least embarrassing topic and Luke needed to know. Kessel looked up from his book.

'Who am I to say?'

'You know about the ballet. Apart from the odd music hall or pantomime, we've nothing to compare.'

'I'm no expert,' Kessel protested.

'Last night, I felt — nothing. Jane was just a girl, dancing.'

'Have you considered her age?' Kessel's eyes were wise. 'Some children develop a precocious talent then, just as suddenly, they fade. Perhaps it's that way with Jane? Last night she failed to move me also but you need a second opinion if I may say so.'

Luke wasn't to be humoured. 'Someone will have to tell her. She's set her heart on becoming a professional dancer.'

'Not you. That would break her heart because she's so fond of you.'

Theodore's own bubble of happiness threatened to explode. Life was sublime! Last night, Charlotte McKie had never looked more lovely. Such elegance, all for him! She'd told him with her eyes that his cause was not lost. He couldn't keep it to himself any longer, 'Talking of hearts, old chap, not a single aorta or ventricle has been injured by my visit; I just wanted you to know.' He hesitated because he wanted to approach the matter delicately. The problem was, to what extent should he confide that he hoped eventually to make Charlotte his wife?

'I hope you did nothing to upset my aunt?' Luke's abrupt pomposity was an attempt to cover embarrassment, 'I don't know what you were thinking of, Kessel. It's not as though you and she —'

'No discussion, please.' Theodore was dismayed, 'My remark was intended to reassure, not invite censure.'

'Nevertheless, I doubt whether Aunt Charlotte will look kindly on Mr Percival in future.'

This was true and Theodore chuckled. 'Did you know the infamous Eustace holds a commission with the Territorial Army? Dr Cullen told me so yesterday. Not suitable behaviour for the successor to Dave McKie, I think?'

Luke was glad yet furious at the same time, which was stupid. Why not let matters take their course? This sudden infatuation between Charlotte and Theo would surely disappear over the coming weeks and might serve as a useful distraction. Yet the rash side of Luke's nature made him blurt out, 'I must say I think it impertinent for you even to consider paying addresses, Kessell . . .' He broke off. Theodore's face was a mask.

'You must allow for the unpredictability of the human heart, McKie. It can do other than simply pump blood, as I have discovered to my cost.'

For the remainder of the journey Kessel didn't look up from his book. Luke was too dismayed to interrupt. They continued in silence to Jesmond. An apology was vital, urgent, but Luke couldn't find the words. A day later, Kessel deliberately left a copy of a letter of thanks where he could see it. It was addressed to John and contained only a brief sentence presenting Kessel's compliments to Mrs Davie McKie but Luke stubbornly maintained his silence and the camaraderie that had been so welcome at the beginning began to wither.

After a few more weeks, when their paths at medical school diverged, neither made the effort to continue their friendship. Kessel was morbidly sensitive over Charlotte. He sent her flowers and received a formal acknowledgement. He told himself he hadn't the right to press her further until he was qualified. It was a time for patience.

As for Luke, the embarrassment at seventeen of considering Theo in his role of Charlotte's husband triumphed over an instinctive desire to apologize. Kessel had no right, he repeated in justification, it had been an abuse of friendship. In early summer he wrote to John that he'd changed his plans and wouldn't be visiting Leipzig, preferring instead to spend the vacation on the croft.

'Father will be pleased,' John told Mary. 'If Ted and Matthew come with us, we can put the place to rights before the winter.'

Jane watched her mother's hair-style subside. Was it over? After the visit to the theatre she and Ted were convinced Theodore had won. When Dorothy had heard of the daring skirt, she confidently predicted an autumn wedding but nothing had happened. Was it to be the dreaded Percival after all? Jane sought out Katriona.

'I don't think you and I should concern ourselves, my pet. These matters sometimes arrange themselves in a way you least expect.'

CHAPTER SEVEN

High Summer

They gazed up at a celestial August sky. The weather had held for over a week; it couldn't last much longer. 'I never want to handle a plough again,' Luke moaned. 'My arms throb . . . there are red hot needles piercing my joints — I'm worn out!'

Ted was scornful. 'You should exercise like we do. We're not a bit tired, are we, Matthew?'

'Yes.'

'Tomorrow we must begin repairs to the croft.' John was even more exhausted but did not dare to stop.

'I think I can improve the conduit.' Ted was arranging pieces of straw in a pattern. 'Grandfather said it kept overflowing in early spring. If I can alter the angle of the pipe . . . and dig a sort of spillage ditch. Got a pencil and paper, Matthew?'

'You must help with the roof first,' John insisted. 'That leak has made the bedroom uninhabitable.'

'Imagine putting up with it for so long! Grandfather said he didn't bother writing because he didn't want to worry you.' Guilt rose afresh in John. It's my fault, he thought, since Davie died I've been so full of my own problems, I've neglected Father.

'The land looks good now, doesn't it?' Luke stared across freshly-tilled earth at the new fencing and gate. 'We should be able to get the potatoes planted before we go. Where are you two off to?'

'We're going to draw a plan,' Ted shouted.

'Such energy!' John grunted. 'It's indecent.'

'We'd best get moving or *your* muscles will seize up.'

'Thank you my boy, good of you to remind me!' John looked at him affectionately. 'Sure you don't mind spending your holiday up here? If you want to take yourself off for a week or two abroad, please say.'

Luke began collecting up the tools. 'I haven't seen much of Kessel lately. He attends different tutorials.' It sounded too glib. 'By the way, how's Aunt Charlotte's admirer?'

'Percival?' John was surprised. 'I've no idea, why?'

'At Easter, gossip was he was ready to declare himself.'

'That was nothing but gossip,' John said firmly. 'Matters now appear to be dormant. Your mother and I are relieved because Charlotte's given up wearing those dreadful skirts.'

She didn't wear those because of Percival, thought Luke.

Alex was mending a creel. With this fine weather, there would be good fishing on the forbidden side of the loch, under the headland near the big house. Not that Alex worried about that. Wee George's grandson was expert enough to ensure he and Ted weren't caught and it might mean a lobster when Helen Shields came to tea.

Alex fretted at the leisurely pace John set. Tilling should have been finished days ago. He began each day at dawn but John stayed in bed until six! As Luke and John came into the yard, he called, 'Will you not make a start on the shingles, John? While the weather holds?'

'Yes, Father.' Which would break first, the weather or his back?

'It's light enough 'til near midnight. We can maybe work late tonight?'

'If you think it necessary.'

'I'd like the roof finished before her visit tomorrow.'

'Father, Mistress Shields is hardly likely to go into your bedroom. It will not matter to her whether it leaks in there or not.'

Alex pursed his lips. 'Maybe so, aye . . . but d'you see where one or two shingles are missing over the fireplace? If it were to rain hard, she'd notice that drip. There's been a pool on the floor before now.'

John turned to Luke who was trying not to laugh. 'Help me get the ladder up and then find Ted and Matthew.'

109

'Ted's going fishing tonight,' Alex reproached. 'He shouldn't over-exert himself this afternoon.'

'I don't think Charlotte will be pleased when she discovers her son has been poaching.'

'Why ever not?' Alex asked innocently. 'Her husband used to. He was better at it than you, John. You were always too nervous of the ghillies.'

The cart jolted over dried mud ruts. It wasn't a comfortable way to travel but Helen Shields couldn't walk far when the rheumatism was bad. She concentrated on more agreeable things, like the view. Where in the world was there another to compare? The carter's back blocked part of it and this prompted Helen's memory. 'Has your cousin had her baby yet, Douglas? She must be near her time?'

'A little boy,' he turned his head proudly. 'Last Sunday morning it was. I saw him yesterday, the image of his father Rory.'

'It's to be hoped the child takes after his mother.' Helen Shields had no use for tact. 'Rory was a dunce but Morag could have made something of herself if she hadn't been so stupid as to marry.'

'Aye, Mistress Shields.' He didn't bother to argue; no-one ever did.

Alex, John and Luke came up the path to meet her. As always, Helen's eyes went straight to John, her 'first-born'. Together they had shared so many hopes and when he'd failed to go to university, her anguish had been as acute as his. Now Luke would fulfil their dreams.

She turned eagerly to greet him but shock froze the words in her mouth. Helen had never known the identity of Mary's seducer but today there was no mistaking it; young Manners smiled up at her out of Luke's face. What a terrible, savage irony for Alex McKie!

The driver lowered the step but Helen continued to sit there. She came to with a jerk and rallied. 'John, you're looking older.' He didn't flinch; he'd known her too long for that.

'I *am* older, I fear.'

'Nonsense, you're only forty-three. At my time of life there can be excuses, but not at yours. How are you keeping, Mr McKie?'

'Very well, I thank you.' There was always a slight hesitancy when he spoke his second language. Mistress Shields could still make Alex nervous, especially today. He saw she'd spotted the likeness.

'And you, Luke?' Luke bent forward and kissed her unexpectedly. It caught her off-guard.

'My word!'

'I'm practising to be a rake, Miss Shields. Licentious fellow-students have infected me with unworthy desires!'

'Indeed?' The tight mouth didn't relax, 'I trust our pure Scottish air will rid you of them as soon as possible. You carry too many hopes, Luke McKie.'

Don't I just, he thought ruefully. She needn't be that hard on a chap. Her skin was as dry as paper under her veil. He followed more slowly as Alex led her toward the croft. Once inside she asked, 'Didn't Ted and Matthew come this time?'

'They are up at the spring re-laying the pipe. They will be here presently,' John apologised. 'Luke, give them a shout — and make sure they are clean.'

As he set off, Luke heard her say, 'Goodness, John, they are of an age to see to that themselves, they don't need you to chase after them.'

Below the spring, operations had reached a critical, muddy stage. Ted was flushed. 'If I could have another half-hour, we're nearly there.'

'Better not,' Luke advised, 'She's in an odd mood today.'

'She'll be all right after she's talked to Uncle John,' Ted said confidently.

'Did you see the way she looked at him? I bet he was teacher's pet when he was at school.'

'Orders are that you are to tidy up and present yourselves,' Luke said ignoring this. 'You can always slip away afterwards when she and Father get to the "do you remember" stage.'

'Good idea! Come on, Matthew, race you!'

The last time she'd seen Ted, Helen had thought how like Davie he was. Today, running toward the croft, she could see much more of Charlotte. He had his father's build and colouring but his mother's determination. He thrust out a filthy paw. 'How are you, Miss Shields?'

'I cannot possibly shake hands with that.'

'Oh, bother! Half a tick!' Ted shot back the way he'd come, grabbing Matthew. 'Come on, quick wash. The cake's on the table.'

Their meetings were so infrequent, idle chatter didn't suffice yet it was all they could manage at first. Helen was full of questions but couldn't find a way to begin. Paternity still confused her then she saw there was a difference after all; Luke had no cruel streak in his laughter and his face was open and cheerful, just like his mother's. Much more composed, Helen accepted a second cup of tea. 'Tell me more about these decadent students friends?'

Listening half-attentively, she watched Ted unfold a diagram. He'd changed for the better; last time he'd been a horrid, noisy little boy but he'd grown up at last. Cake crumbs scattered as he found a pencil and began to improve his new design. Once she might have scolded a boy for that; with age Helen Shields had learned different values. 'Either that, or I'm becoming senile.'

Oh, dear! By their faces, she knew she'd spoken aloud. 'I'm sorry, I didn't mean to interrupt.' Luke had lost his poise and for a moment she wasn't sorry. He'd become a little too confident for her liking. 'How's your schooling, Matthew? I haven't heard from you so far. Lost your tongue?' He smiled, full of his father's charm but something was missing though she couldn't put her finger on it.

'I'm learning to be an accountant.' Helen Shields almost laughed. It was one step better than being a thief, she thought.

John talked of business. The Emporium didn't really interest her, but watching his well-loved face was enough. She avoided Alex and he was relieved that she did. He'd suffered the same shock when he'd first seen Luke and wondered who else might do the same. Only the old schoolmistress, he decided. The Manners family had stayed away

112

from the big house too long for anyone else to remember.

Alex listened for those English words he still understood. His grandsons were incomprehensible to him most of the time, except Luke who spoke slowly so that he might understand. None had the Gaelic, which saddened Alex. Even John needed a couple of days before he was fluent once more.

He saw the schoolteacher's mouth begin to soften. John was telling her about the church bazaar. Something to do with another woman wearing the same hat as Charlotte. 'Both ladies noticed of course.'

'Naturally!'

'Charlotte behaved splendidly. She complimented the customer and said how much better the hat looked on her then she borrowed Jane's beret and wore that instead.'

'How is Charlotte?'

'Very well indeed —'

'She has an admirer.' Luke could've kicked himself. What devil made him come out with that?

'We cannot be certain.' John frowned at the slip.

'He's a rotten egg,' Ted said firmly, 'Mother doesn't like him very much. I'm glad. So's Matthew.'

John was flabbergasted. 'You two haven't discussed it with your mother?' he asked faintly.

'Only with you, Uncle.' Out of the mouths of babes!

Utterly bewildered, Alex asked, 'What are you saying? That Charlotte . . .?'

'It's all right, Grandfather,' Luke reassured him. 'I meant it as a joke. Aunt Charlotte has an admirer in Darlington — which isn't surprising — but she doesn't care for the fellow. I'm sure Ted's right about that.'

'If that is your idea of a joke, Luke, then Newcastle has had an unfortunate influence!' Helen Shields was glacial and her sympathies were with John. 'If she were to marry, I presume that might affect the Emporium, John? Charlotte inherited Davie's financial interest in it, didn't she?'

'That is what concerns me,' he admitted. 'Which is why I sincerely hope, should Mr Percival persevere, she will turn him down.'

113

'You don't need to fuss, Uncle.' Ted was savouring his new role as man of the world. 'Mama's bound to do that because she prefers Mr Kessel, doncher know.' There was no retrieving the situation after that.

Luke's was a makeshift bed in the main room of the croft, John was asleep in the other. In the lean-to bedroom, Alex snored.

Luke moved restlessly; if only he hadn't come out with that stupid remark about Aunt Charlotte. He'd insisted the affair with Kessel was a figment of Ted's imagination but it had set his father worrying. Why hadn't he held his tongue! Eventually, he slept.

Alex McKie needed less sleep nowadays. The first streaks of dawn had always been enough to wake him but he lay still because he didn't want to disturb the others and listened to the early morning sounds. Those of the croft were as familiar as the sea-birds outside. When he heard the squeak Alex knew it was the cupboard door to the left of the fireplace, where Matthew slept. The boy must be awake. Should he go in and make tea for them both? A walk over the hills in the early dawn was the next best thing to paradise. 'I will lift up mine eyes to the hills . . .' Alex murmured his favourite psalm quietly. He had a sudden desire for his grandson to share the same magic. If they went straight away they'd be in time to see the wild anemones before they closed their petals against the sun.

There was another sound. Matthew must be near the hearth because the poker had moved slightly. A few slices of bread, that was all they'd need, Alex would wrap them up with a couple of apples. On the way he would tell the boy legends of the old standing stones . . .

It was an effort to get up. Before his feet had touched the floor, Alex heard something else. It was the tiniest sound and it came from the shelf above the hearth. He was puzzled. There was nothing of Matthew's up there? Another noise, a chink. This time the old man felt cold sickness inside. Surely not? Not the jar? He heard it scrape on the wooden shelf as Matthew lifted

114

it down, the jar used by Alex and his father before him, for money.

Alex McKie had a countryman's finely-tuned hearing and could picture what was happening in the other room. The jar was being tilted gently as Matthew searched for gold among the silver and copper. It was put back on the shelf and stealthy footsteps moved back across the flagstones. Finally there was the self-same creak as Matthew shut the cupboard door behind him.

Alex pulled the blanket over him and lay still but nothing could warm him today, not the sun nor the sweetest flowers that grew on the moor

Helen Shields sent a message inviting Ted and Matthew to tea and adding that her pump needed attention. 'Suggest Ted bring tools,' the note finished.

'This piece that's rotted acts like a diaphragm,' Ted explained importantly. 'D'you know what that means?' Helen bit back sarcasm. Parts of the dismantled pump now littered her yard.

'Can you make it work?'

'I think so, yes. I'll have to try and find a bit of leather or some such to replace it. It's a very old-fashioned design, you know.'

She fixed him with a firm eye. 'It's perfectly satisfactory. It's worked for the last fifteen years.'

'All right,' Ted sighed, 'I'll do my best.'

Matthew was standing in the middle of her room, when she walked back inside, hands in pockets. For a split second it struck her that he was sizing it up. 'There's nothing of value —' Helen began but stopped abruptly. What had made her say that?

Matthew said eagerly, 'I was trying to imagine where you kept the table-cloth. I wanted to set the table as a surprise. Would you like to see my school-books? I brought them especially to show you.'

She watched as the two began the long walk back to the croft, one tall carroty head beside a younger fairer one. It had been the other way round years ago with John and

115

Davie. One thing hadn't changed, though. 'Bless my soul,' Helen said aloud, 'Ted's doing cartwheels, just like his father used to. I wonder what that's all about?'

'I did it!' Ted shouted, 'I used a bit of tarpaulin — and made the pump work!'

Matthew cut across his pride. 'She's very poor, isn't she? She hasn't many things. I wonder if she's secretly rich?'

Ted stared. 'You're always wondering how much people have. I like Miss Shields. She's got a table and chairs and things, enough to be comfortable.' They walked a bit further. 'I think I prefer Grandfather's croft most of all,' he said, 'It's really snug now the roof's water-tight.'

Matthew was disparaging, 'It's the poorest house on the Peninsula.'

'What does that matter?'

'People despise you if you're poor.'

Ted was too full of beans to care. 'I've designed a new culvert, I've managed to mend all sorts of bits and pieces on the croft as well as that pump. I'm going to be an engineer when I leave school!'

'There's not much money in that,' said Matthew.

In the Pump Room at Harrogate, Dorothy Creswell and Jane McKie were extremely bored. Their mothers were talking animatedly to other ladies. In the background, a trio attempted to drown them all with Strauss. The girls perambulated but no one took the slightest notice. It wasn't worth repeating the experiment, Dorothy observed caustic-ally, because the gentlemen present were at least a hundred years old, 'Or over thirty which is just as bad. It makes one wish one was back in Darlington.'

'Oh, no.' Jane wasn't quite as bored as that. 'If we were, I'd be back working in the stock-room. I'd rather be here than doing that.'

'Shall we ask if we can go to the Kinema?'

'Mama's bound to say no.'

'If you were to persuade Katriona to come, we might be allowed.'

'Katriona doesn't like moving pictures. She screamed the first time she went because she thought Pearl White was going to be killed.'

'How silly!' Dorothy was an experienced picture-goer. 'She always gets rescued in the next episode.' They wandered into the entrance hall to stare at the weather.

'I wonder if it's raining up on the croft?'

'It sounds such a romantic place,' Dorothy sighed soulfully. 'Does Luke wear a kilt and shoot stags and things?'

'I don't think so. He didn't last time he went. It's a very tiny house.' Loyalty prevented Jane saying how small. 'They've gone there to help Grandfather as well as have a holiday.'

'How's Ted these days, is he improved?'

Jane thought about it. 'A bit. I'm afraid he'll never be half-decent as a dancing partner.'

'How tiresome.'

'Matthew might, one day,' but Dorothy wasn't interested in anything under sixteen.

'Mama is taking me shopping this afternoon. My dear, the things one needs for finishing school — such lists!' She gave a moue of fatigue, 'One simply asks oneself — will one be ready in time?'

'I do envy you Paris,' said Jane simply.

'I'm not looking forward to all of it.' Dorothy had become a plump, nervous schoolgirl once more, 'You understand French, I don't. I get in a muddle if they speak it quickly!'

'You have to understand it properly for dancing,' Jane explained. 'Six months speaking nothing else — you'll be twice as good as me when you come back.'

'Why don't you come with me?'

'What?'

Dorothy Creswell clapped her hands at the beauty of it. 'Jane, it's the obvious answer. Papa's been growling because I haven't a chaperone. He's even made Mama nervous but if you were with me, neither of them would worry!'

'Mama would never agree to *that*,' Jane said sadly. 'She says my place is at her side.'

'Suppose my Mama were to ask as a favour? We must be among your uncle's best customers,' Dorothy added

117

artlessly. 'I'm sure my Papa would be glad to pay for you as well. Just think dearest, you could see real ballet dancers in Paris!'

In the Kinema Jane whispered, 'Can't asking Mama wait 'til we get home?'

'No!' Dorothy hissed, 'We have to leave in two weeks. You must speak to her tonight.'

'Ssh!' Other patrons wanted to hear Mary Pickford.

'All right,' Jane said bravely. Goodness only knew what ructions it would bring.

It was the day after John and the boys had begun their journey back to Darlington that Helen Shields heard the knock on her door. 'Mr McKie — you've not walked all this way?'

'One of the Hamiltons brought me. He's gone on into Salen.'

'Sit down. It's too hot for a man of your age to be out today.'

Alex held his tongue. The school mistress was forever harping on his age — wasn't she near enough the same herself? Always the woman to put a fellow's back up — no wonder she'd never married. Helen finished what she was doing and settled opposite, indicating he should begin.

'Luke has changed since we last saw him, has he not?'

So that was it. 'I noticed the likeness, of course. I'm sure we're the only ones who did.'

'I did not speak of it.'

'Such things are best forgotten.'

'Aye, aye ...' Alex was reassured. 'All John ever said was — "Luke is my son. I beg you will accept him as such."'

'Luke has inherited far more from his mother.'

'Aye.' Helen could see that wasn't the whole of it. This time, it took much more of an effort for Alex to speak.

'Matthew stole money from the jar. Two guineas, I think it was, I haven't counted it for so long.'

Helen said in disbelief, 'Your money jar?' Everyone knew of Alex's habit. 'What on earth did John say?'

'I could not bring myself to tell him, not — Davie's son.'

118

No, she thought grimly, no more could I.

'If he'd asked, I'd have given Matthew every penny I had, gladly! Is there anything you can suggest, Mistress Shields?' Alex was humble in his distress, 'I thought maybe with you knowing about children and suchlike . . .?'

As she thought of the very few she'd known over the years, whose petty lies and deceits had continued throughout their schooldays, Helen couldn't bring herself to offer false comfort. Alex read something of this in her face.

'Aye, well . . . there it is,' he said softly.

Curse the boy! she thought savagely, for destroying this good man's peace.

Charlotte refused to make a decision while they were in Harrogate and Jane knew better than to press her. Mrs Creswell smiled and Dorothy implored, but to no avail. Once they were home in Darlington, Charlotte promised, she would give her answer. Jane guessed, with a sinking heart, that her mother wanted to turn the Creswell's offer down in the privacy of the Emporium. This was in fact what Charlotte had intended, but there was an unexpected change of plan.

CHAPTER EIGHT

Affairs of the Heart

It was always the same; whenever they returned to the Emporium, Mama resumed her public face. Rarely did they go in by the back way but along the colonnade and in through the front entrance. It was a stately progress, following in Charlotte's wake as she greeted Miss Attewood and bowed to customers. Jane wondered why she didn't enjoy it any more. Then it came to her: it was theatrical, like making an entrance on stage. She did that in her other life as a dancer, she didn't want to do so here. This was her home.

The letter addressed to Mrs Davie McKie was on top of the pile. Jane recognized Theodore's handwriting. Her mother slipped it into her pocket saying she wanted to change out of her travelling clothes. 'Ask Aunt Mary if we might have an early cup of tea, would you, dear? I shan't be long.' She wants to read it by herself, thought Jane.

In the kitchen, Katriona hugged her then held her at arm's length. 'You're looking very smart, miss. I like the new hairbow.'

'It was Dorothy's idea. She and Mrs Creswell want me to go to Paris.'

Mary looked up from her household accounts. 'Does your mother agree?'

'She said she couldn't decide until we get back. I think she wants Uncle John to be on her side when she says no.' Jane perched on the table beside her aunt. 'Could you persuade him to say yes? Oh, and can Mama have a cup of tea?' Mary's stare hinted to Katriona that she needed to talk to Jane alone. Katriona went to the door.

'I'd better go and help your mother unpack.'

'I should leave her for a bit,' Jane said quickly, 'She's had a letter from Theo and she's gone off to read it by herself.' Mary and Katriona studiously avoided one another's eye.

'My dear Mrs Davie,' Charlotte read,

'May I see you? I will be in Durham cathedral next Thursday afternoon, at two o'clock.

I ask most humbly that you meet me there.

Yours very sincerely,

Theodore Kessel.'

Common sense told her it was extremely foolish but in her heart Charlotte knew she would go. She tucked the letter inside her jewel case.

As she poured the tea, Mary said cautiously, 'Jane mentioned the Creswell's offer. It sounds a splendid opportunity?'

'Yes . . .' Thursday, the day after tomorrow! Charlotte wrenched her thoughts back to the present. 'I need more time to consider,' she said, 'We can discuss the matter on Friday.'

It was the most discreet of departures. John and Miss Attewood were given the excuse of a visit to a former employee and Charlotte left by the back way. If Katriona hadn't been taking down curtains for washing, she might not have seen her go.

Dry leaves swirling in the gutter signified an end to summer as Charlotte climbed into a cab. Watching her, Katriona thought what a wonderful outfit it was for a visit to old Mrs Guy. Later, casually, she asked Mary whether the old lady still lived locally.

'She's moved to Durham, apparently. Charlotte said we weren't to wait for her at supper,' which made Katriona even more pensive.

Dorothy Creswell arrived later in the day, impatient to know what had been decided. 'Father says he *must* know soon because of the tickets. Dearest, do tell your mama Jack's accompanying us so we'll be tremendously safe.'

121

Jane said worriedly, 'Mama refuses even to talk of it until Friday.'

'Gosh! That only leaves a week!'

'I don't see why you couldn't ask when your mother gets in this evening,' Katriona said mysteriously. 'You never know, she might be in a good mood by then.'

'After visiting Mrs Guy, d'you mean?' Jane was puzzled but Katriona didn't enlighten her.

The journey back from Durham was too short for Charlotte to recover. She hid her face from other passengers in the Ladies Only compartment. It was far, far too late to wish she'd never gone. Life would never be the same again yet how could she accept Theodore Kessel's proposal? Away from the warmth of his love the difference in their ages danced in bleak rhythm with the wheels; seven years . . . seven years . . .

When she'd seen him, bare-headed, waiting on the platform, Charlotte knew only gladness. They'd walked down narrow cobbled lanes, they'd taken refuge from the rain in a bookshop. Theo had found a travel guide, he'd described the journeys they would make together in Europe once he was qualified — when they could be married.

'Your children will need you less by then,' he'd urged softly. 'but what of your life, Mrs Davie? What of the future?' And when he'd whispered even more quietly, 'I want to care for you so much!' Charlotte had put her hand in his for the very first time.

They'd behaved like young foolish lovers for one ecstatic half-hour, kissing in a deserted doorway, sheltering under Theo's umbrella and laughing at such dreadfully immodest behaviour. Theo's lips had been soft and tender at first but demanded more until Charlotte pulled away, leaning against the cold stone lintel.

'I must go back,' she protested feebly. 'It was folly to come.'

'You love me, you cannot deny that now!' Triumphant though he was, Theodore took her gently in his arms this time. 'Look at me, Charlotte, say the words. It is the truth, is it not?'

She loved him as completely as he loved her and that certainty pulsed in her veins with the beating of her heart.

'I love you . . . but not yet,' she murmured and Theo Kessel kissed her hand to seal their tryst.

'I will wait for you. I will be patient,' he promised.

On the train, Charlotte wanted to cool her face against the glass. 'Seven years . . . seven years . . .'

She slipped in as secretly as she'd departed. Jane was waiting, anxious to speak, but the passage-way was dark and Charlotte hurried past without seeing her. When her mother paused suddenly in front of a mirror, something made Jane hold back. Charlotte raised her veil as if to adjust her hair but instead gazed at her own reflection. Her mother's face was alight with such sublime happiness that Jane caught her breath. In that same moment, she remembered Theo's letter.

She didn't move. Her mother's footsteps receded and the thought nagged; why hadn't Mama mentioned it? And why pay such a long visit today? Former employees were usually treated to half-an-hour plus a basket of groceries from Armitages'. There was so much Jane didn't understand. She tapped on the office door.

'Uncle John? I'd like your help when I tackle Mama tonight. I'm absolutely determined to go with Dorothy.'

John was brought up short by the new steeliness in Jane's tone; it was a vivid echo of Charlotte's. He'd been dreading this moment; the first of the children was about to challenge parental authority.

'Jane, I refuse to take sides. *Provided* your mother agrees, I will do all I can to help.'

'Thank you. I'll go and ask her now.'

Jane thought she'd allowed sufficient time. Even so when she entered the parlour, Mama hadn't switched on the light. 'I have a slight headache,' Charlotte called out quickly. Jane remained where she was. Her mother was by the window and her voice sounded choked.

Jane took a deep breath. 'Mama, I've come for your decision. I know you said I must wait until tomorrow but we need to let Mr Creswell know.' She felt rather than heard Charlotte's agitation and hurried on, 'Uncle John is

123

agreeable. Jack Creswell will be travelling with us. There's absolutely no reason why I shouldn't go. If you say it's because I have to stay with you . . . I think that's jolly unfair. You're surrounded by people here, you'll scarcely miss me at all. It's only for six months and I'll never have such a wonderful opportunity again.'

It wasn't as she'd planned, it was too fierce. Even so Jane added a final, 'I can go, can't I, Mama?'

'Yes . . . I suppose so.'

It was so quiet, for a moment she wondered if she'd heard. She was about to rush across and smother her mother with thanks when Charlotte put up a hand.

'Later . . . not now. I'll be down directly.' Privacy was what she craved, privacy to weep and release the flood of emotion damned up inside. It made her tremble so much she could hardly stand.

Turning her head away, Charlotte looked down into the yard. Billy was examining one of Blackie's hooves. The pony turned to nuzzle his shoulder and this sign of affection released the first tears. She managed to say, 'You may send word to Mr Creswell . . .' before she realized she was alone.

Jane was already half-way to the kitchen. The ribbon was off, hair flew about her shoulders. 'I'm going to finishing school!' she shrieked, 'Mama's agreed. I leave for Paris at the end of next week!'

It was, as Dorothy said when she heard, too absolutely divine!

It was a time of complete pandemonium, of trunks and a passport, of new clothes and shoes needing repair, of packing books and throwing away old toys: a turning point, in fact. Mr and Mrs Creswell spent over an hour closeted with John and one evening Jack Creswell was submitted to the same serious questioning. He did his best to reassure John.

'Quite frankly, Jane is not my worry, Mr McKie; it's Dorothy. She can be frightfully giddy. Jane's influence has always been a healthy one which is why my family are so grateful you've given your blessing. Mind you, once the girls are at the school, all our worries are over. They guard 'em there like dragons. One of my cousins went last year. Came back a delightful young lady so we've high hopes for Dorothy.'

'I'm still unhappy that your father insists on paying both sets of fees, Mr Creswell. I would prefer to pay for Jane myself.' Jack shook his head vigorously.

'Father's pretty stingy at the best of times,' he said cheerfully, 'Now that we've got him to the brink, please don't interfere. He can afford it. If you provide Jane with pocket money, he can cough up for the rest.' John looked so severe, Jack laughed. 'Mr McKie, my father is well-known as a miser in business circles. I'm determined Dorothy shall have her chance and that means providing for Jane as well. Dash it, the course at the finishing school only lasts six months. I'm up at Oxford for two whole years.'

'Jane's welfare is also my concern.'

'You're her guardian, I believe, sir? Must make it doubly worrying for you but have no fear. After five days in Paris, they begin at the school.'

'And during those five days?'

'Hugo Wilton and I will show the girls the sights. I'm quite looking forward to it and I can vouch for Hugo. I've strict instructions from Dorothy that we take Jane to the ballet. We've rooms booked at the hotel my people always use. It's a family-run place in the rue de Crémone.' John was forced to admit he couldn't think of any other objection and Jack Creswell rose to take his leave. 'How's Luke these days? Back at Newcastle?'

'He went back early. He wanted to do extra study before the new term began.' Jack Creswell looked suitably impressed.

'Wish I'd got brains. Fortunately, according to Pa, you don't need 'em in ship-building.' John found this remark very odd.

Luke came back to see Jane depart. It was a grand family send-off from Darlington station. Jane still floated above the ground as she had for the past seven days. Dear, loving faces crowded round the carriage door, smiling and waving, all with a warm embrace except for Charlotte's which was cool and full of last-minute warnings.

125

Leaving home for the first time excited and terrified Jane. Always at the back of her mind was the fear that Mama would somehow contrive to prevent it. She heard the whistle and felt the train begin to move. They were off! She and Dorothy hung out of the window, crying, laughing and making extravagant promises about letters. The engine gathered speed and they fell back inside in a heap. Jack Creswell regarded them with mock severity. 'I hope you two intend to behave? I don't want a pair of silly *schoolgirls* on my hands.'

'We shall be terribly well-bred and adult from now on, won't we Jane? Can we have champagne with our luncheon?'

'Certainly not!'

'You're not going to be mean are you?' Dorothy cried. 'You're not going to be like *Pa*?'

'Mr Creswell . . .?'

'Hey!' Jack smiled good-naturedly, 'Jack's good enough, if I may call you Jane, Miss McKie.' Jane was so nervous she forgot to give permission. The great adventure was using up her stock of courage.

'May I ask a favour?'

'Already?'

'It's money for porters and suchlike,' Jane faltered, 'Uncle John insisted I pay my share but can you do it for me?' Sixpences and threepenny bits were heavy in her new bag.

'I shall be honoured to act on your behalf, Miss McKie.' Quite unselfconscious, Jane counted out the coins:

'Threepence for my hatbox and sixpence for my trunk, that's ninepence. There's King's Cross, then Victoria Station, so that's one-and-sixpence, plus a tip for the cabbie and another when we get on the boat-train. Another ninepence at Dover. And when we get to Calais, you'll have to tell me how much it is in francs. You won't forget?'

Jack smothered his laughter. 'I'll keep an account and we can settle up in the evenings, how's that?'

Relief made her deeply happy. 'Perfect, thank you.' In the dining car she had a final, tiny moment of anxiety. When Dorothy wasn't listening, she hissed, 'Uncle John didn't say anything about tipping the waiter!'

126

Jack leaned forward, conspiratorially. 'I'll give him a penny on your behalf, shall I?' Jane relaxed. Travelling wasn't that difficult after all.

Excitement mercifully silenced Dorothy. The superlatives continued through London, on the boat-train and across the Channel but once the three of them reached the *Gare du Nord*, she was speechless. She remained enthralled but dumb until the following morning, when she and Jane discovered the Rue de Rivoli contained shops. In a street café outside one of them, Jack Creswell and Hugo Wilton ordered two more coffees.

'Fantastic how the sight of a gown can restore the power of speech,' said Jack.

Hugo stirred in sugar lazily. 'Miss McKie managin' to keep up with the translatin'?'

'Seemed to be doing remarkably well, that's why I left 'em to it. The danger as I see it is that Jane will make life too easy. D'you think I'd better drop a hint? Remind her we'd like Dorothy to *parlez* a bit for herself?'

Hugo didn't appear to notice the question. 'Pretty little filly, Miss McKie . . .'

'So you've observed once or twice before, old chap.'

'Have I really?' Hugo looked mildly surprised. 'Must be the eyes. Be quite a looker in a year or two. What are the plans today?'

'An early lunch, then Versailles. Tonight, the ballet. Tomorrow, we tackle the Louvre.'

'Do we, by Jove. Hope I can last the course, old boy. Start to feel my age when I'm presented with a programme like that. Where shall we eat this evening? Champs Elysées, somewhere like that?'

'Let's give 'em the works,' Jack grinned, 'We'll even take 'em there in a fiacre.'

'I think this might be the occasion for my blue silk? Or perhaps one of the new dresses?' It was the most serious decision of the day. Dorothy looked round. 'Can you advise me, dearest?'

Jane came in from the balcony reluctantly. 'Do come out, just for a minute. Across the street, you can see into everyone's home. There's a man just come in from work. His wife kissed him and he gave her a loaf. She helped him put on his slippers — I want to see what happens next . . .' But after a few moments the couple disappeared.

Dorothy said decisively, 'I shouldn't want to live in an apartment, one could never escape the servants. Have you decided what to wear this evening, dearest?'

The choice wasn't difficult for Jane; it was either her taffeta skirt and blouse or her old white organdie. Privately she'd vowed never to wear that again; she'd only packed it because Mama had insisted.

Dorothy's dresses were spread on the bed. Two were brand-new, paid for by Jack. The price had been staggering. Jane reached out to stroke the peach-coloured lace.

'They're so lovely —'

'Yes but which suits me *best*?' I want to ravish Hugo.'

'Try the lavender.'

It had all come true! Jane still couldn't believe it, she wanted to pinch herself but there was no need. Here she was — in a French hotel! It was old-fashioned; the room she shared with Dorothy was enormously high with a vast armoire and two equally large beds with linen sheets! 'We charge at least a guinea a pair for this quality,' she'd whispered to Dorothy as she'd fingered them. 'Maybe even thirty shillings,' and when the housekeeper bowed her way out of the room, she'd nearly curtseyed by mistake. Jane wanted to blush at the memory. Apart from accidentally addressing a porter at Calais as 'Monseignor', she'd coped tolerably well. Far better than Dorothy who simply opened her blue eyes wide, shook her blonde curls and waited for men to spring to her aid. It shocked Jane that they did so without a word being spoken. Never mind, she'd managed. She'd even reminded Jack in the dress shop that he should ask a discount for cash.

They had their own bathroom with a mahogany hood over the bath. There was a row of china knobs to adjust the shower and temperature and as for the marble floor in there . . . Even Dorothy had been impressed. At breakfast, they'd sat on it, picnic-fashion, to eat hot croissants dipped in coffee.

'I feel like *une poule de luxe*,' Dorothy had stretched her arms above her head voluptuously.

'What, a funny sort of hen?'

'No, stupid. It's the name for naughty ladies.'

'Oh, Dorothy!'

'That's the advantage of having a brother who's older,' Dorothy said unperturbed. 'One learns all the interesting words. I don't suppose Ted's any use at all?'

'He mended my bicycle before we left. The seat was loose.' Dorothy scowled.

'I loathe bicycles. My bosoms get in the way and then I fall off.'

Those bosoms were a distinct advantage inside a French gown, however. It had taken only minutes to put on the skirt and blouse but Dorothy needed help with dozens of hooks and eyes. The final effect was breath-taking. 'Oh, Dorothy . . . your blue silk was gorgeous but that's — *devastating*. Hugo will be utterly ravished.'

'Oh, good.' Dorothy went a little pink. 'It's not just that he's rich, I actually like him as well. In fact, I can't quite decide between him and Luke.' She gazed earnestly at their joint reflections in the dressing table mirror, 'D'you think Luke will become *famous* once he's qualified?'

'It's possible.' Jane stifled a jealous qualm. 'If he becomes Dr Cullen's assistant, he'll be very well-known in Darlington.'

Dorothy looked astonished. 'I'm not going to live in Darlington, dearest. I want a rich husband with a very big house in London.' There was a knock at the door.

'Aren't you two ready, yet?' called Jack plaintively.

Each excitement added to the next until they reached the opera house which overpowered them completely. Jane gasped as she saw it. Inside, there was a crush of beautiful, exquisitely dressed women. She and Dorothy crept like mice behind Hugo and Jack. Even the new lavender gown looked rather ordinary in here. From the stalls, Jane stared at the proscenium arch and remembered the Theatre Royal in Darlington. She felt numb. What on earth would it be like when the curtain rose?

129

They were between Jack and Hugo who had arranged it so that Jane sat next to him. He was intrigued to see how she'd react. Already she was concentrating on the stage. When he spoke, she didn't hear. He guessed that nothing would distract her from the performance.

The ballet didn't interest him particularly. Like many other young gentlemen, he used his opera glasses to examine what was on display in the tiers of boxes. Seeing this, Dorothy felt relieved; she'd actually been worried that Hugo was attracted to Jane rather than herself!

Familiar music began and Jane was engrossed. When the curtain fell, Hugo was amused to see that she didn't applaud but sat in a reverie. When he asked if she'd like an ice, she looked dazed. 'Could I have a glass of water?'

Over the girls' heads, he signalled to Jack: 'Fresh air.'

'And a cigarette.'

The two girls promenaded among the fashionable throng long enough for Jane to recover. Hugo watched. The pair were self-conscious as if the entire world watched even though they were completely ignored.

'Miss McKie was overcome, I think.'

'Hardly surprising. Where to, afterwards, old man? Dorothy is determined to have her champagne. I suppose we could indulge her just this once.'

For Jane the evening was one long performance. One curtain fell and she was transported into another theatre, much smaller and full of smoke, where there were singers and waiters dodged in and out with plates of strange food. It was noisy, all she could do was nod and smile, and sniff at the bubbles in her glass while Dorothy flirted.

To her astonishment when supper was finished she discovered they weren't going directly to the hotel even though it was past midnight.

'Got to show you your kingdom, princess,' Hugo announced solemnly. 'It has a certain magical quality at night.' They drove up narrow winding streets. Lights shone through unshuttered windows.

'Isn't it marvellous how you can see the people in Paris,' Jane stared out of the cab. 'They don't hide behind curtains

130

like we do. Oh, look. That lady has stayed up to welcome her husband home.' Jack and Hugo sat up and took notice.

'*En avant!*' Jack ordered sharply. Jane swivelled in her seat to catch a last glimpse.

'She isn't a bit cross even though he's so late.'

Higher and higher, past the last of the tall buildings until they reached the summit where the white dome of Sacré Coeur brooded. Hugo and Jack helped them from the cab and they stumbled tiredly up some steps. 'A little further,' Hugo coaxed. 'It's worth it, I promise you.'

Jane gazed at the glittering lights of Paris spread out before her. The moon had risen, outlining wonders she'd seen for the first time earlier today: Notre Dame inside the silvery ribbon loop of the Seine and, farther off, the Eiffel Tower. Hugo leaned on the balustrade. Behind him, the ornate white façade made an impressive back-drop. 'Quite a kingdom, eh, princess? Does it please you?'

'Oh, yes!'

Dorothy clasped her hands soulfully. 'If only tonight could go on for ever!'

'Tomorrow morning we're going to the Louvre,' Jane reminded her.

Dorothy was miffed. 'I expect it's your age, dearest. You haven't developed any sense of romance.'

'Come on, back to the cab,' Jack called, 'Some of us are ready for bed.'

So much had happened in the past twenty-four hours; there was little conversation now. Once Jack asked if Jane had enjoyed the ballet. 'You were so quiet, it was difficult to guess what you were thinking?'

'I was wondering if I'll ever be as good.'

'Of course you will!' Dorothy cried, 'You're miles better than anyone else at Miss Robson's,' which wasn't quite the same thing.

Perhaps, Jane thought as the cab rattled over the cobbles, if I work harder than ever when I get back — but I must stop thinking of Darlington. I'm here. For the next six months I shall be living in Paris! Nothing quite so wonderful will ever happen again. Impulsively, she leaned

131

across and took Dorothy's hand. 'Thanks ever so much for inviting me, Dorothy.'

'Oh, pooh! Think how miserable I'd have been on my own.'

The elderly night porter was waiting as they came through the heavy glass doors. '*Monsieur Creswell? Il y a deux télégrammes, monsieur, pour la mademoiselle McKie.*' Jane's hand shook as she ripped open the envelopes. She read Charlotte's first —

PLEASE RETURN AS SOON AS POSSIBLE. I NEED YOU BESIDE ME. LOVE FROM YOUR MAMA.

But Ted's was more explicit:

COME BACK. MAMA IN A STATE. CHEERS. TED.

Jane handed them over without a word. As Dorothy began to protest, she said in a tight, pinched voice, 'I knew it was too good to last.'

Charlotte's change of heart was due in part to Eustace Percival. He had decided to make his move. It wasn't easy to summon up sufficient courage, for behind the glossy, booming exterior was a greedy but shy man, and Mrs Davie McKie was a formidable proposition. She was also well protected. At the Emporium, she was surrounded. He had handed in his card on three occasions but couldn't expect her to return the compliment. A widow did not leave cards at a bachelor establishment even when she knew the occupant to be away on business.

He knew Mrs Davie had begun to go out in society once more. She had been seen at the theatre, looking extremely chic. Mr Percival also knew that Darlington schoolchildren were now safely back at school and that every afternoon it was the lady's habit to take tea with her aunt. There was therefore every chance, if he timed his arrival carefully, that he might find Charlotte comparatively unguarded. Mr Percival entered the Emporium at five minutes past four and requested an interview with Mrs Armitage.

Alas, the old lady sent word he might come up and there Charlotte discovered him, standing on her aunt's hearthrug.

'Ah, Mrs Davie — what a happy coincidence!'

Unfortunately, Aunt Armitage decided at that particular moment that there was something she had to tell Bertha. She stepped out of the parlour. Eustace Percival seized the opportunity, and proposed.

Once the old lady had returned and the gentleman had been shown out, not wholly convinced by Mrs Davie's refusal — was he not the most eligible catch in Darlington? — Charlotte became hysterical.

John was away on business. Neither Mary nor Katriona could persuade her to be rational. Jane must come back. This would never have happened had her daughter been at her side. Jane should never have left home. By the time Ted returned from school, the matter was settled as far as Charlotte was concerned.

The occupants of the Emporium showed their disapproval in various ways; Mary was reproachful, Katriona like a thunder-cloud, Mrs Armitage tearful and Mrs Beal tight-lipped but Charlotte wouldn't budge.

Ted listened to the mutterings. He agreed, it was utterly unfair. He also thought his mother was being unreasonable — Mr Percival would surely not try again? He opened his mouth to say so but thought better of it. In her present irrational mood, it might be unwise to provoke her further.

Ted kicked several walls on his way to the telegraph office; it was all so beastly unfair to Jane. After despatching the first telegram he decided to try and clarify matters, with the help of the clerk and using what pocket-money he had.

Jane said bravely she would return alone. She knew Jack and Hugo were planning to go to Switzerland once she and Dorothy were at the finishing school. 'I shall be quite safe; the guard will look after me.' It was an effort to speak without crying but she managed.

'Nonsense!' Jack said kindly, 'I shall travel with you to Calais, Jane. I shan't let you board the boat-train until I've found a suitable lady to chaperone you. After that, we'll telegraph Thomas Cook and their man will meet the train at Victoria and escort you to King's Cross station. Don't argue, there's a dear. Hugo will stay here with Dorothy.

How could I possibly face your uncle if I let you go all that way on your own?'

Suddenly, Jane was very glad indeed. 'Thank you,' she whispered, 'And you will let me know how much I owe you?'

The housekeeper helped her pack while Dorothy sobbed helplessly in a chair. 'Why have you got to go, it's just not fair!' she wailed, which didn't make it any easier.

It was an early start. Hugo sat beside her as Jane drank coffee and tried to nibble a roll. He helped her on with her coat and, seeing the first tears well up, kissed her on the cheek.

'Be brave, princess. You'll take possession of your kingdom one day.'

'Yes ... and when I do, I hope you'll be there.' Jane didn't want to poach on Dorothy's preserve but Hugo had been awfully kind.

'Your wish is my command. Come, let me take your bag.'

He and Dorothy stood, waving goodbye. Inside the cab, Jane clenched both fists until her nails bit into her palms. A large white handkerchief appeared under her nose.

'Blow,' Jack Creswell ordered, then changed his mind and put both arms round her, pulling her to his chest. 'Have a good cry instead if you want. It doesn't matter.' Far better here where no-one could see.

At Calais, a party of tender-hearted ladies declared they would take Jane as far as the Darlington train themselves and she held out a hand to Jack. 'Thank you for looking after me. I'm sorry to have been such a nuisance.'

'Don't be silly.' There wasn't a single tear now, not in public. Jack knew what an effort that must be. Ignoring her hand, he took her in his arms and kissed her tenderly.

'Congratulations on the pluck, you're doing splendidly,' he whispered. Jane stared, lips parted in astonishment, at the first kiss from a strange man.

'Thank you very much,' she said abruptly. On the train back to Paris Jack pondered over those thanks. Jane was a schoolgirl he scolded himself, it didn't mean anything. But, he remembered happily, she was growing up.

Her uncle was on the platform in Darlington. 'Jane, my dear, I'm so very sorry.'

'Mama's got what she wanted, Uncle. Here I am, back home for good.'

'My dear, try not to be bitter.'

Her smile was perfunctory. 'I'll get over it as quickly as possible, promise.'

In the cab John allowed one brief spurt of anger to show. 'Promise me rather that you won't waste your life trailing after Charlotte. She's spoilt things this time because I wasn't there to prevent it. I was horrified when I discovered how selfish she'd been.'

'Was there any *real* necessity for me to come back, Uncle?'

He'd hoped to avoid that one. 'I think it would be better if you asked your mother yourself.'

Jane stared ahead at the familiar street. 'From now on I shall live my life in my own way.' It was quietly said but John noticed for the first time what a resolute chin she had.

They went in the back way. Katriona and Mary were waiting in the kitchen. After the greetings Jane asked, 'Where's Ted?'

'In his room, I think, pet.'

He was pasting pictures of favourite motor-cars into his scrap book. 'Hello . . . I'm sorry you had to come back.' He examined her covertly; she was very, very subdued.

'Thanks for the telegram.'

Ted shrugged, manfully. 'It only cost two-and-three-pence.'

'Oh, Ted!'

'Besides, I thought you ought to have an explanation. Have you seen Mama?'

She shook her head. 'At supper will be soon enough.'

'Yes . . .' Jane had lost all her lovely sparkle. 'I'll go down with you, if you like?'

'Yes, please.' Brother and sister looked at one another.

'I think it was damned unfair!' Ted said hotly. 'It was only because silly old Percival turned up. He got her on her own for a bit and asked her to marry him but she sent him off

135

with a flea in his ear. Then she started yelling at Katriona about being a poor defenceless woman — you should've seen Kat's face! Mama kept it up though — and she managed to blub — but she stopped all of it when she heard you were coming back.' He eyed Jane narrowly. 'You're not going to turn on the waterworks, are you?'

'No.'

He wanted to see her smile. 'Like a bit of licorice?'

She knew he was anxious to help but it had been in his pocket rather too long. 'You have it. I'd better go and unpack.'

Katriona was already putting away the new school blouses, as yet unworn. Jane drifted across to stare out of the window.

'Did your uncle explain why your mother sent for you?'

'No, but Ted did.' Jane sounded indifferent.

'They all think it was because of yon Percival. Your mother will probably give you the same excuse. He certainly came and proposed and she definitely sent him packing. The trouble was, she'd just sent word to that nice Mr Kessel. I'm pretty sure she's turned him down as well.'

'Theodore?' Jane was faintly interested, 'Mama went to meet him, didn't she?'

'I wouldn't know about that.'

'She looked as happy when she got back from seeing Theo as I was yesterday.'

'Uh-huh.' Katriona kept her voice neutral as she lifted out more clothes. 'I'm not saying it was right to send for you as she did, I'm just telling you what happened to help you understand.'

'But I don't understand!' Jane's voice had a harder edge and her face was strained. 'For heaven's sake why didn't Mama marry Theo if she wanted to? None of us would have minded, we're all fond of him.'

'I imagine she thought it was her duty to stay here.'

'That's nonsense!' Jane said sharply. 'We're nearly grown-up. She's using us as an excuse to act the martyr and she's ruined my life —'

136

'Jane, that's exaggerating. Nothing's ruined and you're only a girl yet —'

'I've never been so happy as I was in Paris,' Jane cried passionately, 'Mama's spoiled everything!'

Charlotte was waiting. She'd planned that Jane would come to her in the shop where she would indulge in a tearful reunion. It was a shock to realize her bluff had been called and that Jane was deliberately avoiding her. At suppertime Charlotte found her in the dining-room with Ted.

'Jane . . .'

Jane stood firm. 'How are you, Mama?'

Charlotte had to cross the room to kiss the cool cheek. 'So thankful to have you safely home, my darling!'

'Mr Creswell was very considerate. He arranged a chaperone. I think we should write and thank him for all he's done.'

'Come and see me after supper. We can have a talk.'

'It's been a long day, Mama. I'd prefer to go to bed.' It was a small victory but it marked the new gulf between them.

Alone in her parlour, Charlotte wept. She'd convinced herself she'd done what was right: she'd denied herself for the sake of the children. It wasn't the uncertainty of marrying a younger man she told herself, nor the newly burgeoning warmth of love — that could be quenched given time; instead Charlotte had chosen the path of duty and now Jane had spurned her sacrifice.

It was windy and cold in Newcastle. Luke hurried into the lodgings. The post was fanned out on the hall table. He collected his weekly letter from John and noticed there were more than half-a-dozen for Theodore Kessel. He saw with dismay that one was from Charlotte. Was she attempting to renew the acquaintanceship? Luke's face exhibited what William Cullen called his 'Puritan look' as he began to climb the stairs. It was embarrassing to imagine what his aunt might be up to.

He began John's letter distractedly. A phrase stopped him and he went back over the last few lines. John's style was terse. Percival's unwanted proposal and Jane's return took only a couple of sentences but Luke re-read them several times. Why had Jane been forced to return? He searched for a reason but his father had none to offer. Charlotte had sent for her daughter in a fit of pique and had earned the obloquy of the entire Emporium in doing so but Jane was behaving with great dignity.

Luke recalled Jane's ecstatic face less than a week ago, and seethed. How selfish! How thoroughly unjust. He walked about, trying to rid himself of anger and think of some way she could be compensated for the terrible disappointment.

He became aware of noises next door; Kessel had obviously returned. Luke remembered he'd been attending a course at a London hospital, hence the neglected mail. He thought again of the letter from Charlotte. Had that been written in a fit of pique and if so, what indiscretion might it contain?

Luke almost convinced himself he had the right to knock and demand the envelope be returned unopened. He shivered. He'd been standing too long in the cold room. He'd need the blanket over his knees before he could begin studying tonight. No, hang it all, he'd light the fire. Once in a while he deserved a bit of comfort and he could think more clearly if he were warm.

As he stooped to put a match to the kindling, Luke heard more sounds coming from Kessel's room. In his prim mood of certainty he told himself he needed to know what Theodore was up to. A cupboard backed the flimsiest part of the wall. Luke opened it. He could hear quite clearly now: the sounds were of a man in despair, sobbing his heart out.

Luke ran through the facts a second time slowly, and re-interpreted them. He was no longer self-righteous; instead he felt ashamed.

'Kessel loved her and she's rejected him, that's what the letter was about. Poor old chap,' he whispered. 'I'd no idea he was so smitten.' The tormented sobs unnerved him, the idea that love could unman someone so much. It also occurred to Luke that Charlotte had turned down what was possibly her last chance of happiness. 'Small wonder she wanted Jane,' he whispered.

The street lamps made patterns on the wall before he summoned up the courage to tap on Kessel's door. There was a sound but he wasn't sure if he'd been bidden to enter. Luke opened it cautiously. The room was in shadow but flames rose in the grate where Theodore crouched over a burning pile of papers. A half-empty suitcase lay on the bed.

'Yes . . .?' Kessel didn't look up from feeding the flames.

'I came to ask if you were all right?' Kessel didn't reply. 'And to apologise,' Luke said heavily. 'I should have done so ages ago. I'm sorry. It was no concern of mine what you and Aunt Charlotte —'

'No.' Kessel struck the burning scraps savagely, sending fluttering ashes into the air.

'I'm so very sorry,' Luke repeated lamely. He held out his hand.

Kessel ignored it a moment, then muttered, 'It's too late.'

Luke was red-faced with guilt, his arm leaden at his side. Was it his fault then? He retreated awkwardly. Had his small interference caused so much misery?

He could no longer concentrate and went to bed and a fitful sleep. In the early dawn there was a knock. Kessel looking gaunt and tired, stood there in his travelling clothes.

'I came to thank you for your apology, McKie. I should have done so last night but . . . I'd just received bad news.'

Stupefied, only half-awake, Luke stared. 'Are you off somewhere?'

'I was offered a position in a French teaching hospital while I was in London. I've decided to accept.'

'It's a bit sudden, isn't it?'

Theodore turned away, scarlet-faced. 'I can't bear England at present, McKie. I've a request before I go, however . . . Oh, and here's my address in France, should — anyone — ask for it.'

It was easy enough to comply with the request. Luke handed over the photograph in exchange for Theodore's card. 'Is there anything else,' he asked embarrassed, 'Anything I can do?'

'Just your hand, old chap. Last night I was too upset . . .
you must forgive —'

Luke seized his. 'It's all my fault!'

'Not so, I fear.' Theodore swallowed and managed a
grin. 'I cannot vent my disappointment on you, Luke, for
it's not that simple. It's circumstance, convention, call it what
you will but your esteemed aunt is reacting as any proper
woman should.'

'Give her a little more time,' Luke begged, 'She'll change
her mind once Ted and Jane leave home, you'll see.'

'Perhaps . . . and if you could bring yourself to mention
my name occasionally . . .?' He broke away from Luke's hug
and picked up his portmanteau. 'Meanwhile, farewell for the
present, old chap.'

Luke listened as the footsteps crossed the hall and the
front door opened and closed. He looked at the card in his
hand. 'As soon as there's an opportunity,' he promised the
empty air but he tucked the card at the back of his pocket-
book because that was the easier thing to do.

CHAPTER NINE

The End of an Era

Ted was to remember that time as an end to childhood. It did not happen suddenly, but by Christmas changes had taken place. A year ago everyone had been counting the days until Luke's return. Now they were accustomed to his absences.

Jane had changed; she didn't smile as readily as she used to. Ted hadn't realized how much he'd enjoyed their former spats but Jane was much more adult and refused to be provoked. Since her return they'd become closer, partly out of antagonism to Mama. Ted would have scoffed at that idea too, a year ago. Then girls had been something to be despised — but not any longer. He was secretly proud to have a pretty sister. He never said so of course, that would have been really soppy but he mentioned casually if her hair was a mess, saying he preferred it when it wasn't. That was the sort of helpful advice women expected from a chap.

They had discussed Mama's behaviour and Jane astonished him. 'If we'd been living in Paris, Mama would have accepted both Mr Percival *and* Theo.'

'Can you have two husbands in France?' This was interesting information indeed.

'You only have one proper one but you can have as many callers as you like. Ladies who do are called '*Poules*'. I saw one, as a matter of fact.'

'Golly! What was she doing?'

'Greeting one of her friends. He gave her a loaf and she helped him put on his slippers. Actually, he may have been her real husband,' said Jane with regret. 'I don't suppose callers have slippers.'

'I think it's cheating.'

'All the same, I wish Mama had someone to be fond of instead of relying on us.'

'It won't be so bad when you go to London.'

But Jane surprised him a second time. 'I don't think that will happen. I'm not a good enough dancer.' Which as Ted said to Luke when he came home for Christmas, was a bit of a facer.

'We've got to think of a way of cheering Jane up. She could go into a decline if she sits and mopes. You see young women like her in advertisements, drinking tonic wine against debility.'

'I don't think there's any danger of that!'

Ted said pugnaciously, 'You and I must put our heads together, Luke. Otherwise Jane could end up helping Mama in the Emporium.'

'Jane has one more year at school first.'

'Yes, but this is the time when she must decide what she really wants to do, so she can present Mama with a *fait accompli.*'

Luke chuckled at Ted's new sophistication. 'I promise to give the matter thought.'

Ted strolled through the festive, crowded Darlington streets. That younger, boisterous self who had eaten hot potato cakes seemed part of another life. In one way, he was glad; such behaviour would not be tolerated now he was a Prefect. Uncle John no longer talked of a future in the Emporium, either. That was to be Matthew's province. For Ted, extra lessons in science and physics would, it was hoped, bring an engineering apprenticeship. Motor cars! The new passion could stir him just as bull's-eyes once had but was far more satisfying. Imagine being able to work on engines all day long, build them even? On Saturday afternoons when he wasn't needed for deliveries, Ted would make himself useful in Bowdon's Garage, the nearest place he knew to Paradise.

Jane had come to a surprising conclusion about Luke and his attitude toward Theo. With her new-found ability to appraise the situation she explained her reasoning to Ted and tackled Luke when he returned for the holiday.

'Is Theodore coming for Christmas?'

'Why d'you ask?'

'He's awfully good fun. I'm very fond of him.' Her gaze didn't waver. 'Nearly as fond as Mama.'

Luke didn't like the scrutiny and tried to be off-hand. 'Kessel's left Newcastle. He had the chance to do research at a French hospital and decided to take it.'

Jane stared. 'I thought he was planning to qualify over here?'

'Yes, he was. It's a frightful shame.'

'He was spoony over Mama. I hoped she'd marry him.'

'Good heavens, what a thing to say!' Luke blustered. Jane's eyes became very cool.

'Why pretend? You knew how much they liked one another, and he made her laugh. Did you try and put him off?' Luke couldn't think of a tactful reply. 'If you did,' Jane said angrily, 'I think it was beastly to interfere. I might have gone to finishing school if Mama hadn't turned Theo down.'

'That's true,' Ted said judiciously, 'So was it all your fault Jane had to come back?'

'No, it wasn't.' Luke was annoyed at the inference.

'I think you should write to Theo and invite him to visit,' Jane insisted. 'If she knew he was coming on holiday, Mama would have something to look forward to. She's been very difficult these past few months.'

'Hear, hear!' Ted agreed. 'I'd like to see Theo, too. He was a good egg.' It was his highest accolade.

Dismayed, Luke defended himself against their united attack. 'I did make it up with Theo the day he left. But if you really think inviting him would be a good idea . . .?'

'Yes, I do.'

'Why not ask Aunt Mary first,' Ted suggested. 'She can be very sensible when it comes to dealing with Mama.'

But unfortunately Mary was cautious; Charlotte was beginning to settle after what had been a time of upheaval. 'I would leave it a little longer, dear,' she told Luke. 'Perhaps we can invite Mr Kessel next year rather than risk another upset so soon?'

When she heard, Jane was disappointed. She still hankered after France. If Theo and her mother became friendly once more, might he not persuade Mama to let her go? At supper that evening, it galled her to hear Luke chatting so confidently about medical school. 'I suppose you'll be helping Dr Cullen again this holiday?' she demanded.

'If he'll let me,' Luke's easy confident smile was the final straw.

'It's so unfair!' Jane exploded, 'Boys can always escape. They can choose what they want and go away and do it. Everyone applauds — tells them what fine chaps they are. Girls have to obey their mothers for the rest of their lives!' There was a flurry of black stockings and petticoats as she ran from the room. Ted immediately leapt to his feet and rushed after her.

Oh Lord, thought Luke guiltily. Ted was right, they must put their heads together and find a way of improving Jane's prospects.

At Easter he suggested, 'Why not spend summer on the croft with us? Father's written saying Ted, Matthew and I would like to go and he'll come for a couple of weeks when he can. It'll do you the world of good to escape from Aunt Charlotte.'

'Where would I sleep? There's nowhere unless I went in the hay loft and I don't fancy that.'

'I'm sorry, I hadn't thought of the practical side,' Luke apologised. 'But if you'd like to go, I'm sure we can think of a solution.' He could see Jane was wavering. 'Ask Katriona what she thinks.'

It was unfair to invoke such a biased opinion. Katriona declared at once that of course Jane must go to Scotland. 'It's high time you learned how civilized people behave. Besides, the water's so much better up there; there's no typhoid and it looks like being a bad summer for that down here.'

Luke also recruited Mary and John as allies. 'It will mean Jane can escape Harrogate as well as Charlotte,' Mary pointed out.

'There is the problem of sleeping arrangements. The boys and I will be packed like sardines as usual. I wondered if we could ask the Hamiltons to have Jane?'

'I'll write to Mistress Shields,' John said promptly, 'She'll be glad of the company.'

Oh, lor . . .! thought Luke, I doubt if Jane will appreciate that.

She didn't; she resisted up to the last minute. She would prefer to stay at home, she declared. Dorothy was due back after an extensive tour of France and Switzerland. Jane wanted to spend the next few weeks hearing all about it.

It was a hot day in early summer. Kitchen windows were wide open but the atmosphere was oppressive. Jane was helping Katriona clean the silver when Charlotte entered. 'Is it today Dorothy returns?'

'Yes, Mama. Jack has gone to Paris to fetch her. Their train's due in Darlington at four and Mrs Creswell has invited me over for tea.'

Her mother put down her library books and peeled off cream leather gloves. 'Just think,' she said idly, 'If I'd let you stay in Paris, I would be looking forward to your return this afternoon, just as Mrs Creswell must be with Dorothy.'

Before leaving for tea at Haughton Green, Jane wrote asking Helen Shields if she could stay for the entire summer.

'Did Charlotte mean to hurt Jane's feelings?' John asked later.

'I don't think she understood in the least,' Mary replied, 'But I shan't forget the look Jane gave her.'

'What was Charlotte's reaction to that?'

'Bafflement.'

He sighed. 'As well as thoughtless, Charlotte's much more short-tempered nowadays — it's having a bad effect on Ted. I shall be glad when the children are away.'

Luke travelled directly from Newcastle, arriving ahead of the rest. Alex McKie had never been alone with Mary's son before. He was nervous as well as eager and the dog caught his mood, whining and fidgeting until Alex shut him in the byre for a bit of peace.

'Hallo, Grandfather. It was such good weather, I came over the moor.' The silhouette, rimmed by the evening sun, was almost that of a stranger until Luke moved and Alex could see the eager handsome face.

'How's John?' Always the first question reflecting the perpetual prayer: Let me see my beloved son once more, for I am an old man.

'He's well, Grandfather. He sends his dearest love and will be with you toward the end of the month.'

'Aye . . .' To hear the words spoken brought the time closer. 'It will not be long, now.' The careful English, practised for days. 'And are you still enjoying medicine?'

Luke's face was transformed. 'It's fascinating! You've no idea what improvements have been made lately in tracing diseases of the blood . . . But don't start me off, Grandfather, I can go on for hours.'

Alex caught the excitement even if he didn't understand. 'I want to hear. What is it like to be in a hospital? You must tell me for I have no notion.' Then, forgetting his good intentions, he lapsed into Gaelic: 'Come inside. You are welcome in this house.'

Luke was dozing after the effects of the journey when his grandfather asked, 'Does your father believe there will be trouble?'

'With the Fenians?' Luke said, dazed.

'In Europe. Last Sunday the minister preached that war was unthinkable. When you consider how often the poor man's been mistaken in the past . . . It makes you doubt life eternal when he guarantees it, never mind anything else.'

But John agreed with the minister:

'I fear the church could be wrong,' he wrote in his weekly letter to Alex, 'but I'm sure it will be prevented for such a prospect is too dreadful to contemplate.

'Charlotte has begun a campaign to stop Matthew going to Scotland. She told Mary privately she could not bear to be without one of her children this summer. When Matthew returned from boarding school yesterday,

146

she suggested he might like to work in the Emporium — for a wage!

'I discovered this *fait accompli* (as Ted calls it) and have struck a bargain. Matthew will go to Scotland but can return when I do and work until the start of his next term. One cannot deny that such experience will be useful to him . . .'

Always the slight hesitancy, thought Luke. Father wasn't completely convinced Matthew had turned over a new leaf. He handed the letter back to Alex. The old man sat a long time with it. Had the time finally come to tell John about the theft from the money jar? His eyes were misty as he gazed at Luke. This grandchild was such a fine young man; it brought consolation.

Helen Shields watched Jane unpack. The request had delighted her. After the lonely, dark winter months, she'd been counting the days. Now Jane was here, and with her the sunshine.

How tall the girl was and with such a mass of hair! 'You favour your grandmother,' Helen said decisively. 'Her curls were the same dark shade and always in a tangle.'

Jane felt pleased that she didn't resemble Charlotte. 'It's obstinate hair, it won't stay up.'

'Then let it hang loose. Your grandmother used to. Your father and uncle were extremely proud of it. In one of Davie's first compositions he wrote, "My mother has beautiful, dark brown curly hair, very long down her back."' Helen shook her head. 'Too many adjectives. Come through to the parlour when you're ready.'

Careful preparations had been made to the small white-washed bedroom, Jane saw. A row of wooden pegs had been hammered into the wall behind the door. Paintwork and varnish looked suspiciously fresh and there were two new rag rugs. On the sill was a bowl of sweet-peas. Perhaps it wouldn't be too bad after all? 'Could you manage a few scones with your tea, Jane?' Helen called, 'With fresh cream and home-made jam?'

Half an hour later, her mouth blue with familiar bilberry stains, Jane leaned back, replete. 'I couldn't manage another mouthful. I'd no idea I was so hungry,' she apologized, 'I seem to have eaten an awful lot.'

Helen looked satisfied. 'I've become a reasonable cook, over the years. Now, I'm not expecting to see much of you during this holiday, Jane. You're here to fill your lungs with good fresh air — so see that you do. The daily walk to and from the croft will help. I've no doubt your grandfather wants to feast his eyes on you as often as he can.'

'I love the summer!' Jane stretched ecstatically, 'when you can feel the sun through your clothes!'

'It's almost too hot,' Helen grumbled. 'Borrow my old straw hat, otherwise you'll be burned like a gipsy. D'you want to talk about your future?'

Abrupt and to the point. Jane fiddled with her knife to give herself a breathing space.

'Charlotte can't keep you beside her forever. You don't intend to sit at home arranging flowers and waiting for "Mr Right" do you?'

'Certainly not!' Jane blushed.

'Thank goodness you've got that much spunk. So . . . what are your plans?'

'Since Paris, I haven't really made any.'

'Disappointment is no excuse,' Helen reproved her. 'What sort of school report was it this term?'

'"Could do better" in arithmetic. Top in French and English.'

'What I would expect of Davie's daughter but we'll work at the arithmetic.'

'You're not going to give me lessons, are you?' Politeness gave way to alarm.

'How can you face the future, Miss, if you cannot add up?' Jane wanted to mutter she'd managed very well so far but held her tongue. 'Luke tells me you've changed your mind about dancing, which I must say made me thankful. While you're here, we'll discuss other possibilities. Your uncle wants you to have the same opportunity as the boys so stop worrying about your mother, Jane. Once you've made up your mind what you want to do, John and I will deal with Charlotte.'

148

As she prepared for bed, Jane had a pang of conscience: was it underhand to plot against Mama like this? Then she recalled Charlotte's callous remark and decided it wasn't.

Ted and Matthew had their bikes this year. One of Jane's tasks each morning was to provide them with sandwiches. Gradually, over the weeks, the two explored the Peninsula and it was Alex's delight each time they returned to tell them the history of the landscape.

One overcast afternoon, they found a lifeless grey stone house, open to the sky.

'Grandfather said it's to avoid paying taxes,' Ted balanced precariously on top of a wall.

Matthew squinted up at the surviving chimneys. 'What a waste, taking off the roof. If the place were let, at least there'd be rent coming in. I suppose no-one wants to live up here?'

'I wouldn't mind. It's a super view.'

'How could you run a garage profitably? We've only seen one motorcar since we came.'

'Yes, a Buick,' Ted said happily, 'but there could be plenty more before the summer's over. Anyway, I don't want to *run* a garage, I want to work on the engines.'

'That won't make you rich,' Matthew observed shrewdly. 'Why don't you ask Uncle John to help you set up in business for yourself?'

'I don't like asking him for money.'

'You're stupid. I shall when I'm qualified. I want my own private office as well as working in the Emporium. You and Luke don't want to help so it all depends on me,' he ended plaintively.

Matthew almost made it sound as if Ted had failed in some way. He protested, 'Uncle John was jolly pleased when I said I wanted to be an engineer.'

'Quite. But Uncle will need me when the time comes for him to retire. After all,' Matthew said piously, 'it's for all our sakes, really, if I keep the Emporium running smoothly. But in return I shall expect to be made manager.'

Ted looked uneasy. 'Is that all you'd do? Keep it running smoothly?'

'Of course!' Matthew was all bland innocence, 'It'll be up to me to expand when the time is right. Uncle's lost his way. He should have re-invested in other shops years ago. He could have had several by now, maybe even one in London.'

'He had to pay Mr Wilkinson's debts,' Ted reminded him. 'That set him back.'

'He should never have laid out a penny,' Matthew replied crisply. 'The bank told him at the time he wasn't legally responsible.'

Ted thought this sounded like treachery. 'But it was to ensure all the employees had a pension when the factories were closed? So that no-one starved?'

'That money was part of our inheritance. It should have been reinvested for *our* future.'

Ted leaned against the warm grey stones and tried to fathom the logic. He watched a bird spiral up in a hot air thermal. Matthew was very positive when he talked about business. As for the collapse of Mr Wilkinson's factories, it was so long ago, Ted couldn't remember the details.

'I don't care,' he said at last, 'Uncle John wanted to be fair, that's why he did it. You and I haven't suffered so why keep moaning? There's enough for you to go to university as well as for my apprenticeship.'

'I want more than that. I want to be rich,' Matthew replied.

Life was timeless on the peninsula, thought Luke. Here we are one year later with the hay cut and spread to dry, about to plough up the land again. And I'm just as exhausted as I was last year; even the aches in my back feel the same.

Jane emerged from the croft with mugs and a pitcher of lemonade. That at least, was an improvement. He watched her walk across the stubble, anticipating the cool sweet-sharp taste of the drink on his tongue. What a lovely lazy end to a summer day.

She had on her oldest clothes protected by a smock made from one of grandfather's shirts and her hair was swathed in a cloth as protection against midges. Luke supposed it was Charlottes's influence that she should continue to look elegant. Miss Shields' old bonnet had had no effect, she was as brown as the rest of them. She waited until he'd drunk then refilled his glass.

'D'you know where the Balkans are, Luke?'

'Mmm . . . think so, why?' he answered hazily.

'Miss Shields was trying to find them on the globe last night.'

'Uh-huh.' He watched a ladybird climb one of the stubble stalks. Should he save her a useless journey? There was nothing but a view from the top. Luke tried to imagine having the same multi-faceted eyes: how vast a world did they encompass, six inches from the earth?

'It hasn't been too bad, staying with Miss Shields. We've had some jolly interesting chats.'

'Miss Shields is a jolly interesting old bird,' he murmured. Jane glanced at the sleeping John. 'Bet she was frightfully strict when he and father were at school!'

'Decided what to do about your future, yet?'

She sat up and hugged her knees. 'No, but we're nearly there. Miss Shields said we must approach it logically. She made me write down all the things I prefer doing, at school and in the Emporium.'

'And?'

'We made another list of the jobs open to women and the qualifications each would require — *that* didn't take long.' Jane was a prim echo of the schoolmistress. 'It's absolutely scandalous that women are prevented from doing so many things because we haven't got the vote.'

Luke wasn't to be led down that thorny path. 'What happens next?'

'By tonight I'm to have all my thoughts ready, then she and I will discuss every possibility and come to a decision.'

Luke smiled to see her so serious. 'I look forward to hearing what it is.'

The following day, the last of John's holiday, Jane was in buoyant mood. She set off for the croft, calling affectionately that she wouldn't be late. Her feelings for Helen had changed completely since that first day. Last night they'd talked themselves dry but it had been worth it; a decision had been made which Jane was sure was right.

It hadn't rained for weeks and the earth was baked brown and dusty. Jane had left off her petticoat and vest days ago, revelling in the heat through liberty bodice and blouse. Later, when the chores were done on the croft, she would go for a swim in the loch. If they had the place to themselves, the boys didn't bother with bathing suits. It was tacitly understood that Jane would neither look nor tell Mama. As she pulled on her old navy costume that clung so heavily when it was wet, Jane decided this was another aspect of life which was shamefully unfair.

John's last day was to be spent with Miss Shields. Jane met him on the way to the cottage, soberly dressed in waistcoat and shirt, his jacket over his arm. It was strange to see him in his Darlington clothes again. He kissed her good morning with a smile, 'I keep meeting this gypsy girl every time I come this way . . . Heaven knows what my wife would say if she knew!'

'Shall I tell you your fortune, kind sir?'

'I don't believe in superstitious nonsense.'

'You're having fresh salmon for your tea, and bannock cakes. How's that?'

'Very good!'

'As for my fortune, Miss Shields wants to tell you that herself.'

John looked pleased. 'You've decided what you want to do?'

'She's going to tell *you*, I'm off to break the news to Luke. Bye!' Jane hurried away along the path, happier than he'd seen her for months.

Alex McKie saw the figure emerge through the heat-haze. He was resting with his dog when the dark-haired nymph appeared, dancing and waving. There was a sudden pain in his chest. 'Jeannie . . .' he whispered, 'Jeannie, is it you?' A moment later he knew who it was and felt glad; this was Jeannie incarnate and he had lived to see it.

'Grandfather, I found some different ones today. Tell me what they are . . .' As she put each wild flower into

152

his palm, Alex would say the Gaelic name and Jane would repeat it.

'Now do you remember those from yesterday?'

When it was finished, she asked, 'Are you going as far as the crossroad?'

'I thought I would, aye.'

'It's awfully hot. Don't stay out too long, will you?' And she was off on the final stretch of road to the croft.

Luke was making an attempt to pack Matthew's clothes. 'Thank goodness you've arrived,' he called cheerfully. 'Why is it that garments double in size when I try and fold them?' He caught sight of her face. 'You look cheerful?'

'Oh, I am. Miss Shields is a positive dear, did you know?'

'I've heard her called several names but never that.'

Jane seized Matthew's jacket from him and began to refold it. 'You know how depressed I'd become? Partly Paris but mainly because I couldn't be a dancer? Last night, Miss Shields began by scolding me — "Don't say you're not good enough, Jane. That's no excuse. You must try harder."'

'I don't quite see how that makes her a dear?'

'It didn't. But when she'd finished scolding, she said, "Anyway, it's perfectly obvious you couldn't become a professional dancer even if you wanted to because you're too tall." Which I am, but fool that I was, I'd never noticed!'

'Are you?' Luke's eyebrows were raised. 'I know you've grown a lot —'

'Last night, we measured me and proved it.' Jane gave a little laugh, 'It probably sounds feeble but you've no idea how relieved I was. I *knew* I'd never be good enough, but being too tall, five foot seven in fact, I can stop feeling guilty.'

'Oh, Jane, people change their minds all the time about what they want to do. Look at Ted? First a boxer, now a mechanical engineer —'

'I'm going to be a nurse.' It was out. 'Are you pleased?'

Luke's expression was mixed. 'If that's what you really want . . .?'

'Yes, I do. We talked and talked. Miss Shields even offered to take me on a visit to a hospital to see if I liked it,

153

the way she did for father that time. I said it wasn't necessary, that I'd ask Dr Cullen. You don't think he'd mind?'

'He'd be delighted. He thinks very highly of women who take up nursing. But Jane, it's an awfully hard life.'

'We discussed that. I've spent a great deal of mine on my feet, you know,' Jane said gravely, 'Both dancing and in the Emporium. As for the sad side of nursing, I know a bit about pain. I used to help Katriona with father, remember. It might hurt less when you don't love a person.'

'There are children to nurse,' Luke said softly. 'It can tear at your heartstrings when they don't get well.'

She nodded. 'We talked a lot about facing up to death last night but neither of us were sad. Miss Shields is very practical, you know. Do you still believe in God?'

'Yes, of course.' Luke was defensive, caught out by her question.

'I hope *I* do,' she surprised him. 'Sometimes I wonder. But I couldn't be a good nurse if I didn't believe. You'd need to be able to comfort a person if you knew they were going to die.' The large brown eyes were so solemn, Luke leaned across and hugged her.

'Dear Jane! Promise you'll never turn into one of those terrifying ward sisters, all starch and squeaky shoes. They frighten the life out of me.'

'No I won't.' For some reason he didn't understand, she'd blushed. 'D'you think it possible you and I might work together one day?'

'It depends where you apply,' he began but was interrupted by a shout.

'Hoy, Jane!' It was Ted, yelling as he raced Matthew up the slope, a wet towel trailing on the ground behind him. 'Are you there? Oh, you are — marvellous. Matthew and I decided we couldn't wait, we've already been for a swim. The trouble is, now we're *starving*!'

Jane tried to sound stern. 'When you've rinsed the mud off that towel and hung it out to dry, Ted McKie, I might find you each a stale crust.'

'Jane's going to be a nurse.'

'Are you?' Ted was astonished then thoroughly pleased. 'I say, what a thundering good idea! What on earth made you think of that?'

'Miss Shields said it was obvious.'

'But why?' Luke was intrigued. 'You didn't explain.'

'I like looking after people. I used to help Katriona with father, and with old Mr Armitage when I was little.'

'Mama's good at nursing,' Matthew said, unexpectedly. 'When I had diptheria, she was ever so gentle. I expect you take after her.'

Ted looked at him in surprise. 'I'd forgotten she did that. It was ages ago.'

Mama loved me best of all then, thought Matthew. She never left the room and I had her all to myself. It's never been the same since. He heard Ted ask, 'Will you nurse at Greenbank Hospital, Jane? Next time I break a leg it would be nice if you were there to look after me.'

'I want to work in Paris, eventually.' She'd astounded them this time. 'Miss Shields said it might be possible if I keep up French at night school.'

Ted giggled. 'Will you be a *Poule*? With millions of callers?'

'Hark at us!' Luke joined in the laughter, 'A doctor, a nurse, an engineer and an accountant? Did you ever hear the like?' They began ridiculing one another, four tanned happy faces with a limitless future before them.

'And Matthew's going to be rich,' Ted crowed, 'As rich as Croesus before he's finished.'

'I wouldn't be at all surprised,' Luke agreed. 'Anything's possible today.'

There was a movement outside the window. 'That's not Gip back already?' asked Jane. They crowded to the doorway to look. 'What's happened to grandfather?'

Outside, the sheepdog scurried round the yard, sniffing to discover what had changed. Matthew went over to fondle his ears.

'What have you been up to? You haven't deserted grandfather, have you? Bad dog!' Luke stared back up the track.

155

'It's too far for grandfather to go to the crossroads in this heat. I did warn him . . .' He looked round worriedly, 'Come on, Ted. You and I had better —'

'There's grandfather now. Uncle's with him.' They stared where Matthew's finger pointed.

'Both of them? That was a short visit to Miss Shields.' Jane sounded puzzled rather than worried.

'Grandfather's walking badly . . . Father's helping him. Come on.' Luke made as if to go and help but Jane clutched his arm.

'Something's wrong. Look at their faces. Something awful's happened.' Her voice trailed away. No one moved. 'What is it, d'you think?'

'I don't know.'

Two generations, full of sorrow, helped each other over the last few yards. In the sunlight, John's haggard face looked as old as Alex.

'England is at war with Germany.' Tears rolled down his face. 'Swear to me, Luke, for Mary's sake, you will not go and fight.'

CHAPTER TEN

War

' "Momentous Day in World's History".' Emily Beal had unwrapped the vegetables and crumpled bits of of newspaper were spread on the kitchen table. Her mother scraped carrots jerkily. ' "Nations are arrayed against Nations." '

'Momentous nothing! He's not a full shilling.'

'Who isn't?'

'The Prime Minister. And the Kaiser. They're both as bad.'

' "Kings's Message to the Fleet — 'The Sure Shield of Britain and her Empire." '

'I don't want to hear. If Mr McKie says it's wicked —'

'Listen to this bit, "Chancellor Describes Scheme to Insure Food and Work for England. All Parties Voice Approval —" '

'Who says?' demanded Mrs Beal. 'Did they ask me? Did they ask Mrs McKie? No, of course they didn't, they just went ahead and started a war.' Like many another these days, Mrs Beal found herself, alternating between anger and tears.

'It's to save "Gallant Little Belgium",' Emily reproved her. 'They're sending refugees over here. "Plans afoot to offer Hospitality." ' Mrs Beal swept the carrots on top of chopped swedes and turnips.

'Scrag end, that's what it'll mean. If they come here, they can eat it same as we do. I'm not cooking anything fancy.'

The atmosphere in the Temperance Hall was electric. There was silence as the vicar's wife cried, 'Are we all agreed, ladies? Sewing parties to make comforters for British and

Belgian soldiers to be held each night in the Friends' Meeting House in Skinnergate, commencing at 7.30 p.m.? Please tell your friends. Anyone willing to join our enterprise will be most heartily welcome!' There was wild applause and some shrill cheers.

'Before we go . . . Remember our motto.

"Leave your change,
Every Copper Will Help" .'

Dorothy Creswell rushed to empty the contents of her purse into the plate. Following more soberly, Jane added twopence. It was their third meeting in a week; so far the war was proving extremely expensive.

'Isn't it heavenly! So exciting! Shall I call for you this evening, dearest? If it's raining, I'm sure Pa will send the car.'

'I can't. My Red Cross class is at seven.'

'How horrid! I don't want to go on my own!'

Jane stared. 'Dorothy, the entire female population of Darlington will be there tonight.'

'Oh, you know what I mean. Anyway, how did you manage to enrol? I thought you had to be seventeen to be in the Red Cross?'

'I lied,' Jane told her calmly, 'and if you say one word to Mama, I'll never speak to you again.'

By the first week in November the Recruiting Sergeant had interviewed too many to worry about this one.

'Age?'

'Eighteen.'

The lad wasn't of course but the Sergeant asked the next question without waiting for a reply. Finally he ordered, 'Sign or make your mark,' and five minutes later Billy Beal was outside, slightly disappointed. He'd been rehearsing his new date of birth all the way to the train.

'Don't worry. You're in, that's all that matters,' Ted urged.

'Wiv' the 'orses?' Ted had promised him that.

'Bound to be. The cavalry need recruits to assist the farriers. You'll be selected when they see how good you are.'

'An' you'll 'tend to Blackie?' Billy's anxiety was profound; Ted had been known to forget her feed.

'Promise. Come on, let's get back.' The need for discretion had taken Ted and Bill as far as Bishop Aukland. Ted guessed what would happen when Uncle John learned what they'd done; that discovery must be delayed as long as possible.

It was very hard, being the son of a pacifist. His fiery nature wasn't peaceable and he longed desperately to 'do his bit.' When Billy confided that it was his dearest wish also, Ted felt honour-bound to help.

There were posters everywhere. It was one's *duty* to enlist and it was common practice to lie about one's age. Billy hadn't committed a crime. In fact, Billy hadn't committed any offence whatsoever; it was he who'd schooled Billy to lie. He'd even marched with the Church Lads Brigade to see a machine-gun being fired at Neasham Territorial camp. He'd lied about that too but war made everyone's conscience more flexible. And now he'd helped Billy Beal become a soldier.

The first hero emerged unexpectedly when John was handing out the wages one Friday. Young Allen from Mens' Sundries stood before him, stolid and expressionless. 'I've had my papers, sir. I'm a reservist, you see. I have to report on Wednesday.'

John took off his pince-nez and rubbed the sore spot on his nose. 'You have a brother at home, I think.'

'Sister, sir; Gladys. She'll look after mother while I'm gone. Back by Christmas, they reckon.'

'We must pray that is so,' said John earnestly. 'Your position will be kept open.'

'Thank you, sir.'

'You'd better finish here Monday and spend Tuesday with your family. Here's two shillings. Treat them to tea in Hinton's.'

Something like emotion appeared behind young Allen's acne. 'That's very good of you, Mr McKie.'

'Don't thank me,' replied John tersely. 'I disapprove of war. If you can return without having fired a shot, I shall think more highly of you, remember that.' This was beyond Thomas Allen. With a final mumble of thanks, he disappeared. When Hart arrived, John said, 'We'll have to find a temporary replacement.'

'Would you consider bringing in Mr Matthew?'

'Not for the present. If for any reason, Allen isn't back by Christmas, he can help out then.'

'I'd no idea it would be so *boring*!' Dorothy's blue eyes rolled helplessly. 'All we did the entire evening was practise rolling bandages with our handkerchieves. Honestly, Jane, such a waste of time. And I saw cook and Bessie in a corner. We didn't speak of course but I didn't realize just *anyone* could go. I don't think I'll bother again. What did you do?'

'We began studying for our Home Nursing Certificates.'

Dorothy smothered a yawn. 'That doesn't sound particularly exciting?'

'Last night we learned the correct way to sweep a floor.'

'Goodness, I've never had to do that.' Dorothy shook her head in exasperation. 'Isn't it maddening? The men are having all the fun as usual.'

'I don't understand, Jane. I gave you my permission to attend classes once a week.'

'But now it's Wednesdays as well as Fridays, Mama. We must all qualify for our certificates as soon as possible.'

'I don't see why . . .' Charlotte frowned. 'You surely don't intend to *do* anything with them?'

'Of course,' Jane said calmly, 'if the hospital nurses become overworked then we will volunteer to assist.'

'Thank heavens there's not the slightest likelihood of that happening!'

The meaning behind her words was implicit and Jane looked at her levelly. 'If it does, I shall volunteer, Mama. Whatever you say, I shall do my bit and you won't stop me.' She picked up another trayful of dishes and took them to the sink. It was Emily Beal's night off and she was helping with the washing-up.

Sitting at the table, Mary kept her eyes firmly on the household accounts. She was acutely aware of Charlotte's shock at this small act of defiance. Charlotte opened her mouth to argue but was baffled. For Jane to turn her back as well? Eventually, common sense returned; what hospital nurse would tolerate a schoolgirl cluttering up her ward? Slightly relieved that she didn't have to pursue the matter, Charlotte left the kitchen. At the sink, Jane's taut back relaxed. She began to hum as she worked.

They're growing up, all of them, thought Mary. This war has given them all energy and purpose, but Charlotte can't accept it because she doesn't understand.

The Emporium was bustling: bunting was doing very nicely thanks to the country's response to Kitchener's call. McKies' had been first as usual and had sold out twice over.

Bring and Buy sales were planned, concerts, street parties — if their suppliers didn't fulfil the new order, they'd be reduced to selling the red, white and blue flags Mr Hart had used (against Mr McKie's wishes) to deck out their Patriotic Window. Mr Hart was in a pleasant state of fluster as he thought about it.

There was a stir; whispering counter-hands attracted his attention. Mr Hart looked round. There, in an ill-fitting shoddy greatcoat, a piece of wood at the slope in lieu of a rifle, stood Billy Beal!

Mrs Beal's feelings had undergone a considerable change. At first she'd championed her employer. She'd known him for over twenty years, surely Mr McKie couldn't be mistaken over something as important as a war?

But Emily discovered so many articles with a differing point of view, and there was so much excitement in the town — surely it was only right that our boys should go and teach the Hun a lesson.

Women had been raped in Belgium. Refugees confirmed they'd read those same reports. Innocent little babies had been decapitated by bestial young Fritzes who drank human blood! When Emily read that out the scales fell from Mrs Beal's eyes. Her son stood before her now in all his glory: 'Oh, our Billy!' she whispered and burst into proud, happy tears.

161

In the office, Ted faced a furious John.

'It was disgraceful to persuade Billy to enlist. You don't deny you were responsible?' Ted remained silent. John's voice was tight but he tried to be reasonable. 'You were too young to understand when Davie asked for your promise. I will explain why it was so important to both of us. Your great-grandfather was ordered to fight at a time when the Laird could demand a man's life as rent for a croft. I know you've heard that part of the story many times but now hear the rest of it.

'Your ancestor believed right to be on the other side and refused to fire when ordered to do so. He was given fifty lashes before being executed. The Laird gave out he was a traitor but we were proud of him. I hope you prove worthy of his courage.'

Ted felt sick but he had to make John understand. 'It's different this time. Right is on *our* side, everyone says so. Last night Mr Martin Harvey made a speech in the Opera House in Middlesbrough — I read it in the *Gazette* — "The Empire faces the gravest peril but will emerge, stronger than ever!" '

At the sight of his shining face sorrow weighed John down. 'Old men have preached that tale since mankind began, to convince the young to fall on one another like beasts. Does a German boy deserve to be killed any more than Billy Beal? For that's what war means, Ted: killing and being killed.' When Ted didn't reply, he asked, 'Do you intend to break your vow to your father?'

'You needn't worry. A promise is a promise.' The office door slammed then, a few seconds later, the one to the yard.

What use were words against 'patriotism', John wondered bitterly.

Mary protested, 'Billy Beal hasn't the least understanding of what it means.'

'I doubt whether that will worry the war machine in London. They must be grateful for such docile fodder.'

'Thank God Luke is safe.'

'Amen,' John sighed. 'We'll have to revise our plans. Once Billy has gone, Ted will have to do the deliveries. I'm loath to bring Matthew home. He's begged to be allowed, of course, he knows we're short-handed. If he were to give up boarding-school and move to Darlington grammar, perhaps he could work in Menswear in the evenings. . . ?'

'Charlotte wouldn't mind, not now. All her children have become very precious. And it would only be a temporary measure, until Thomas Allen returns.'

The turnover in woollen underwear that season had never been greater as mothers, aunts, sisters and brand-new fiancées purchased for loved ones facing the worst winter in living memory among water-logged trenches in Flanders.

'We shan't need to reduce a single item for the January Sale, Mr McKie, in fact we scarcely need run a Sale at all. They've been queuing up to buy — I've never seen anything like it! How soon can we expect the additional order for merino combinations?'

'When the war is over,' John said curtly. 'Supplies of wool are no longer reaching the mills because of enemy activity. Would you kindly ask one of the assistants to copy out this list from the evening paper.'

Mr Hart's face fell. 'Not more for the Patriotic Window?'

'I fear so.' John gazed sorrowfully at some of the names. 'Not as many as le Cateau and Mons, thank God. Somewhere on the river Aisne where there were several Darlington Pals . . .'

He broke off because Ted could be heard shouting outside. Neither man moved as the office door burst open.

'The Hun's been bombarding the coast, Uncle John! Scarborough, Whitby and Hartlepool have all been hit!'

Mr Hart clutched the desk for support. 'My God . . . suppose they invade? We might lose!'

But the excitement didn't last and Dorothy Creswell grew bored.

'You can always knit,' Jane suggested.

'I loathe knitting, I want to *do* something. What did you learn today?'

'How to make beef tea. Invalids need sustenance.'

163

'Mama was planning to give me a dance this month but Jack's been moved to another training camp and most of his chums are already in France. Never mind, it won't be long before he's home on leave.' Dorothy's hands were clasped ecstatically. 'I shall see Jack in uniform, at last! Oh — that reminds me, have you any decent belts in your shop? He says the standard issue looks frightfully cheap.'

'I'll ask Mr Hart.' Jane put away the last of her sewing and stretched cramped fingers.

'Did I tell you that our application for convalescent soldiers has been accepted? We're to be allowed six — I can't wait! Mother's ordered the sweetest bonnet with a white organdie veil and I shall wear a white apron — they might take me for a nurse!'

'When Luke comes at Easter, I'm going to ask him how to join the VADs. I shall be sixteen then.'

Dorothy's eyes widened. 'That'll mean leaving school — what will your Mama say!'

'I shan't tell her until it's too late,' and Jane fixed her with a stern stare.

'I know, I know,' Dorothy said petulantly. 'If I utter one word, you won't be my friend.'

That summer, Luke dreaded returning to Darlington. How to break the news? He couldn't bear to at first and went in through the main entrance knowing John would probably be in the office. There were far more changes now. The war was nearly a year old and only two familiar faces remained among those in Menswear. Matthew's sleek head was bent over an elderly customer choosing a shirt. He exerted his charm and the women decided on both garments. Luke waited to see the transition completed then chided himself. Father had written that so far there'd been no problems.

Who am I to criticize anyone, Luke asked silently, when I'm about to desert them?

He summoned up his courage and went to the office. John heard him in silence. 'I'm going as a medical orderly, father,' Luke kept the explanation brisk and business-like. 'According to the interview board, it's the lowest form of life but once they realized I couldn't be bullied, they had no other choice. It's what I wanted.' His heart lurched at the sadness in John's eyes. 'Please, try to understand. I couldn't go on watching from the sidelines, not knowing whether it was cowardice. Everyone else at Jesmond has gone. My place at university will be there when I return — at least I'll be helping to heal the sick.' He gave the ghost of a smile. 'There are plenty by all accounts, and a sad shortage of doctors.'

John pulled himself together. 'Couldn't you have gone . . . as a doctor?'

Luke shook his head. 'I'm not sufficiently qualified and it would have meant enlisting.'

'Yes, of course.'

'So . . . I shall "do my bit" and gain experience at the same time. It might enable me to finish more quickly when I return, one year instead of two perhaps?' His voice shook as he said, 'I hope you'll be able to make Mother understand.'

'So do I.'

'I asked Mother if I could be a proper nurse like you but she said it would ruin my hands,' Dorothy grumbled on the way to Haughton Green.

'I'm only a Volunteer, not a VAD. I read aloud to the patients and write letters for them.'

'Why can't they do that themselves?'

'Some have had their arms blown off. Two of them are blind.' Jane swallowed. 'They don't smell awfully nice, either. Sister says it's because their wounds are gangrenous.'

Dorothy wrinkled her *retroussé* nose. 'Urgh! Our wounded have been carefully selected, Daddy insisted on it: nothing too beastly. Thank you, Saunders.' The chauffeur held open the door and Dorothy stepped out. As a special treat, Jane had been invited to view the first intake of convalescent patients. Once inside Dorothy said, 'One moment, dearest,' and shed both jacket and hat before donning a dainty overall. 'I daren't go in improperly dressed. Nurse Thompson is strict! There.' Jane followed her into the ballroom.

She saw at a glance that these soldiers had suffered lightly by comparison with those she had encountered. Each had his own attendant, although these ladies appeared more concerned with flower arrangements at the bedsides. Many of Mrs Creswell's friends had insisted on being allowed to help; nevertheless Jane shared the men's embarrassment.

'D'you know, most of the boys left their belongings behind in France,' Dorothy whispered. 'Mother gave them a proper scolding. We even had to buy suits of pyjamas. Those who are in blue are officers, cream is for other ranks. Don't they look sweet? And they're so grateful.'

Jane remembered the screams as dressings were changed in the real ward and the sharp 'If you're going to be sick, Miss McKie, go home and don't come back!'

She stayed by the door as Dorothy sallied in and chatted to one particular patient. 'I'm trying to be extra-nice to Charles,' she murmured when she returned. 'He's so nice but terribly afraid. According to Nurse Hawkins, he's *malingering*. Saunders and I are taking him for a drive tomorrow, to try and buck him up.'

They were served tea in the morning-room. 'I was awfully glad to hear Luke had gone to France, dearest. People do talk if they don't go.'

'He's gone as a medical orderly, not to fight,' Jane said warmly.

'Yes, I know. But one needn't say so, need one? It's a pity Ted's grown so tall and manly. I saw him in the town yesterday.'

'Several of his admirers have given him white feathers.'

'Oh, dear!'

'Ted pretends to see the funny side. He keeps them in an elastic band. Whenever someone gives him another he flourishes the bunch as if it were a bouquet.' Jane finished her tea and stood up. 'I must get back. Thank you for letting me see your visitors.'

Dorothy was dismayed. 'We're not quarrelling are we? I know this isn't the same as a real hospital . . .'

'Would you like to see where I work, if I can arrange it?'

'No, thank you.' Jane's tone had been sharp. 'I may not be as brave as you, Jane, and it might sound a pretty feeble war effort, trying to help that boy conquer his cowardice but at least it stops me worrying over Jack.'

'I'm sorry, I didn't mean to be unkind!' Jane kissed her impulsively. 'It's just that I feel so angry for Ted. At least I don't have to fret about him or Luke.'

'Have you heard from Luke?'

'He's in what they call a Stationary Hospital. It's only tents. He says it's awfully wet and muddy.'

'Are you going to the fund-raising Garden Party on May the first?' Dorothy asked, brightening at the prospect. 'They're digging a real trench in the park, with periscopes and rifles and things. Some of our boys are going to make tea over a camp-fire! Won't it be fun?'

'No osprey feathers?' The customer was scandalized. 'Miss Attewood, I have subscribed many times over to the National Relief Fund in support of our merchant shipping.'

'I'm extremely sorry, Mrs Carlisle. We are having difficulty obtaining supplies.'

'Can I help?' It was Matthew, smiling and smooth. 'How are you, Mrs Carlisle, looking very well I see.' Miss Attewood, watched caustically as he feigned horror at her complaint. 'No osprey — I don't believe it! Miss Attewood,' Matthew snapped his fingers and the lady buyer stiffened. 'Miss Attewood we cannot disappoint our most valued customer.'

'No, Mr Matthew.' There wasn't a single osprey feather left and he damn well knew it!

'This hat must be re-trimmed according to Mrs Carlisle's express wish.'

'But . . .'

'Mrs Carlisle has made sufficient sacrifice by making her straw last two seasons. If I could have the hat-box?' It was passed across and the buyer's lips compressed into a thin, tight line.

'I knew I could rely on *you*, Mr McKie.'

'Of course, Mrs Carlisle.' Matthew's eager expression remained until she was out of sight. Miss Attewood waited, stubborn and silent. 'Take this to the work-room,' he ordered, 'use the feathers from one of my mother's old hats and charge Mrs Carlisle seven guineas.'

'Seven! The wretched thing only cost five originally.'

167

'Supply and demand, Miss Attewood,' Matthew said silkily, 'As you so rightly observed, we are having difficulties. But please don't argue in front of a customer in future. It gives such a bad impression.'

In the leaking tent near Camiers, Luke tried to ignore the terrified faces as they watched the dressing trolley approach. It had never occurred to him before he arrived in France that there would be no anaesthetics. The ward sister had reprimanded him. 'There is morphia, Mr McKie. That is kept for patients in dire need.'

And how would you define this chap? Luke wondered sadly. He positioned the demi-john ready for use. Did it really prevent gangrene, swilling out raw wounds with this cold, lime mixture? That wasn't the worst of it. Before they could irrigate, the old dressing had to be removed. It was his task to hold the youth steady. What was he, twenty-two or three, about the same age as himself in fact. With both buttocks shot clean away. The dark-haired nurse began to tug gently at pus-soaked gauze, masses of it, coming from a gaping hole with no sign of healthy flesh. Luke used his strength to hold the lad and closed his ears as the girl inserted the tubes and pressed the plunger home. Thank God Jane was only a probationer. She was too young to come to France and surely no English hospital contained horrors such as these.

His diary entry read: 'Heavy rain today and bedding soaked.'

Dorothy couldn't contain her indignation. She flung herself into a chair while Jane continued to darn stockings. 'Both of them left without working out their notice to work in a munitions factory near Luton!'

'Did they say why?' asked Jane, tiredly.

'The pay is much better than maiding, apparently. Fourpence an hour plus a bonus. Most earn at least thirty shillings a week. One of the creatures has an aunt living in nearby and they intend to lodge with her.'

'It's a deal of money. Far more than Uncle pays our counter-hands.'

168

'But Mama and I haven't a maid between us. Mrs Metcalfe's agency can't help because of this beastly war!' Dorothy's eyes filled with tears, 'Who's going to see to my clothes?'

Jane pushed the darning aside. 'Dorothy, I had to hold a stump this morning, because the senior probationer wasn't there, while they rebandaged it. The smell was awful. I shall probably have to do the same when I go on duty this evening so don't come here complaining of a lack of maids.'

'Oh!' Dorothy thought she might gag but the sight of Jane's tears stopped her. In her misery, Jane rocked to and fro.

'I know I lied about my age because I wanted to be a nurse but I didn't know it would be like this! They're all so young and brave, Dorothy . . .'

'There, there,' Dorothy said helplessly.

Luke lifted his head. It was the wind that brought the sound so close. The thirteenth 'Last Post' so far; yesterday there had been twenty. He hunched under the blanket. The palliasses were closely packed but that same freezing wind penetrated every corner of the tent. How long? There was already a glimmer of light outside. Another half-hour and he would have to face the ward again. The Hun were using a dreadful new gas which caused men's lungs to fill. They 'drowned' as they sat up in bed, and they understood what was happening; they knew there wasn't a cure. Luke shivered. That wasn't all; word had got out about his pacifism. For some men it was the same as being a coward and they didn't attempt to hide their contempt. Luke gave them a focus for all their frustrated anger and terror. As for him, the dying men were his own front line whenever he went on duty. An 'enemy' he was doing his best to help.

Jane crept into the sleeping Emporium and began to climb the stairs. It took a long time, she was so weary.

'Hallo . . .' Ted was at the corner of the stair and she sank down beside him.

'Something wrong?'

'Not really.' He blew soft white feathers out of his palm and caught them as they floated down again; it hurt her every time he did it. 'I've had a post-card from Billy Beal.'

'That's splendid!' Jane examined the colourful picture; a love-lorn soldier stared up at a lace-edged bubble where a young woman gazed down on him soulfully. 'I don't suppose Billy had much of a choice,' ShesDShe laughed.

'I think that bit is him thinking about Aunt Mary. His message to me is on the back.'

Jane turned it over, saying, 'I'd forgotten he could write.'

'Someone else has done the address.'

She read it: 'Ted, McKie Bros, Darlington, England.' Opposite, the message was 'B.L.A.C.K.I.E.' followed by a row of crosses.

'Dear Billy . . . he must be dreadfully worried about her.'

'I would write back and reassure him if I could,' Ted said fiercely, 'but he hasn't said where he is.'

'That was probably too difficult. He'll be home on leave soon, so don't worry about it.' She hauled herself to her feet. 'Ted, I must get to bed, I'm worn out.'

'I can't go on like this, Jane. You, Luke, Matthew, even Dorothy Creswell — she brought some of her convalescent soldiers into the Salon today but I sneaked off before they could see me.' Jane's heart went out to him.

'I know it's not easy. You heard about the letter Aunt Mary had? Men spit when Luke goes into the wards because they've found out he's a pacifist.'

'I wouldn't care if they chucked bricks if only I could *do* something!'

'It's fear. They're all absolutely terrified of going back. No-one could possibly hate Luke —'

'Jane, I've got to go!' Ted muttered, 'I might kill the next Biddy who gives me a feather.'

'Ted. please!'

'Something'll have to happen soon or I'll burst!'

In the comparative comfort of a half-roofed barn, four soldiers sat playing cards.

'All I'm sayin' is, I don't reckon he should be shot, that's all.'

'Ain't your responsibility. 'E's been found guilty: *kaput.*'

'But he's stoopid!'

'Who says?'

'I do. An' you know 'E is, an' all, Corp.'

'That ain't got nothing to do with King's Regulations. Keep your 'ead down, stick by the book an' try an' survive this bloody war.'

They played on in silence. The private was soon out of the game. He lit a carefully preserved dog-end. 'D'you remember what the charge was, Corp?'

'Cowardice. Running away in the face of the enemy.'

'But 'e wasn't runnin' away, not reely runnin'. 'E was upset. Four of 'is 'orses got killed by a whizz-bang, that's all 'e cares about. 'e was goin' to tell this woman 'e keeps on about. When they asked if 'e'd anythin' to say 'e says, "Got to tell Miss Mary 'bout the 'orses." '

'Stop it!' The young corporal was fearful. 'You shouldn't 've been listening back there. If 'e's so stoopid to care more for 'is 'orses than 'isself, that's 'is lookout, right?' He stood up suddenly, spilling the cards. 'Termorrer, we carry out orders, right?'

The private squashed the butt flat. 'Only 'ope 'e's too bloody stoopid to know what's comin'.'

Billy Beal stood beneath the small barred window. Something terrible was going to happen. He knew about it. They'd told him but he pushed it away. His body shook with fear. He sucked his fingers as he looked at the stars. Pieces of candle-flame. When he was little he'd had a bit of blanket as a comforter. Something terrible . . .

The noise richochetted in a ragged echo. The officer in charge watched as crumpled legs twitched. He'd have them on a charge for making such a mess of it. Slowly and deliberately he unfastened his holster. Equally calmly he walked across, took aim and fired. He replaced the pistol and returned to his original position.

'A coward,' he said, loud enough for the men to hear.

'Beg pardon?' The padre had made a great effort to detach his thoughts from the matter in hand.

171

'He did nothing but cry as he faced the guns.'
Poor bastard, thought the man of God.

The firing party ran round and round the square in full kit. The private's feet were bleeding. 'If I ever get out of this, I'll find 'is ma and tell 'er . . . She deserves to know it wasn't 'is fault . . . *if* I ever get out of this . . .'

Luke pushed his way through the crowds in what was the hub of the Empire these days; platform number 7 at Victoria Station, where trains arrived from the continent. Surely someone had come to meet him? He'd sent two telegrams to make sure. Perhaps it was expecting too much but he was surrounded by other people's happiness as the tide of relatives reached out to hug and touch those who'd survived.

'Luke! Luke!' Jane struggled to reach him. Despite his gladness, he had to ask, 'Are father and mother here?'

'They had to stay with Mrs Beal. Billy's dead. Your telegrams arrived at the same time as the one from the War Office.'

'Oh, no! Ted must feel rotten.'

'He's in a dreadful state. Oh, Luke . . .' She clung to him, trying to hide her tears and smile. 'It's not much of a home-coming for you, I'm afraid. I've a taxi waiting. If we hurry we can catch the five-thirty-five.'

Luke hesitated. 'What time's the last train? Isn't there one about midnight?'

'I've no idea.'

'Look, I've been surrounded by misery for months. It's sad about Billy but if your number's up, that's it.'

'I know what you mean. It's dreadful but I've almost got used to death at the hospital.'

'You?' He was shocked. 'You're too young.'

'It's my own fault, I know. I told lies to get accepted and even more shocking ones to escape for twenty-four hours! I've perjured my soul to meet you, Luke!'

'Tut, tut,' he grinned. 'Well, let's be even more wicked and enjoy ourselves. I'm not being callous about Billy but I want to go to the theatre, have a decent meal, that sort of thing. Most of all, I want a cup of tea and a bath! I've dreamed of *that* all the way from France.'

'Aunt Mary's arranged an absolute banquet.'

'It'll keep,' he said firmly. 'I can't stand the thought of all that grief, not yet. Come on, let's find a hotel.'

He'd changed. There was a new hardness about him. Remembering the letter to Aunt Mary, Jane thought she understood. He took her arm as he strode out of the station and commandeered a cab.

The driver found them a small, family-run hotel where the owner's wife insisted Jane warm herself in front of a huge fire while Luke had his bath. He discovered her fast asleep when he finally came downstairs. In repose Jane's face had lost the strain of Billy's death and was the one Luke remembered. When the proprietor brought in their tea he waved a toasted tea-cake under her nose. 'Wake up. There's enough here to feed a brigade.'

They sat and ate, growing easier together with every mouthful. Jane tried to shut Mrs Beal's anguish out of her memory. Tonight was for her and Luke, a blessed space in time for them to be happy together.

But a theatre wasn't the place to escape the war, not this year. 'Join up, join up', posters and programmes urged. In the foyer, women shook collecting boxes. 'For the War Fund!' With the rest of the audience, they had to stand aside to allow wounded soldiers and their nurses through to seats in the front row. Luke watched the group warily. His eyes grew ever more bleak when after a first half of singers, jugglers and acrobats performing to patriotic songs, the curtain rose on the final act. Jane heard his muttered, 'Oh, no!'

On stage, a male impersonator strutted up and down in front of a backcloth of the trenches;

'Good-by-ee . . . Good-by-ee!
Wipe a tear soldier dear
From your ey-ee . . .'

Down below, the wounded were urged out of their seats. When the last stood reluctantly beside her, the artiste gave a signal. From behind the cloth came realistic explosions and flashes. One soldier shouted hysterically and a nurse

173

rushed to calm him. The impersonator nodded swiftly at the conductor.

'We don't want to lose you but we think you ought to go. . .' She waved her arms imperiously and the audience joined in.

'For your King and your country both need you so. . .
       We shall want you and miss you,
       But with all our might and main,
   We shall cheer you, thank you, kiss you. . .'
She planted a kiss deliberately on the youngest in the line. Jane felt Luke shudder at the sight of the scarlet mark on the boy's cheek.

'When you come back . . . again.' The audience rose and above the wild applause, Jane heard Luke's voice.

'Come on, let's go home.'

He slept on the train, wrapped in the heavy woollen scarf Aunt Mary had given him. 'I'm always cold,' he said, 'It's living in those damned tents, I never seem to be warm. The chill eats into your bones.' Then, 'I'm sorry our evening was such a failure — I wanted to treat you to a champagne supper, the lot, and all you end up with is a cup of tea and a bun!'

'It doesn't matter. There'll be another time.'

'You're a dear . . . We couldn't forget Billy either, could we?'

'No,' she agreed softly, 'He was always part of our lives.'

'Would you make sure I'm properly awake before we get to Darlington? I'm so deuced tired.'

She picked up the end of his scarf now and printed a kiss on it. 'Dear Luke, I love you so much. Please don't change any more. Don't let the hatred make you bitter.'

John was on the platform. At the sight of them his face cleared. 'Luke, my boy, welcome back! Thank God you and Jane are safe. Ted's disappeared.'

174

CHAPTER ELEVEN

Home Thoughts

'Reason it won't start . . . could be an air-lock.' Ted's lips weren't working very well. The young man in smart motoring clothes looked at him with distaste. To be accosted by a stranger in this quiet country lane made him nervous.

'You're inebriated.'

'Yes . . .' Ted agreed equably. 'Got any tools?' The man unclipped one of the headlamps and held it up.

'Come over here where I can see you.' Ted shambled across. 'Why should I risk letting you touch my 'bus?'

'Very sporty . . .' Ted patted the bonnet appreciatively before undoing the strap. 'Very nice . . . Had her long?'

It took an hour. The mouthful of fuel Ted sucked in by accident sobered him. The owner of the 'bus thumped him on the back and produced a thermos from the wicker basket in the dicky. 'Have some coffee . . . It's not hot but it'll help remove the taste.'

Ted swilled tepid liquid round burnt gums. 'Thanks . . . beastly stuff. Gone down my gullet — excuse!' He rushed to the side of the road and vomited into the hedgerow.

'I say — are you all right?' The young man was tall, fair, slightly older than Ted with protuberant short-sighted eyes.

'Shall be . . . hang on a minute.' The car owner moved a discreet distance away. Eventually he heard Ted mutter, 'Made an exhibition of myself.'

'Nonsense! You've been a great help. Will she start now d'you think?'

'Should do.' Ted grasped the starting handle. 'Ready?' It took several hefty pulls. The young man shouted above the engine noise, 'Climb aboard, I'll drive you home.' He fiddled

175

with his goggles and adjusted the windscreen. 'I'm afraid I can't see awfully well — sing out if you see anything. Hit a cow last week. I say, you don't drive by any chance?'

'I've always wanted to!'

'Fine!' They swapped places. 'By the way,' — the young man held out a gauntlet — 'Cavendish, Archie. Not of this parish.'

'Ted McKie. Where are we anyway?'

'By Jove, you must've been kippered! We're on the outskirts of Sadberge.'

As they slid into the first field, Archie Cavendish called out, 'Not to worry, often happens to me!' but by the time they approached a bridge Ted was more cautious. Once across, relief made them voluble.

'I hope you weren't worried.'

'Not at all! One grabs hold of these loops without thinking. Er, do you recall your actual intention, old chap?' Cavendish asked tactfully. 'You were *en route* to Darlington, I take it?' Ted hunched his shoulders as memory flooded back. Oh, God! Billy . . . The car trickled to a halt.

'A pal of mine is missing, presumed killed. The telegram arrived this morning. If it hadn't been for me he wouldn't have enlisted — I couldn't face his mother or my family, that's why I pushed off. Trouble is, I don't think I can face going back either.'

'Beastly things, wars,' Cavendish agreed sadly. 'One loses a lot of chums. I've just been chucked out by my family, as a matter of fact. I'm a lowly private in the RAMC because I don't choose to fight. Came home on leave — Pater demanded I become a soldier — "fight like a man" etc., etc. "A stretcher-bearer, nothing but a disgrace." Tried to explain. No use. Upshot was — "Never darken my doorstep again". Have to find a temporary billet for the rest of my leave. Called at a friend's house tonight but he's at the front and his Mama screamed that I was a traitor.'

'Why not come and stay with us?'

'I couldn't possibly —'

'Listen, Cavendish, you could be an enormous help. With this new Act, I'll be called up anyway — and I *am* going to do my bit — but I refuse to fight. Partly because of Billy, and a promise I made to my father, but mainly because I think the whole business is pointless. So if that means it's a choice between stretcher-bearing or cleaning up after the cavalry, I know which I prefer. Could you help wangle me into the RAMC?'

Archie Cavendish became very serious indeed. 'I can tell you where to apply, but for God's sake be certain of your beliefs before you do, McKie. Doing battle with the Tribunal is worse than facing the Hun.'

'Are you part of the No Conscription Fellowship or have the Quakers got at you?' the sergeant sneered.

'I gave my word —'

'Cowardice, is it?'

'That's unfair!'

'Unfair?' a burly man exploded, 'That's a new one. Got any sisters?'

'A brother and a sister.'

'Supposing the Boche . . .' the sergeant leaned across unpleasantly, 'Suppose they were to rape that sister of yours? What would you do? Stand by and let it happen or shout "Help, Help" for someone else to pull the trigger?' Torn between fear and anger, Ted stood his ground.

'According to my uncle, most of those rape stories are nonsense —'

'Are you calling me a liar?'

'And if the Boche are licentious soldiery then the Allies are probably just as bad,' he quoted bravely.

The sergeant looked as if he'd like to break Ted's neck. 'You could be subject to a court-martial, McKie. If found guilty, you would be asked whether you are prepared to be shot for your convictions. How would you respond?'

Terrified and with a dry mouth, Ted clung to the fact that if Cavendish had survived then he still had a chance.

'Whatever the consequence, I believe it to be morally wrong to kill.'

'Take him away.'

The cell was cold. They'd stripped him of his clothes leaving nothing but his overcoat. A uniform lay on the bunk and the sight of it made Ted furious. 'How dare they . . . how damn well dare they!'

He heard a key in the lock. 'Exercise drill. Follow three paces behind the next man and do not attempt to speak — here! You can't do that!' Ted had flung aside the coat and was racing past other prisoners.

'Come on!' he yelled, 'I'll show you how to keep warm.' Within seconds the yard was full of leaping naked bodies. The duty officer swore.

'Get that red-headed Conchie off my back!'

On Luke's last day of leave everyone made deliberate efforts to be cheerful. Mary told Mrs Armitage ten times over, 'Dr Cullen says it's excellent experience, invaluable . . .'

'Bound to be, my dear. Why, he'll be as good as qualified by the time the war's over!'

Jane had obtained grudging permission to be absent for an hour. 'I can't come to the station, there isn't enough time,' she said as she hugged him. 'Thanks for not telling Mama I lied about my age.'

Luke shook his head over her roughened hands and strained face. 'I wish I had now. Dr Cullen and I both know you're far too young to be involved, Jane. Some of the wounds, they turn my stomach —'

'Ssh! Don't let them hear! They're worried enough as it is over Ted, and I can manage, honestly.'

'Keep your fingers crossed Ted doesn't lose his temper. In a military jail, it could be fatal.'

Charlotte waylaid Luke near the office. 'Could I ask one last favour, my dear?'

'You've just time, Aunt. I want to say goodbye to Father —'

'I won't keep you. It's Mr Kessel's address. . .' In the half-light of the passageway, Luke sensed her acute embarrassment, 'I would like to write.'

'Yes, of course.' He was full of guilt that he'd failed to pass the information on earlier and fumbled for his

178

pocket-book, 'I've been wondering whether to tell you . . . the day Theo left — we'd made up our quarrel by then — he asked if he might have the photograph I had of you. I hope you don't object?'

Charlotte was overcome by this and couldn't speak as he handed her the address. 'I wish . . .' she began but had to clear her throat. 'I do so wish you'd told me that before.' The guilt he'd managed to suppress rose up and confronted him.

'It's my fault again. I've been remiss and caused even more hurt. I'm so sorry, Aunt. Poor Theo was in such a state that morning. He understood your reasons for refusing but he did so hope you'd change your mind eventually. I should have told you.'

'Oh, Luke! We've wasted so much time! I realized almost at once I'd made the wrong decision — if only I'd known how to contact him, I could have told him how I felt!' This came from the heart.

'I'm so sorry,' Luke repeated lamely. 'I'm sure he's safe,' he added hastily but Charlotte was hurrying away, trying to hide her anguish. Damn my laziness, he cursed. If I'd told her immediately, they might have been together by now.

'Goodbye, Father. Look after Mother for me.'

'I will. I'm very proud of what you're doing, my boy. It cannot be easy facing up to other men's contempt.'

Luke was still sore. 'Don't make me out to be brave. I've a sneaking feeling I am a coward underneath. Mercifully, I haven't had to put it to the test.' Thank God! thought John. He glanced at the clock.

'Yes,' said Luke, 'time to go.'

'You have everything?' This broke the mood and made Luke chuckle.

'I shall be the best-equipped orderly in the entire Medical Corp, thanks to you!' There was something important that he'd never had the grace to say until now but he wouldn't let pride stop him this time. 'You've been far too generous all my life. You gave me your name. No-one could have asked for a more honourable one.'

John was stunned. He stuttered, 'It was a long time ago, Luke. Gratitude isn't necessary . . . you and Mary have given me far more in return . . . You'll miss your train.' Luke picked up his kit. 'You won't do anything — foolhardy?'

'I won't.' He was the taller and stooped to kiss John's anxious cheek. 'I've already said goodbye to Mother, she's with Aunt Armitage.

There was so much more but the words remained unspoken. At the door Luke managed, 'I love you, Father.' It was enough.

'The reason I survived,' Ted said in answer to Archie's question, 'I kept thinking if they try this hard, war must be really evil.'

'I'm glad you withstood it, nonetheless.'

Ted grinned. 'You didn't stay with us long but certain aspects of my Mama's character must have struck you, Cavendish? What she's passed on to me helps stiffen the backbone, doncha know?' He was sombre when he said, 'Some poor devils were ordered out of hospital to go back to the Front. One was so crippled he could scarcely walk. It was drills and fatigues non-stop. Any spare time, we had to clean boots and buttons. If we weren't spick and span it was punishment drill. It was so rough after three days, one fellow tried to kill himself.'

'There were six successful suicides during the time I was at Aldershot,' said Cavendish. 'Even the coroner complained.'

'One man hit an officer. They hushed it up of course but I heard he ended up in the Harwich redoubt.'

'That redoubt . . .' Cavendish told him, shivering at the memory, 'is built inside a hill. The cells are pitch-black, water runs down the walls and there are rats.'

'You were sent there?'

'Only for four days apparently but it was difficult to judge. Great advantage, short sight,' Cavendish finished cheerfully. 'Never expect to see anything so don't worry if I can't.'

'Why didn't you warn me what it would be like?'

'With your temper, I didn't dare risk it.'

'Yes ... I was beginning to hate those sergeants more than any German. Anyway,' Ted said jauntily, 'the worst must be over, now.'

It was a misfortune that Ted had such conspicuous red hair and a boxer's physique, thought Cavendish.

'They'll probably still try and rile you once we get to France,' he advised, 'They're only waiting for an excuse to put a rifle in your hands. Stick it out a little longer and you should be all right.'

'I'll remember.'

'Come on, let's take a look at Southampton. Last chance before we sail. I wondered if I might send a postcard to your sister?' Since being introduced, Archie Cavendish had carried Jane's image in his mind. 'It wouldn't be an impertinence?'

'I should think she'll be jolly pleased.'

'Ripping girl, your sister.'

'She used to be a dancer,' Ted told him proudly. 'She was as pretty as a picture on the stage.'

Dr Cullen was so engrossed he forgot to drink his whisky. 'All this that Luke writes about treatment for gangrene — it's fascinating.'

'He left the diary for all of us to read but I haven't had the courage to show Mary. There are some terrible experiences.'

'My dear old friend, Luke writes of war as he finds it, not the way the politicians would have us believe. Give this not only to Mary but to any who would dispute the lists in your "Patriotic Window". I've seen women stand and stare at a loved one's name in there. For some, it's the only comfort left to them, poor souls. Thank heaven Luke has the strength to face these horrors. Part of that strength he gained from Mary so let her read the diary.'

'I heard him urge Ted and Jane to write down their thoughts for Charlotte.'

'Good heavens! I hope Ted's are fit for her to read! How is Charlotte since Jane left?'

'Low in spirits, as you'd expect. She and Matthew seem to be closer, which is a blessing.'

181

'Ye-es . . .' Like many another, Dr Cullen slid away from any discussion of Matthew McKie.

16th March, 1916
Property of E. McKie, Private, RAMC, 65th Field Ambulance.
In the event of the owner being whizz-banged, crumped, bombed, bayoneted, or trampled on by the short-sighted A. Cavendish, Esq., please foward (without risking Base Censor) to Mrs Davie McKie, McKie Bros, Darlington, Co. Durham, England, The Empire, The World!
Crossed over to France on paddle-steamer La Margarite. *Arr. Le Havre midnight, proceeded up river to Rouen. V. wet. Cold rations. Hot tea at No. 5 camp. Bell tent collapsed 3 a.m. due to wind & rain.*

DARLINGTON GAZETTE:
Debate at the Mechanics Institute on the subject of *Patriotism.*
During heated exchanges in the chamber yesterday evening one member drew attention to a permanent display of the names of the fallen. This display in a prominent position in Darlington does not contain the word 'Victory'. The honourable member responsible was urged by fellow members to include this word plus other suitable patriotic embellishments, to encourage those about to enlist.

The Military Hospital, Dover. 30 May 1916.
Dearest Mama,
At this hospital we receive the wounded direct from hospital ships, some alas, very ill indeed. I now do straightforward dressings unsupervised because we're short-handed. I still have to report for uniform inspection — Matron is an absolute tartar about my hair!
Have you heard from Luke? Archie Cavendish sent a card from the River Somme, all fresh and green in the Spring. He says Ted is working in the laundry at Meaulte. Please remind Dorothy to write. She's a rotten correspondent and it's been ages since her last letter.

Love to everyone, especially great-aunt Armitage,
Jane.

Warm sunshine shone through stained glass, spilling colour
lavishly. Charlotte stood beside Mary and watched the
bowed black figures in the front pews. At long last, she
knew Theodore Kessel was safe. It had taken six months for
his note to reach her: a note hastily scribbled by Theodore
as the Boche arrived, tossed to the villager baker as he was
marched past with others on their way to a prison camp,
and kept safe by the baker's wife until British Tommies
recaptured the village.

Her unknown benefactor had explained this in a brief
covering letter, adding; 'Posted on leave in Wolverhampton.
Sorry for undue delay.' Six months! But her lover was safe,
somewhere in Germany.

Above her a voice prayed that the Almighty would accept
the soul of Jack Creswell, called to God in the Service of his
Country, buried now in French soil. Charlotte knelt. The
few precious words danced in front of her closed lids:

'I will love you always, Theodore Kessel.'

She stood in silence as Mrs Creswell leaning on her
husband's arm passed down the aisle. Dorothy followed,
looking neither to right nor left, a heavy black veil over
her blonde hair.

Jane hadn't yet replied to the letter telling of Jack
Creswell's death. Charlotte wondered how many tears had
been shed. Once, in Harrogate, she and Mrs Creswell had
talked fondly of their children's futures. Charlotte had
wondered then about Jack and her daughter. It was too late
for such thoughts now. Perhaps it was merciful that Jane was
too far away to attend today's memorial service.

Charlotte had tried to forbid the transfer to a Dover
hospital but Matthew had dissuaded her. 'Let Jane go if it's
what she wants, Mama.' Charlotte was about to insist she
needed Jane beside her when he'd smiled and said, 'You
have me, remember. I'll never leave you.'

Matthew had done his best to fill the gap left by Ted, too,
she knew, but however hard she tried, Charlotte could not
feel any affection for her youngest child. Ted brought down

183

her wrath upon his head time after time but she loved him because he reminded her of Davie; Matthew could never do that. Please God, keep Ted safe, she prayed. She felt so lonely, then she chided herself; how much more desolate the Creswells must feel!

Mary was ready to leave. She saw Charlotte's cheeks were wet and squeezed her arm; Charlotte shook her head guiltily. 'I wasn't thinking of poor Jack.'

'What then, dear? You're not worried about Ted? His postcards are always so cheerful.'

'I've heard from Mr Kessel, too.' On an impulse, she took out Theodore's letter. 'He still loves me.' As Mary read the torn scrap and understood for the first time the depth of feeling between them, she heard Charlotte say, 'When this dreadful war is past . . .'

'When it is, dear,' Mary agreed, 'The children will be grown-up, and it will be time to consider your own happiness.'

'Then you don't think it wrong of me?' Mary handed back the note and kissed her.

'Mr Kessel has been steadfast. God keep him safe until the two of you can be together.'

'Bless you, Mary!'

They followed the rest of the mourners to where sheaves of lilies lay.

'Such a fine young man,' Mary whispered softly.

Meaulte. June 12th 1916, Ted's diary entry read:

Billeted in a filthy stable! Blackie's is a palace compared to this. Found two mice in the butter tin; no prisoners taken! Our task today was to empty sandbags but the Hun raked the parapet with constant machine-gun fire. 'Some' task! 12 REs killed by one single crump two trenches along from ours. Remains of one chap had to be put in sack for interment.

Cavendish and four other COs were paraded at 1000 hours and marched off with their stretchers up the line. I shall miss him. He won't miss me because he takes his spectacles off whenever firing begins. He says he's much braver if he can't see.

184

Casualty Clearing Station No. 23, June 25, 1916, wrote Luke:

Big push expected soon. Massive bombardment day and night to 'soften' the enemy. We are so far forward we can see our shells landing on the German trenches. I'm 'acting' anaesthetist, 'acting' assistant surgeon plus anything else that's required — how Kessel would laugh! One of our tents caught a whizz-bang and six MOs were killed. We try and joke about it.

Our operating table has a distinct list to port because the rain has made gullies and there are no spare duck-boards.

Three suicides today among those marked down as 'fit'; all successful. The telegram is always the same: 'Regret inform you x died today after a relapse.'

On June 30th, still billeted in the stable near Meaulte, Ted climbed up the ladder to claim his tiny piece of floor and found it already had an occupant. 'Cavendish! I thought you'd disappeared for good. Put your glasses on you silly old owl, it's me!'

Archie peered at him myopically. 'McKie? God, there can't be two heathens with red hair!'

'How are you?' Ted's hug threatened to crush his ribs. Archie rubbed them tenderly.

'I think I'll live.'

'But what are you doing here?'

'All available personnel have been ordered to Aid Posts in this area by GHQ at Beauquesne. It's sheer coincidence I ended up back in this salubrious establishment —'

'Rum ration!'

Men in the crowded hayloft looked at one another. 'This is it then?'

'Reckon so.'

Soberly, they stood in line with their tin mugs. Cavendish carried his back up the ladder and began to unwind his puttees. 'Only discovered these beggars don't care for rum last time we had a ration.' He dribbled the liquor down the first leg and lice dropped onto the floor. 'Super way to go. Not quite a butt of malmsey but beggars can't be choosers. What do you do with yours? Brush your teeth?'

185

Ted laughed and drank instead. 'It's better than cocoa. Just think, last term at school they were trying to make us sign the pledge; now we're positively encouraged to drink!'

'Dutch courage,' muttered someone.

Ted watched Cavendish rewind methodically. 'I'm surprised you can see to do that in here.'

'Full moon, hadn't you noticed? Bound to be if there's a push coming. HQ only issued with out-of-date calendars.'

'It's scheduled for 7.30 tomorrow morning.' Heads turned and voices were hushed. The man who'd spoken nodded quietly. 'Our guns cease at 0700 and the Infantry go over at 7.30 hours.'

'In daylight?' Ted couldn't keep the wobble from his voice.

'Very sensible,' said Cavendish loudly. 'They might trip over the barbed wire in the dark.'

In the Casualty Clearing Station, Luke wrote: *The push starts in an hour. The ground has shaken non-stop for days from the pounding of the guns, it will be a relief when it's over.*

TO WHOM IT MAY CONCERN:
This diary plus my personal effects, to be given to my father John McKie, the best and most decent of men. My dearest love to my mother, Mary McKie. God bless you both.

'Time for a last pipe, I fancy.' Cavendish stared at the increasing daylight between the rafters. 'Only decent present my father ever gave me, this pipe.' He puffed contentedly. 'Never told you about my people?'

'Only that they live near Gainsford. Kindly put your mark here, for my folks in Darlington.' Cavendish glanced at the postcard of a kitten gambolling with a ball of wool. Turning it over he read, If weather continues fine, Archie and I might manage a bit of cricket, love Ted. 'Don't want them to worry unnecessarily,' Ted explained apologetically.

'Of course not. Don't bother writing to mine,' Archie commented, signing the card. 'They aren't the sort to worry anyway. They're stinkin' rich, not just ordinarily but stinkin'.

One big problem, though . . . can't stand one another. Don't speak at all.'

'What — never?'

'Never,' said Cavendish firmly. 'House, silent as the proverbial.' Ted began to laugh. 'No, seriously. Mater one end of the table, Pater the other, nod to the butler. No-one utters a sound. I thought it was normal until I went away to school . . . found chaps actually encouraged to talk. So refreshin' meeting your family. Everyone babbling at once. By Jove, what a noise!'

'Scolding me, you mean,' Ted grinned.

'Rippin' dark eyes your sister has,' Cavendish puffed. 'Flashed them at your cousin no end. He didn't seem to notice.'

'Luke? Don't suppose he did. He was tired. He'd only just got back from France.' Cavendish thought not even the most dire fatigue would prevent *him* responding to Jane McKie's eyes.

Ted opened Mr Armitage's watch and listened to the silvery chime. 'Seven o'clock,' he muttered. Two minutes later the pounding ceased. The silence that followed was tangible. Men sat and waited. No-one spoke. Then, in the soft morning sky, flares began to burst, illuminating every leaf and blade of grass for miles.

'The Hun must've heard about my little disability.' Cavendish emptied his pipe. 'Showing me the way. Jolly decent of him.'

'Stretcher-bearers!'

Wave after wave, shoulder to shoulder, at a steady pace in the hot summer sun, men walked towards the German guns; guns which should have been pulverized but had been hidden in deep underground shelters. Within twenty-four hours, out of a total loss of 57,450 casualties, over 24,000 wounded had crawled or been carried into field ambulances or over-flowing casualty clearing stations.

Ambulance trains had not been brought so far forward because it was judged they wouldn't be needed so the wounded lay on open ground beside the medical tents, some of which were within sight of the front line.

'Immediate evacuation . . .' The officer's voice could be heard above the inferno but those working inside the tent didn't bother to look up. For over twenty-four hours, in a choking cloud of ether and iodoform, nurses slit uniforms from mangled bodies, orderlies sponged torn flesh and Luke struggled to keep up with the surgeon's frenzied commands. Underfoot it was slippery with blood.

'This salient is being evacuated,' the officer repeated.

The big push had been a mockery but it wasn't over yet. 'Those wounded who can be got away will leave . . .'

Inside the tent, one by one they paused, dull-witted from exhaustion as his meaning began to penetrate. What would happen to the rest? How could they possibly "leave" with so many desperately wounded men?

'All medical personnel to withdraw immediately.'

'I'll stay.' Luke heard his own voice speak the words; inside, another one shrieked, I'm a coward! I daren't stay, I could be killed!

'Are you a doctor?' The officer was sharp; there was no time for heroics and qualified men couldn't be spared.

'No, an orderly.' Their eyes met; each knew what it meant.

'Good luck, then.' Luke managed to calm his terror a fraction; 'first time anyone's saluted *me*!' he whispered through trembling lips.

Newly hired female counter-hands filled the empty places at the big dining table. It was breakfast-time; the morning post had just been delivered and Charlotte seized the envelope beside her plate. After almost a week, a letter from Jane! There were murmurs of satisfaction as she announced the fact.

'Is she well?' John asked as Charlotte skimmed through it.

Miss Attewood said eagerly, 'May we know her news? Miss McKie is always so cheerful — and interesting.'

'And so lucky! Nursing "our boys".' Charlotte looked up; this from one of the newcomers, taken on when Gertie had gone as a land-girl.

'You think so?' she asked quietly. From the opposite end of the table, John saw how pale she was.

'Perhaps this is not the time —' he began but the newcomer interrupted.

'Oh no, please Mrs Davie! I do so envy your daughter! How wonderful to smooth the men's pillows and comfort them.' Charlotte glanced at her briefly, then at John.

'I fear much of what Jane has to tell us contradicts what is in this morning's newspapers. However . . .'

' "The Military Hospital, Dover, July 5th 1916

Dearest Mama,

The wounded have been pouring in for four days and nights. Someone said the trains full of injured men go as far as Scotland now that English hospitals are full. We have two men to a bed and above them, another in a stretcher balanced on the rails. The corridors are so full one can scarcely squeeze past. I hadn't the strength to undo my shoes today. Another girl cut the laces for me but my feet have swollen to twice their size so I can't put them back on." '

'Dear me, how will she dance?' asked Miss Attewood, startled.

' "One VAD had to have her stays levered off because the whalebone was embedded in her skin —" '

'How ghastly!'

' "I had planned to fall into bed but my hair was riddled with lice. Some soldiers have been in the trenches for weeks without water and their clothes run with vermin. I nearly cried but soaked my hair in disinfectant and now feel much better." '

Up and down the table half-eaten bacon and eggs congealed as young ladies reached for their handkerchieves.

' "We've had more badly wounded than anyone can remember," '

'Ah . . .' The newcomer's eyes were closed and her face ashen.

' "including one poor brave man who had most of his face blown away," ' Charlotte continued inexorably. ' "We've been warned the chaos in France is dreadful and worse is to come . . ." '

She paused again. 'The remainder merely concerns family matters. I fear those newspaper reports you read out to us,

189

indicating a successful outcome to this latest battle, may be premature.'

'I fear so,' John murmured. He saw Charlotte's hand tremble as she refolded the letter. 'Dear Jane . . .'

'She *would* go!'

'Yes, indeed.' Charlotte walked swiftly to his end of the table, handed him the letter and left the room. One by one the counter-hands followed. John read the rest of it alone.

'No word from Luke but another funny postcard from Archie Cavendish, "somewhere in France". He says he and Ted are managing famously. Please write and tell me how Dorothy is. She hasn't managed a line since Jack died. I'm not surprised. It must be difficult to imagine what an everyday occurrence death is, back in Darlington. It keeps on happening here because they're too badly wounded and there's so little we can do except ease their passing. We try not to cry, it's unfair on the rest if we do but sometimes we can't help it. They're so young and so very brave.'

Some of the forbidden splashes were evident on the page but Jane's last words strove to be cheerful.

'I'm sorry this scrawl is so clumsy. Please tell Mrs Creswell next time you see her, she was right; nursing does ruin your hands!'

John found Charlotte in her parlour and put the letter in her lap then kissed her cheek. It was something he never did except on birthdays or at Christmas.

'Try not to worry. Just be very, very proud.'

In a pack stores near La Bourse, Ted spat cheerfully on the first hot iron. 'Attack about to commence, Corp.'

'Present h'arms!' Ted saluted, the iron dangerously close to his ear. 'Fire!' shouted the corporal. Ted brought it down smartly on the seam of a trouser leg.

'Got 'em,' he crowed. 'Sizzle, sizzle . . . die, you little blighters.' Insects sped across the cloth ahead of the heat.

'You done those rifles, yet?'

'Yep, Corp. You can see your face in 'em.'

'Top Brass is due again today.'

'Crikey!' Ted looked up from his ironing. 'This place must be safe — twice in a week? Enemy must be a thousand miles away!'

'Well stop looking so cheerful, otherwise they might think you want to go back to the line.'

'I was just thinking, me — cleaning rifles? Funny sort of job for a CO. Mind you, after four months' stretcher-bearing, I deserve a bit of luck.'

'You deserve nothing.' The Corporal attempted severity. 'Not prepared to defend your country.'

The smile left Ted's face. 'Still think that way, do you?' he asked quietly.

'No I bloody don't but that's unofficial. You never heard me say that, McKie.'

'Pity all the dead boys didn't say it, loud and clear, then the Brass might have listened.'

'What happened to that pal of yours, the one with the glasses?'

'Caught a Blighty at Mametz Wood.'

'Now that's what I call real luck,' the Corporal said enviously. Not what I would, thought Ted.

'Archie's left arm was blown off. He managed to get a message back. Told me he should never have stopped to pick primroses and violets that morning.'

'Here, what you doing with that Oxford powder?'

'Some of these blighters won't succumb.' Ted was shaking the canister vigorously.

'That won't do any good!' The Corporal came across with candle and matches. 'Hold the trousers where I can see.' He ran the lighted candle up and down, burning off the insects. 'These are French lice, McKie. They thrive on Oxford powder because they're too ignorant to read what it says on the packet, they think it does 'em good. Now, you carry on — an' hurry up!'

'Yes, Corp.'

The prison camp was in a forest, three rough wooden huts in a compound surrounded by barbed wire and the stifling quiet of hundreds of square miles of pine trees. French, British and Italians had been herded together for months

191

but today there was a new menace. A new intake of Russian prisoners included one who was obviously seriously ill.

Luke and the only other doctor, Etienne Chabal, broke the news to representatives from the other two huts: 'Typhoid!'

'We think so, in fact we're sure of it,' said Etienne. There was a burst of terrified chatter then a prisoner shouted above the rest, 'We must demand they give us medicine. It's our only chance.'

'I agree about that but when have they ever listened before?' Luke was silent as the argument went back and forth, remembering Etienne's dispassionate verdict on the Russian.

'This man is our executioner, McKie. He brings death. I wonder what the guards will do once they discover it?'

'They might want to kill him. We must try and prevent that.'

'We can do nothing. He has undoubtedly infected others by now — we cannot conceal an epidemic. As for the guard, I think they will desert rather than risk their own lives.'

There had been no medicines for the wounded who'd survived the terrible journey. Luke and Etienne had done what they could but there was a row of graves along the edge of the compound.

As month dragged into month men had begged, implored, demanded more food, medicines and letters via the Red Cross. It was known that supplies of food and clothing had arrived because prisoners had seen cartons but the guards denied it.

'No doubt they are sending the food back to their own families,' Etienne declared cynically. 'And why not? They are peasants, McKie. They're one degree above the bread-line themselves, why should they give *us* anything?'

Luke and he were elected by the rest to tend the sick. When the guards cut the prisoners' rations still further, they were requested to perform another, far more disagreeable task.

'If a man is sick . . . very sick . . . why give him the same as the rest?' the spokesman asked.

Etienne stared. 'I don't understand.'

Another member of the deputation explained. 'It's for everyone's sake, captain, to give the rest a better chance. You and the English doctor, you must decide. If a man isn't likely to live, he can have water but his food must be shared.'

Dear God, Luke prayed, let them not ask us to do this; survival of the fittest — we'd be no better than animals!

That night, when he and Etienne finally gave in, Luke McKie wept. He thought his tears would never cease. All his pride in his skill, his delight in healing seeped away like grains of sand. From now on at the sight of the two of them, men would shrink away in fear. It was far worse than being spat at for being a pacifist, it was a denial of all Luke believed in.

'How can we do it?' he demanded passionately, 'How could either of us practise medicine in future if we do?'

Etienne Chabal shrugged. 'I'm glad you think there is a future, McKie. For me, the present is sufficient.'

The Military Hospital, Dover. 15th December, wrote Jane;

Dearest Mama,

A miracle! I begin a fortnight's leave in three days' time! It would be heavenly to find Luke or Ted at home when I arrive, preferably both. I make the same wish morning, noon and night!

Another quaint message from Cavendish written by someone else. He's been wounded but doesn't say how badly. He lost touch with Ted during the Somme.

No word from Dorothy. She must have taken Jack's death terribly hard. In a way I dread seeing her but I must of course, to try and bring a little comfort. It took ages before I could bring myself to write — Jack was so kind to me in France that time — but I expect she understood.

I'm dreaming of nothing but gallons of hot water and one of Katriona's heavenly plum puddings! Don't laugh! We've had no sugar or jam for ages.

Mrs Armitage took Bertha with her for support. 'Mr Collins, I ask you not to interrupt, however shocked you are.'

'Ma'am?' His former employer looked so grave that he trembled. What now? She put a curious list on the marble slab and because there was one other customer present, dropped her voice to a whisper.

'These are the essential ingredients for a pudding according to Katriona. And this . . .' Mrs Armitage slid the crinkly white paper across the marble slab, 'is a five-pound note. I order you to procure every item, using *bribery* and *corruption* if necessary!'

'Mrs Armitage, if there was any way in which I could —'

'You will succeed!' Field Marshall Haig couldn't have been more emphatic. Mrs Armitage gripped Bertha's arm to give her extra height, 'It is for Jane . . . who was named after poor dear Charlotte's mother . . . She gave her baby to me to care for all those years ago. Her grandchild shall have the best pudding Darlington can provide. And if there is need of another five pounds, so be it.' The shrunken bosom heaved with emotion causing the jet to shimmer. 'If the Kaiser is enjoying one for his dinner this Christmas, I hope to God it chokes him!'

CHAPTER TWELVE

A Casualty

'Awfully kind of you to take me in,' Cavendish said for the third time. 'Exceedingly embarrassed, turning up unannounced and all that. Felt sure Ted would be due for leave about now. Bound to be here, I thought. Stupid of me.'

'Mr Cavendish —'

'Archie, please!'

'Archie, then. There's a nice fire in the dining room so why don't we go in there?' Mary said firmly. Archie lurched behind her, not yet accustomed to his unbalanced body. When he saw the room was empty, he said with something like relief, 'Family disappeared up the chimney?'

'Not quite,' she smiled. 'My husband's in his office. Charlotte and Jane are visiting the Creswells, Mrs Armitage is taking her nap and everyone else is in the Emporium. Christmas Eve is a very busy day!'

'I know, and now you're landed with an uninvited guest!' Archie groaned penitently.

Mary reached for his remaining hand. 'Archie, you're more than welcome. Frankly, I see you as a Christmas angel from a generous St Nicholas! If you can ease Charlotte's mind, the rest of us will be so grateful. Not that she's really worried about Ted because his postcards are always the same — how wet it is, how he's looking forward to "a spot of Blighty" — but seeing you will bring him that much more close.'

''Fraid this particular angel is short of a pinion feather or two. Hope this won't sicken her,' Archie moved his stump. 'Turned my Pater's stomach, that's why he told me to get

195

out. Always throwing me out. Heigh-ho. Sometimes I feel like a pregnant housemaid! Mary's smile froze but Archie didn't notice. 'I hadn't warned Pater, d'you see. Should've done of course. He reacted predictably. "Disgrace not to be an officer", equally disgraceful to be maimed while carryin' a stretcher apparently. Tried to explain — shells damn difficult things to avoid. No use.'

His grimace was so comical, Mary had to laugh this time. 'Oh dear, I'm sorry!'

'No, please . . . like to see pretty ladies laugh. 'Fraid the stretcher in question was empty,' Archie said softly. ''Nother chap and myself, tryin' to reach a fellow on the wire. Neither of them were terribly lucky.'

She swallowed. 'How dreadfully sad.'

'When I woke up, tried to find my arm. Extremely pleased when a Welsh fusilier turned up and offered to lead me back to our lines. Wasn't sure how to say "My left arm is missing" in Hun. Need two hands to surrender. Could've been a bit awkward.'

He babbles away because of his face, thought Mary. And he's watching that door for Jane. What a terrible shock when she sees the scar — I do hope she manages to be kind.

'So glad Luke's safe,' Cavendish said unexpectedly. 'A rippin' Christmas present for you. When did you hear?'

'It wasn't an official source but a letter from a soldier who saw him captured months ago, at the fall of the Somme. It didn't arrive until yesterday because he himself had been left for dead when the dressing station was evacuated.'

'Splendid news, however long it took,' Cavendish repeated. 'Bet Hun prisons have better food than ours. Luke's probably swiggin' hock and keepin' the other fellows amused with stories about patients. Stick to the rules, sit tight and wait for peace to be declared, that's all they have to do.' He leaned forward and offered a handkerchief. 'Chin up, pretty lady. Won't be long before you have him back again. Any Christmas card from fearless Ted?' Mary shook her head.

'According to the last postcard, he was in a "cushy billet".'

'Glad to hear it, especially this time of year. Hun not very active during the winter. Burrows deep like we do. Hope Ted doesn't get bored and thump the sergeant. How's Mama Charlotte?'

He's the only one who dares call her that, thought Mary, but when is he going to ask about Jane?

'Charlotte's very well.'

'Smartest lady I know. Could teach those French desmoiselles a thing or two. Mind if I smoke my pipe?'

'Wouldn't you rather have tea with Mrs Armitage? Bertha usually takes it to her about now. I know they'd both be delighted to have a visitor.'

'At your service, ma'am.'

She wants to warn Jane, Archie thought. I'm such a terrifying sight she can't bear to let anyone see me without telling them first. I should never have come. Nevertheless, he followed her obediently along the passage and down the back stairs.

'I could always find an hotel.'

Mary turned round quickly and hugged him, 'Archie, never, never say that.' She kissed him gently. 'Next to Luke and Ted, there's no-one I'd rather see. You must look on this as your home from now on, until your father relents.'

'Dear lady . . . could be t'other side of eternity before that happens!'

'Good!' They smiled like conspirators. Outside the parlour, to Archie's surprise, she didn't go ahead of him but tapped on the door, calling, 'Mrs Armitage, you have a visitor. Go on, in you go, my dear.'

The old lady cried with delight as soon as he entered. 'Oh, how lovely! Bertha, look, it's dear Mr Cavendish! Oh, your poor arm — never mind, you can manage a piece of cake? How splendid! What a lovely surprise for dear Jane!'

Why does no-one mention my face, thought Archie desperately, is it so frightening they can't bring themselves to speak of it? 'Dear lady, as young as ever, I see . . .'

'Mr Cavendish, you're not wearing your spectacles again!'

Jane heard the laughter as she approached the parlour. Aunt Mary had issued brusque instructions: 'Be very

197

kind and gentle, Jane. Archie's so nervous his whole body trembles and the scar looks raw! I'm sure it's not healing properly. I've sent word to Dr Cullen and he'll be here at supper. We'll all pretend he'd been invited so that Archie isn't upset.'

'You think the damage is mental as well as physical?' John asked thoughtfully. Mary had summoned them to the kitchen.

'I'm certain it is,' she answered warmly, 'and his father is responsible — he's treated Archie in a disgracefully callous fashion.'

'Archie's probably suffering from shell-shock. Most of them have nightmares after a spell in the trenches.' Jane was having difficulty marshalling her thoughts; the outing to the Creswells had been a disaster. She tried to concentrate instead on Archie's problems. 'Why did his father throw him out this time?'

'Because of his injuries, so please do your best not to notice them.' Mary gazed at Jane steadily; she could see something was amiss. 'We can talk about the Creswells later but at present, Archie needs our love and care. Katriona's made up Ted's bed for him and lit a fire.' She turned to John, 'Will you warn Charlotte? She's probably gone to her room.'

'We're overrun with customers!'

'Five more minutes, that's all.' Mary gave him a push. 'And find a present for Mr Cavendish to put under the tree!'

How many maimed and disfigured men have I seen? Jane wondered. They came off every boat and it was always the same: their eyes would be full of hope and a fear of rejection. It was the sternest test for any nurse but you had to meet their despair without flinching.

Yet friendliness could also bring problems. After seeing abhorrence in the faces of their families, many soldiers clung to the nurses, begging them to be their 'special girl'.

Is that what it was this time? I don't suppose Archie sends anyone else funny postcards? What an effort it must have been to keep sending them while he was in hospital?

It hadn't occurred to Jane before that Archie Cavendish had made several special efforts on her behalf.

It isn't fair, she thought wildly. I have to go back to the hospital in three days' time, I can't take any more emotion, not after what happened this afternoon . . . She tapped on Mrs Armitage's door.

Mrs Armitage watched as Jane clasped Archie's hand and told him how happy she was. But she didn't look well, she was very pale. What a terrible time these poor young things were having.

'I want you both to know we've managed a real Christmas pudding for tomorrow, my dears. It's supposed to be a secret but I can't keep it to myself any longer!'

Jane laughed. 'How marvellous. I must thank Katriona.'

'It was your great-aunt that did it,' Bertha said darkly, 'She bribed Mr Collins.'

'I say! Mrs Armitage, I'm surprised and shocked.'

'It was only a little bribe,' the old lady said comfortably. 'My war effort, you might say. And it wasn't for Mr Collins *himself.* He is incorruptible, otherwise he wouldn't be where he is today . . . No, he had to *induce* one or two of his suppliers to part with raisins and mixed peel!'

'Resourceful fellow,' Archie said with approval.

'Oh, he is! I begged him not to tell me how he did it for I should have felt hugely guilty. Now, it's time we all dressed for supper, my dears. We have the dining-room to ourselves on Christmas Eve, Mr Cavendish, once Mr McKie has closed up and everyone has gone home.'

'There's plenty of hot water and if you need any help . . .' Jane's voice trailed away. In the awkward pause, Archie said evenly, 'Thanks but I can manage.'

Damn! she cursed as she led the way, imagine me being as clumsy as that!

How Jane has changed, thought Archie. All eyes and so nervy she looks as if she could snap. She's far too young to be nursing wounded fellows like me. Ahead of him, Jane had opened the door.

'You're in here, Archie. It's Ted's room, hence the rather battered state. I'm next door and we both share the bathroom with Matthew but he won't be up for ages. He

199

works full-time in the Emporium during the holidays.'

'From what I remember, he must be nearly old enough to enlist.'

'Not for another nine months but as for that, Matthew would never risk his neck. He'll find a way round it somehow, when the time comes. Your bags are over there ... have you everything you need? Phew!' she fanned herself, 'Katriona certainly built up that fire! She must have a secret coal supply.'

'Or bribed someone,' said Cavendish lightly. 'Thanks, see you at supper.' He closed the door.

I've upset him terribly, Jane thought, but I can't help it. What with Dorothy's ghastly behaviour, Luke in some unknown prison camp — and the thought of going back to all that agony on Monday, I just can't cope with his feelings!

Archie leaned against the shabby paintwork. Why did I make the effort to come, he moaned, what's the point? The way she looked at me just now — nothing but pity!

He lurched over to the bed. Someone had unpacked his things and towels were warming in front of the fire but tender care didn't help the pain in his heart.

He struggled out of his travelling clothes. In the bathroom, water had already been drawn, steaming hot. He sank into it gratefully, taking care with his bandaged stump. The shrapnel wounds were still livid down his left side and leg but at least they were healing whereas his face ...

Out of the bath, he rubbed away the condensation on the mirror. The puckered gash looked grey and unhealthy. I'll pack, Archie thought. First thing tomorrow, I'll slip away and find a train. York or London, it doesn't matter where. He eased the dressing gown over his shoulders and went back to Ted's room.

He heard Jane go past as he sat, despondent. So much for telling her he could manage. He couldn't begin to fasten a stud!

There was a knock. 'It's me, Archie, Katriona.' She bustled in uninvited, laden with bowl, ointment and bandages. 'I've come to see to your arm, dear. Now, let's have that old dressing off.' Before he could object, she had uncovered the wound, her harsh Scots voice soothing away any awkwardness. 'Mr John paid for my training at the hospital years ago in Inverness . . . I've been chief nurse and bottle washer here ever since. Talking of washing, that hospital was the first place I ever saw water come out of a tap . . . I thought it was a real miracle. Well now, that scar on your face looks a wee bit inflamed. Let's see what we can do about that, too.'

The heat of the poultice drew out the pus. With it, Archie felt tension and pain begin to drain away. 'Should have had it seen to,' he mumbled. 'They warned me at the hospital but I insisted on discharging myself.'

'Didn't want to add to the burdens of the nurses at Christmas?' Katriona asked shrewdly.

'Not exactly.' He reddened. He felt transparent and as helpless as a baby in her skilled hands. It was when she'd redressed him and was dealing with the wretched stud, he blurted out, 'I shouldn't have come. I'm so damn useless.'

'Hush! Now, you listen to me — and don't fidget while I tie this, you're worse than Ted. It so happens you're a godsend as far as we're concerned, because of Mrs Davie.'

'Yes, I know. Mrs McKie explained.'

'No, it's not about Ted. Someone else. Mrs Davie has a — friend, a young gentleman, over in France. She's been weeping for more than a week because he's been taken prisoner and she can't send him a Christmas card. *We're* not supposed to know how much she cares but we do. And when this war's over, she's going to marry that nice Mr Kessel because we can't stand it if she doesn't.' Katriona shook her head, 'Charlotte McKie's been a *very* difficult woman since she fell in love, Mr Cavendish.'

He found himself grinning. 'And what am I supposed to do?'

'Why, distract her of course. You're a young man yourself, aren't you? I've always been told that one in hand was worth two in the bush. Look at the effect you've had on Mrs McKie — *she* looks ten years younger since you arrived. Do the same for Charlotte and the rest of us will be eternally grateful.' Katriona scooped dirty dressings into her apron and picked up the bowl. 'It's a pity you can't do the same for Jane,' she said non-committally, 'with her so

201

worried about Luke . . .' She snatched a quick look to see the effect her words had had and, satisfied, went on, 'It's a childhood thing, this fancy she has for him.'

'It's lasted long enough,' Archie muttered before he could stop himself.

'Aye . . . but Luke doesn't feel the same, take my word for it.' Katriona paused at the door. 'Jane's in for a lot of hurt when she discovers that fact, Mr Cavendish, she'll need a friend. I hope you'll not be far away when she does.'

Archie's emotions felt as raw as his flesh. 'How could I ask any girl to live with this!' He thrust the scar toward her. 'Oh for goodness sake, you were never an oil-painting. Men! Nothing but vanity from the day they're born!'

'And this?' The empty sleeve moved slightly.

'Haven't you another that works perfectly well? Mother Nature must've known men would always be fighting, that's why she provided them with spare parts. Now, is there another reason for you to feel so sorry for yourself? Are there any *vital* pieces missing you haven't told me about?'

Nurses! They were always the blasted same!

'All in working order, thank-ee,' Archie said sheepishly.

'Glad to hear it. I know what's best for this family. Now, you run along and practise some of your charm on Mrs Davie. Be sharp!'

'Aye, aye, captain.'

Laughter stifled any doubts and fears that evening because they all intended it should but when the meal was over and four of them were left in front of the blaze, Dr Cullen put an arm round Jane's shoulders.

'You've been miles away from the rest of us tonight, princess. Not still worried about Luke, are you? Not now we know he's safe?'

'No . . .'

As Jane hesitated, Charlotte said quietly 'The visit to the Creswells upset us both.'

Jane nodded. 'It certainly did! I've never been so shocked. You remember them, don't you, Dr Cullen?'

'Didn't they lose a son. . . ?'

202

'Their only son, Jack, in the spring offensive.' Charlotte paused because she too found it difficult to continue.

'What happened this afternoon?' Archie asked Jane.

'I haven't heard or spoken to Dorothy, Jack's sister, since he was killed. We used to be the greatest of friends ... she was terribly close to her brother. He was an awfully kind person, a really good sort,' Jane's voice trembled and William Cullen tightened his hold. 'I wrote to Dorothy, of course, but she never replied. I assumed it was because she was still too upset. I didn't know what she and her mother had been up to ...'

'What was that?' asked Cullen.

'They've been trying to get in touch with Jack,' Jane burst out, 'What they invited us this afternoon wasn't tea but a séance!'

'What on earth's that?'

'It was disgusting,' Charlotte snorted.

'You sit, hands touching, round a table,' Jane explained. 'The curtains are drawn and one of them — she calls herself "Madame Clara, Society Palmist and Clairvoyant" — but I've seen her about the town. She's a little woman who lives in East Raby street. She used to do alterations for us.'

Amused, Archie asked, 'And what does Madame Clara, palmist and former dressmaker, get up to?'

'She calls up the dead.'

'What!'

'She pretends she's talking to them. She goes into a trance and speaks in a funny voice. She *claims* she was speaking through what she called a "spirit guide" — to Jack.'

'How beastly!' Jane shivered.

'Yes, it was. What made it worse, they all wanted to believe it. All the other women there had lost someone. It was desperately sad I know, but it made me feel ill!'

'It was macabre!' Charlotte said flatly.

'Think one's chums should be left in peace,' Archie murmured. 'Once the bugle's sounded, nice long rest. Wake up refreshed on Judgement Day. I say!' — he brightened up — 'None of those chaps she chatted to mentioned my arm, I suppose? Like to know what happened to it.'

'Mr Cavendish — really!' But he'd broken the ugly spell and made them laugh.

It was Katriona and Dr Cullen who put him to bed but Jane who, in the darkness, heard the whimper followed by a sudden cry of fear. She put on her wrap and went next door, soothing without waking him. When he was quiet, she curled up in front of the dead fire. Nightmares like his could last most of the night. She had a sudden thought: what on earth would Mama say if she knew? Jane yawned. Before the war, if she'd been alone in a man's bedroom, half clothed. . . ! Oh well, times had changed.

Archie had been such a dear tonight. He'd helped calm her about Dorothy and persuaded her to ignore the séance. 'I'm sure your friend will get over it. She must still be frightfully unhappy but time heals, you know. It always does.'

'You're not only kind, you're awfully nice, Archie Cavendish,' Jane whispered into the darkness, 'You sent us all to bed feeling cheerful — I haven't felt this good for weeks.'

Would he ask her to be his 'special girl'? If he did, I shouldn't mind, she decided. It's not the same as I feel about Luke of course. He'll always come first but Archie would be such a marvellous *friend*.

From time to time, weary though she was, Jane wiped away the sweat of fear as he slept and whispered softly as she'd learned to do on the wards, 'It's all right. You're safe now. No more war.'

In Haughton Green, Dorothy's pillow was wet. She hadn't had the courage to tell Jane beforehand; how she wished she had! In the great empty house alone with her grieving parents Dorothy felt desolate.

If only she'd replied to Jane's letters! She'd pretended it would be all right — once Jane knew, she would understand, and forgive. She might even invite Dorothy over to the Emporium for Christmas. Oh, the bliss of escaping from this terrible gloom for a few short hours!

'It was stupid of me,' Dorothy sobbed. Jane's face, the horror when she had understood, had shocked Dorothy back to reality. 'I shouldn't have argued with her, either. Jane was right: what we're doing is wrong!'

And what good did any of it do? It couldn't bring Jack back. At first, Dorothy had been willing to believe in it but not any longer. Jack would never have sent such silly messages, and there was another thing. Dorothy blew her nose impatiently. Never mind how much 'Madame Clara' poo-poohed, Jack could spell; if it really was him dictating those words, it was amazing how often they were incorrect. 'What an incredible hash the medium made of it today!' Dorothy scolded herself into a semblance of cheerfulness, ' "Beeutifull thoughts" indeed!'

She thumped the pillow and turned it over, 'Try a few beautiful thoughts of your own, for heaven's sake!' Another worry was Mrs Creswell, who had drifted from unhappiness into deep melancholia and now depended on Dorothy. 'If only father didn't have such awful moods. You were always the one to bully him back to being normal, Jack, I can't manage it! Will I ever be able to escape?' Dorothy was suddenly terrified at the thought, 'Now you're gone, Jack, will I be stuck here for the rest of my life?'

Outside the prison huts snow blanketed the forest, isolating them completely. It concentrated their thoughts on sounds, from the human misery inside the camp, to the sudden sharp death cries of wild animals. It was a bitter irony to starving men that now bird and animal tracks could clearly be seen up to the very edge of the wire, as if to taunt them. During daylight nothing ventured so close but with the darkness forest creatures, at least, grew bolder.

The typhoid had run its course but a terrible apathy remained. Close on three hundred had been imprisoned at the beginning; less than two hundred and fifty remained. The guards had behaved as Etienne predicted; most had fled. Those who remained were without hope themselves and treated their captives with brutal indifference.

To survive, a man needed food as well as hope but soup and bread were distributed only twice a week. There was no longer any need to withhold anyone's share: those who reached a certain level of starvation could not survive an interval of four days.

There was nothing to ease the pain. Luke sat beside one bedside after another through the night hours when the human spirit was at its lowest ebb. Tonight, it was a tough ex-miner from northern France whose will to live had been as strong as his body was weak. He had lain on his bunk for almost three days but Luke knew he could not last much longer. It was talk of his former life that had finally broken his spirit; when he'd recalled the misery and fear of working at the coal face, it brought an inevitable change. With only that to look forward to, why fight on, he demanded of Luke.

'More water?' The miner could no longer answer. Luke raised his head so that he could sip.

'*Merci.*' It was very faint and Luke bent closer.

'Just a little longer, please try . . .' The man looked at him with something like contempt. 'Please,' Luke begged, 'Only one more day before they bring us food.'

'No.' Just as he'd willed himself to stay alive, the man had decided it wasn't worth the pain. His rasping, shallow breaths grew less frequent. He knew Luke was still there. Before he slid into unconsciousness, he whispered, 'You live . . . but I win . . . I am free!'

Etienne was still awake when Luke sank down tiredly on the bunk beneath.

'He's gone?'

'Yes . . .'

'Some of them were arguing what day it was.'

'Next food is the day after tomorrow.'

'No, I mean the date.'

What did that matter, thought Luke? What did anything matter, they would all die in the end.

Outside, a faint sound came from the guard-hut. Singing? He listened: up and down the hut, prisoners began to nod. Etienne said quietly, 'We were right about the date. That is a German carol; it must be Christmas.'

CHAPTER THIRTEEN

Aftermath

The atmosphere was fraught; rumours about food rationing were rife and Mrs Beal declared it would be the final straw once too often. Mary lost her temper. Emily Beal gossiped. By lunch-time everyone in the Emporium knew there had been 'words'. In the kitchen the three of them washed up in a hostile silence.

'Mary, can I speak to you a moment?'

She followed John into the dining room. 'Emily Beal is an absolute menace!'

'I dare say she is but there's a young fellow downstairs wants to talk to Mrs Beal. He claims he was there when Billy died but I can't make up my mind about him.'

Mary immediately put bad temper aside. 'What sort of fellow is he?'

'Penniless,' John said decisively. 'Whether or not he's a rogue . . . He claims he was invalided out because of trench feet. In other words he doesn't qualify for a pension. I can't decide whether he told me that in an attempt to cadge money from a sorrowing mother.'

'I'll stay with Mrs Beal while she sees him. What shall I give if he is genuine? Would a pound be too much?'

'Make it ten shillings and a hot meal. More and he might spend it all on drink. What's Emily done to upset you?'

'Oh that . . . nothing, a storm in a tea cup. I do hope the man's genuine. It's been dreadful for Mrs Beal; not even a note from Billy's regiment to say what happened. Most families get those and it is some consolation.'

'I'll send him up.'

At first, the three women were slow to understand. 'You say you were there when Billy died?'

'God help me, I never killed 'im. Fired lower down. It was the officer did that. But I swore if ever I got out, I'd come and tell you it weren't Billy's fault. 'E never meant to run away, he was worried about the 'orses, that's why 'e did it. *They* were in a terrible state. A shell 'it the transport waggons, blew half of the animals to pieces. "Got to tell Miss Mary 'bout the 'orses," that's what 'e kept saying. It's all 'e said when they asked 'im at the court martial.'

Mary's throat was suddenly dry. Emily looked puzzled. 'Billy was "Missing, presumed killed".'

''E was killed all right.' The ex-soldier was nervous as he recognized her ignorance. 'It wasn't me who did it, though. Not yours truly. Honest.'

'I don't understand,' said Mrs Beal plaintively, 'What did the Germans do to Billy?'

The man licked his lips 'Nuthin'. "Cowardice in the face of the enemy" but it wasn't true. It was because of the 'orses —'

He was interrupted by Emily's wild scream. 'They killed our Billy!'

Mrs Beal stared at her. 'What's the matter with you?'

''Ere, I can't stand this,' the man muttered. The one who he knew to be "Miss Mary" looked close to fainting. 'I'm sorry,' he said, 'but I'm off. I only come 'cause I swore I would . . .' He hobbled toward the door. 'I'll see meself out. The stairs was this way, right?'

Mary controlled her trembling long enough to nod and the man disappeared. In the kitchen Mrs Beal begged, 'It's not true, tell me it's not, Mrs McKie?' as understanding finally reached her.

Mary and Katriona sat with Mrs Beal throughout the day and into the night until she declared she was ready to go back to Coburg Street. Mary stayed until Dr Cullen had called before returning home. John took her into the office.

'You're worn out, my darling. Sit here. I'll ask Katriona to bring us tea.' When it came, he asked 'Is there anything we can do?'

'Very little. Dr Cullen has given her a sleeping draught but I doubt whether Mrs Beal will ever recover.'

'So wicked . . . How could anyone accuse Billy? Surely his simpleness and lack of wits were obvious?'

'I'm sure they were. John, I just don't understand. What crime could Billy Beal possibly commit? There was nothing I could say to help.'

'If we could prevent the news getting out —' but Mary was already shaking her head.

'You're forgetting Emily, John. She's a good kind girl and I wish I hadn't lost my temper with her this morning but it's not in Emily's nature to keep a secret.'

Mary was right; the news spread like wildfire. The McKies did what they could to defend him but Billy Beal's childlike nature was forgotten in the excitement at his fate.

The Sunday following the soldier's visit, Mary and Charlotte decided to accompany Mrs Beal to Morning Service. 'It's dreadful to think she might be attacked in church but some of the remarks, from some of our oldest customers!' Charlotte shook her head, 'Unbelievably vitriolic. Poor Billy! No-one will ever convince me he deserved it. If Field-Marshal Earl Roberts ever dare set foot in Darlington again, I shall demand an explanation! I suppose I shall have to write and tell Ted now it's widely known?'

'Not while he's in France, dear,' Mary advised. 'Remember how he reacted when he heard Billy was dead? Ted is a very tender-hearted young man.'

'Hrmph!' said his mother.

'Even if he does conceal it by annoying you constantly,' Mary smiled. 'And when he comes home on leave, Billy's death will no longer be the principal topic of conversation.'

'I dread the effect once Ted does learn of it,' Charlotte sighed. 'I wish there was some way we could spare him. However . . .' She picked up her elegant umbrella. 'Shall we go?'

Mrs Beal hovered, discreetly hidden behind a clump of privet in the graveyard. Emily had refused to leave the house this morning and Mrs Beal certainly lacked the

209

courage to go into church alone. She saw her two protectors coming towards her and stepped out to greet them.

Inside the church porch another woman waited, full of venom. She too lived in Coburg Street. Her entire life had been devoted to her husband and only son. Both were 'Missing, presumed killed' but some unknown German wasn't to blame, she knew that now. Headlines shrieked their message: The Enemy within. The whole nation was at the mercy of those cowards who refused to fight. She remembered the shambling, dribbling little boy. Touched by the devil at birth, he'd been. Everyone knew that. She would cross the street rather than pass by on the same side as Billy Beal.

He had betrayed her man and her son! He alone was responsible. Hatred filled the vacuum of her life and made her cry out for vengeance.

'Here! Put these on your son's grave, if you can find it!'

Mrs Beal shrank from the fistful of feathers. The crazed woman chased after her, clawing at her with both hands so that the air was filled with whirling scraps of white. Mary stepped off the kerb to interpose herself between the two just as a terrified, half-blinded cab horse reared up, bringing its hooves down onto her back.

Charlotte heard the scream and the crack as the cab shafts split. She used her umbrella to push people aside, issuing instructions in a loud clear voice: 'You — fetch Mr McKie. Boy, run for Dr Cullen in St John's Crescent, tell him it's urgent and when you've done that, find a policeman. Is there any gentleman who will lend me his overcoat?'

Mrs Beal knelt beside Mary, 'Are you hurt, Mrs McKie? Can you get up?'

'Stay where you are,' Charlotte said quickly. Her skirt fanned over the wet cobbles as she sank down opposite. 'Be as still as you can, dear. Help is on its way. Ah, thank you ...' Coats were thrust at her and Charlotte's fingers automatically selected the best quality cloth. 'If you could cover Mrs McKie with it?' She leaned a little closer to ask, 'Is there much pain?'

'No.' Mary sounded surprised. 'None at all.'

Drizzle thickened into rain. Umbrellas were unfurled as Charlotte continued to talk calmly.

'Can we make you more comfortable? Would you like a pillow? Just whisper and I shall hear.'

'Could you . . . take off my hat?'

'Of course. Mrs Beal?' Fingers removed hatpins tenderly and lifted off the best winter felt. Charlotte spread her scarf beneath Mary's head. A few more minutes passed.

Mary murmured, 'I'm very cold, Charlotte.'

'Yes of course.' She made no mention of the first coat but signalled there should be another.

Dr Cullen had been at table and still had the napkin tucked in at his neck. Mrs Beal moved and he crouched beside Mary. 'Now then, Mrs McKie, what have you been up to?' Charlotte was about to speak but he shook his head and began to probe. When he reached her spine, Mary gave a sudden gasp and stared up at him. There was a moment of recognition, of complete understanding between them, then he spoke.

'Has John been sent for?'

'He'll soon be here, Mary.'

William Cullen turned to the group, 'Give Mrs McKie a little more air. You three, cover us with your umbrellas, please; the rest to move further back.'

Mary's thoughts were perfectly clear. 'Charlotte, could you come a little closer?' She found it difficult to focus now but the familiar silhouette was bending over her. 'My dear, you must mind what I'm going to say. Remember to tell Luke I was thinking of him. He is to care for my beloved John, always. Thank Mrs Armitage for all her kindness — and Charlotte . . . when the time comes, I hope you and Mr Kessel will be very happy together.'

She knows she's going to die, thought Charlotte, terrified. Mary knows and she's giving up without a fight.

'Mary —'

'No more, my dear. Not now.'

The circle continued to watch as Charlotte, her back ramrod straight, gripped Mary's hand. When she saw the

211

syringe, Mary managed to whisper 'Not until John comes,' and Dr Cullen put it back in his bag.

We're ghouls, thought Charlotte, sitting here waiting for her to die! And she stared at William Cullen, willing him to perform a miracle.

John arrived, breathless and without a jacket. Watchers saw the almost imperceptible shake of the doctor's head then John flung himself beside his wife, the rain mingling with his tears. 'Mary!'

She opened her eyes. 'I'm so glad you've come, my darling. Don't worry, the pain isn't bad. My dearest love to Luke.'

'No!'

But although she continued to gaze, Mary's eyes were lifeless.

The following day, shocked passers-by saw in the Patriotic Window, a name added to the list of those who'd lost their lives as a result of the war; it was in John's hand-writing, directly beneath that of Billy Beal.

Ted rotated each aching shoulder in turn. He'd tried to pad the back of his neck but permanent, deep red weals marked where stretcher straps had bitten into his skin. His nerves were bad these days. This shelter, a former German sap-head with half the roof timbers missing, didn't offer enough protection. There were no steps. A group of them had tumbled down the greasy muddy slope in their anxiety to escape the bombardment.

Overhead, 5.9s began to explode again, shattering the universe. Ted was frightened but his brain still worked; he was in a trap, he must get out! If the roof caved in they would all be buried alive! He began scrabbling frantically.

'What's wrong?'

'Going to find a better 'ole, chum. Get us a leg-up.' As he heaved himself out, earth splattered, filling his eyes and mouth. 'Not going to choke to death . . . the bastards aren't going to do that to me,' he swore fiercely.

He stumbled on, the imaginary conversation a ploy to give himself courage. 'You wouldn't believe how much the Hun wants to finish me off, Mama . . . Everywhere I go —'

This time the shell-burst knocked him flat and the shock wave ripped through his body, bursting his ear-drums 'I can't go on!' he whimpered, half-crazed by the terrible pain.

He wouldn't give up! After all this time he simply would not give in! Smoke thinned to show the lip of an empty trench ahead with a half-dug cavity at the bottom. Ted rolled over the edge and crawled inside.

The next explosion left him senseless. He regained consciousness at dusk, dizzy and unsteady. Rain had turned the ground into a quagmire with few landmarks. He attempted to listen but his ears hurt desperately. He nursed them with muddy hands, full of fear at this strange new, silent world. Where were the enemy? Where was his own line? Ted strained his eyes for a movement in the desolate, derelict landscape with its burnt-out skeletal trees. Was he the only one left? He moved off, guided by instinct, to rejoin his pals.

At the edge of the saphead, he waited. It was half-full of mud under which nothing stirred. The rain was much heavier now.

'Weather continues unseasonal,' Ted's voice said inside his head. 'Four orderlies and one stretcher-bearer lost . . . Privates Worthington, Ball, Hesketh . . . and Jimmy Maddocks, who owed me three francs.' He wiped moisture away with his sleeve.

A wild-eyed man appeared through the curtain of rain. 'The Boche are coming!' He shook him hard and Ted collapsed like an empty puppet, feet dangling over the void. 'The Boche!' the man shrieked again as he staggered away.

'. . . and Private Bolton . . All killed at Braye, where we were three years previously.'

In the prison hut, hollow-eyed, gaunt survivors stared in disbelief. '*Oui!*' the French prisoner repeated excitedly. '*La guerre – fini! Le Croix Rouge est arrivé.*' They followed, half-demented into the November chill. The lorry was in the compound, the emblem so glaringly red and white it startled them. Luke stopped – the prison gates were open! With

213

both hands he shaded his eyes against the sky; the guard tower was empty.

More shouting. Another man was waving his arms and pointing. RAMC orderlies were already handing out food. One had a sack of letters! Luke attempted to run, Etienne caught him before he fell, 'Careful! Easy now . . .'

Luke retreated with a mug of soup and his precious bundle, cradling it to his breast. A feeble pull and the string parted. In date order, the letters went back to the month of his capture. The latest one, in his father's hand, he kissed and opened first.

'My dearest boy, I take up my pen with the heaviest of hearts. Your dear mother, my darling Mary, died today as the result of an accident . . .'

CHAPTER FOURTEEN

Brave New World

'What we need to do is replan our strategy,' Matthew thrust both hands in his pockets, his fingers sensitive as always to the feel of different coins. John nodded absently and Mr Hart gave a cough.

'What particular aspect of strategy had you in mind, Mr Matthew?'

'We must plan for the future. What type of store do we want? We cannot go on in the same old way — the world outside has changed. Our customers have changed. Young women don't dance attendance on their mothers nowadays — they want to shop for themselves. So far, we don't cater for them. The Emporium is far too old-fashioned!' he cried impatiently. 'We must move with the times.'

John roused himself. 'There's something in what you say, of course. I'm afraid I hadn't given the matter much thought. What about you, Mr Hart?'

Before the deputy manager could reply, Matthew plunged in again: 'The Salon must go. It doesn't bring in enough profit. Women sit in there all day, brooding like *crows*!'

'It is for the benefit of our customers,' Mr Hart was shocked, 'A place of refreshment where respectable ladies can meet their friends —'

'But it isn't profitable and it occupies valuable floor space. I think we should rip it out. Also, I think I should visit our suppliers and explain our new policy: McKie Brothers needs new blood.' It brought a chill to Mr Hart to hear Matthew say so. 'I take it you've no objection, Uncle?' Matthew asked.

'I beg your pardon, my boy . . .?' Not for the first time,

John admitted, 'I fear I wasn't concentrating.'

'I'm sorry,' Matthew touched his arm lightly. 'I know it's too soon but you must let me help with the business worries. I want to have the Emporium back on its feet by the time Luke and Ted come home.' He gave one of his brilliant, charming smiles. 'They've done their bit. Now it's up to me to do mine.'

Mr Hart gave him a sideways look. It was common knowledge that Matthew had avoided serving king and country not from principle but by pleading weakened lungs due to diptheria.

'I'm glad you feel strong enough —' he began before he could stop himself.

Matthew's glance was cool. 'Oh, I'm full of energy to do what's best for McKies, Mr Hart. Please, Uncle?'

'I'm afraid I'm still not clear . . .'

'I'd like to make the round of all our suppliers. Leeds first, maybe Manchester then Glasgow. Explain our new ideas and ask for theirs into the bargain.'

Matthew has such enthusiasm, thought John. He's full of the energy I once had when Mary and I . . . He was interrupted again by one of Mr Hart's little coughs.

'Might it not be an idea . . . ? With all deference to your experience, Mr Matthew, you are still rather, er, young. And as you pointed out Mr Ted will be returning soon.'

'Ted wants to work in a garage, not the Emporium,' Matthew answered briskly.

John thought it time to intervene. 'We must see how things are. Ted may have changed his mind —'

'But time marches on, Uncle,' Matthew insisted. 'So, have I your permission? I'd like to make the round trip of the warehouses, leaving here on Monday.'

After supper, John sought out Charlotte, now in the kitchen planning menus with Mrs Beal for the following day. 'When you've finished,' he said deferentially. He knew how Charlotte resented having to fill Mary's role. Her pleasure was to be in the Emporium discussing fashion. Nor, despite his gratitude, could John shut his eyes to the way things had changed.

216

There was a lack of harmony in their living quarters nowadays and Mrs Beal's constant reminder that she only stayed, 'because of what your dear wife did for me . . .' had become exasperating. Even Katriona managed to ruffle him. 'We can't go on like this, Mr John. Something will have to be done.'

Matthew was probably right; they had to make drastic changes, but where to begin? When Charlotte began, he listened patiently to her grumbling.

'I don't know why Mrs Beal can't manage on her own – she's been dealing with shopping lists for years.'

'That, according to Matthew, is part of our trouble; we have all become too staid.'

'That's because we're run off our feet,' his mother said shortly. 'I notice he's taken himself off to the Kinema again tonight?'

'He's promised he will recommence accountancy evening classes when the spring term begins but before then, he wants to replan the entire shop floor.'

When John finished describing the proposals, Charlotte sighed. 'What an upheaval. Will it be worth it?'

'I hope so. I must work out estimates with Clough and think it through very carefully indeed. I fear I have let things slide, Charlotte.'

She examined her finger-nails. 'Mary's been sadly missed, no doubt about it. And you and I must continue to do what we can, for the sake of the children. I suppose we must accept some of what Matthew says. He's certainly been bubbling over with ideas lately.'

'Then I take it you've no objection if he begins by visiting our suppliers?'

In the warm darkness, Matthew gazed at the goddess on the screen. For two brief hours, she was his, spreading her glamour like a cloak, thrilling him with her fears and hopes, all glistening white satin and golden hair. In his fantasy world, she reached out her soft arms filling the void of his loneliness with love. Twice a week Matthew sought and found solace at the Scala. Here he wove his dreams but the time for that was past. Now he must

217

act, quickly; establish himself as John's successor before Ted returned.

It was Matthew's secret intention to be the sole member of the family on whom John would depend. Sharing the Emporium with Ted wasn't part of his plan at all. In future Luke, Jane and Ted would have to depend on Matthew for favours, they would learn to respect him instead of despising him for being a thief. 'I don't steal any more!' he cried silently to the golden one on the screen. Attempting to take over the Emporium was a different matter altogether.

It happened simultaneously; Mrs Armitage developed a temperature and in a letter full of guarded official phrases, John was informed that his son would be arriving in two days' time at Victoria Station.

'I wanted to go to France and bring him home myself,' John told William Cullen in agitation, 'but then the old lady took to her bed.'

'Liuke can't come here.' Dr Cullen was adamant. 'It looks like influenza to me. How old is Mrs Armitage?'

John thought for a moment. 'Eighty next birthday.' He waved the official letter, 'This suggests Luke is weak and may need a long period of convalescence.'

'I'm as anxious to have him back as you are, Mr McKie, but at present it's too dangerous. In that condition he needs to be away from contagion and fog. What about Saltburn? Or your family place up in Scotland?'

John was forced to smile. However carefully he described it, Cullen could never grasp how small the croft was. The doctor warmed to his own idea. 'Scotland would be ideal; fresh air and wholesome, nourishing food. Why don't you go with him? And what about Jane, can she arrange some leave, to help with the nursing?'

'I've sent a telegram asking if she can. One thing troubles me. I don't yet know whether my letters ever reached Luke.'

Cullen put a hand on his shoulder, 'My dear old friend, if they didn't, he will need you as never before. Bertha and Katriona can nurse the old lady. Charlotte and Hart can run the business. Once Mrs Armitage is recovered, we'll send word to bring Luke back to us. What a home-coming, eh!'

Dr Cullen wasn't as sanguine after his second visit to the sick-room. He spoke to Katriona privately. 'Mrs Armitage is worse than I thought. She should be in the fever hospital.'

'Bertha's shivering and complaining of a headache.' The doctor swore under his breath. 'Doctor, leave Mrs Armitage where she is,' Katriona pleaded. 'Hospital would be the finish of her.'

'If you're sure you can manage? There's no treatment apart from compresses and as much liquid as you can persuade her to drink. See that Bertha is confined to her bed; we'll decide what to do about her later.'

He found John in his office. 'Go to London immediately and wait for Luke there; that way there's less chance of passing on the infection.'

The matron masked her disappointment with severity; this particular probationer had been promising. 'I'm extremely disappointed, nurse McKie. After all your insistence that nursing was your chosen profession . . ?

Jane's chin went up. 'I don't believe I've given cause for complaint during my time here?'

'But why leave now? You're not one of those silly young women, full of patriotism, and a desire to wear a uniform. They're leaving in droves now the war's over — thank heavens, because a hospital needs dedication. There are many, many young men who still require our help and who will do so for years to come.'

That's the whole point! Jane wanted to cry out, nothing but more and more coming home to die — I can't stand it. I've had enough and Luke needs me. She said aloud, 'My uncle informs me my cousin is being repatriated and may require medical care —' The matron brushed this aside.

'Your uncle can hire someone else. Your place is here.'

'I wish to leave,' Jane repeated stubbornly.

'Then it will be entered as an unfavourable mark on your record, nurse. I insist you reconsider before making an irrevocable decision.' But when Jane went back to her cubicle she immediately began to pack.

They waited by the entrance to platform 7, a tall slim girl with a mass of dark curly hair whose face was eager despite its palor, and a slightly stooped man wearing a black armband.

It was cold. Jane rubbed her hands inside her muff and stamped her feet. This smart outfit wasn't suitable for the weather but she'd been saving it for Luke's return. If there'd been ice and snow, Jane would have still turned out in the grey jacket with its high persian lamb collar.

Last night at dinner, John had noticed how attractive she looked. 'Shall we go to the theatre tonight? I'd like you to enjoy yourself.' When she smiled and shook her head there was a new brittle tightness which saddened him. 'I've missed the sound of your laughter, Jane. You've had so little fun. I think of you in the same way I do Ted and Luke, squandering your youth for the sake of your country. Is there nothing I can do to make up for it?'

'Dear Uncle! We'll learn how to enjoy ourselves as soon as both boys are safely home.'

'What about the nursing? Are you certain you don't want to return?'

'No, I've not finally made up my mind,' she admitted. 'I was too young when I began at the hospital and the life was cruel but we didn't have much choice. There wasn't really time to think. Now I need a respite. Suddenly all I want is to take each day as it comes. To be lazy for a change.'

'I promised your father I would do all I could —' John began. Jane reached across.

'You kept your promise but I absolve you from it. I'm a young woman now; you must let me find my own way.'

'At least let me help? I'm increasing your allowance. Why not travel and see the world before you decide? You could always go back to Paris.'

There was a shadow behind her eyes as Jane remembered Jack Creswell. 'We'll see,' she compromised.

Signals changed. The group at the platform barrier had swollen to a small crowd. Busy travellers hurried past, eyes averted. Not another hospital train — the war was over!

220

It emerged from the smoke. No smart paintwork but dull grey. Those who descended were the wreckage of the war. A line of ambulances waited to receive them.

John recognized him first. Jane couldn't forgive herself afterwards. All those years she'd been in love, all the waiting for Luke to return and now she looked straight past him. She watched those walking toward the barrier, eagerly searching every face. She felt John stiffen. Even then Jane didn't notice the figure in the wheelchair; when she did her heart filled with pity.

Luke reached out exhausted, emaciated arms.

'Father!'

'Luke — your mother . . .'

'I know. I had your letter.'

'My dear son!'

In a carriage on the way to Leeds, Matthew was so excited he could only pretend to read. Uncle had agreed to the first part of his scheme without argument. He was brimming with confidence. By the end of this trip, he would be firmly established with all their suppliers as *the* contact at McKies. After that, he could really begin to make changes. Clough could redesign the shop floor. If Ted was back by then, he could help with the drawings, as long as he didn't interfere.

Matthew shivered slightly; Ted's personality was so much stronger, he must ensure his own position was unassailable.

The two other passengers in the corner seats had loud northern voices. 'This war's been good to me, I cannot deny it.'

'Shoddy trade'll never be the same now great-coats aren't wanted.'

'Change the colour, that's the thing,' the first business-man advised, 'Folks don't want to see or smell khaki. How's shirting?'

'Same as shoddy. We'll have to put our thinking caps on.' He leaned forward to keep it confidential. 'Trouble was, I thought t'war'd last another couple of months.' He dropped his voice a fraction. 'What did they want to call an armistice for, half-way through t'bloody season? They could've waited until Christmas, couldn't they? I went ahead and re-ordered.'

'Oh dear me!' The first tried to sound sympathetic. 'Got much of a problem, have you?'

'Excuse me . . .' There was hostility in the two stares but Matthew smiled disarmingly. 'I'm sorry but I couldn't help overhearing. I'm in the retail business myself.'

There's one born every minute, thought the first Yorkshireman.

William Cullen took an enormous breath. 'Can you hear me, Archie?'

'Rather. Clear as a bell. To what do I owe the pleasure, doctor?'

'How are they treating you at Roehampton?'

'Splendidly! I've got three arms now. Two and a spare, if you know what I mean? And several contraptions in lieu of a hand but they don't bolt on terribly well so I'm hoping Ted can modify them when he gets back.'

'It's about Ted that I'm telephoning . . .' Dr Cullen gripped the mouthpiece in an effort to shout as far as London. 'His mother's had a telegram to say he's on his way home. The trouble is, we've got infection here. Mrs Armitage is extremely poorly. John and Jane have had to take Luke to Scotland — he sounds as if he needs a lot of care, poor chap. Charlotte's got her hands full. Can you meet Ted in London?'

So Luke had survived and Jane was with him? Archie Cavendish forced himself to sound cheerful. 'Sorry to hear about Mrs Armitage but I shall be delighted to do the honours. When's Ted due?'

'Tomorrow. Arriving at Victoria on the six o'clock boat train. I don't know what sort of state he's in.'

In her aunt's bedroom, Charlotte watched dawn break through a gap in the curtains. Memories flooded back of childhood, the years spent behind the cheese and butter counter in Armitages' with her aunt watching over her from her cashier's cage.

222

In the old-fashioned mahogany bed, Mrs Armitage's lips had faded from grey to blue. Bronchial pneumonia had followed influenza. 'Nothing to be done,' Dr Cullen warned, 'It's the pattern of this epidemic. The dear old lady hasn't the strength to combat it.'

Charlotte yawned. She must visit the hospital today and take Bertha a clean night-dress. She opened the curtains. The sun was beginning to show, it might even be fine. And Ted was on his way home! Despite the sadness, gladness and hope began to flow through her. Ted was safe!

Imagining she heard a sound, she glanced at the bed but Mrs Armitage hadn't stirred. Katriona came in, tying on her apron. She bent over the pillow then murmured, 'They sent word from the hospital half an hour ago.'

It took Charlotte a moment to grasp what she meant. 'Bertha?' She framed rather than uttered the word.

'I'm afraid so. She died in her sleep, pet. Don't worry about Mrs Armitage, she can't hear and I'll see to her. You go and have a cup of tea. I'll call you if there's any change.'

But Katriona and Dr Cullen left Charlotte to sleep on in the kitchen rocking chair. The sun had risen in a bright windy sky when she returned to the sick room. Her aunt's hands were folded against her breast. It seemed odd that they should be holding Mr Armitage's photograph, not clutching at jet buttons.

'It was peaceful,' Dr Cullen said quietly. 'She just slipped away, the same as Bertha. I'm rather glad they were together at the end. You must try not to be sad, my dear.'

Charlotte remembered the many times Bertha had dried her tears when she was a little girl. 'I shall give instructions for both Aunt and Bertha to be interred alongside my uncle. It's only fitting since Bertha devoted her life to them.'

'I agree. You haven't heard from Scotland, if Luke is any better?'

'There hasn't been time. I shall have to telegraph John to return.'

'Yes.' Dr Cullen came to a decision, 'As regards Luke and Ted, I'd prefer them both to stay away. I realize how hard it is on you but even healthy people are being decimated in this epidemic. Let Mr Cavendish take Ted where the air is clean and free from contagion. We will send for them as soon as it's safe.' He grasped her shoulders, 'I wouldn't ask unnecessarily, Charlotte.'

It was an impertinence he rarely committed, using her Christian name. She knew it must be serious.

'If you think it best.'

'I do.'

Only a week or so ago and Jane was standing here, Archie thought ruefully; same platform, probably waiting for the same damn train! No bad thoughts, old boy, he scolded, nothing but silly bright chatter to welcome old Ted.

As the train drew in Archie wondered about him. 'Hope he's in better trim than I am. God! Supposing he's lost an arm or a leg?'

'Hey!' A bear-hug and the wild red curls were towering above him.

'Good life, McKie – you haven't grown, have you?'

'It's the rest of the world that's shrunk, that's all!' Ted bellowed joyfully. 'Am I glad to see a friendly face!'

'Welcome home. I'm standing in for Mama Charlotte, plus everyone else,' Archie apologized. 'I'll explain once we're in the cab. We're staying in London tonight.'

Ted heaved his kitbag under one arm but kept hugging his friend with the other. 'We got through,' he kept shouting, 'Archie, we made it! Back home for good!' Crowds turned at the joyful roar and once in the cab, Archie said diffidently, 'I say old chap, there's really no need to raise your voice.'

'You'll have to speak up,' Ted yelled, beaming at him. 'My ear-drums have gone. They should heal but I can't hear awfully well at present.'

Oh lord, thought Cavendish.

He'd chosen the hotel with care; it was discreet and very, very quiet. 'My friend's war has been rough,' he'd explained when he'd made the reservation.

'Not a case of shell-shock?' the reception clerk inquired delicately. There had been one or two unpleasant disturbances and the hotel had its reputation to think of.

'I don't think my chum will break up the furniture but I can't guarantee it,' Archie replied callously. 'Just give us a couple of rooms and arrange for a valet.'

'Certainly, Mr Cavendish.' The elderly clerk was piqued; returning warriors imagining they could carry on ordering people about. 'With a bathroom?'

'Make it a suite then we can have our meals in peace.' Polite table manners hadn't been a feature of the trenches.

They entered the hallowed portals and Archie watched cynically as staff scurried before the force of Ted's gale. The elderly reception clerk, his back to the wall, handed over their keys.

'Telephone?' Ted thundered genially and the man pointed with a trembling finger.

They had arranged in the cab that Ted would speak to William Cullen.

'Haven't they got an instrument in the Emporium yet?'

'Not so far. It's a new acquisition as far as the doctor's concerned, too,' Archie mouthed so that Ted could lip-read. 'He hasn't quite mastered it.' And when the two of you begin, he thought as Ted went into the cubicle, I shall sit far away from any glass which might shatter.

To his relief, Ted wasn't unduly upset by Mrs Armitage's death, partly because Archie had warned him but also because, in his words, 'She'd had a good innings. Chaps with influenza were dying like flies over in France. Healthy men who'd gone all through the war.'

'Poor old lady . . . and Bertha,' Ted wiped his face with his hand. 'I'd like to have seen 'em again of course but there it is . . . Mother is going to feel it, you know.' It was over and Ted began to talk of something else. The pair of us have become inured to death, thought Archie.

They were to stay overnight then head for Scotland as soon as possible.

'I've warned the garage to have the old 'bus ready. We'll stock up with one or two items before we leave.'

'I'm rather glad we're going away for a bit. I don't think I'm fully house-trained, if you know what I mean?'

'I do indeed.' Ted vibrated with restless energy, part of it the excitement at being in England.

'Just a quick glimpse of the family then off we go. You'll love it on the croft, nothing but fresh air and marvellous views.'

Archie began to laugh; the mood was catching. 'You haven't changed, McKie! You've taken all the army could chuck at you, plus the Hun and you've beaten 'em both.'

Ted joined in. 'My God, Archie, but it was hard work being a Conchie. The times I wanted to thump the Top Brass! Had to keep my fists in my pockets, I can tell you.'

In the privacy of their suite and stripped of his clothes, Archie saw the deep scars on Ted's shoulders; stretcher-bearing had left its mark after all.

For his part, as he sat up to his neck in steamy water, Ted considered Archie Cavendish.

He'd been shocked at the puckered scar, and the sight of the artificial arm brought home his friend's plight. Archie had a nervy twitchiness that Ted recognized too. They both needed to escape from sudden noise. 'All right for me,' Ted muttered. 'Can't hear a blessed thing half the time. Poor old Cavendish nearly jumped through the roof when that waiter dropped that salver.'

Up on the croft, he thought, that's what'll quieten the old nerves. Give my ears a chance, too. God, what wouldn't I give to hear a skylark again!

The hired valet called out, 'I'll be back to shave you in fifteen minutes, Mr McKie,' and began to collect the scattered clothes on the sitting-room floor. 'Will the gentleman be needing these much longer, Mr Cavendish?'

'I sincerely hope not. Planning to get him some decent togs if there are any in London that'll fit.'

The valet looked at him shrewdly. 'Got enough brandy, sir? The first night back is often a bit unsettling, in my experience.'

'A bottle wouldn't come amiss. I've only my flask. Here.'

'Thank you, sir. I'll fetch it when I bring the shaving things.'

226

If we can drown our sorrows, I might even manage a bit of shut-eye, thought Archie. Wonder how bad Ted's nightmares are?

In the wholesalers in Glasgow, two clerks were discussing Matthew McKie. 'He's got his uncle's drive all right, and some of his father's charm but I can't take to him, Mr McIver. You should hear him patronizing me. As if I didn't know what I was talking about!'

'It's the new generation; they want to make up for lost time. One of us will have to look after him this afternoon, by-the-by. He's catching the late train and wants to see the sights. Will you do it?'

'Why not let young Cunningham, Mr McIver? They're nearer the same age . . . and it is raining cats and dogs.'

'You're right, the young don't feel the damp the way we do.' He called out, 'Mr Cunningham! Could you step this way a minute, please.'

Matthew and young Cunningham had driven up and down Buchanan Street, Argyle and George Streets with Matthew doing his best not to appear impressed. Now the taxi nudged its way through a crowded, less salubrious area. 'Paisley's Corner did you say?'

'Aye. Broomielaw and Jamaica Street . . . not the best part of Glasgow but as usual, powerful busy.'

'Uh-huh.' Matthew's legs were nonchalantly crossed and his hat was tipped forward. Through the window he glimpsed a tattered pre-war hoarding advertising holidays on the Côte d'Azur. 'Thought I might visit Monte this summer . . . Depends on business of course.'

'Monte Carlo?' Mr Cunningham's eyes were gratifyingly round, 'For a holiday, d'you mean?'

'Provided McKie Brothers can manage without me.'

'It must be an awfu' responsibility?'

'It can be.' Matthew tilted his hat even further over his brow. 'That's the river, I can see over there?'

'Aye, the Clyde. There's a bonny trip doon the watter when the weather's fine.'

'What happens when it's raining?'

227

'The steamers still go, I suppose.' Mr Cunningham was unsure.

'Can one get a cup of tea?'

'Oh yes, they serve tea in the saloons on all the steamers.'

'That settles it, then.' Matthew tapped on the partition.

There was a sprinkling of other passengers, mainly elderly. Two women, a mother and daughter, sat alone. The mother nudged her daughter as the two pairs of legs came into view down the stairway. The young woman made a quick assessment of the quality of the trouser suiting and directed her smile at Matthew. He smiled back. Mr Cunningham didn't see any reason to smile.

'Will we stay this end?' he murmured.

'Think we'd get a better view down there.' Matthew led; reluctantly, Mr Cunningham followed. Staring ahead over Matthew's shoulder, he saw two identical pairs of calculating eyes, two mouths which even lip rouge couldn't soften and, on the younger woman, bright gold hair — in a bob! Mr Cunningham had imbibed certain rules of survival at his mother's knee. Unfortunately for Matthew, Charlotte hadn't thought them necessary.

The bell clanged, paddle wheels moved rhythmically and the four of them set off on a voyage of discovery.

For Mrs and Miss Macgregor, this was no idle way to pass an afternoon, nor were they admirers of scenic beauty. Theirs was more in the nature of a trawling expedition, for three days previously, Miss Macgregor's current protector had vanished leaving nothing but bills behind.

'So this is your fist visit to Glasgow, Mr McKie?' Mrs Macgregor's voice could rasp the paint off our front door! thought young Mr Cunningham inelegantly.

'He's leaving tonight, aren't you, McKie.' Mr Cunningham was beginning to feel the weight of responsibility Mr McIver had imposed and recognized it was up to him to deliver their customer back intact, at least as far as the railway station. 'On the seven-thirty-five, you said?' he reminded Matthew.

'Maybe . . . I haven't quite decided.'

Mrs Macgregor said coyly, 'Did you hear that, Effie? Mr McKie hasn't made up his mind yet?' The daughter re-crossed her ankles in their high buttoned boots. The golden-brown tunic dress with fur edging was warm against Matthew's knee. Gold hair shone guinea-bright, dazzling him.

'Effie? What a pretty name.'

Ye Gods! thought young Mr Cunningham.

'What's yours?' Effie Macgregor had drawn Matthew into her web.

'Ah, I spy activity at the tea-urn, McKie! Will you excuse us, ladies? It's the reason we came on this boat, such a powerful thirst we had!' If he could get McKie out of range. Up on deck if it wasn't too wet. Mr Cunningham was on his feet, full of urgency.

'My ... I just could wet my lips with a cup of tea!' Mrs Macgregor's hard eyes defied him to prize Matthew away, 'I'm sure Effie is desirous too, aren't you my precious?'

The daughter turned her graceful neck so that Matthew could admire her other profile. 'Did you speak to me, mother?'

'Mr Cunningham is kindly offering to buy us refreshment, hen. Make sure they add the milk to the tea, Mr Cunningham. Effie cannot abide it the other way round. Two lumps.'

Young Mr Cunningham watched the disaster develop from the safety of the tea counter. Effie Macgregor must be at least twenty-five or six! And McKie was behaving as though he'd never seen a girl before. If there'd been a way of scuttling the vessel, donning a life-jacket and dragging their customer ashore, Mr Cunningham would have done it. He tried transmitting thought messages but it was useless. Matthew was spellbound: his glamorous, golden goddess had stepped down from her screen and was sitting beside him!

Mr McIver demanded threateningly; 'Where's McKie now? Don't say you've lost him altogether, Mr Cunningham.'

'I couldn't help it, sir. Mrs Macgregor has what she calls "an apartment" somewhere in Bridgegate. The three of them got into a taxi and disappeared.'

'Dear me!'

'I offered to take him to the station,' Mr Cunningham protested. 'They whisked him away before I had a chance. I'd say those two ladies have been up and doon the watter on the lookout for an innocent wee laddie for years.'

'Tut, tut! You should have taken greater care, Mr Cunningham.'

'But, sir —'

Mr McIver tapped a telegram lying open on his desk. 'This arrived and I took the liberty of opening it. I sincerely hope McKie does catch that train this evening. He's due at a family funeral tomorrow and now that we've no idea where he is . . .'

Young Mr Cunningham still marvelled at the naivety. 'When Matthew McKie got on that steamer, he'd his future before him . . . when he got off, he was doomed.'

'Let's hope he extricates himself before it's too late.' Mr McIver pointed to the *Glasgow Evening Citizen.* 'There's two Breach of Promise cases reported in there tonight; it took a thousand pounds before one young man was free.'

'A thousand. . . !'

'Plus costs,' Mr McIver added impressively, 'I'd hate to think what John McKie will say if he finds his nephew has that sort of noose round his cocky young neck.'

Dr Cullen gave in to pressure from Charlotte: if Ted and Archie were breaking their journey, Ted could at least spend the night in his own bed. 'Provided the rooms are fumigated, he can. Do you expect him to attend the funeral?'

'I told him I'd rather he didn't,' Charlotte said. 'It's better if he and Archie set off for Scotland first thing in the morning. Matthew can accompany me to the church.'

'When does John return?'

'Tonight.'

'I shall go to the cemetery.' Dr Cullen jammed on his dilapidated hat, 'Your dear aunt so disapproved of doctors, I owe it to my profession to attend.'

When John arrived, Charlotte took tea down to his office. He made a clumsy effort to rise.

'There's no need for you to wait on me, Charlotte.'

'Sit down and enjoy it,' she said briefly, 'You look worn out. How is Luke?'

'He weighs less than seven stone. The journey to Scotland was a nightmare.'

Charlotte thought instantly of Theodore Kessel: 'It's a wonder he survived!'

'It's a wonder any of them did,' John said sombrely. 'Luke told us of one poor creature who knawed off his fingers he was so desperate with hunger.' Charlotte's cup rolled to the floor. 'Oh, my dear, I'm sorry. I shouldn't have told you.'

She said earnestly, 'Go back to Scotland, John. Stay with your son. We can manage here.'

'I don't think I could face the journey again immediately. Jane does well and the Hamiltons are very kind. There's no real worry any more. Luke told us he'd dreamed of being back on the croft. Waking each morning in those peaceful surroundings will help as much as anything.'

Charlotte collected the cups. 'I still think you should go.'

'Once the danger of snow is past, perhaps. Oh, Charlotte, thank heaven he was spared! With Mary gone, I think I might have lost my reason.' The pince-nez were polished unnecessarily.

'Thank heaven Ted and Archie will be here tonight. You and I need cheery faces, however brief the visit.' Charlotte paused in the doorway. 'Where does Jane sleep? Is she staying with Miss Shields?'

'It is too far and the weather too bitter. She has a mattress in front of the fire. Luke shares Father's bed.' John managed a joke: 'Truth to tell that's another reason I wasn't sorry to leave, I'm too old for draughty haylofts.'

'When Ted and Archie are there, Jane will have to stay elsewhere.'

'Maybe the Hamiltons can fit her in?' he suggested vaguely.

He listened as her footsteps receded and the lift weights made their familiar reverberation, then opened his desk and took out Mary's picture. 'Your boy is safe, my darling.'

231

CHAPTER FIFTEEN

One Step at a Time

'The croft is not well equipped, Mr Cavendish, that's why I want you to take spare bed-linen.'

'Dear Mama Charlotte!' Archie pointed to his 'bus', 'What with us and our luggage ... the old girl ain't got one spare inch. We've a couple of rugs apiece, we shall be warm enough. Look what we've had to do with my spare arm!' It was lashed to the bodywork. 'Ted's idea,' Archie said proudly, 'If we fall in a river, we use it to paddle ourselves ashore. Now, don't you worry. By the time he comes back, he'll remember to use a handkerchief and why the knife and fork were invented. Speciality of the Cavendishes, etiquette.'

'If only he wouldn't shout so . . .' She was still bewildered. Like so many, Charlotte had grasped little of what war had actually meant. The reality of the trenches was too shocking to comprehend.

'Ted will be quiet as a mouse next time you see him,' Archie promised extravagantly. 'He'll slide in and out of rooms like a housemaid.'

Charlotte's eyebrows rose.

'Don't change him beyond all recognition, I'd like *some* small fault to remain.' Archie kissed her as she added, 'And don't keep him from me too long. Send me Jane as soon as she can be spared.'

'I will.'

'You have your ration cards? You might need them in Scotland.'

'We nipped over to Gainsford this morning, extracted a few items from the pantry. Butler a friend of mine,' Archie explained. 'Thought supplies might be a bit tight up in Scotland. Ah, here he comes!'

Ted emerged in his new motoring clothes and Charlotte folded him in her arms. 'Come back to me soon!' she shouted so that he could hear.

Ted made an effort to tease; 'Chin up, old lady. Hope Matthew gets here in time — give him a thump from me, to remind him I'm home.' He tried to smile but it wasn't easy. At Charlotte's request, John had broken the news about Billy Beal. She saw how deep the lines were on her son's face; we've turned him into an old man, she thought. After all Ted's been through, we had to inflict that on him. He guessed what she was thinking.

'Mrs Beal's to have half my allowance.'

'Oh Ted, no. It's not necessary.'

He held up his hand; 'No arguments, please. Uncle's arranging it. It might seem like blood money but I want it done. Poor old Billy, I let him down in every possible way. Didn't even stay to look after Blackie . . .'

Charlotte said awkwardly, 'It was about nine months ago . . . She was a very old pony by then and fodder was difficult to come by. The vet advised us it was for the best.'

'Yes, of course.' Ted hugged her again to hide more tears. 'If there's any justice in this mad universe, those two are enjoying a celestial clover field and the Top Brass are burning in Hell.'

'All set, McKie?' Archie grasped the starting handle. Ted climbed in behind the wheel.

'All set.' The engine started explosively and Ted beamed through the tear-stains, 'I heard that!'

Archie picked himself up and climbed on board. 'Blasted garage must have added dynamite to the petrol! Shall I release the brake? That's it — Tally-ho!'

Matthew was wonderfully, gloriously happy. He'd never had such a wonderful evening. For the first time in his life he'd been the centre of attention: the Macgregors had been so kind! When it came to dinner, they knew the perfect restaurant. It seemed churlish not to suggest

233

a box at the theatre afterwards but my goodness, the cost!

He'd stayed near the station and caught the earliest train the following morning — both ladies had been there to see him off! Since arriving in Darlington, however, he'd thought of several reasons to delay his arrival at the Emporium.

He took another peep at his new picture. What an inspiration of Effie's! There they both sat, side by side, in front of the classical landscape in the photographic studio in Sauchiehall Street.

'Two copies,' Effie had said in her sweet high-pitched voice, 'one for you and one for me. I shall be there whenever you think of me, and I shall think of you, too.'

'Isn't that wonderful, Mr McKie! My precious — how I shall miss you when you go to live in Darlington.'

'That can't happen for several months!' Matthew was gasping; one step at a time! Goodness, how Mrs Macgregor liked to rush! He experienced a tiny stab of panic. 'I shall have to explain to my mother and uncle. It could take time, especially for Mama to understand.'

In Darlington it was now late afternoon: problems began to nag. How to explain six dozen overcoats and eight dozen shirts from Leeds for a start. He'd have to hide the photograph where his mother wouldn't find it. Only when the Emporium was reorganized and he was John's official deputy would Matthew reveal his goddess: Effie Macgregor.

Odd how in this light the picture didn't do her justice. Effie's hair looked dull instead of bright gold and those little curls at the nape of her neck — Matthew shivered, she'd actually permitted him to touch them! To his surprise, they felt stiff, not as he'd imagined — they looked artificial in the photograph. He put it aside and took out the writing paper he'd brought at Dressers. In a corner of the library, Matthew began his first love letter.

'My own dearest darling girl . . .' but he didn't know the words for love, he hadn't had to use them before. What he could express were his plans for the future. The pen flowed over page after page as he described those.

It was hunger that finally decided it. That and the knowledge that his luggage had probably arrived on the station dray. He would go via the Post Office. Matthew's hand hovered in front of the slit; Miss Euphemia Macgregor, Second Floor, No 14 Bridgegate, Glasgow.

It had been a sordid set of rooms. Mrs Macgregor shared his indignation that her tender plant should have to dwell in squalor. She'd flourished a powder puff — Matthew was fascinated, he'd never seen his mother use one.

'Mr McKie ...' Mrs Macgregor flicked away the pink specks. 'The tales I could tell you about lawyers, Mr McKie ...' Her eyes rose to heaven. 'The day Effie and I receive what is due to us, we shall leave this *bothy* on the instant! I intend we should go to Richmond Street, Mr McKie!' It was the promised land. 'One meets a *very* superior class of person in Richmond Street. If a young gentleman with that address were to invite my precious for an evening of refreshment and entertainment, I shouldn't have a single qualm. Not one. Provided I went along as chaperone, of course. Effie's reputation is a sacred trust, Mr McKie. It is her mother's best jewel.'

Miss Euphemia Macgregor, No 14 Bridgegate? Where was the harm? The envelope disappeared.

Matthew took the shallow steps up Prebend Row in a bound. Sauntering, hands in his pockets, he kicked open the gate and went the back way. Hunger was much stronger now. In the kitchen Mrs Beal was emptying scones onto a plate. She stopped as soon as she saw him. Matthew stuffed one into his mouth. 'My word, I'm famished! How's great-aunt Armitage? Any better?'

'She and Bertha were buried this morning.' Mrs Beal waited for a reaction but Matthew's face was a mask. 'She's left you her share of Armitage's.' He felt a pounding excitement begin inside, pulsing with his blood, and let out a long slow breath.

'What a marvellously kind old thing she was.'

Mrs Beal was appalled. 'Aren't you sorry she's dead!'

Matthew considered the question. 'Great-aunt was old. I don't suppose she expected to recover.'

A fortnight later, head bent against the snow, Jane hurried across to the peatstack in the lee of the byre. Soft flakes

235

fell thickly. She'd filled every bucket. It didn't matter if the water froze, she and Luke could manage. Their food stocks were good. Grandfather was safe with the Hamiltons. He'd gone there so that Luke could have the soft feather bed to himself. Jane had been sharing a room with Hester Hamilton but not tonight, it was too dangerous to try and struggle through the drifts.

She dropped extra peats on the mat inside the door and pushed down the latch. 'There! It can snow a blizzard if it likes!' She shook glistening drops off the old piece of sacking she used for protection and knelt to warm her hands. 'Urgh! It's cold out there tonight!'

Luke was snug under blankets in the old fireside chair. He regarded her anxiously, 'Shouldn't you be making tracks? Before it's too deep?'

'It already is.'

'Oh, Jane . . .'

'Don't fuss!' She said it carelessly so that he shouldn't worry. Presently he heard her begin peeling vegetables for their supper.

'All the same, you must go over to the Hamiltons tomorrow and stay there. I can manage, I'm strong enough. Aunt Charlotte will be furious if she discovers we've allowed this to happen.'

'If the snow clears, I will.' Jane finished chopping some carrots and threw them into the stewpot. Let it snow forever! she implored. But even if it did, would Luke understand how much she loved him?

'I shall be sorry to see t'Salon go,' Mr Clough admitted, 'I remember when we built it. I argued wi' your uncle, thought it sounded too fancy. But it's been popular; become quite a landmark in Darlington.'

'It was so much my great-aunt's domain,' Matthew said smoothly, 'for ladies of her generation. We must move with the times. And we need the space for our new Spring lines.'

John had been furious when he'd discovered what those were; why such a huge order from suppliers whose goods were of unknown quality? Matthew evaded questions as best he could — he certainly needed to sell off the cheap coats fast, to redeem himself. He'd succeeded in rousing John out of his apathy, the last thing he wanted.

'I'd like the whole area to look as tempting as possible, lots of bright warm lighting, Mr Clough.'

'Tell you what I'll do. You've given me an idea what you want. I'll tek it away an' price it up. Send it to Mr McKie. Once he's satisfied, we can go ahead.'

'It's my plan, Mr Clough. You send the estimate to me!' Matthew was over emphatic and the builder stared.

'It's Mr John I work for, always have, so don't you start ordering me about. I'll let meself out. I know the way because I replaced every rotten door in this place before you were a twinkle in your daddy's eye!'

There had been another letter from Effie today. Matthew could feel it inside his waistcoat pocket. The pink envelopes were arriving with increasing frequency.

If only she hadn't misunderstood, if only he'd waited before describing his plans! Effie immediately assumed they would carry them through together — she talked of a Spring wedding! One step at a time! In his dreams, Mrs Macgregor's face was there, behind Effie's shoulder. Matthew had always been able to wriggle out of difficult situations before but this time things might prove tricky.

He moved to where Mr Hart was serving a customer. 'Slipping along to the office, Mr Hart. On business.' He bestowed his most charming smile on the customer. 'We shall have our new line of Spring coats in next week. Top quality and very reasonable; all the latest shades. Perhaps we can tempt you?' Mr Hart watched Matthew disappear. What was he up to this time?

'Well now, I could treat myself to a coat,' said the customer, 'Especially if they really are a bargain?'

Mr Hart replied blandly, 'I couldn't say, sir, I'm sure but we're all interested to see Mr Matthew's selection.'

Matthew relaxed in John's chair. He didn't suggest Thomas Allen take the other. The former employee said angrily, 'Mr McKie promised my place would be kept open.'

'I'm sure my uncle fully intended that it should. Unfortunately circumstances have changed —'

'What circumstances? I was in the department this afternoon. Mr Hart was busy but there were only girls helping him out. There used to be three of us in there before and none of 'em women.'

'Customers' tastes change, Mr Allen. Before the war, gentlemen wouldn't dream of being served by young ladies. Now, as you may have noticed, they don't mind nearly so much. In fact, some of them prefer it.' Besides, employing women meant Matthew's swift promotion was assured. And once he managed to get rid of Hart . . .

'Mr McKie give me his word,' Allen insisted. 'Four years in the trenches — I've earned the right to come back.'

'Right? Can you show me a written contract?'

'Of course not. Mr McKie give me his word —'

'Without one, I'd say you hadn't a leg to stand on. Good day to you, Mr Allen.'

Matthew heard the outer door slam. He took out Effie's latest missive.

'My darling boy,

I am almost ready to name the day when I can stand beside you as your bride in a sweet little chaplet of orange-blossom. . . 'It was the signature that frightened Matthew the most

'Your loving fiancée,
Effie Macgregor.'

All things considered, thought Archie, we're not doing badly. They'd taken nearly two weeks to reach Crianlarich because of what he politely referred to as 'mishaps'. A blacksmith had straightened the chassis without much difficulty. Until the thaw was over they would stay in Fort William. Somewhere with hot water and plenty of whisky. No point in risking the 'bus' on flooded roads. Besides, he'd learned a few more details about the McKie family 'property'.

'Going to be a bit crowded isn't it?' he asked mildly. Ted thought for a moment.

'We can sleep in the hayloft. Grandfather doesn't keep any beasts nowadays. Remember the time you and I were billeted in one?'

'Vividly. Began that day with two hands to light my pipe.'

'Sorry,' Ted apologized.

'Let's stop in a hotel first. Don't object to a hayloft, you understand, but not while it's so damn cold.'

They were staying the night in an isolated homestead where the only sounds were of wind and distant sheep. With luck, a few pints of the farmer's brew and a smoke, they would both sleep peacefully.

Ted had changed; some of the boisterousness had disappeared for ever after he'd been told about Billy Beal. Gradually he and Archie were managing to tease each other back towards normal behaviour but there was no way Ted would ever forget. Archie prayed that the army doctor had been right and Ted's ears would eventually heal. He had plans and the deafness might be a problem.

Things are looking up though, Archie told himself. 'Ted's improving. He even remembers to check whether there are passers-by before unbuttoning his trousers — and in a week or two, I'll be feasting my eyes on Jane! Yes, up; quite definitely.'

The thaw had spread throughout the peninsula, filling the dykes. Any remaining snow was in deep clefts in the hills. Behind the bitter wind was the relentless surge of spring. Tiny plants sprang up, sheltered by the ancient standing stones of Clach Chiarain and Camas nan Geall. On the highest tide, a token of the latest war was washed up above the water-line. The crofters took the unknown German sailor and buried him among their own dead, as their forefathers had with other warriors since time immemorial.

Some woman would be waiting, Jane thought sadly, a sweetheart praying for a miracle. For Jane, the thaw had washed away her last hopes. She and Luke had been snowed up for five days but never once had he responded to her shy demonstrations of love.

Nor was he confined to the croft. Today he'd managed to stagger outside using grandfather's sticks. 'I'm worse than a new-born lamb! No! Don't take my arm, I can manage.' He'd broken free.

She walked up the path hearing excited birds in bracken and hedgerow. Letters were left in a hollowed-out boulder on higher ground. Soon it would be dry enough for the postie to reach the croft. For everyone else in this far-flung community, he was the most welcome sign of all; the end to another winter of isolation.

It was ironic; three years in hospitals with young men pleading for her affection and trying to push love-letters into her hand. Jane's answer was always the same: she was someone else's 'special girl', but it just wasn't true. It was a childhood notion she'd cherished, that was all. When she'd woken this morning and saw the winter was over, she knew in her heart that Luke would never love her.

There were two letters in the hollow; one from Charlotte, the other post-marked Fort William. Ted and Archie would be arriving at the croft tomorrow; the idyll, such as it had been, was at an end.

Hester Hamilton was the first to wade across the mud and ice. 'Your grandfather is very anxious to come back. He wants you to stay with us from now on, Jane. He's been fretting these last few days.'

The implication was clear: Jane looked at her steadily 'There was no need, Hester.'

'Aye, well . . . you can come home with me now the snow's melted.'

'Tomorrow. It'll give me a chance to wash the sheets. Luke will need to have my bed in front of the fire so that grandfather can have his own back.'

'Ted and his friend will soon be here,' Luke called cheerfully. 'Between the three of us, we can look after grandfather.'

He's ignoring me already, thought Jane. Now that he's better, I'm only an irritating reminder of how helpless he was.

'It'll be the best tonic the old man could have,' Hester assured him. 'Ted'll put new life into Mr McKie, he always does. Will I help you with those sheets, Jane? It's a fine drying wind, right enough.'

'I can manage.'

Tonight will be our last night together, she thought.

She cooked lavishly and set the table with glasses and a bottle taken from Alex's cupboard.

'What's this?'

'Whisky. Grandfather won't mind and I thought we deserved it.'

'You do, certainly.' Luke poured out two measures. 'Bless you for all you've done, Jane. I couldn't have come this far so quickly without you.' He raised his glass. 'To the kindest nurse in all the world!' I will not cry, Jane thought fiercely.

'The stew has venison in it tonight.'

'A feast, by Heavens! You know, I used to dream of every aspect of this place; that's what kept me sane I think. The thought of being able to talk to grandfather again. After the horrors of that camp, I need his wisdom to help me start again. There's so much I want to discuss —'

'Shall we have some more whisky?'

'Why not?'

She cleared away and washed the dishes, listening to the familiar sounds as Luke undressed for bed, hearing the occasional chuckle at his wobbly clumsiness; the whisky had left him mellow.

Jane knelt in front of the fire with a bowl of warm water and sponged her slender body. She pulled on her night-dress and brushed the thick hair until it crackled, then she rose and walked deliberately through the doorway into the bedroom beyond. Luke lay with his hands behind his head, gazing at the stars beyond the uncurtained window.

She was finding it difficult to breathe but not because of the cold. When Luke spoke he sounded incredibly sad; 'Dear Jane, it's no use. I tried to tell you days ago when I first realized how you felt but you refused to listen.'

'I love you!'

'Please go away before it's too late.'

'No!' She nearly choked from the pounding of her heart. 'I'm grateful for all you've done but it's not the same thing.'

'Please! Let me stay with you tonight.'

'I beg you to go away, Jane.' But he made no move to prevent it as she climbed in beside him.

It was love-making of a kind; there was guilt on one side, guilt mixed with desire, and eagerness on the other. Jane was so loving with her caresses that instinctively Luke wanted to respond. She was as beautiful as he'd always known she must be — but it was all so wrong! Tension built up inside and he became hard in response to her tenderness, but all the while Luke's conscience screamed at him to stop: it felt as if he were violating his sister. Jane tried not to cry out when he hurt her for Luke couldn't help himself now. It was soon over and he pulled himself away, curling up in misery as far from her as he could, bitterly, angrily ashamed.

'I'm sorry, so terribly sorry. Oh Jane, we should never have let it happen. Your wonderful sweetness was meant for someone else.'

She lay for a while, listening to his sobs, the full realization of what she'd done filling every particle of her mind. It had achieved nothing. It had spoiled everything. Eventually she crept back and lay on her mattress beside the fire and waited for daybreak.

Helen Sheilds tied the yellow duster on her gate as a signal to the next carrier who passed. John's letter had finally reached her with the news of Mrs Armitage's death. It also contained other information; Jane had been left to tend her grandfather and nurse a helpless Luke. On the croft in this weather? The two young people must come here instead — the Hamiltons could be relied on to care for Alex. Come here as soon as it could be arranged, Helen decided. Luke would be more comfortable and she could share the nursing with Jane. Full of zeal at her plan, Helen opened her door to a diminutive boy in a vast checked cap. 'Yes?'

'May I be of assistance, Mistress Shields?' He gave her back the duster.

'You're never *Tommy* Hamilton?' Helen stared; had the carter's son been reduced by the cold?

'No, he's ma brother. I'm Dougie. I'm helping out because Tommy's back at school today.'

'Oh, I see. Well, Dougie, I want you to deliver this note to a Miss McKie who's staying on her grandfather's croft.'

'Old Mr McKie is staying with *ma* grandfather.' Dougie said importantly. 'He came over before the snow set in. He does most winters, you know.'

'Yes, but I didn't realize he had this year.' This was a nasty shock. 'In that case, I want this note delivered into Miss McKie's own hands *as soon as possible*.'

'Mary Hamilton's son came back from the war real bad. Jane McKie's been looking after him. She's a nurse. She was sharing my aunty Hester's room until she got stuck over there because of the snow.'

She was also a personable young woman who had no business to be alone with a young man, however ill and whatever the meteorological conditions. What a misfortune John had had to go hurrying back to England. Helen's frown became extremely grim.

'Ma auntie Hester tried to get across to them for five whole days but the drifts was *terrible* bad.'

'Were, Dougie, not "was".'

'Aye they were.' He tucked the note in his pocket. 'She's got through yesterday, though. Will I wait for an answer?'

'You will. Tell Miss McKie I will expect her this evening, *without fail.* How is Luke, is he any better?' She couldn't leave a helpless invalid without succour.

Dougie gave his considered medical opinion, 'He can totter as far as the wee hoose now when he has to do what's necessary. I'd say he was on the mend.'

'How did your aunty find him?'

'She thought he was looking quite frisky. She asked if they needed any help but Jane McKie said she could wash the sheets herself. Luke sounded awfu' pleased his grandfather was moving back in. Did you know Ted McKie and another gentleman are coming from Fort William?' Dougie kept the best bit till last. 'In a motorcar!' He paused in vain for Helen to be impressed. 'Ma father was thinking *we* ought to invest in a motorcar one of these days.'

'Yes, well, you run along, Dougie, and don't forget my message to Miss McKie.'

Dougie whistled and waited at the top of the path as the mare searched for new shoots in the winter-brown verge. When Jane emerged, Dougie hailed her. 'I've a message for ye. The old schoolmistress says you're to go and stay wi' her.' He fished the note from his pocket. 'Here y'are but that's what's in it.'

Jane opened the envelope and Dougie watched a bird spiral upwards before diving toward the heather. He made a

243

mental note where he might expect to find a clutch of eggs in a week or two. 'If I were you, I'd do what it says. Otherwise she might come for ye on her broomstick.'

Jane couldn't bear another night here. This would be a solution, however imperfect. 'My suitcase is packed. Can one of you bring it over?'

'Aye . . . You'll maybe get it after school, when Tommy comes past.'

'Thanks, Dougie.'

He jerked his head toward the sky. 'It's a grand day.'

'I hadn't noticed.' Without another word Jane walked back down the path and closed the door.

Women! He was inclined to agree with his brother, they were a pretty stupid lot.

Archie Cavendish sat a little distance from the car to smoke his pipe. He was glad they were nearing the end of their journey. They'd begun very early that morning, laden with cans of petrol as well as food. As the 'bus lurched from one pot-hole to the next, he prayed they wouldn't ignite. Having survived the Somme, it would be careless to disappear in a puff of smoke in the Highlands of Scotland. 'Is it serious?' he yelled.

Ted slid out from beneath. 'Don't think so. Can you pass me the tools?'

'You never mentioned how spectacular the scenery was,' Archie shouted. 'What d'you want first?'

'Spanner.' A few grunts later, Ted said. 'Dreamed about this place when we were over there. Thought, if ever I get out alive I'll go and walk on those hills . . . Luke probably felt the same.'

'I'm not surprised,' Archie said to himself, adding, 'and we're all going to be together. Wonder how it'll be?' He raised his voice, 'Ever thought about what you want to do afterwards? After your walk?'

'No.'

'Had a bit more time to consider — oh, sorry. What next?'

'Wrench.' Archie put it into the outstretched hand which then disappeared. 'As I was saying, I had a bit of time to think while I was in hospital. Wondered where you and I might end up, in fact. Been thinkin' again these past few days. Fancy coming into business with me?'

'Is that bit of rag about?'

It's like talking to myself, Archie thought crossly; might as well wait until he's finished. He tapped his pipe against a stone, thrust it into his ulster and began to search for the disgusting piece of filth without which Ted was unable to finish any repair. Ted shot out from under the car like a bullet.

'Hey! Do that again.'

'What?'

'What you just did,' he demanded excitedly. 'Tap . . . tap . . . tap.'

'With my pipe you mean?' Archie fished it out. 'I was emptying it . . .' He repeated his actions.

'That's it,' Ted shrieked, 'that's what I heard. You were bawling your head off, then I heard tap . . . tap . . . tap.' Archie stared at him incredulously. 'Don't you see — my hearing's come back! I'm not going to end up deaf after all!'

A foreigner might have imagined he'd stumbled on a fearsome ritual as two men, one his face smeared with cryptic marks, danced round and round, arms clasped, uttering wild cries; then the foreigner would recall with relief that he was in Scotland.

They were on their way again when Ted asked, 'What were you babbling about anyway?'

'Oh, yes . . . I wanted to know if you'd like to join me in business?'

'Doing what?'

'Garage, of course. What you've always wanted,' Archie said promptly. The 'bus slewed to an alarming halt. 'Steady on! Give the old girl a heart-attack doing that.'

'Do you mean. . ?'

'Get hold of my trust fund when I'm twenty-five,' he explained. 'Find the right site, build what we want. With a workshop. You'd be in charge of repairs. I'd smoke a pipe. Might even sell the odd 'bus from time to time.'

'I'm not a trained mechanic.'

'Not yet but you can start an apprenticeship or whatever as soon as we get back. I'm not twenty-five for another eight months. What d'you think?'

'I think it sounds ripping!'

'Good. Hurry up and get us to our destination. The air's a bit nippy this morning.'

A few miles further on, Ted shouted above the engine, 'Did you ever think about Jane when you were in hospital?' Not very subtle, my old pal, Archie thought wryly.

'Once or twice.'

'According to mother she resigned from nursing.'

'Don't blame her,' Archie shouted back. 'Real gorgons, some of those sisters.'

'There's another particular gorgon we have to visit,' Ted reminded him. 'Not a nurse: Miss Shields. We go past her front door in about twenty minutes.'

'Oh, the school teacher! Any chance of cadging a cup of coffee? Breakfast is but a memory.'

'Why not? Her bark's worse than her bite. Don't be surprised if she orders you to wash behind your ears.'

Outside Helen's cottage, Ted turned off the narrow road and slapped the 'bus affectionately. 'Not much further now, old girl.'

'Actually, it might be a good idea if we were to wash,' Archie hinted. 'Rather a strong smell of oil, don't you think?'

'Don't be so fussy! Come on.' Ted strode up the path. 'Miss Shields? It's me, Ted McKie. I'm back!' Archie waited a little nervously. The door opened and the stern tall figure caught her breath.

'Oh, you're so like your father, Ted!' She put out her hand, 'Welcome home! Where's this famous automobile they've told me about? Imagine driving all the way from Darlington!'

'You can inspect her in a moment but meet the owner, my friend, Archie Cavendish.' Helen took in the scar and the artificial arm.

'How d'you do, Mr Cavendish. I've heard about you too, from John McKie. Now, Ted will show you where to wash while I put the kettle on.' Archie avoided Ted's eye.

Archie was amazed at the repast but then he had as yet very little understanding of the way news travelled in the

246

peninsula. John's letter and Dougie's remark had reminded Helen to bake extra in anticipation of a visit.

Scones, cake and biscuits disappeared rapidly. Ted did the talking for both of them. I've almost cured him of shovelling food down his gullet, Archie thought, satisfied. He pulled out his pipe.

Helen Shields's voice cut through his absent-mindedness. 'You may smoke over by the sink, Mr Cavendish, provided you open the window and empty the ash outside.'

Did anyone ever argue with Helen Shields? Standing, staring at the view, Archie listened as the conversation shifted from the marvel of Ted's restored hearing to discussion of Luke.

'I've sent word for Jane to come and stay with me. Luke's fit enough to fend for himself apparently and your grandfather wants to move back home.'

So Jane and Luke had been alone together? Archie puffed thoughtfully, remembering how Jane used to sparkle in Luke's presence. A man could scarcely fail to notice those wonderful eyes marooned in the cramped space of a croft.

'You and grandfather will get on famously, Archie. He taught me to poach.'

'You forget how long ago that was. He's an old man, Ted.'

'And Luke is better?' Archie asked, carelessly.

'He can walk again, so I'm told. He must still be very weak.'

'Archie and I will take him for a spin,' Ted grinned, 'that should increase the urge to stay on his feet.'

Archie tamped down his tobacco. 'Miss McKie must be an excellent nurse. To achieve so much in so short a time.'

'No doubt she is,' Helen answered carefully, 'Now, I've never had a chance to examine a motor vehicle at close quarters, Mr Cavendish. I'm very curious to know how they work.'

Ted was midway through a stream of explanation when the latch clicked and Jane stood there, obviously startled by the sight of them.

'Jane!'

'Oh, Ted — I'm so glad you're safely home!' Brother and sister hugged and kissed. 'I've been so anxious, even though I knew you were safe.'

247

'I know, old girl. I gave the Hun every chance but he kept missing me — Here . . .' Ted broke off. 'I dare say Archie's even more pleased to see you than I am!' Steady! thought Archie.

'Good to see you again, Miss McKie, how are you?' He stood, cap in hand, smiling foolishly.

'Hello, Mr Cavendish . . .' They shook hands and Jane reddened, 'I'm glad to see you're so much better.'

Archie touched his scar. 'It's not healed too badly, thanks to Katriona and Dr Cullen of course.'

Watching them, Helen Shields thought, 'Go on, my girl. Reassure him, make pleasant chit-chat, it's what he needs.'

Jane said awkwardly, 'Good . . .' and that was all.

Ted was puzzled. Not much of a welcome. 'When shall we call and take you both for a spin?' he demanded cheerfully, 'I want Archie to see the whole of the peninsula in easy stages if the weather stays fine —'

'I shan't be staying. I'm catching the next ferry.'

'Oh, no!' It was Archie's turn to go scarlet.

'Here,' Ted was hurt. 'Not when we've only just arrived, Jane. It was a damn long haul —'

'Ted!'

'Sorry, Miss Shields, but we've been looking forward to seeing Jane *all* the way from England!'

'I'm tired, Ted. I want to go back to Darlington.' I have to escape, to wipe away the memory!

'Poor old Sis! Nursing Luke must have been jolly hard work.'

His sudden concern made her want to cry. 'I hope you've brought enough food.'

'Archie's bus is laden to the gunwales! Please stay, Jane. Just a little bit longer. Archie and I would take it as a kindness if you did.'

The tears were flowing as Jane shook her head. 'Please don't ask me, Ted. I'm awfully glad to see you, truly. Both of you.' She turned to Archie; this man who'd made so many efforts to show his affection in the past, who stood before her now, as embarrassed as she was. If only last night had never happened! 'Another time, perhaps . . .' Jane excused herself incoherently and fled from the room.

Oh dear, oh dear, thought Helen, I wonder what that's all about. Briskly she said, 'You two must be on your way. Remember me to Mr McKie and Luke. Leave Jane to me. I'll try and calm her down.'

'Make her stay,' Ted insisted, 'for Archie's sake.'

Archie Cavendish was red as fire. 'You must forgive my friend. Lost all his finesse in the trenches, doncha know.'

'Ted McKie never had any, Mr Cavendish,' Helen snorted, 'I'm surprised you haven't discovered that fact until now.' But Ted had put her in the picture as to what the problem might be. Helen Shields stood, waving them off, thinking, poor young man: why does Jane waste her time imagining Luke's fond of her when this one's head over heels — Oh, what a silly girl!

Archie grasped the starting handle. Katriona had suggested he stay to pick up the pieces but if Jane couldn't even bear the sight of him, what was the use? It's my stump, he thought, morbidly self-conscious, Jane managed to mention the scar but not the stump, that offends her too much.

Ted was puzzled, but not enough to worry. 'Take you for a spin another time, Miss Shields! Right Archie. All set.'

Seconds later as they rattled past the gate, he waited for Archie's usual 'Tally-ho' but this time it never came.

That evening, John asked Charlotte to join him for half-an-hour. She was fraught after dealing with a difficult customer.

'It's about Miss Attewood,' he began mildly, 'I fear she's given in her notice —'

'Oh, no!'

'I have however, persuaded her to rescind it.'

'Thank goodness. What on earth caused that after all these years?'

'Matthew had apparently tried her patience once too often —'

'Drat the boy!'

Charlotte looked so annoyed John couldn't prevent laughter. 'I'm sorry. It's too serious for that.'

'I'm surprised you can laugh with Mr Clough's dismantling the Salon. What with the banging and the dust, no wonder our customers are fractious.'

John leaned back in his chair. 'I know you find that hard to understand, Charlotte but Matthew does have a point. I looked at the figures. The Salon was extremely wasteful of space and no longer paid for itself. In fact ours has become an extremely old-fashioned establishment altogether.'

Charlotte frowned. 'I thought you were angry with Matthew.'

'Oh I am. I shan't forgive that business in Leeds in a hurry. No, I said he had a point about the Salon, that's all. But the sooner we pack him off to college, the better. Some of his ideas . . . frankly, I was shocked. And the way he's been behaving with staff behind my back — Miss Attewood poured out her heart this evening.'

Charlotte was miffed that she hadn't come to her with the problem. Guessing this, John asked thoughtfully, 'Tell me, how do you see the future? Do you wish to continue working here?'

'I?' Charlotte was nonplussed.

'It seems to me that there will only be you and I from the family, plus Matthew of course, working at McKie Brothers eventually.'

'You don't want me to ask Jane —?'

'Certainly not, nor Ted. They must decide on their own futures. But so must you and I, Charlotte. You for instance are still young and, if it won't offend you, very handsome.'

'Thank you, John.'

He'd reached a delicate stage. 'Mary once mentioned that you and Mr Kessel . . ?'

Charlotte's heightened colour prevented him probing further. After a pause, she said, 'It is true, once the children are settled . . . I had hoped to visit France —'

'Then you mustn't waste any more time.' John took her hand in his, 'We will visit the travel agent tomorrow.'

'But how on earth will you manage?' she asked flatly. 'With Mrs Beal barely able to decide whether we should have shoulder of lamb or fish pie.'

'I intend to ask her the same question: does she wish to continue or would she prefer retirement?'

'But we can't *all* go!' Charlotte stared. 'How would the Emporium carry on if that happened?'

'That is my problem, Charlotte. I simply ask you to follow the inclinations of your heart and leave those worries to me. You have worked here since the day you were married and at Armitages' before that. It's time for a proper holiday. I must confess I shall be delighted to meet Mr Kessel once more.'

Despite the brisk, brave words, once the workmen had left that night and the Emporium was empty, John wandered through the half-dismantled Salon. Mr Clough's team had been quick; already there was no trace of the pink and blue tracery left.

'Like the Palace at Versailles!' Davie's reaction all those years ago echoed in his mind: 'Man, it's a poem!'

There was no room for poetry now. According to Matthew, retail space was the only sensible objective. John tried to put aside his dislike. Wasn't this what he'd always wanted? A member of the family with new ideas who would share the burden of running the business?

Helen Shields sent Jane to bed early that night, with cocoa and a hot water-bottle. Now was not the time to scold.

Despite a conviction that she would not sleep, Jane was surprised when a cup of tea was thrust under her nose the following morning and Helen moved to draw back the curtains.

'There's a jug of hot water in the kitchen but you'll have to fetch it yourself, Jane. My hands are too stiff.'

Jane washed, dressed and thought of the inevitable inter-view with dread. She walked through into the parlour and Helen examined her critically.

'That's better. Yesterday you looked so miserable, you even depressed Ted and that takes some doing. Now, eat your bacon and egg and have two cups of coffee. A firm foundation, that's what I always say. The world appears much more tolerable after bacon and egg.'

But when Helen began to talk, apparently inconse-quentially, it was not of the future but of the minutiae of life on the peninsula, of a generation of young women who'd lost sweethearts, who were anxious to find new partners. Having sown disquiet, she led Jane to the question of what she intended to do next.

Jane was obediently drinking her second cup of coffee. 'You and I seem to have these discussions every three or four years.'

'Why not? I gather we didn't make the right decision last time?'

'I think we might have done if I'd been in a *normal* hospital, if there hadn't been so much agony and death.'

'I understand, my dear. And I think you're wise. You can always return to the profession if you change your mind. How old are you now?'

'Nearly twenty-one.'

'Well that's young enough to start again but what you need first is a holiday. Nursing Luke has worn you out.' Jane turned extremely pale. And whatever else you got up to, thought Helen severely.

'Uncle suggested I might like to travel.'

'Excellent. I'd suggest at least six months.' Helen got up and moved to stare at her favourite view. 'For Luke and Ted, their renewal is up here; for Mr Cavendish, too, I imagine. You need somewhere more sophisticated. Yes,' she went on serenely, 'having three personable, unmarried men about will be a Godsend to every mother in this district, especially Hester Hamilton with her bonny daughters. There'll be invitations galore —'

'Ted's too young to marry!' Jane burst out, 'And as for Luke . . .'

'Oh, I wasn't speaking of them. I meant Mr Cavendish. Now, it's time you were gone, Miss. You may come and stay next time you need advice but that ferry's usually on time these days and as you're determined to catch it . . .'

She watched the girl leave on her stubborn, solitary journey toward the jetty.

'Luke isn't for you,' Helen scolded the figure vigorously. 'Archie Cavendish might fill the bill if he isn't snapped up by someone else but it will need a far stronger woman to cope with Luke.' And it came as a surprise to Helen that it would need someone as resilient as Mary McKie had been.

CHAPTER SIXTEEN

Revelations

'It's time we tackled the question of your future, Matthew. Tomorrow I propose to enrol you in college. You can begin full-time accountancy classes at Easter. Once you cease earning a wage here, I shall increase your allowance in line with Ted's and Jane's.'

'I'd like a little longer to think if over, Uncle,' Matthew felt the familiar panic churn inside. He couldn't manage on an allowance. Already he was sending money regularly to Effie, in response to various appeals. Inside his pocket was a bill from Samuels of 134 Buchanan Street, Glasgow for what Effie had described as 'a dear little ring, two pretty diamonds and a ruby, only £5.19s Od.' How could he begin to pay that out of an allowance?

'Actually, I'd prefer to continue gaining experience by working here.' The blue cats-eyes smiled winningly. 'I learn much more being with you and Mr Hart.'

John was not to be cajoled. 'You're no use to me unless you're qualified.'

'Surely there's no real need? By working here I shall gain sufficient experience to become a partner —'

John was startled. 'On the evidence so far, Matthew, that day is still a long way off. These plans of yours for revamping the Emporium ...' He pushed the folder across the desk. 'They contain basic mistakes. Look at the figure you've put down for wages. We pay out far more each week.'

'You needn't,' Matthew muttered. 'You needn't pay such high wages.'

'Matthew!'

'That's why we mustn't take on men, Uncle. Women can do the work and cost less.'

John stared. 'But you've written down the amount we used to pay before the war.'

'Why not?' Matthew was defiant. 'It's common sense. There's plenty begging for work and it would mean a higher profit.'

'There's such a thing as morality!'

Not in business, Matthew thought scornfully, that's where you're so stupid. But he must remember to hold his tongue, he couldn't afford to upset John!

'Another of your mistakes was to engage that young girl for Men's Outfitting without consulting me. She will have to go once young Allen gets back. No, the time has come for you to go to college. Prove to me you are capable by passing the examinations. After that you can begin a proper apprenticeship under Hart's supervision.'

'But that could take years!' Matthew burst out. 'I must become a partner sooner than that.'

John was very angry. 'You've been spoiled. Hart was right, I should have insisted you work in the stock-room instead of letting you loose with our suppliers. That disastrous visit to Leeds and Glasgow has gone to your head.'

Hmm! John thought as the door crashed shut. If Matthew didn't change his attitude soon, there would have to be even more fundamental changes! Hart had murmured a warning days ago. 'Too er — cocky, if I may put it that way, Mr McKie.' John drummed his fingers in annoyance. Here he was, deep in plans for reshaping the Emporium and trouble where he least expected it. Last year, Matthew had been so keen to finish his accountancy studies.

He pushed the offending folder into a drawer. Matthew had to be taught a lesson. Two years at college should do it, maybe eighteen months if he worked hard, and a six months' apprenticeship. The boy was nineteen. Good Heavens, twenty-one was early enough to think of any 'partnership'!

He went to see if the afternoon post had brought a letter from Luke. There was an envelope, addressed in Charlotte's hand to Theodore Kessel at a hospital in France. It had been franked 'addressee unknown'. A sadness stole over John as to what this might mean. I can't face Charlotte's disappointment when she sees it, he thought, I need some fresh air.

The pavements were wet with spring showers. He tramped up and down trying to harness his ideas. With Matthew at college John needed to hire temporary staff so that he and Hart could take long-overdue holidays themselves. His colleagues at the Lit and Phil might know of suitable people. It was true there were plenty returning from the war. It saddened him to see so many with pathetic trays of matches and bootlaces. Surely a country that owed them so much could provide better for its sons? A land fit for heroes. It didn't appear that way to John.

'Mr McKie?' He stared blankly at the man who'd interrupted his reverie. 'Could I have a word, Mr McKie?'

'Thomas Allen, isn't it?'

'That's right, sir. I apologize for speaking to you in the street.'

'Not at all,' It was difficult to reconcile the slow-spoken youth with the firm lean face in front of him. 'I'm extremely glad to see you safely back, Mr Allen. Have you been home long?'

'Several weeks, Mr McKie.'

'Indeed.' He was surprised. 'Have you found another position? If so, Mr Hart or I will be happy to furnish a reference.'

'There's no work to be had, Mr McKie. I had hoped you would redeem your promise, sir. Mr Matthew said it wasn't possible.'

'Matthew?'

'He interviewed me two weeks ago.'

'I wasn't aware . . .'

'He said circumstances had changed and you were only employing female counter-hands. I notice you've already engaged another. That means there's no place for me, I suppose? I'm sorry to beg, Mr McKie, but that's what I am doing . . .'

John's emotions were in angry turmoil. 'Leave it with me, Mr Allen. I'll have to see what can be done. I take it you've no objection to undertaking whatever work I can offer you?'

255

'Anything, Mr McKie. I'm that desperate.' John's hand reached automatically for his wallet. Thomas Allen tried to back away, 'No, I didn't mean —'

'Please, take it,' John said curtly, 'Are you at the same address? Good. I'll send word when I can. Good-day to you, Mr Allen.'

'Thank you very much, sir!' Gratitude was too much on top of all the rest. John nodded and quickly walked away.

In Gents' Outfitting, Matthew was trying to quiet a customer.

'I'm afraid we cannot accept —'

'You told me these coats were a bargain.'

'So they are —'

'And I paid good money —'

'Very inexpensive, considering the quality —'

'But I've only had it a fortnight and look at it. Three days' rain and it's useless.'

'These garments are designed for the spring, sir, not for *bad* weather.'

The man leaned heavily on the counter. 'Well, lad, it may have escaped your notice but in Darlington, there's bad as well as good, in t'spring. An' this coat won't stand up to any of it. If t'wind blows, I can feel it right across me kidneys because the cloth's so poor. So if it's all the same to you, I want my money back and you can put this' — he flung the coat at Matthew — 'in t'bin. Look how streaky it's got! It weren't even dyed properly. One pound three shillings and tenpence three farthing.' He stuck out a belligerent hand as Mr Hart appeared.

'Any problems, Mr Matthew?'

'Not at all, Mr Hart.'

The customer didn't agree. 'Oh, yes there is! *You* said you'd be interested in seeing these coats. D'you call this quality?'

Mr Hart shook his head. 'No, I do not.'

'I always thought I could rely on McKie Brothers.'

'You can indeed, sir. I apologize both for any incon-venience and your disappointment. Allow me.' Matthew

256

moved aside sullenly. Mr Hart seized the pad from under the counter and wrote out a refund.

The customer read the figures upside-down. 'That's more than I paid.'

'Naturally. As a token of our good faith. An unfortunate mistake has occurred. McKie Brothers pride themselves in rectifying any mistakes.' Mr Hart snapped his fingers. The leather bucket sped along the wire and returned immediately with two pound notes.

'The price you paid, sir, plus a small sum as a token of our goodwill. In future, garments such as these will retail at a substantially reduced price as an indication of their inferior quality.' He accompanied the customer through the shop and bowed him through the door.

Back in the department he spoke to Matthew in a very different tone. 'We sell quality in this establishment. That policy isn't going to change because *you* think it smart to make a quick profit. Get me a sales card.' Matthew stared. '*Now!*' roared Mr Hart. Avid assistants pretended to be very busy indeed.

When it arrived, Mr Hart sketched out the words and handed it back. 'Fill in the lettering neatly then put it on a stand.'

'SPECIAL OFFER,' Matthew read, 'UNWANTED STOCK. NOT OUR USUAL QUALITY AND THEREFORE SOLD AS SUCH, BELOW COST: ONLY FIVE SHILLINGS AND ELEVEN-PENCE THREE FARTHINGS PER GARMENT PLUS TWO FREE SHIRTS.'

'We'll sell at a loss!'

'I'm glad that point hasn't escaped you. It's less than these coats are worth but at least McKie Brothers might keep their reputation. Now finish the lettering and put that card where everyone can see it — at the double!'

'Dearest Effie,' Matthew began that evening, 'This letter may come as a bit of a surprise but I hope you will understand. In order to abide by my uncle's wishes, I have to return to college next week. The visit you and your mother proposed making to Darlington, will therefore have to be delayed . . .'

CHAPTER SEVENTEEN

Decisions

'John, I'd like Jane to accompany me if you've no objection. You know my letter was returned? I thought if I went to Mr Kessel's address myself, and made enquiries . . .'

'Of course.'

Charlotte's colour was high and she looked as awkward as a girl. 'If Jane is with me, she can translate.'

'I'm glad she's agreed to go,' John said sympathetically. 'The change will do her good. She's been very pale since she returned.'

Charlotte was dismissive of her daughter's state of health. 'I've given her two doses of senna.'

'You *will* treat it as a proper holiday? Allow yourselves plenty of time in Paris? You both deserve new hats and it might be just the tonic Jane needs.'

'Oh, John!' She embraced him so rarely that John blushed. 'You're a kind man.'

'I wish you every success in your search,' he mumbled.

'You don't consider I'm behaving — foolishly?' The truth was painful to acknowledge. 'No doubt Mr Kessel sees himself as a young man. I shall soon be forty-one.'

This made him smile. 'How many more grey hairs d'you have?'

'Very few,' she answered tartly. She probably knows each and every one, he thought amused. Charlotte was her usual elegant self. She was too voluptuous for current fashion but shorter skirts had revealed what Davie had always boasted, that his wife's were the most elegant legs in Darlington.

'I can't see any deterioration, Charlotte, and I doubt whether Mr Kessel will either. D'you have sufficient funds?'

258

'I shall withdraw two hundred pounds of Aunt Armitage's money. If Jane would like to stay on in France, then she can.'

'That's very generous of you,' John said frankly, 'I know how you've come to depend on her.'

'Parents must learn to let go,' Charlotte shook her head, 'I saw Dorothy Creswell in the town. Mrs Creswell did nothing but cling to her arm. It made me realize I mustn't behave that way with Jane.'

Up in Jane's room. she and Katriona were sorting and repacking clothes. 'You'll not need much. Your mother's planning to do plenty of shopping.'

'Yes . . .'

'Well, cheer up!' Katriona was indignant. 'It's Paris you're off to, not the salt mines. I wish it was me instead.'

'I'm sorry . . .' There was silence for a time.

'What's wrong, pet? Are you sickening for something?'

Jane jerked away from her. 'No!'

'I was surprised you didn't stay in Scotland once Ted and Mr Cavendish arrived.'

'I'm all right!'

Katriona could see that she wasn't. 'It's not Luke, is it?' At the change in Jane's expression, she asked, 'You and he. . . ? Oh, Jane you weren't daft, were you?' Just as she'd withdrawn, Jane now reached out for comfort. Katriona understood and held her close. 'He never was the man for you, pet,' she said sadly.

'I know!'

This came from the heart and Katriona couldn't chastise her. I should have done years ago though, she thought, then I might have prevented this happening. 'Are you overdue?'

'Yes! I should've started two days ago!'

'We'll keep our fingers crossed.'

'But I can't go to France —'

'We'll keep praying,' Katriona repeated firmly. 'Three more days before you leave, that could be time enough.' And there was me hoping Archie Cavendish would be the one . . .

'You won't tell Mama?' Jane implored.

259

'What d'you take me for? Haven't I always done my best for this family? Now finish that packing and wash your face, I've other things to do. And Jane . . .'

'Yes?'

'Perk up a bit. Otherwise your ma will get suspicious.'

Heavy-hearted, Katriona went in search of Charlotte. Another of her brood was giving cause for anxiety.

'There's one of those pink envelopes, Mrs Davie. Same Glasgow postmark.'

Charlotte took it with the tips of her fingers and sniffed. 'It's scented!'

'Aye, so were the others; it's a bit early for love letters.'

'Don't be ridiculous, Katriona!'

'I thought as you would be away from here for the next few weeks . . .'

'Put it with the rest of the post. I'll speak to Matthew this evening.'

Charlotte ordered him to come to her parlour. 'Ladies do not use perfumed writing paper, Matthew. Kindly cease that particular correspondence immediately.' He stared but said nothing. It never occurred to Charlotte that her order would not be obeyed.

The following morning, Jane could be heard singing. Her mother was smug. 'I always say, you can always rely on senna.'

Katriona agreed drily. 'Aye. It's marvellous what miracles those wee pods can achieve.'

When she came in to breakfast, Jane said innocently, 'Our travellers' cheques should be ready. Would you like me to collect them?'

'Yes please, dear.'

In the High Row, Jane heard someone call and turned to find Dorothy Creswell. 'Jane, how lovely to see you again!'

'Oh, hello . . .'

There wasn't much warmth and Dorothy said hesitantly, 'Are you busy? Have you time for a cup of coffee?' They had not met since the séance. 'It seems such ages since that ghastly afternoon! I avoid spiritualism nowadays.' Dorothy spoke as though the question had been asked. 'I'm trying to wean Mother away from it.'

'I'm so glad.'

'Jack would never have sent such silly messages! Madame Clara claimed his spirit had sent instructions that I must always wear silk next to my skin! My own brother, talk to me about underwear?'

Jane said gravely, 'I never knew Jack was an expert on ladies' combinations.'

'Oh, Jane!' They laughed, not easily but at least with relief that tension had dissipated. 'Where shall we go?'

'Wherever you like,' Jane was light-hearted, 'I warn you I haven't much more than ninepence until I visit the bank.'

'Neither have I.'

'What?' She noticed for the first time Dorothy's rather drab coat.

'Hadn't you heard about Pa's shipyard? Most of it was shut down when the politicians decided we didn't need any more battleships.'

'I'm glad,' Jane was serious, 'Anything to do with war should be consigned to perdition.'

'Yes, but no-one considered what was to happen to the men,' Dorothy countered. 'Those who came back found their jobs had disappeared. As for us,' she pulled a little face, 'so much of father's money was invested — that's all gone. Our house is up for sale and I've been taking typewriting lessons in Middlesbrough.'

'Oh, heavens — Dorothy!' Jane kept her sympathy until they were discreetly hidden at a corner table in a cafe, 'Surely there's some money left?'

'I'm sure there is but Pa's always been a miser. If Jack had survived . . .' She tilted her head in a way Jane remembered. 'He was the only one who could talk Pa round. Mother's in too much of an emotional state these days.'

'Is there no-one you can ask?'

'I went to the solicitor. Instead of keeping it confidential, he told Pa.'

'How mean!'

'Women are chattels, my dear, hadn't you heard? It's men who make the decisions.'

'Oh, what absolute piffle! What about the decisions nurses had to make when there weren't enough doctors to go round.'

'Ah . . .' Dorothy wagged her finger mock-solemnly. 'The war is over, dearest. Everyone's supposed to return to the good old ways — women are, at least. We're expected to resume the role of arranging flowers and waiting for "Mr Right". Madame Clara saw my "Mr Right" in the tea leaves.'

'Goodness!'

'He never turned up. He's probably still over there . . . in "some corner of a foreign field", like all the rest,' Dorothy sighed then brightened, 'At least the typewriting lessons have provided an escape — and I'll be able to earn my living. Think of it, Jane: independence. Heady stuff! Anyway, that's enough, especially as you are paying for these. What's been happening to your family? I heard Luke was very ill?'

Jane took a sip of coffee before saying, 'He's recovering, up in Scotland.'

'And Ted?' Dorothy asked, suddenly pink. 'I heard he'd gone as a Conchie, that must have taken a lot of spunk.'

'Yes it did. We were jolly worried he would forget and thump an officer.'

'Heavens! That could've been fatal.'

'He's in Scotland too with a chum of his, Archie Cavendish.'

'There was a boy called Cavendish at Durham school when Jack was there.' Dorothy wrinkled her nose. 'Dreadful parents — terribly rich but never spoke to one another. Sounded simply ghastly. He was an only child and rather sweet.'

'One and the same, I'd say.' Jane was colouring now. 'An awfully nice chap.'

'Awfully nice,' Dorothy agreed, slightly surprised. 'Thank God one or two have survived.'

'Archie's lost an arm but he manages to joke about it.'

'Hugo Wilton died last month. He'd been gassed and didn't survive the winter. Do you remember him in Paris?

262

He wanted to be your beau but you only had eyes for Luke.'

Jane had a sudden vivid recollection of asking Hugo to be in Paris the next time she went there. She swallowed, 'So many you and I won't see again.'

'No,' Dorothy said softly, 'But they can rest in peace from now on as far as I'm concerned. What are your plans?'

'I've given up nursing. Mama and I are off to France before I decide what to do next. D'you remember Theodore Kessel?'

Dorothy immediately put two and two together. 'Is that why your mama . . . ? My dear, wedding bells at last — how lovely!'

'We have to find Theo first! He was taken prisoner but he managed to send Mama a message.'

'So romantic!' Dorothy clasped her hands then remembered. 'Whatever happened to Mr Percival?'

'D'you know, I've no idea!' Jane chuckled, 'It sounds dreadfully callous but I don't. He disappeared from our lives during the war.'

'I saw him in Darlington once, shiny and pompous, strutting about with his officer's cane — oh my! Thank goodness you were spared him, Jane!' As the two of them rocked in their chairs, Dorothy gasped, 'Are we being terribly unkind?'

'Probably, but isn't it a relief to be able to laugh!'

When they separated, Jane's mood was buoyant. She'd wept for thankfulness that morning. Guilt and shame were still intense but oh, the relief! And now she and Dorothy were reconciled. The sun shone, in a few days she would be in Paris and Dorothy had promised a list of useful addresses. 'My dear, a divine dress-maker and a milliner inspired by Paradise! In return, if you hear of anyone needing a type-writing assistant . . . ?'

'Dorothy, do you think I could learn?'

'Goodness dearest, if I can, anyone can. I'm jolly nervous at the thought of that first day, though. In an office! Suppose I can't cope? Oh, but I must, I must! And in future I can claim to have a *trade*.' She smoothed on mended

263

gloves, 'Just imagine — four years ago I was bemoaning the loss of my maid.'

Jane watched the tam o'shanter go bravely down the street. Independence was a mixed blessing for a woman, she decided. 'All the same, I must make up my mind. At least I have a choice now! What would I have done if I'd been pregnant? The same as any woman I expect, cry my eyes out, not that that would have done much good.' She gave herself an impatient little shake. No doubt Luke would have offered to do the decent thing — 'but I couldn't have married him — it wouldn't have been fair! Poor Luke, he couldn't even bear to touch me afterwards,' she whispered to herself.

She was conscious of her body beneath her clothes, smooth and slender; now it would remain that way. 'I've been so lucky ... but I've ruined my chance with Archie. Shop-soiled, that's what you are, my girl; he's clean and decent. And it's all your own wretched fault!'

In a further desperate effort to make Effie understand, Matthew despatched a second, carefully-worded letter to Glasgow. Mrs Macgregor scanned it quickly. 'He says he'll be attending college for at least eighteen months.'

'He's a boy,' Effie sulked. 'Nineteen! He told me he was twenty-one.'

'He's still his uncle's heir, hen. The best thing you and I can do is move ourselves to Darlington. We cannot stay on here anyway, the rent's due.'

Effie was so shocked, she trembled. 'Leave Glasgow? What good will that do! Matthew says he's no money now he's a student.'

Mrs Macgregor was more robust. 'But when he sees you again maybe he'll find a way? Or ask his uncle for some. Remember how fond Matthew was of you?'

Effie still wriggled uncomfortably at the prospect. 'We can't go all that way. We haven't enough for the train tickets.'

'We'll send every stick of furniture to the auction rooms. If we're not staying, we might as well risk it.'

'You promised we'd never have to do that again!'

'Just this once,' Mrs Macgregor wheedled. 'Trust your old mammy.'

'But he's only a boy,' Effie wailed.

'Boy or no, Matthew McKie must either marry you — or pay for the privilege of breaking his promise. Oh, wipe your eyes, my precious.'

But Effie, frail butterfly that she was, couldn't bear the thought of so much upheaval. 'We'll stay here. I'll find myself another man.'

'Look at yourself,' Mrs Macgregor pushed her daughter close to the mirror. 'Take a good look. We told Matthew you were twenty-three but you are twenty-seven. All the men you used to know are dead in Flanders.' Effie groaned. 'Don't worry. It'll be all right, I promise. We'll not leave a thing in this midden and they'll never think to search for us in England!' Mrs Macgregor's spirits were rising by the minute. 'Just think, hen — marriage! No-one's ever offered that before. It means security!'

'Thought we'd take Miss Shields for a spin. Bring her over to visit grandfather, what d'you think?'

'Rippin'. Could we persuade one of the charmin' Hamilton ladies to bake a few cakes? Stocks are runnin' low.'

'It's Luke's fault. He never stops eating.' They were in the byre, engaged in what Ted described as 'de-coking' the 'bus. I must look damn rum, thought Archie, a one-armed assistant motor mechanic?

There was another rum thing: Luke McKie. Archie had had the fiercest imaginary conversations but when he'd actually met Luke, he couldn't help liking him.

He'd been touched by the way Alex McKie cared for his grandson, with a hand under Luke's elbow whenever the wobbly legs gave out, urging him to eat, to build up his strength; it was so tenderly done, Archie felt his eyes grow moist. If only his family had been like that. He tried to imagine the scene at Gainsford — and laughed at the improbability.

One day, when he'd been helping Alex build up the peat fire, the old man said slowly, 'I hope I live to see Luke a doctor.'

'I'm sure you will, sir. I can understand what it must mean but Luke's improving by the hour. He speaks of returning to his studies in the autumn.'

It took time for the old man to translate then he asked, 'You and Ted are to have a — garage?' Alex wondered what on earth a garage was.

'Rather! Can't wait to get started.'

Alex McKie was examining Archie closely. 'It is for Jane's sake too, I believe?' Alex paused. 'Ted confided your hopes as well as your plans, Mr Cavendish. I trust you are not offended? Jane is young. It will do no harm to wait a bit.'

Archie was scarlet. He gave a nervous 'Yes, quite . . .' and found his hand being shaken. I can't spoil his dream, he thought. How can I tell him Jane can't stand the sight of my stump?

'Fancy coming fishing tonight?' Back in the cow byre Ted had interrupted his reverie.

'Rather!' Fishing would not be in the orthodox manner Archie had learned at Gainsford but stealthily, by night, with quietly-spoken crofters intent on filling the larder rather than casting a fly.

Another memory of Gainsford amused him. How many rooms in that house? Fifteen? More? Yet in this dwelling everything fitted into one small space.

'What's the joke?' Ted asked.

'It's the croft . . . I still find it incredible.'

'A bit shabby,' Ted was apologetic, 'I intend to make a start on it as soon as we've fettled the 'bus.'

'You misunderstand. I meant it's perfect.' Ted stared. 'It fits the people who've lived there like a glove. Close your eyes and picture it, you'll see what I mean.

'You go through the door — not forgetting to duck — and immediately on your right, that's where the boots are stacked, the hats and coats, the buckets, the yard broom — all the outdoor things. Then there's the bench —'

'With fishing tackle beneath.'

'Spare rope and twine kept in the lobster pots. Oars laid against the wall. An incredible collection of tools. Leather, tacks and an awl for mending shoes. The table in the centre of the room —'

'There was always a plant or some flowers on it when grandmama was alive.'

'Now there are your grandfather's books.'

'The Bible, an English dictionary and *Pilgrim's Progress.*'

'Near to the table and in front of the hearth is his chair.'

'You're forgetting the cupboard beds on either side.'

'No, I'm not, you're ahead of me,' Archie protested. 'Then comes the shelf across the end wall without a square inch of space. Candles, matches, the oil lamp, the money jar. Family photographs, bits of driftwood, a tin for documents —'

'The penknife with the horn handle, the watch that hasn't kept time for more than half a day as long as I can remember.'

'There are the pans stacked on the hearth, with the peats and the poker.'

'The big cupboard against the far wall for clothes and blankets. Judging by the way the door won't shut, I shouldn't think grandfather's thrown anything away in his life.'

'That's because any one of those things might come in useful,' Archie said. 'That's his whole philosophy, whether it's a skill or a wornout weskit, I don't believe your grandfather has wasted a scrap throughout a long useful life. He manages on very little.' He glanced at Ted. 'That's not by way of criticism. I've never met a more generous man. He welcomed me into his home like royalty.'

'I knew you and he would take to one another,' Ted wasn't offended in the slightest. 'You haven't moved on past the big cupboard.'

'Another bench with bedding and rugs stacked beneath, your grandmother's chair, shelves with all the plates and cooking things including, let us not forget, the one glass tumbler; a curtain across the opening to the bedroom then more shelves for utensils, the kitchen table under the window and we're back at the door once more.'

'Well done! You've forgotten the lines across the ceiling. There's nothing but shirts and vests hanging on them now but grandmama used to hang all kinds of stuff up there to dry. Matthew and I would lie in our beds and sniff

267

mint and sage, seaweed and onions . . . I could evoke
those smells when I dreamed of coming back. It's always
felt like home up here; you can be at peace, not like
the shop.' A thought occurred. 'How does it compare
to your place?'

'I was thinking about that,' Archie confessed. 'Fifteen
rooms or so. I'm not certain of the top floor.'

'Servants?'

'The usual.'

'Yes but how many?'

'Butler, footman — he went to the war and didn't
come back — housekeeper, two maids, two women from
the village who come three times a week to do the laundry and things. Gardener and under-gardener plus a boy.
Coachman — he left years ago. I think that's the lot. Oh,
and my mother has her personal maid and I had a tutor
when I was young.'

'That's thirteen . . .' Ted checked on greasy fingers, 'To
see to the comfort of two adults and one child?'

'They saw to our material needs. We were, I think, the
most miserable three people on God's earth.'

Ted roared with laughter. 'You must tell grandfather! I'd
hate him to miss that joke! What's the time?'

Archie looked at the gold hunter he'd been given on his
twenty-first birthday. 'Half past twelve.'

'How about a spot of grub? Hester brought eggs
and bread this morning. There's also the remains of
the gammon.'

'Marvellous!'

They were half-way across the yard when Luke emerged,
white-faced. 'Grandfather's ill. I think it's a stroke.'

Looking out of the tram window, Jane saw the 'for
sale' boards. Behind them, the paintwork was shabby and
the shrubs needed pruning. Dorothy opened the door as
she approached.

'Don't take your coat off, wait 'til we're upstairs.' The
vast cold hall spoke eloquently of economy. There were no
banks of hot-house flowers but because of the memories,
Jane asked, 'How is your mother?' It seemed impossible

that Mrs Creswell might not emerge from the ballroom, all warmth and rich elegance.

'We might see her at tea-time,' Dorothy replied evasively, 'if she's well enough. She stays in her room most days. Here we are.' She opened the door of one of the smaller bedrooms.

'Isn't this where Mademoiselle . . ?'

'That's right! I moved in because it was easier. As you can see, it's cosy. You can take off your coat now if you like.'

There were tub chairs in front of the fire. On a table, Jane recognized the old gramophone. Instead of her carved tester bed, Dorothy now had a small divan against one wall. 'I moved that in here because single sheets are less bother to iron.'

'Goodness!' It popped out before Jane could help it.

Dorothy gave a wry grin. 'I know. Who would have thought, et cetera, et cetera. I shall have to find somewhere to rent when the house is sold. Does your uncle still let rooms in Coburg Street?'

'You can't live there, Dorothy!'

'Beggars can't be choosers.'

Inspiration came. 'Why don't we ask Dr Cullen? He's bound to know of somewhere.'

'It has to be cheap. I shall be lucky to earn more than seventeen and six a week.'

'Here . . .' Jane pushed the greaseproof-wrapped package at her friend, 'From Emily Beal.'

'Pikelets — how scrumptious! Wait, I have a fork. There we are. You toast while I go in search of butter.'

There was no further suggestion that Mrs Creswell might join them, Jane noticed. She knelt in front of the fire and threaded the first pikelet onto the fork.

Hanging outside the wardrobe were four or five evening dresses. Jane recognized one. It had been the envy of everyone in the dancing class; beaded pink silk. Today it looked old-fashioned. How styles had changed as well as everything else!

Dorothy returned with a laden tray. 'It's nicer if we have tea here rather than the kitchen. You don't know anyone who buys that sort of thing, do you?' She indicated the pink dress.

'Miss Attewood might. I know beading is fearfully expensive.'

'If I manage to sell them, I might have enough for a new blouse. Help yourself to sugar.'

'Thanks. Has your dress allowance been stopped?'

It was an indelicate question but Dorothy didn't seem to mind. 'Yes. Pa grudgingly paid for my typing lessons but that finishes when I qualify. Mmmm, these are heavenly. Please thank Emily for me.'

'Of course. Look, Dorothy, promise you won't be offended?' The head tilted in the familiar way. 'You know my clothes come from stock, as a sort of advertisement. One new outfit each season. I have a skirt and jacket that could be altered, especially if you're going for interviews. And I'll tell Miss Attewood you want to trade those gowns against a new blouse. How would that be?'

'Absolutely wonderful!' Her friend appeared genuinely pleased and Jane's anxiety disappeared.

'Come round on Friday. We leave for Paris first thing on Saturday.'

'Will Ted be there?' Dorothy asked idly.

'I shouldn't think so. He and Archie don't intend to hurry back.'

Helen Shields had been jolted the eight miles to the croft. It was progress, and she must get used to it. Ted's request meant she couldn't refuse.

'We called in the doctor from Fort William. He wanted to send grandfather to hospital but he refused. He wrote "Luke" on his slate so that settled it.'

'And is Luke capable?'

Ted hesitated. 'I think so. When this happened, it sort of changed him. He took charge of the medicine and tells Archie and I what to do. He's still as weak as a kitten but I can lift grandfather and Archie helps. We're coping.'

'And now your grandfather has asked for me?'

'He wrote your name on the slate.'

'I see. Well, I'd better get my hat.'

Ted held out Archie's leather motoring coat. 'Do put this on. It can be chilly when the air rushes past. Absolutely exhilarating! I had her up to thirty miles an hour downhill in the Lake District.'

'Ted McKie, if you dare go fast whilst I'm in that contraption —'

'I'm a careful driver!'

Helen looked pointedly at the dents and scrapes on the bodywork.

'Hmm!' she said.

The croft hadn't changed. If Jeannie McKie had been alive, her one good table-cloth would have been on display and fresh scones ready on the hearth. Today there were slabs of bread and a jar of Gentlemen's Relish from Fortnum and Mason. Archie had done his best.

Alex McKie sat wrapped in shawls. At first he looked the same but then Helen saw the other, twisted side of his face. She came close, took his good hand and began talking, pausing every now and then for him to convey he'd understood.

'I can see you're well looked after, Mr McKie. I doubt very much whether a hospital could have done better.' The rheumy eye found Luke. She nodded. 'It's what I would expect, of course. Now, shall we send John a telegram? I am sure he would want to be here?'

Inside his useless shell, Alex's energy was fading. He stared at the slate and chalk; mercifully Helen understood. 'I think Mr McKie wishes to speak to me alone. Do you three wait outside until I call. Mr Cavendish, you can put the kettle back on the hob, please.' It had been the first lesson she had learned when she came to the peninsula; how long it took for water to boil over a peat fire.

Archie murmured, 'Before you arrived, he wrote that on the slate.' She read C...H...I...L...D...R..E...N as the door closed behind them.

'You must mean grandchildren, I think?' The eye agreed. After a moment's thought Helen said, 'Well now, you and I will not concern ourselves with Matthew for there's nothing we can do.' She looked at him steadily. 'Luke,

271

Ted and Jane gladden the heart; think of them and be proud.'

Alex was satisfied. He managed to lift his hand and indicate the shelf above the hearth. What on earth did he want among all that clutter? Helen began to peer along the length and then spotted the photographs. Of course! She put the one of Davie into his hand.

Close to, the full extent of Alex's frailty became apparent. Helen Shields tightened her lips to prevent them trembling; John must come at once.

She sat until wisps of steam trickled from the spout. She had been privileged to share the harshest as well as the most joyful moments in this home. Her life bound up with that of crofters? A daughter of the manse! Helen almost smiled. But what an enormous achievement Alex's life had been compared to her father's futile existence. It was a sad irony that, at the end, this good man was not destined to see his dearest wish come to fruition.

Helen blew her nose and warmed the teapot; Luke must describe the future to his grandfather; his was the one that mattered most. She went outside to call them in from the byre.

'Ted, Mr Cavendish — go and see to the tea, please. Not you, Luke. I want a word.' When they were alone, she said with an effort, 'I shall advise your father to come as quickly as possible.'

'It would be wise.'

'You must warn Ted and Mr Cavendish.'

'They've already guessed.'

'You alone can ease his passing, Luke. Describe your plans once you're qualified.'

'Of course.'

'He is my oldest friend . . .' She'd never even thought of it before. Her voice came dangerously close to breaking but she pulled herself together. 'Do what you can to make him happy,' she ordered and walked out of the barn.

In front of Miss Attewood's critical gaze, Dorothy rotated slowly. 'It isn't the colour I'd have chosen for you, Miss Creswell, being so fair in contrast to Miss Jane but let us

see what a gaily coloured piece of chiffon will do.' The
manageress tucked the scarf inside the collar. 'There we
are, much better.'

'Oh yes.' Dorothy relaxed. The tailored jacket was severe
but with pale peach roses at her neck the effect was
charming. She sighed with pleasure. 'I hate to admit it, Miss
Attewood, but I do have a penchant for *expensive* clothes.'

'I understand. Turn round for me again ... yes, I
think that length is better. Might I suggest plain grey
cloth gaiters? In an office, it would not do for an *ankle* to
be too explicit.'

'Oh, quite.' Dorothy was wondering how to explain she
couldn't afford them when Miss Attewood produced a pair.

'These were used in a display so no charge, Miss
Creswell.'

Dorothy reddened. 'Thank you.' Was it charity?

'Miss Jane mentioned you were having to increase
your wardrobe *before* your first interview — so difficult.
We always dispose of items from window displays among
family and friends.'

What a relief! 'Thanks very much *indeed.*'

Jane was explaining Dorothy's predicament to John. 'Isn't
there anything we can offer her?'

'I write my own letters, Jane, I always have.'

'Yes, but what about my old Saturday job, tying parcels?'

'Surely Miss Creswell would expect a more superior
position.'

'Uncle, until she finds full-time work, she'd be delighted.
Honestly. Won't you interview her before she goes? Please!'

When Dorothy was seated, John said, 'I fear in the stock-
room you would find yourself at everyone's beck and call.'

'It will be a useful experience, Mr McKie. I'm so grateful.'

Outside in the passage, she embraced Jane. 'You are a
brick, dearest.'

'Nonsense.' Jane could be as brisk as Charlotte on
occasion. 'You're not getting off scot-free. I rely on you to
look after Uncle while Mama and I are away.'

'I don't suppose I shall see anything of him.'

273

'He'll poke his head into the stock-room, he always does. Remember to ask if he's changed his socks and is eating properly.'

Dorothy was round-eyed. 'I couldn't possibly ask a gentleman about his socks, Jane.'

'Oh, dear! Nursing must've coarsened my fibres!' She gave Dorothy a hug. 'Tell Ted I'll send him a view of the Eiffel Tower. If you should see Mr Cavendish, please give him my regards. Goodbye Dorothy — and good luck!'

Charlotte and Jane departed next morning; Helen Shield's telegram arrived at midday. John summoned Mr Hart. 'I shall leave immediately for Glasgow, to catch the earliest connection tomorrow.'

Mr Hart responded to the crisis. 'Pray remain in Scotland until you are easy in your mind about your respected parent, Mr McKie.'

'It'll mean leaving you short-handed.'

'I have one or two suggestions, sir. First, young Allen. May I re-engage him on a temporary basis in Gents' Outfitting? If he combined that with stock-room work it would mean an increase in remuneration.'

'Bring in Allen by all means and pay him accordingly.'

'Thank you, Mr McKie. And Mr Matthew to assist with deliveries when he returns from college? He has a bicycle.'

'An excellent idea.' If there were tantrums, Hart could deal with them. 'It's a relief to know the Emporium is in safe hands.'

'Its continued prosperity means as much to my family as it does to yours, sir.'

Over a hasty meal John decided to leave Matthew a note but he was on the train before he thought of it again. Oh well, Hart could break the bad news. John had a sneaking feeling that without his presence, Mr Hart would govern with a much firmer hand.

CHAPTER EIGHTEEN

Arrivals and Departures

Alone in the waiting room of Glasgow Central Station, their worldly possessions at their feet, Mrs Macgregor embarked on a difficult subject.

'My precious, you remember I boasted to Matthew that your reputation was my finest jewel?' Effie's lip curled slightly. 'That was because I could see what a nice innocent boy he was.' She eased herself inside her uncomfortable stays, 'An inexperienced fiancé is going to expect his betrothed to be unsmirched.'

'Then he's in for a disappointment,' Effie said shortly.

'Please! Don't even *think* like that, Effie. One hint that you're not pure as a lily and we could be on the next train back to Glasgow!'

Worn out after a night sleeping on bare boards, Effie asked sullenly, 'How long before we come back anyway?'

'My precious, we might not, if Matthew really wants to marry you.' Mrs Macgregor shifted under Effie's stare. 'And I don't think he will try and take *advantage*. It will be marriage or nothing with that boy.'

'So I'm to go on pretending, is that it? I couldn't keep that up.'

'Now don't be silly, Effie.' Mrs Macgregor attempted to be more conciliatory. 'Suppose you grow to like him? He's that fond of you, you could twist him round your finger.'

'I'll *have* to tell him about the others. It's bound to slip out —'

'Effie!'

'When he asks how we lived, how we paid the bills?'

'That life's behind you —'

275

'It might catch up!'

'Effie!'

The train was announced. They collected their belongings and proceeded without another word to the platform. Buffeted by fate though she'd always been, Effie Macgregor had lived by her own rules. There were the good times, when she was pampered and money flowed. These didn't last because men were fickle but she accepted that. Matthew had been shy and affectionate, not the sort she was accustomed to, a temporary respite in fact, and the 'engagement' only a ploy in the game. Belatedly Effie realized she was now expected to play another role, one that could prove beyond her capabilities. She boarded the train for England very reluctantly indeed.

Alex McKie was trying to capture thoughts which eluded him. If his prayer was answered, John would be here in time. If not, Jeannie would console him. She appeared in front of him now, fleetingly, as he'd first known her, solemn-faced at the pump in the yard of the Big House. He'd helped her fill two buckets. She had beautiful dark hair and grey eyes with brown flecks. She'd whispered her name. Alex repeated it now, 'Jeannie . . .'

Luke stirred and opened his eyes. Inside his dying husk Alex knew Luke checked that he was still alive. When Luke peered at his watch, Alex wanted to tell him it was about an hour before dawn. He tried to move but the pain was very bad. Please let John come!

'I think you're awake, grandfather? Proper doctors are supposed to tell their patients to rest but what use is that to you? I'm sorry I fell asleep.' Luke yawned and pulled a blanket round his shoulders. 'Miss Shields said I was to tell you my plans. I've been trying to sort them out since her visit.

'Once or twice, in the darkest days, I wanted to give up medicine. Being with you has cured me of that, thank heavens. I guessed you'd have the wisdom to do it — but I hadn't expected it to be like this.

'I've been remembering how arrogant and priggish I used to be. Everything was possible provided I worked, that was all there was to it. Only it just wasn't true. It was thanks to you and father every step of the way was made easy.

'Once I'd accepted that, the rest fell into place. We can't live in isolation, we depend one on another but it's given to the lucky ones to help the less fortunate. At least, that's how I see it. But the conundrum remained — why did I survive the camp when others did not?'

'I kept thinking of another prisoner, a miner. I couldn't save him. I *might* be able to help others, so that's my decision. I hope you approve? I love you grandfather. Thank you for all you've done.'

Alex had another sharper vision of Jeannie as pain stabbed. He managed to make a sound. In his head he was shouting; all Luke heard was a sigh and moved quickly to the bed.

'What is it?' He could see all the signs of distress and asked urgently, 'Can you show me?' The half-blind gaze was directed at where Alex knew the slate to be. 'Is that what you want?'

Uncertain, Luke gave him medicine and propped the slate under his hand. Outside, he could smell the first warm winds of the year. He filled his lungs in guilty enjoyment at being alive.

Ted stumbled out of the byre and stretched. 'You're up early. How's grandfather?'

'Not too good.'

Ted stared. 'Can he hang on long enough?'

'I'm not sure. I don't think so.'

'Poor old grandfather. You can see what's in his mind. He looks toward that blessed door with so much hope.'

'I know.'

'Get some kip, Luke. Archie and I will see to him.'

'Talk all you like. I think it helps.'

On their second morning in Paris, Charlotte and Jane visited one of Dorothy Creswell's 'divine' establishments.

'Mama?'

'Yes?' Charlotte was engrossed in a very wide straw hat with velvet ruching round the crown.

'Mama, I've just calculated how much this toque actually costs.'

277

'Please!' Charlotte said firmly, 'I'd rather not know until I've made my choice. It could influence it; adversely.'

All the same, thought Jane, seven guineas!

'Oh, look!' It was her mother's glad cry and she was instantly alert.

A mannequin had emerged from behind the screens in a printed afternoon dress topped by an enormous black silk hat with a jaunty red ribbon tied in a bow. 'Jane, I have never seen anything so exquisite! Can you imagine wearing that in St Cuthbert's?'

Jane could. 'I think it would be better,' she said to the *vendeuse* in her correct schoolgirl French, 'If you were to show my mother those outfits more suited to her age.'

The woman was older than Charlotte. She gave an exquisite shrug. 'But we do, mademoiselle. This model is too elegant for your purpose.'

The approach to Darlington from the north was not inspiring. Mrs Macgregor gazed out on rolling mills and engineering works. She demanded of the taxi driver, 'McKie Brothers Emporium. D'you know where that it?'

'Yes, madam.'

'Did you hear that, Effie? It's big enough to be *known*.'

The cab trundled past the colonnade. Mrs Macgregor saw the windows: it was better than she'd dare hope. 'Oh my . . . Effie!' But Effie hung back when her mother addressed Mr Hart.

'Mr John McKie? This is Miss Euphemia Macgregor, Mr Matthew McKie's fiancée, and I am her mother.'

Of all the crises Mr Hart had had to face, this was the severest. He bowed.

'I am Mr McKie's deputy, madam. I regret to inform you Mr Matthew McKie is at college and the rest of the family are away at present.' He waited, noting the reactions carefully. The younger woman looked as if she would cut and run but the mother stood her ground.

'We will stay until Mr Matthew McKie is returned.'

'Certainly, madam.' Mr Hart sent a minion scurrying for Thomas Allen. When that reliable young man arrived, Mr Hart drew him aside and briefed him discreetly. 'Bring a couple of chairs and place them in the corner behind the coat rail.'

'Yes, Mr Hart.'

The deputy manager looked at the clock; another hour at least before Matthew would be here. 'Nip upstairs. Ask Emily Beal to bring them tea. And Mr Allen . . .'

'Sir?'

'It needn't be best Darjeeling.'

But Emily was shy; her place was in the kitchen. Fortunately Dorothy Creswell had called to thank her for the pikelets.

'I'll take it to them, Mr Allen. Who did you say they were?'

'A Mrs Macgregor and her daughter, miss. Friends of Mr Matthew, I believe.'

'How strange they should turn up unexpectedly.' Mr Allen kept his thoughts to himself and when Dorothy approached the corner, she thought she knew why. She couldn't decide what astonished her most: the dazzling gold of Miss Macgregor's hair, her scarlet lips or her blue eyelids. One thing was certain; these were not the sort of ladies one was 'at home' to, whatever the circumstance.

In the hotel room, Jane sat amid mounds of tissue paper. 'You've been exceedingly generous, Mama. I've never had *three* new hats in my life.'

'Neither have I. I think we should be extremely careful how we break the news to John.' They giggled like children, Charlotte at the dressing table in the coveted black silk with its jaunty bow.

'The trouble is,' said Jane, 'I believe we're doing this the wrong way round. We should go and find Theo first, *then* spend time in Paris.' She saw her mother's troubled face. 'I'm sure there's a straightforward reason why he hasn't written.'

Charlotte was unable to express her real fears. 'You'd prefer us to defer all the sight-seeing?'

'Yes I would. It would be much more fun if Theo were with us. Shall I go and enquire about trains?'

Luke closed Alex's eyes and led John into the other room. 'Stay here by the fire ... Hester promised to come and help. I'll ask Archie to go for her. Please, Father, don't be too sad.'

Ted waited until John had recovered slightly before handing him the slate. 'Grandfather obviously wanted you to know what was most important in his life,' he said, matter-of-factly, 'No-one could say if you'd be here in time so he wrote that this morning.' Through misted glasses John read J. . .O. . .H. . .

Ted kept his tone conversational. 'These past few days, we've been telling grandfather all about our plans. Luke's decided to try for a practice in a mining area — I'm certain grandfather was cock-a-hoop when he heard that. Archie and I are going to have a garage. Grandfather even guessed how keen Archie is on Jane. I'd say he was a happy man at the finish.'

In the depths of his sorrow John found joy; all the young recovered and ready to begin again. Ted was right; in a way it was a renewal of life, not simply an end.

As Archie strode across the turf his thoughts turned away from sadness, to Jane. Overhead the early evening sky was a soft deep blue. 'Hope the dear girl is enjoying herself; hope she doesn't fall for some damn Frenchie.'

Matthew dawdled on his way home; accountancy was fascinating. His imagination soared to new heights as dreams of a future when the Emporium would be one of a chain of stores seemed tangible.

Did he think of Effie in all this? Only occasionally. College had shown him new horizons but also confirmed certain misgivings; one step at a time, that was the way to succeed. He and Effie were secretly engaged; that was enough. He could visit her on business trips to Glasgow — a delicious prospect — but as for matrimony, that would have to wait.

He dallied until it was nearly seven o'clock. Mrs Beal was in the kitchen; 'You're to go to the office. Mr Hart's waiting for you.'

'I'm not making deliveries on that damn bike!'

'Language! Anyway, it's not to do with parcels.'

'Can I have something to eat?' Matthew switched on his most charming smile. 'I've been studying so hard, my brains are famished.'

'Nothing, that's what you'll get. Now, hop it.'

'When I'm a partner,' Matthew muttered savagely, 'I shall sack that silly old bat and her snively daughter. Everyone who's ever been rude to me in my life!'

Waiting had not improved Effie Macgregor. The dawn start after a sleepless night, the *maquillage* applied and reapplied and finally the delay. She'd had far too much time to think; the reality of her situation became horribly clear. She and her mother daren't return — they had very little money; it all depended on Matthew McKie.

Weary tears made runnels through eyeblack and powder. Effie's ankles were swollen in the tightly laced glacé shoes. She hadn't looked in her mirror but she knew she must look a sight.

Matthew flung open the office door. He saw Mr Hart sitting at John's desk and beyond him — Effie! She got to her feet and half staggered towards him. 'Oh, Matthew, don't send me away, please don't.' It was the opposite of what Mrs Macgregor would have advised but she held her tongue. Matthew stared in astonishment as Effie, weeping and forlorn pleaded with outstretched arms. Under the electric light, her hair glistened pure gold.

'Please . . . you're the only one there is!' It wasn't what she meant to say, it was the stark truth but Matthew understood it differently. Suddenly he was a man. No-one had ever needed him before. His face suffused with tenderness, 'Darling Effie . . .' All those wonderful plans for the future were forgotten; he was in love.

Mrs Beal offered sympathy. 'I don't think they should have been put in Mrs Armitage's old rooms.'

Katriona was tight-lipped. 'I warned Mrs Davie . . . I knew there was something fishy when those letters kept arriving — why can't they be sent straight back to Glasgow?'

'There's reasons why not, apparently. They're to stay here until Mr John or Mrs Davie gets back.'

Katriona almost laughed. 'If I were Matthew, I'd be on my knees for Mr John to be the one to get here first!'

'I've had another postcard from Ted.' Mrs Beal fetched it down from the mantelpiece. 'He says he and Archie are driving all the women mad up in Scotland and we're to be sure and tell Jane. He doesn't say how his grandad is or whether his uncle got there yet.'

Katriona examined it. 'This was sent before we had the telegram. Before we even knew those wretched females existed!' Exploding with anger, she grabbed her coat from the peg on the kitchen door. 'I need some fresh air. It's a disgrace having women like that under this roof!'

Mrs Beal listened to her footsteps. 'Let's hope it is Mr John as gets back ... I hate to think what it'd be like with Mrs Davie.'

Charlotte and Jane reached the address, that of the hospital where Theodore last worked, on a day which would have passed for summer in England. The building was austere and grey, part of a convent and staffed by nuns.

They waited in a small white-washed room with windows onto a garden. Jane was conscious of bees. In England it was too early for so many.

Charlotte sat upright. They'd come so far yet was she at the end of her journey? Her emotions were in turmoil; she wanted to tug open the neck of her blouse for the unaccustomed warmth stifled her. Instead she sat absolutely still, ankles crossed, hands in her lap, apparently passive.

An elderly nun entered and began to cross-examine Jane politely. Charlotte listened to the ebb and flow without understanding. When the nun looked in her direction, she flushed dull red. Suppose Theodore had married after the war? Was that why her letter had been returned? She was nothing but a silly middle-aged woman who'd come on a wild-goose chase. Jane was speaking to her.

'We've come to the right place ...' For some reason she looked at the nun rather than at her mother, 'Theodore was working here up to the time the Germans arrived. They took him away.'

Why is she telling me this, wondered Charlotte? We know what happened? The covering letter explained.

'After Theo had disappeared, his mother was taken ill ... The nuns cared for her here but she died during the influenza epidemic.' Jane hesitated and the nun asked a question.

'Yes, I'm coming to that, *ma soeur*. Theo was brought back after the Armistice.'

And suddenly, Charlotte knew.

'He's buried near his mother because the nuns thought that is what he would wish.'

Bees' humming and the scent of flowers filled the room. Charlotte remained upright in her chair. Neither Jane nor the nun dared speak.

'May I see the place?'

She walked stiffly because there was nothing left to hope for. They were led through the cloisters to a small walled cemetery where several small white crosses were set apart from the rest. When the nun explained, Jane translated.

'These were people who died as a result of the war. They've given Theo pride of place because he didn't leave his patients here even though he knew what might happen.' The nun had passed in front of one of the crosses.

'*La mère*?' Charlotte nodded that she'd understood. A couple of paces further but this time no words; the nun made the sign of the cross then left them. Jane waited. Her mother moved forward and leaned forward as if to read the inscription. How can she see through her veil, Jane wondered? The grave was surrounded by bushes full of pungent spring blossom. She could hear birds; it was difficult to imagine such a spot overrun by soldiers.

They'd been so innocently happy that wonderful evening in Darlington. She was going to be a great dancer, Theo was about to discover a way of taking away pain ... if only there were a palliative for the way Mama feels now, Theo dear!

Poor dear Mama! At least when I get back, Archie will be there ... and then, biting her lip, Jane wondered if she had the right to think so. A movement caught her eye. Her mother had picked up some of the blossom. She took a folded piece of paper from her bag and tucked the flowers inside; she was ready to leave.

Jane didn't follow immediately but went for a last look at the small white cross.

THEODORE KESSEL
1887–1918

Goodbye, Theo

Helen Shields had not been on many picnics and she certainly hadn't expected to enjoy this one. Sadness compounded her arthritis. It was an enormous effort to negotiate her stiff hip into the confined space of the passenger seat but after that, Ted had coaxed the battered 'bus further than she had been for years. At the summit of the moor, Archie spread their rugs.

Dreading what was to come, Helen concentrated on deep breaths until her pulse had quietened after the excitement of the drive. Beside her, Archie unpacked the wicker hamper. 'We might have forgotten one or two items.'

'Like cups?' said Ted flippantly.

'No, all present and correct. One tumbler, one without a handle and the yellow one that's a bit chipped.'

'I shall use the tumbler as a measure,' Ted warned. 'I don't trust the way you pour.'

'Oh, good. We *have* remembered the food. And the tin-opener. Here, Ted, I can't quite manage it. Let me pour the wine.'

'So. . . ?' Helen asked, unwilling to defer it any longer. 'Tell me about yesterday?'

'It was magnificent,' Archie said simply. 'The grandest sight I ever saw. Everyone came.'

'We had a proper wake the night before. No-one went to bed but I didn't feel tired.'

'Neither did I. People sat and talked, all the things they could remember. It was happy as well as sad because the old gentleman was so well-liked.'

'The first thing I'd like to do this afternoon, is to give you both a toast.' Ted handed Helen the tumbler. 'To a giant among men, to Alexander McKie.'

'Hear, hear!' cried Archie.

284

Oh dear, thought Helen, suddenly shaken, I don't think I can stand it after all. An enormous slab of bread landed on her knee.

'Have one of my sandwiches,' Ted said companionably. 'Hope you haven't got dentures. Chap lost his once when I'd been a bit generous with the cheese.'

Helen tucked her handkerchief away. 'My teeth are my own, thank you.'

'Good. Do drink up. There's claret to go with the next course. We took grandfather on wee George's cart over the old coffin route. We stopped once or twice for the women to sing to us.'

'I've never heard anything like it before,' Archie shook his head.

Helen nodded. 'Mouth music. It was new to me when I first came to the Highlands. A lament can be — evocative.'

'There was a chanter playing when we got to the churchyard.' Ted helped her to more wine. 'That was pretty marvellous, too. I think the Minister was scared. There were so many of us and we must've looked a pretty heathen lot.'

'We didn't take Mr McKie into the church either because we knew he regarded it as a mean-spirited place.'

Ted chuckled. 'He had his revenge on them yesterday, churches and ministers alike. I was near the fellow and could feel his quaking! Uncle John had insisted we have the service where everyone could see the handiwork of God so we hauled the cart on top of the mound. It looked pretty special too, because we'd decorated it with boughs of spruce and sea grass.'

'Silhouetted against the mountains and the sky, it was as though a warrior was being laid to rest,' Archie said quietly.

In her mind's eye Helen saw it. She thought she understood; not a hidebound ceremony but a pagan return of a spirit to the earth from which it had sprung.

'How did the Minister react? I hear he has a degree from Edinburgh University. Second class.'

'He managed,' Ted grinned, 'and we got down to the real business after he'd finished. So many wanted to say their piece. Archie and I couldn't understand half of it of course, but uncle John did and it meant such a lot to him. Hester Hamilton told me one chap praised grandfather for taking more salmon out of the river than any ghillie. I did feel proud!'

'What a good thing the Minister doesn't understand Gaelic!' Helen didn't notice that her tumbler had been refilled.

'There was more greenery in the grave and each of us held a white cord; Uncle and Luke, wee Georgie Hamilton and myself. It should have been Matthew but he couldn't get here in time.'

Helen said, with unexpected vehemence, 'I'm glad he did not!'

Ted decided to ignore that. 'There was a wonderful skirl of the pipes at the finish, not mournful at all, like a march. And then we all went home,' he finished lamely. 'Don't know about you, Archie, I thought it all went splendidly?'

'A most triumphant exit.'

I must remember that for these two, death has been such an everyday occurrence. Helen drained her tumbler and held it out. The sun felt warm on the back of her neck.

'And John wasn't too upset?'

'What helped,' Archie explained, 'was that Luke had managed to make his grandfather understand the sort of medicine he intends to practise.'

'Ah!'

'Knew you'd be pleased,' Ted said happily. 'Said to Archie, mustn't forget to tell the old girl — Oh lor! Have some more claret.'

Helen's hat slid ever so slightly over one eye. She pushed it to the back of her head. 'You have a dreadful way of expressing yourself, Ted McKie.'

'Haven't I just? Have a piece of gingerbread?'

We've managed it, thought Archie as they slithered and bounced back across the heather. She's heard all about it and she doesn't feel sad any more. In fact, she's feeling very cheerful! They hit a stone which jarred every tooth in his head. Helen Shields gave a merry laugh.

Bottles crashed and Archie clung on with his remaining hand. 'Tally-ho!' cried Ted. 'Tally-ho,' echoed Archie. Provided they didn't break their necks, all Miss Shields would suffer tomorrow would be a sore hip and a headache.

CHAPTER NINETEEN

'Not fourteen annas to the rupee'

'Dorothy? It *is* you, isn't it?' An unseasonal north-east gale made Dorothy's eyes water. She was anxious to catch her tram but when she saw who it was, she gave her friendliest smile.

'Ted! How are you?'

'All the better for seeing you. Did you know your nose is bright red — and would you feel compromised if I suggested a cup of tea?'

'How dare you — and yes, please!'

'Pity the Salon doesn't exist any more. I could have flaunted you in front of Darlington society.'

'No you couldn't because I would have refused,' Dorothy said firmly. 'Where are you taking me anyway?'

'In here. They do a luscious repast and there's room under the tables for a chap's legs.' Ted led the way into a cafe near the market. 'Pot of tea for two, masses of toasted tea-cake and a selection of cream buns, please.'

'Not for me —'

'No, for me. I'm starving. How's the typewriting business?'

'I have two certificates of competency,' Dorothy said primly. 'I exhibit them at interviews. Actually I've been offered two jobs which is extremely flattering for a beginner.'

'Are you going to type love letters for Rudolph Valentino?'

'In Darlington? I shall be in a typing pool with six other girls,' Dorothy said severely, 'and I'm a business woman,

Ted McKie, not a floozy.'

'Glad to hear it,' Ted said comfortably. 'Have you found somewhere to live?'

'I was on my way to see Dr Cullen. He knows of a possible place in St John's Crescent. When did you get back?'

'About an hour ago. Dropped Archie off at Gainsford — Ah . . . here we are. All those cakes are for the young lady but you can bring me a plate of biscuits, if you'd be so kind.'

'Ted!'

'My, your nose has gone pink this time —'

'Ted McKie, *will* you behave!' She'd subdued him but only temporarily. He felt amazingly cheerful sitting at a table with Dorothy Creswell.

'Can I have just one of those cream buns?' he asked penitently, 'I really am extremely hungry. All that motoring, doncha know.' They chatted about his various exploits. 'Uncle John and Luke are staying for a few more days. They haven't had much time together since Luke got back and there's lots of clearing up to do. It seemed like a good opportunity.'

'I was awfully sorry to hear about your grandfather, and from Jane in Paris. What a sad shock for your Mama.'

Ted nodded. 'Rotten luck. Because of Luke we were all convinced Theo must be recovering somewhere.'

'Have you met Mrs Macgregor or her daughter yet?' Dorothy asked carefully.

'You're the fourth person who's asked me that today.' Ted bit cheerfully into an éclair. 'The answer is "no" but I've never been more intrigued. Fancy young Matthew having a lady-friend!'

'I met them when they arrived. And I work in the stock-room on Saturdays. That's a splendid place for gossip!'

'Oh lord, so you do. I'd forgotten.'

'Mr Allen regales me with the latest happenings.'

'Who's Mr Allen when he's at home?'

Dorothy said sweetly, 'Did you know you've a blob of cream on your tie? Heavens, I shall be late.'

'You're not going!'

'Dr Cullen is expecting me — and Mr Allen is a dear,

by the way. I shall be interested in your opinion of the Macgregors. Thanks for giving me tea.'

Ted strolled back to the Emporium deep in thought. As soon as he'd arrived, Mr Hart had sought him out and apologized for offering accommodation to the Macgregors. 'It was at Mr Matthew's insistence, Mr Ted. I hope I did what was right.'

'Don't see you had much option, under the circs.'

'Thank you.' Mr Hart was growing daily more anxious. 'I fear Mrs Davie may not see the matter in the same light.'

'Where are the ladies now?'

'They visit the picture palace most afternoons. In the evening, they and Mr Matthew usually go dancing at Miss Betts or the Queen's Hall.'

'What a gay social whirl.'

Katriona added another interesting fact. 'They drink. Mrs Macgregor tried to hide the bottles under the bed but Emily found them.'

There was very little which could remain hidden in the Emporium. 'Think I'll give Archie a tinkle,' Ted decided as he walked in through the yard. 'He might fancy popping over for supper. I'd like his support when I meet these two.'

Archie was delighted to accept. 'Any chance of me moving back in for a couple of nights?'

'That didn't last long,' Ted laughed, 'What's your father complaining of this time?'

'Told him about our plans for the garage. Not a suitable profession for a gentleman, apparently.'

'Oh, lord!'

'Not to worry, he can't interfere. But I'll bring my pyjamas if it's all the same to you. Tomorrow I shall look for a couple of rooms to rent. How's the redoubtable Katriona?'

'Suffering from a surfeit of lowlanders. She'll be glad to welcome you back. See you later, old chap.'

Ted was with Mrs Beal when Effie took her tray back to the kitchen. She and her mother had fallen into the habit of eating alone rather than confront Katriona in the dining-room.

At the beginning, Mrs Macgregor tried to persuade her daughter into new ways, rising each morning to eat breakfast but after more than a week cooped up in Mrs Armitage's rooms, Effie had fallen back into her usual routine. She stayed in bed until noon and on days when there was no change of cinema programme, didn't bother to dress until evening in time for Matthew's return. She was in *deshabillé* now as she entered the kitchen. Seeing Ted, she stopped in alarm.

'Oh . . !'

'How d'you do. You must be Miss Macgregor. I'm Ted McKie.'

'Effie . . . Please call me Effie.' It was automatic, as was the smile and the tweak at her hair. Effie wished she'd remembered to comb it and pulled her wrap together coyly. 'I didn't know anyone had arrived.'

'Only me at present,' Ted said cheerfully, 'the rest of the battalion should be here by the end of the week, not forgetting Mama and Jane.' It sounded like the massed hordes of a clan.

Miss Macgregor went a little pale. 'Mother and I are most grateful,' she began weakly.

Ted nodded understandingly. 'I gather you needed a roof and thought of Matthew,' he said blandly.

Miss Macgregor opened her mouth to say there was more to it than that but shut it again quickly. 'Please tell Matthew I'm in my room when he returns,' she said and left.

After a pause, Mrs Beal said, 'There you are then.'

'There we are indeed.'

Matthew raced up the stairs to wash and change. He'd promised Effie he wouldn't be late because they were due to go dancing. The passage was littered with trunks and bags. He could hear laughter and knocked at Ted's door. The room was thick with smoke from Archie's pipe. 'Hallo, young 'un,' Ted called genially. 'How's the budding businessman?'

'I didn't know you were back. Is Uncle John downstairs?'

'He and Luke should be here by Friday.'

291

'Oh, I see.' Matthew attempted nonchalance; it was an answer to one worry. Charlotte hadn't yet sent word when she would return.

'I met your lady friend by the way,' Ted said casually, 'We had a little chat. Rather — mature, I thought.'

'She's twenty-three!' Matthew shouted and his brother grinned.

Jane and Charlotte went back to Paris. Charlotte needed time to recover. 'You don't mind?' she asked hesitantly.

'Of course not.' It was unusual for Mama to be so considerate, but then it was a strange situation.

They went for walks but as her mother's melancholy lessened Jane grew daily more impatient to return. There was nothing more to be done here. Despite its pleasures, Paris was a way of marking time. Ted and Luke knew what they wanted; Jane did as well. Spring was over and she was anxious to begin.

'You've made up your mind?' Charlotte asked one morning over breakfast.

'I want to be independent. Typewriting would make that possible.'

'I need to be independent too,' said Charlotte. Jane was puzzled. 'I can't return to the Emporium after what's happened. It's not simply the pity . . it's the thought of the future as well.' Charlotte straightened her back. 'When we came here, I imagined I might remarry, Jane.'

'Yes.'

'Those same years lie ahead; years of widowhood, in England not in France. I don't intend to be a burden to you or Ted nor do I want to spend them in Darlington.'

'Where will you go?' Jane was bewildered; they'd always lived in Darlington.

'I'm undecided. I'll discuss it with your uncle when I return.' She caught sight of Jane's face. 'You want that to be soon?'

'Yes, please!'

As they packed, Jane said tentatively, 'When I'm qualified, I'd like to leave the Emporium and live on my own. Would you object?' It was a daring request.

'Aunt Armitage would never have dreamed of allowing me the same freedom.'

'Times change, Mama.'

Watching young French women walk arm in arm along the pavement without a chaperone in sight, Charlotte was forced to agree.

Ted and Archie leaned on the balcony rail and watched dancers perambulate below. 'There goes the waiter again, over to their table,' Archie observed. 'The mother has a powerful thirst. Must be quite a strain on your brother's finances.'

'But what a dainty way Mrs Macgregor has with her little finger.'

'Quite a glow, too,' Archie said solemnly, 'especially in the region of the proboscis.'

'Port emerging through the pores?'

'Very likely,' Archie agreed.

'Know what the daughter reminds me of? One of those *demoiselles* from la Maison Toleree!'

''Fraid so, old chap. I'd say those two ladies ain't exactly fourteen annas to the rupee.'

CHAPTER TWENTY

A Perfect Match

Effie always dressed with care before visiting the kitchen nowadays. On this particular morning there was a stranger, tall and attractively haggard with dark hair in need of a trim. She gave her most winsome smile. Mrs Beal introduced them reluctantly.

'This is Miss Macgregor, Luke. Mr Luke McKie.'

'Effie.' She smiled again. Luke's remote air was irresistible.

'Your tray's ready,' snapped Mrs Beal, but Effie was not in any hurry.

'Matthew's talked so much about you, Luke.' Matthew hadn't said a word about how handsome he was!

Mrs Beal was indignant at the familiarity. 'Your food's getting cold.' Effie waited for Luke to hold open the door. When she'd disappeared, he said, 'What a dreadful creature. Where on earth did Matthew find her?'

'You haven't seen the mother! I'm that thankful your father's back.' The weight slid from Mrs Beal's shoulders.

'Dr Cullen's invited me to use his spare room. He thought I'd find it easier to study in St John's Crescent. I'd say he was right! Can I come back here to eat? I think Father might need a bit of support.'

'Bless you, of course you can!'

Luke hugged her suddenly. 'You know, much as I love the croft, I always feel I'm home, once I've set eyes on you.'

'Eee, pet, not much of a welcome this time. Never mind, your father'll get rid of 'em.'

In the office, Mr Hart had nearly finished his tale. 'There is one other matter although I am loath to add to your problems, Mr McKie.'

'I would prefer to know the full extent of them.'

'Mrs Macgregor has selected various items in Ladies' Mantles. I ordered Miss Attewood to withhold the garments and prepare a bill. I trust that meets with your approval?'

'Definitely.' The deputy manager was relieved. 'We've known each other for many years, Mr Hart. I am most grateful for your support on this occasion.'

'H'as to that, Mr McKie, I regard this establishment with as much pride as you yourself, I believe.' And he withdrew, majestically.

John sat in his office, alone. Oddly enough, he wasn't particularly disturbed. He'd recovered from the initial surprise that Matthew had invited two unknown ladies to stay and mulled over Mr Hart's phrase that neither was 'quite *comme il faut*, Mr McKie'.

John had listened attentively to the catalogue of misdemeanours but knew that in the hothouse atmosphere of the Emporium, little upsets often grew out of all proportion. He was more preoccupied with another conversation, heard on the croft. Listening to Luke, Ted and Archie chatting about their plans, it became obvious that all three would soon need capital.

John was determined Ted would match Archie pound for pound in the garage enterprise; in his experience, joint responsibility enabled a partnership to flourish. As for Matthew and Jane, he would give them the same amount because he always had. And Luke, when the time came, must have his share to buy into a practice. All this would require a great deal of money. Charlotte's plans were as yet unknown.

'But what do *I* want?'

Good lord, John thought surprised, I haven't asked myself that for years. And back came the answer, 'I'm blessed if I want to continue working here for Matthew's sake.' It brought him up with a jolt. Was that all it amounted to these days? Had the Emporium become nothing but a burden?

Any final decision must be deferred, but the options could be considered. John brooded and began to jot down figures. The account that Mr Hart had referred to lay on the desk top. His eyes focussed on it and the name Macgregor; these two unknown women from Glasgow. (Mr Hart had not thought it prudent to mention the word 'fiancée'). It occurred to John that Matthew had never invited friends home before. When he'd asked Hart why they weren't staying in an hotel, his manager had become a little vague. Certainly one of them had gone too far, expecting credit. Hart would deal with that. John saw his problem as merely establishing the duration of the visit. He sent word that Matthew should come and see him on his return from college when Katriona arrived with his tea.

The message filled Matthew with excitement; at last! He was nervous but not unduly so. He'd rehearsed the forthcoming scene until he was word-perfect.

He toyed with the idea of visiting Effie first. Her encouragement would bolster his confidence but there was also Mrs Macgregor. By early evening she'd sometimes consumed more than was wise. Effie denied it half-heartedly but, once the bottles were discovered, claimed her mother did it simply out of boredom.

Matthew had forbidden alcohol this evening. He'd impressed on Effie how essential it was all three of them make a good impression. He was confident she'd understood.

Feeling better, he washed and changed. Supper was at seven which gave him just enough time to announce his engagement to John. And after supper? He'd take Effie to the Palais de Dance for a celebration! The thought of holding her in his arms made Matthew's heart sing!

Luke, struggling with books and a suitcase, surprised him in the passage. 'Hello? You coming or going?'

'Both,' Luke replied, 'Moving in with Dr Cullen for a while.'

'Oh here, let me help.' Matthew seized the suitcase, eager to speed him on his way. Effie had praised Luke far too often for his liking. Luke dashed his hopes.

'I shall be here for meals. I need peace and quiet for study and I gather that commodity is in short supply nowadays.' Matthew dropped the case and walked away.

'Hello, Uncle. Welcome home.' Matthew's smile stayed in place even though Katriona was there.

John nodded. He was much more grave. With the tea had come explicit details of the Macgregors' behaviour as well as a telegram from Charlotte. John continued his conversation with Katriona. 'According to this, Charlotte and Jane arrive back tomorrow at six. I shall be at the station to meet them.'

'I'll see that everything's ready, Mr John.'

'Thank you.'

Matthew listened; so Mama was on her way home. Good. He waited until Katriona had gone then braced herself. John forestalled him with the bill.

'These friends you've provided accommodation for, Matthew. Please explain to them that we do not allow credit unless references have been taken up, particularly with strangers.' Matthew opened his mouth then shut it again, completely baffled. John had him at a disadvantage. 'I do not recall you mentioning them before? Whoever they are, they've caused a great many upsets. Presumably you offered the rooms as a temporary arrangement and are in the process of booking an hotel?'

'I . . . er . . .' Again Matthew foundered.

'I realize it must have been an emergency although I find it reprehensible that you should do such a thing without informing either your mother or I —'

'We're engaged.'

'I beg your pardon?'

All the fine words he had rehearsed, disappeared. Matthew stuttered, red-faced, as John continued to stare. 'I met Miss Macgregor in Glasgow. We became engaged.'

'After one afternoon? You are referring to that visit, I take it? You haven't been back since?' Matthew didn't reply. 'You cannot be "engaged" to anyone, Matthew,' John said reasonably. 'That would indicate some form of betrothal.'

'We met on a river-boat steamer . . . Effie was with her mother, it was perfectly respectable!' Matthew was close to

297

tears in his frustration. 'She's beautiful . . . I love her! She loves me!' he shouted.

John shook his head at the pathetic phrases. He tried to let the boy down lightly. 'Matthew . . . There can be no possible question of an "engagement" —'

'I've asked Effie to marry me!'

'You are under-age.'

'I've bought her a ring!'

John's countenance changed. 'Then you have been extremely foolish,' he said, coldly. In the distance they could hear the gong. John rose. 'I will speak to Mrs Macgregor privately later. As soon as supper is over you will go to your room and stay there until I send for you. That is an order, Matthew.' There was grim authority this time. Matthew opened his mouth to protest but no words came. He flung out of the room. John stood for a moment, baffled and angry. He found he was still holding the bill and stared again at the neatly written name: Mrs Macgregor.

Effie's nerves weren't strong enough to withstand neglect. She and Matthew had discussed the coming interview with John many times. Her lover had boasted how simple it would be but Effie wasn't convinced; she wanted to be sure Matthew knew what to say.

Away from the familiarity of Glasgow, her confidence had waned. It was restored a little by the warmth of Matthew's passion but Effie had never had such a young, inexperienced lover and his naive boasting added to her uncertainty. How could he be so certain of his uncle's approbation? The instructions concerning her behaviour this morning had been those of a nervous boy rather than a confident heir, adding to her doubts.

Inside her comfortable prison Effie exhausted herself, filling in the time until Matthew came. She'd spent the afternoon trying on dresses. Once discarded they were hurled aside. She'd done and redone her face, her hair, her nails — where was he?

When he finally stood before her she lost all control. His face told her what had happened. 'Why didn't you come here first!' It was a frenzied scream and Matthew stepped back.

'Hen!' warned Mrs Macgregor but Effie was too worked up.

'You *promised* me you'd come to me first.'

'Effie, please!' He hadn't seen her like this and it frightened him. 'Pull yourself together. I have to introduce you to Uncle —'

'What did you say to him? Was it all right?' Feverish anxiety consumed her. 'If only you'd discussed it with me!'

There were beads of sweat under the powder. Why did she insist on using paint when it made her look old? Matthew felt so tender and protective, it hurt him to see her made ugly. 'Please, Effie, wash your face and come to supper. I'm not supposed to be here — Uncle's waiting to meet you.'

'Wash! My precious spent hours making herself look beautiful —'

'Look, we must go down,' he begged.

'What happened?' Effie clutched his arm, 'What did you say to him?'

'Effie, it's gone seven o'clock.' As he hustled them into the passage, she cried desperately, 'What did he say?'

'He said I was under-age and wanted to know about some damn bill for clothes!'

The shouting was audible from the dining room. John and Luke stood on either side of the fireplace. Katriona, arms folded, waited to serve the soup. They could hear Matthew's high-pitched indignation as the door burst open and for the first time, John saw how matters stood.

Mrs Macgregor had planned to be extremely gracious but she'd fallen back on her usual remedy. It came as a surprise to find herself in a chair with a plate in front of her.

'As I was saying, Mr McKie, my daughter Effie — her mother's most precious jewel incidentally — opened her heart. She confided how deeply in love she was ... with Matthew.' Mrs Macgregor found herself staring at Luke and wondered if maybe Effie had been a mite hasty? She discovered her mouth was open too, adjusted it and returned to her theme. 'Although Matthew is young,

299

I gave their engagement my blessing. You do understand?' John passed the bread to Luke. 'This is why we came to Darlington, Mr McKie,' her voice rose in an effort to make him understand.

John asked mildly, 'May I ask what your immediate plans are, Mrs Macgregor?'

She'd never guessed it would be so easy. 'I have no intention of returning to Glasgow. I shall stay with Effie and Matthew once they are married . . .' Mrs Macgregor remembered Matthew had not yet heard of this and reached for his hand but encountered the water jug instead. 'Jesus, how did that get there?'

'Ma!'

Luke was already on his feet. Emily Beal came in with a cloth and Katriona collected the soup plates.

Mrs Macgregor tried again. 'Where was I. . . ?' It was annoying that Mr McKie would make no comment at all. He and his son sat at the end of the table in black ties and armbands like the undertaker's men. Of course! Mrs Macgregor had been remiss. She rushed to make amends.

'What a dreadfully sad time you must've had in Scotland, Mr McKie. Matthew told us you and Luke were attending your father's obsequies.'

'That is so,' murmured Luke.

'The poor old gentleman! And what was Matthew's share of the Will?' Mrs Macgregor had taken a genteel mouthful of pigeon pie but the clatter of Luke's fork made her choke.

'I think you must have misunderstood, madam,' John said quietly. 'My father was a crofter.'

Completely undeterred, Mrs Macgregor asked between coughs, 'But there must have been some property to divide between the family?'

John put down his napkin. 'Would you excuse me?' and left the room.

Mrs Macgregor was sympathetic. 'Dear me, I'd no idea he'd still feel like that. What a sensitive man your uncle is, Matthew.'

The following day as he waited on Darlington station platform, John thought sadly of the letter he'd received that

300

morning from Jane. So Charlotte's chance of happiness had disappeared after all. When he'd first met her all those years ago, he hadn't noticed Charlotte's beauty, only her chin. Well . . . she'd needed that chin, never more so than today.

The train stopped and the porter opened the carriage door. John offered her his arm.

'Dear John, how very kind of you.' The hand was steady, the gaze didn't falter, above all the chin was up. Charlotte McKie would not exhibit weakness in public.

'Welcome home, Charlotte. What an elegant hat!'

'Yes . . . and I've several more besides.' It was bravely said.

'Jane!' She appeared sophisticated but the next moment it was the girl he remembered hugging him between kisses, whispering, 'I'm so sorry about grandfather! Ted wrote and told me.'

'Don't be, my dear. It was a good end, surrounded by those he loved. Now, tell me, will one trolley be enough or should I engage a second — and how many cabs?'

They chided him and tried to belittle the mound of hat boxes. 'One couldn't possibly visit Paris without making one or two purchases,' Charlotte protested.

'Of course not. I have a surprise. Once your luggage has been despatched, we have been invited out to tea before returning to the Emporium. I hope you're not tired because I've already accepted on your behalf.'

'It sounds intriguing.'

'Then let the mystery continue!' John twirled an imaginary moustache and cane. 'Come, let there be two cabs, porter. Luggage to the Emporium, the other to St John's Crescent.'

'Oh, it's Dr Cullen,' said Charlotte, satisfied.

But they drove past the surgery and saw Dorothy Creswell at an open front door. 'Jane! Welcome to my new abode.'

'Goodness!'

'Mrs Davie, I'm so glad to see you. Won't you come in?'

When pleasantries had been exchanged and the tea brewed, John explained, 'Miss Creswell was kind enough to offer assistance in our predicament. A temporary refuge where we can discuss what is to be done.'

301

'Rather!' Dorothy cried from behind the teapot. 'It's all hands to the pump, to rescue the sinking ship.'

'What — ship?'

'The Emporium, Charlotte.'

Matthew's attention wavered in class. Last night the dance hall had brought a temporary respite: ecstasy in Effie's arms. And she had shared his passion as never before, wrapping her arms around him and begging him never to leave her — as if he could! That happiness had soon been blighted, however. Once home, Mrs Macgregor talked of nothing but her need for new gowns.

'You can pay for the bill for me surely, Matthew? I want to look my best when I meet your mother. Just a wee few dresses? A present for Effie's old mammy?'

'Use your own money,' he said petulantly.

'We haven't any,' Effie replied flatly.

'What?'

'We've nothing left. We're penniless.' She was exhausted after the tensions of the day. 'Look, why not make me a proper allowance, Matthew? It would save all this arguing.'

'Yes, then Effie and I will know exactly how much we have to spend.' The beauty of that idea appealed to Mrs Macgregor immediately.

They were in the parlour where nightly he was permitted a few chaste kisses, in Mrs Macgregor's presence. He was appalled to learn of their poverty. He'd laughed when Effie told him of selling the furniture, thinking it a clever trick. It never occurred to Matthew that that was all the money they had.

Who would provide for Mrs Macgregor in future?

As the truth slowly dawned he gazed about in despair at the slovenly state of the room. 'I think you should tidy this place at least, before Mama arrives.'

'Oh? And do we have to pass some examination before we're fit enough to meet your precious mother?'

'Careful, Effie!' Annoyed though she was, Mrs Macgregor was cautious. 'We know how excited Matthew must be — and we want to make a good impression. Maybe this place could do with a clean? Would you arrange it with the servants please, Matthew?'

'The *servants* won't set foot in here. I advise you to see to it yourselves. Goodnight, Effie.' As the door slammed, Mrs Macgregor was full of chagrin; Matthew had escaped without settling the matter of her gowns.

In Dorothy's lodging, she and Jane went upstairs to view the other half of her 'abode'. It was a comfortable bedroom with a chair and wardrobe from Haughton Green. 'That's all I brought with me, that and my clothes. The rest has gone under the hammer. Maybe someday I'll benefit from the proceeds — unless father leaves everything to the missionaries!'

Jane shook her head in admiration. 'You've got guts, Dorothy. I couldn't have coped.'

'Yes, you would. It's amazing how one can learn to when necessary. Your Mama is a remarkable example.'

'Yes . . . She bottles it up inside but she wouldn't dream of letting it show.'

'Here . . . Ted sent me a birthday card.'

'I'm sorry, I forgot the date!'

'It doesn't matter. Besides, I'm far too old for such nonsense.' But for some reason, Dorothy looked extremely pleased and continued to hold onto the card, 'Isn't it comical?'

'Motor cars?' Jane asked.

'Hadn't you heard? He and Mr Cavendish have found a piece of land for their new garage.'

'So they *are* going ahead with the idea?'

'Rather! Isn't it marvellous?'

Archie Cavendish would be living in Darlington! Jane realized with surprise how the weather had also improved lately.

'I wonder . . . I know it sounds frightful cheek but I wonder if Ted and he will need a typewriting assistant? When the business is established?' Dorothy looked at her seriously, 'Mr Cavendish would be such a dear to work for, d'you think I'd have a chance?'

303

Jane saw too that Dorothy had regained her looks as well as her independence. 'I'm sure you would,' she said gallantly. She even managed an encouraging smile.

Downstairs, in Dorothy's sitting-room, John listened as Charlotte insisted, 'Matthew is under-age and I shall refuse permission.'

'Unfortunately he has bought the woman a ring and expressed his intentions in various letters. Mrs Macgregor has spoken of having that correspondence under lock and key.'

'What a monstrous way to behave!'

'In law, Matthew may be deemed to have made a contractual engagement.'

'In law?'

'Mrs Macgregor has, I fear, every intention of profiting by it if we try and prevent the marriage.'

Charlotte jerked upright. 'That cannot be allowed to happen.'

'And I have to tell you I see no way of preventing it because Matthew is so determined. He comes of age next year, as I'm sure the Macgregors know. It's Morton's Fork, Charlotte and you and I can do nothing about it.' Charlotte stared.

'As bad as that?'

'I'm so sorry . . . especially after your own tragic disappointment.' She brushed aside any reference to Theodore Kessel.

'Not now, John. Some other time.' Personal sorrow would have to wait.

'I'm afraid I have to press you on one matter: have you considered your own future lately?'

Charlotte asked slowly. 'Does that mean you have a plan?'

'An idea, certainly. Before we discuss it, I would like to know your wishes. If it is too soon to ask, then I will wait.'

'I've already told Jane . . . When I realized the emptiness that lay ahead, I decided I wanted a complete change.' Charlotte reached for his hand, 'It may seem like desertion but I want to leave Darlington, John.'

304

To her amazement, he said simply, 'I'm so glad. Because if you agree, I think we should sell the Emporium.'

In the taxi, John told them, 'Mrs Macgregor and her daughter usually remain in their rooms apart from visits to hairdressers or the picture palace. I imagine we shall not encounter them until supper-time.'

'I want to see Matthew the minute he returns.'

'Yes, Charlotte.'

'And I'd like you to be there, John.'

Nothing but storm clouds ahead, thought Jane. I am glad Ted's home.

'Mama?'

'Goodness Jane, you made me jump!'

'Can I invite Dorothy this evening? To keep me company?'

'An excellent idea,' said John, 'and I think we might include Dr Cullen if he's free? He might prove a match for Mrs Macgregor!' They managed faint smiles. As they reached the colonnade, John remembered. 'By the way, Archie Cavendish has moved back in temporarily. His father's being difficult over something or other. It's cheered us all, having him here.' Judging by the way Jane blushed, she wasn't unhappy either. She disappeared upstairs in search of Katriona.

'That's better!' Katriona held her at arms' length. 'That's the start of an improvement. Keep it up.'

'I don't know what you mean!'

'Of course you do, my pet. You'd let yourself go. That's a nice new hairstyle — how are your hands?' Katriona shook her head over the rough skin. 'Still nurse's hands. We'll use glycerine and lemon every night. How's your mother?'

'Bearing up wonderfully.'

'Then please God, may it continue! These — Macgregors!' It became a term of abuse the way she uttered it.

'Dorothy's coming to supper and Dr Cullen if he can.'

Katriona looked at her narrowly. 'Luke's staying with the doctor but he usually has his meals here.'

'Good,' Jane replied evenly, though her colour increased.

'Just thought I'd better warn you.' She followed Jane into her room. 'There's one more thing and then I won't speak of it any more. Luke came to see me as soon as he got back, worried sick about you, as well he might be. I told him you were all right. He hadn't written because he was scared your mother might want to read the letter.'

'I understand. That was decent of him.'

'He still got the backside of my tongue,' Katriona announced cheerfully.

'It was mostly my fault —'

'Aye, well. You were both stupid — and damn lucky. Now, did you know Mr Cavendish was staying here?'

Jane was fiery red. 'I don't see what that has to do with anything!'

'Oh, for pity's sake — do you want some other girl to snap him up?'

Jane thought of Dorothy Creswell. 'If she loves him, why not?' she said heroically.

Katriona exploded, 'Sometimes I could shake you, Jane McKie!'

Charlotte searched for a certain gown in her wardrobe but couldn't find it. When Katriona called that her bath was ready, she decided there were more important matters and chose a sober, plainer one instead. She must hurry. Matthew would soon be home and waiting for her in John's office. However unpleasant, it was an interview that couldn't be avoided.

'I don't remember you trying that on yesterday.' Effie blew on her nails to dry them. 'It suits you though.'

'It's my colour, isn't it?' Mrs Macgregor preened herself in front of the mirror.

'How did you get the old skinflint to let you have it?' Effie asked the question again because her mother hadn't heard.

'Oh, I managed,' Mrs Macgregor answered evasively, 'Have you decided what you're going to wear tonight?'

'This . . .' Effie slipped off her wrap and turned round to demonstrate the full effect.

'Oh, my! That'll make them sit up, that's really sophisticated! But it's awfu' short, Effie, is it meant to be like that?
I can see the darn in your stocking.'

Her daughter swore. 'Lend me a pair.'

'I cannot. I'm down to lisle myself, my silk are beyond
redemption. Wear your green beads, eh? They won't notice
the darn if you have those on.'

She never makes any attempt to kiss me, thought Matthew,
it's always I who have to go to her. Well, this time I won't.
'Good evening, Mama.' He smiled charmingly but the blue
eyes were opaque.

'I won't pretend I'm glad to see you, Matthew, not after
what I've been told.'

'You never were "glad", Mama, let's have an end of
pretence!' Excitement made him feverish. This time, she
would dance to his tune.

Charlotte recoiled at the vehemence. 'No, I've never
cared for you in the same way I have for Ted and Jane,' she
admitted, 'I tried, Matthew but I don't believe it's possible to
love you all equally. You were never as open with me as the
other two were . . . However that is not what we are here to
discuss. This so-called engagement —'

'It's not so-called! I am going to marry Effie Macgregor!'
Careful, careful, he could feel the familiar panic begin and
tightened his grip on the gold in his pocket. 'Unlike you,
Effie *does* love me.'

'And if I refuse permission?'

Matthew's eyes glittered; he'd been waiting for this.
'I shall tell everyone what you've been up to in France.
Chasing after a dead lover! I shall tell people it's your
own disappointment that makes you want to interfere with
my happiness. And if anyone says again that Effie is older
than me — I shall make sure they know how much *younger*
Theodore Kessel was than you! Seven years!'

Spittle spurted like pus from a wound. John cried
out but Charlotte raised a hand that he shouldn't interfere.

'Is that the best you can manage, Matthew? A feeble
attempt at exposure? Tell me, how much *older* is this Miss

307

Macgregor? I never sought to hide the difference between Mr Kessel and myself.'

Matthew was shaking and nervous. In his imagination Charlotte should have wept and begged forgiveness. Instead she was waiting, scornfully, for an answer. 'Effie's twenty-three,' he whispered.

'Nonsense!' John cried, 'the woman's at least twenty-six.'

Charlotte saw her son cringe and part of her was full of sorrow. 'Are you certain of your feelings? Do you love her, Matthew?'

'Yes!'

'Then I shall do nothing to prevent your marriage. Love might transform you into a decent human being.'

Jane and Dorothy were in the dining-room, conversing as though neither had a care in the world while each wondered what was in the other's mind. Will Ted notice me, Dorothy thought in anguish, and if he does, will it mean anything? I mustn't forget I'm as poor as the proverbial church mouse and no great catch for anyone!

Can I bear it if Archie likes her more than me? Jane wondered. Dorothy's my best friend! It will be terrible but it's my own fault; I should never have chased after Luke.

The door opened and Matthew walked in, followed by two women. He had what Jane thought of as his glittery look.

'This is my sister Jane and her friend, Miss Creswell. May I introduce my fiancée, Miss Macgregor.'

Effie saw two girls with pale serious faces, one dark, the other fair, their hair unfashionably long, wearing plain, high-necked dresses. Such frumps!

'Don't be so formal, dearest. Your sister must call me Effie,' she gushed. This was going to be easy!

From behind, her mother cooed, 'Why if it isn't the shy lassie who brought us tea when we first arrived, D'you remember, Effie?'

Dorothy Creswell caught the full force of the brandy-laden breath. 'Good evening. I hope you are enjoying your stay in Darlington?' She was resolutely polite.

Jane was slower to recover. 'How d'you do, Miss Macgregor.'

'Effie, please! And I shall call you Jane.' Mrs Macgregor was satisfied. By comparison with these two, Effie was dazzling. If Mrs Davie McKie were as dull as her daughter, why worry?

'There aren't many easy chairs in this room, Matthew.' Mrs Macgregor looked at them critically. 'I hadn't noticed before but you really could do with new furniture in here.' She moved over to the table. 'I think Effie should sit nearer the fire tonight. That gorgeous new dress — such pretty georgette, isn't it, Miss Creswell? We know this wee dressmaker in Glasgow, charges practically nothing —'

'I shouldn't sit there,' Jane said quickly, 'That's my mother's chair.'

'Dear me, what a fuss!' Mrs Macgregor gave an angry smile. 'Not very polite, if I may say so? Where did you get your dress, Jane?'

For one wild moment, Jane considered tearing it off and thrusting it into her hand. 'I can't remember,' she muttered. 'It's years old.'

'Yes, I can see that.' Mrs Macgregor put her head on one side. 'You know if you took an interest, you could make something of yourself. Be more modern, like my Effie.'

'Heaven forfend!' breathed Dorothy in her ear.

'Did you speak, Miss Creswell?' Dorothy's mouth remained tightly shut.

'Have you a cigarette, dearest?'

Matthew blushed. 'I'm sorry, Effie, I think I've some gaspers up in my room. I'll fetch them if you like.'

'No matter. You can bring me one after supper.' He relaxed, visibly. He's like her tame poodle thought Jane in disgust, and she's older than Matthew. What will Mama say about that frock? Up to her knees — and you can see the shape of her nipples through the bodice!

The door opened again: John and Charlotte walked in followed by Dr Cullen who swooped on Jane and gave her a hug. 'Old man's privilege,' he announced.

Effie simpered and extended a limp hand at a wooden-faced Charlotte. Before Matthew could make a move, Dr Cullen had plunged back into their midst.

'Mrs Davie, may I do the honours and present Matthew's two guests, Mrs and Miss Macgregor who've come all the way from Glasgow on a visit. This is Mrs David McKie, ladies.' He peered closely at Effie's chest, 'My word, Miss Macgregor, shouldn't you be wearing a vest? There's quite a chill in the air tonight.' Dorothy giggled.

Charlotte was stunned; despite what John had told her she hadn't comprehended the extent of the disaster. These two were adventurers, the daughter a painted trollop not fit to be in the same room as Jane and Dorothy. Slowly she transferred her stare from daughter to mother; the shock was profound.

'That's my gown!'

'I knew you wouldn't mind, Mrs Davie. We had so little time for packing and when I discovered we were the same size . . .' Mrs Macgregor's confidence began to fade under the terrible accusatory stare . . . 'Effie and I left Glasgow in such a rush!' Affectation slipped and grew shrill. 'If you'd been home earlier, of course I would have asked you . . .'

Effie grasped the enormity of what her mother had done. 'You stupid bitch!'

In the dreadful silence that followed, Charlotte's words were splinters of glass.

'I think Mrs Beal is ready to serve.' But no-one moved. As Dorothy confided later, 'My dears, I completely forgot to breathe!'

Ted and Archie saved the day. They came in at a rush, full of apologies for being late. 'We were planning the layout . . . never heard the gong. So glad you're home, Mama — and looking marvellous!' Ted seized his mother affectionately and Archie shyly kissed her cheek. They began the round of introductions, starting with Dorothy. 'This is Miss Creswell, Archie, a definite improvement on the tubby specimen I used to know.'

'How d'you do, Mr Cavendish . . . I think you knew my brother, Jack.'

Archie gripped her hand more tightly. 'I did indeed, Miss Creswell. He was very kind when I was at Durham . . . fine chap. I'm honoured to meet his sister.' He moved on to Jane.

'Miss McKie. I'm glad to see you again. I trust the visit to Paris was enjoyable.' It was stiff and formal but his eyes conveyed more than his words.

'I'm happy to see you, Mr Cavendish. Yes, Paris lived up to expectation.' Jane was rosy. Arriving at the Macgregors, Ted stopped precipitately at the sight of the frock.

'Good lord!' Archie collided with him and Ted pulled himself together. 'Let me introduce you to Matthew's friends, Mrs Macgregor and Miss Euphemia Macgregor.' Archie found himself gazing short-sightedly at an inadequately veiled pair of nipples.

'Yes, I see . . .' It was an apparent slip of the tongue and he over-compensated with his handshake. 'How d'you do, very pleased to meet you . . .' Jane felt Dorothy and William Cullen quaking beside her and daren't take her eyes off the carpet.

Charlotte had recovered. The theft would never be forgiven but she had a difficult supper party on her hands. 'We won't wait for Luke.'

'Please don't, dear lady, I've left him with one of my most tiresome patients. Allow me.' The doctor held out her chair and they took their places.

Excitement plus the brandy made Mrs Macgregor dizzy. Charlotte terrified her — and Effie should never have spoken like that. But now these two boys had arrived — she wasn't sure if the maimed one hadn't slighted Effie in some way — there were so many people and Mrs Macgregor was unaccustomed to society. She wished she were sitting where Mrs Davie couldn't stare so pointedly, as if it mattered, borrowing an old wee rag like this . . .

She looked for something to put in her glass. Effie whispered fiercely, 'There's only ever water.'

'Oh, for God's sake!' Mrs Macgregor hadn't meant it to be so loud! Up and down the table, conversation lurched then resumed awkwardly as Luke slipped in, apologized to Charlotte and took his place beside John.

Effie's nerves were quivering; Charlotte McKie despised her. She'd gazed at her new dress with such disgust, Effie wanted to scream. As Matthew's mother, she should have welcomed them; instead, she'd been as haughty as Luke. Effie watched jealously as he nodded to Jane and murmured something. Jane blushed and nodded back. How dare they all be so patronizing and how dare they ignore *her*! Wasn't she the guest of honour?

'How are you enjoying Saturday afternoons in the stock-room, Miss Creswell?' John was asking courteously, 'I fear it must be very tedious?'

'Oh, no I love it, Mr McKie. My office job finishes at one o'clock so you see, it fits in beautifully. I hope you'll allow me to continue? Mrs Beal spoils me. She insists I have a cup of tea as soon as I arrive.'

'Quite right too,' John smiled.

'Then you are a shop-girl, Miss Creswell?' Mrs Macgregor was determined to avenge the snubs.

'Shop-girl *and* office girl, Mrs Macgregor. Why, do you know,' Dorothy leaned forward, blond curls framing her face, 'Mr McKie actually pays me a shilling an hour! How could I possibly give up a job like that?' Smiles broke out as she added light-heartedly, 'Besides, I couldn't disappoint Thomas Allen.'

Dr Cullen smote his brow. 'Miss Creswell, tell me I'm not too late?'

'I'm afraid you might be,' Dorothy gave a mock-tragic sigh, 'Although he has a wife and ten adorable children, I fear.'

'Good heavens!' Mrs Macgregor clutched her napkin affectedly. 'Are you enticing a married man away from his family, Miss?'

Above the hoots of laughter, Charlotte said coldly, 'A joke, Mrs Macgregor. I'm glad to say Miss Creswell cannot be suppressed for long. Yes, thank you, Katriona.' Soup plates were collected and the main course arrived.

'I'm thankful my Effie has never had to sully her hands. I must say I'm surprised that your mother permits it, Miss Creswell? You appear to have been respectably brought up?'

312

'Oh I was,' Dorothy answered pinkly, 'Fortunately it hasn't prevented me from earning an honest bob. Otherwise I might have been tempted to become a kept woman.'

Oh well done, cried William Cullen silently and Ted's mouth twitched. Mrs Macgregor ignored Effie's kick under the table.

'A mother who has her daughter's welfare at heart,' she announced sententiously, 'must guard her child's reputation from all evil for it is her finest jewel.' At this, none dare catch one another's eye.

'Matthew told us you'd rushed off to be a nurse during the war, Jane?' Effie said shrilly, desperate to intervene.

'Thank Heaven so many brave women did "rush off", Miss Macgregor, William Cullen reproved. 'Thousands of men survived who wouldn't have had a chance otherwise.'

'But soldiers, doctor?' Mrs Macgregor smiled coyly, 'How could any mother who has her daughter's reputation at heart, allow her to mix unchaperoned with the hoi-polloi of an army?'

'They treated us with gentlemanly respect, Mrs Macgregor,' Jane cried hotly.

'I think you were jolly brave,' Dorothy added her twopennorth, 'I wouldn't have had the courage to do what you did.'

'And Miss Macgregor? What work did she do during the war?' Dr Cullen's voice was creamy and set Effie's nerves jangling.

'My daughter had not the slightest need,' Mrs Macgregor said quickly. 'She was with me.'

'What, not even comforts for soldiers?' he murmured. Oh, God! thought Effie, surely they'd all understood that?

Charlotte frowned, for she did not. 'Would you pass Miss Macgregor the cabbage, Dr Cullen?' But Effie's appetite had disappeared.

'I'm so glad you've found work for Thomas Allen, Mr McKie,' Dorothy dimpled deliberately at John. 'He doesn't complain but I think he had a pretty frightful time in France. He's so grateful, and such a dear.'

'I wish I could have offered more but Matthew had already filled his position.' Charlotte's eyebrows went up.

313

'Why did you do that?' she asked.

'I found someone cheaper to employ.'

'But I gave my word it would be kept open for him,' said John.

Matthew shrugged. 'He had no written contract, Uncle. Why should he expect it? Times have changed. Counter-hands come and go, you don't need to provide attics for apprentices or meals for everyone else. It's a buyer's market. You hire cheaply and once they demand more money, you hire someone else instead. It makes economic sense.'

'And Thomas Allen, He supports his mother and sister —'

'Oh, he'll be all right,' Effie sniggered. 'He has Miss Creswell making eyes at him.' No-one laughed at her joke.

'Is that how you would run the business, Matthew?' Charlotte asked thoughtfully.

Matthew was full of confidence now that he held Effie's hand under the table-cloth, 'When it's McKie Brothers — *and nephew* I shall work like a Trojan to prove I'm right.'

John ignored the suggestion. 'And you, Miss Macgregor? Do you agree with Matthew's philosophy?'

'What?' John had caught her off-guard. Effie looked up and found she was the centre of attention.

'Uncle means when you and I are managing the Emporium, do you agree we should pay as little as possible to the shop assistants?' Matthew asked boldly.

This time Effie understood. 'Oh, yes. Why waste money? It's hard enough to come by.'

'You don't believe in such a thing as loyalty?'

'I do not!' Effie's voice was as hard as her mother's. 'When has anyone ever been loyal to me?'

'Until now, my precious!' Mrs Macgregor jumped in hastily, 'Matthew has been as loyal a fiancé as any mother could wish.' She rushed on now she had the opportunity. 'Mrs Davie, can I assume that you and Mr McKie have no objection to the engagement?'

She gathered herself, ready for battle, but Charlotte's swift reply astonished her.

'None at all. I advised Matthew he should proceed with the marriage. Would you prefer sherry trifle or apple tart, Miss Creswell?' Charlotte shied away from discussion

314

of such a delicate matter in public, and she could bear Mrs Macgregor crowing victorious over what was still her dining-table. Her full attention centred on Dorothy: 'Isn't trifle your particular favourite?'

William Cullen waved his spoon cheerfully. 'Miss Creswell, at whatever risk to your reputation, I demand to be your partner here whenever sherry trifle is on the menu.'

At his end of the table, John relaxed. The meal was nearly over and tomorrow he'd ensure other arrangements were made, for the sake of his digestion.

'I'd adore some, thank you, Mrs Davie. May I ask, did you visit that divine dressmaker in the rue Dedier? You'll never forgive me, Mr McKie, but I encouraged Jane and her mother to be extravagant!'

'I'm glad to hear it,' John said cheerfully.

Dorothy beamed. 'Dr Cullen, you must implore Mrs Davie to show you her new hat. But please keep yourself under tight control, sir. It's so delicious, you'll want to eat it.'

Their laughter compounded Mrs Macgregor's frustration. She didn't understand why Charlotte had capitulated, and that cheeky blonde girl continued to be the centre of attention while she and her daughter were being ignored!

Dorothy was unstoppable. 'I shall be madly jealous when you appear in your wonderful new clothes, Jane. Tell me, did you buy much in Paris?'

'Oh, no!' Luke pulled a mock-horror face. 'Miss Creswell — Dorothy — I have admired you from afar all these years but please, I beg, do not begin talking fashion; I don't think I can stand it.'

'Hush,' Dr Cullen scolded, 'Look how starry-eyed Miss Creswell has become. I could die of love and she wouldn't even notice.'

'Ted and I bought some frightfully smart gauntlets today, Miss Creswell,' Archie put in. 'Dark-brown with just the teensiest hint of a suede cuff.'

Effie in her fashionable new dress and everyone ignoring her!

'I could show you a glimpse of my new socks too, if you like, Dorothy?' Ted stuck his leg in the air and began

315

inching down his trouser. 'But don't blame me if the sight overcomes you.'

'Steady, steady,' Archie implored. Dorothy pretended to faint. 'Stretcher-bearers!' he roared and he and Ted leapt to their feet.

Mrs Macgregor's vision was clouded with brandy and misunderstanding. 'Effie . . .' She was on unsteady feet, pulling at her daughter's arm, 'Matthew, you've no business to let them insult your fiancée . . .'

Ted lowered his arm from its frenzied salute. 'What's up?' he demanded.

'Sit down, you two,' Charlotte chided, 'Mrs Macgregor, it's only high spirits, please don't be upset.'

'Mother!' Effie hissed but Mrs Macgregor was too confused to retreat.

'I will not stay while this *rabble* ignore Effie. We have been *insulted* . . .' She saw Effie's face and knew she'd overstepped the mark; tears began to fall. 'Your mammy's only got your best interests at heart, hen . . .' She was level with Charlotte now. 'Will I give you this rag back tonight?'

'Keep it, keep it.' Charlotte waved an agitated hand, desperate to end embarrassment, 'Katriona, perhaps Mrs Macgregor would prefer to go to her room —'

'You keep your hands off me!' Mrs Macgregor staggered angrily away. Effie followed, helplessly. At the door, she spoke with the dignity of despair.

'My mother's tired. She'll be better in the morning.'

The door closed. After a brief pause, Matthew left the table and hurried after them. No-one spoke. Dorothy and Jane stared at the table-cloth.

A tear ran down Charlotte's cheek and fell with a plop into the trifle dish. In the silence, William Cullen reached across and folded her hand in his. 'Dear lady, don't. Please. Salt water will ruin it and I'd like a second helping.' He'd turned tragedy into bathos; Charlotte couldn't sustain her sorrow as their ripples of tender laughter flowed toward her.

'Oh, really!' But it was no use and she had to join in.

'I know what all that custard is doing to my adipose tissue but I do not *care* ! And neither must you,' Dr Cullen added with special emphasis. Katriona began to clear their

316

plates but he clung to his. 'Be off, you old spoil-sport, I will have some more!'

'But what is to happen?' Charlotte demanded, attempting to be serious. 'That dreadful woman .. ?'

'Every young man deserves a mother-in-law, especially Matthew,' Dr Cullen told her comfortably. 'Yes, Katriona, you may add extra cream ... Just think, Mrs Davie, you'll be in the same position yourself one day ... maybe the respected in-law of one of these young people?' He leered wickedly at Dorothy Creswell.

'Mrs Davie, Jane, would you mind awfully if I made tracks? I have to be up rather early for the office.' Dorothy, charmingly pink, began thanking John and Luke for a pleasant evening.

'Escort party, Fall- - -In!' Archie called suddenly. He and Ted were on their feet, raggedly to attention. ''Shun! One–two–one–two–one–two. Gentlemen to adjust dress before leaving —'

'What?!' Ted was scandalized.

'Young female party, subject of escort, cannot stand the sight of socks therefore braces to be lowered one inch,' Archie ordered imperiously. 'Young female party — to get — HAT!'

'I think,' said Charlotte severely, 'They are offering to take you home, Dorothy.'

'I rather think they are!' She kissed Charlotte and with Jane, Ted and Archie, set off happily for her 'abode'.

Archie could be heard complaining in the passageway. 'I'm not going to wear my glasses in future, then I won't be frightened by the sight of Miss Macgregor's thingummybobs —'

'*Mr* Cavendish!'

The atmosphere for those remaining in the dining-room was mixed. Katriona piled the last dishes onto her tray.

'There's one thing you've missed in all the commotion tonight,' she told Charlotte, 'Matthew's fond of that hussy. He really does want to marry her and she seems fond of him. They could turn out to suit one another.'

As she left them, Luke said thoughtfully, 'D'you know, I think Katriona could be right.'

317

CHAPTER TWENTY-ONE

Matrimony

'Such a frantically busy few days . . . I must say, Dorothy, my head feels swimmy!'

'Have a digestive?'

'Thanks. Uncle talked the whole thing over with Mama, Luke, Ted and I, then asked that we go away and think about it. Last night we discussed it for ages. We're all agreed: the Emporium will be sold but it's to be kept secret until a buyer has been found.'

'What about Matthew?'

'He's not to be told a word! Uncle made us promise. He'll get his share of course but it would upset things properly if a whisper reached the Macgregors and they tried to interfere. Did you hear about Uncle's revenge?'

'No?'

'The morning after that terrible supper party, he booked the two of them into the *Temperance* hotel in Coniscliffe Road. Mrs Macgregor nearly had a fit but Uncle's paying and they have no money so there they stay.'

'When's the wedding?'

'The fourth of next month. Mama suggested a quiet affair but Mrs Macgregor insists "her precious" walks down the aisle in a white veil.'

'My word!' Dorothy pursed her mouth in a very prim manner. 'I wonder if she understands the significance?'

When they'd done laughing, Jane said 'We're being too unkind.'

'Not at all,' Dorothy protested but Jane was serious for a moment.

'You know, it doesn't take much for a girl to change into someone like Effie, especially coming from such an awful place. Matthew told me about it. I'm sure she was decent once.'

'I disagree.' Dorothy was stubborn. 'It's the same choice every girl has sooner or later. Why couldn't Effie have earned her living and kept her self-respect? No wonder she clings to Matthew, he must have seemed a godsend.'

'It's mutual,' Jane said absently, 'He's terribly fond of her, . . .' But she shrank from telling Dorothy what had happened on the croft so didn't continue.

On a Saturday afternoon in the stock-room, surrounded by brown paper and string, Dorothy conversed quietly with Thomas Allen. 'I shall miss all this. Fortunately, I can manage without my shilling an hour. How about you?'

'It's all right, Miss Creswell. Mr McKie has promised he'll find me a place. *He's* always kept his word. I know he's found positions for most of the others so I'm not worried.'

'I hope it's something more interesting next time because you deserve it.'

'Bless your heart for saying so, Miss Creswell,' he said cheerfully. 'Now, are those two packages ready for Albert Hill?'

If asked to describe his nature, Thomas Allen would not have used the word 'resentful' yet the trait was there, buried deep inside. And it festered, grateful though he was for his incredible luck, for on the following Friday evening, Mr Allen celebrated his engagement to the sweetest girl in the world.

She, together with the next sweetest girl, Miss Creswell and her friend Miss McKie, gathered with former comrades of Mr Allen's in his mother's modest dwelling. As the evening wore on the gentlemen discovered they were uncommonly dry and, on being given permission, bade the ladies farewell and took themselves off to The Green Tree at the corner of Skinnergate. This hostelry had a liberal reputation, the only clock having an unfortunate habit of running down five minutes before closing time

319

without anyone noticing it. Thus it was nearly midnight when Mr Allen and his friends were finally told they must go. Conversation eddied as they ambled along. The general topics were the sale of McKies and the forthcoming nuptials of the despised member of the family.

'You wouldn't think they were related . . .' Beer had fed Mr Allen's resentment. 'Mr McKie's a gentleman . . . Miss Jane's a lady . . . but him?' He expressed his opinion into the gutter. One or two of the others followed suit. By the time the party were at the other end of Post House Wynd, all had reached the same conclusion: Matthew McKie was a wart on the face of the earth. It was Matthew's misfortune to be walking home along High Row when they did, and one of the comrades spotted him.

Mr Allen would not describe himself as either resentful — or vicious. Indeed his mother knew him to be the kindest of sons and his sweetheart found his kisses extremely tender. Perhaps it was as well both ladies were peacefully asleep. Not that the comrades were unfair. Discipline prevailed and when Mr Allen had thrashed Matthew to their satisfaction, they left him and went quietly away, model citizens every one.

Jane discovered her brother at the foot of the back stair. She and Katriona helped him into the kitchen and bathed his wounds. They used arnica and witch-hazel, they used cold water compresses but the following morning, dressed in his wedding clothes, Matthew McKie was a pitiful sight. Those bruises and swollen lips were Effie's first sight of her bridegroom for he hadn't thought to send her a note.

'. . . Those whom God hath joined together let no man put asunder.'

Swathed in ninon and lace, Effie listened to the words and realized their significance; she smiled tentatively at Matthew. He was hers for life now. She hoped she'd be able to stick it out. He gazed back, full of wonder and love; he had gained his heart's desire.

Afterwards, Dorothy and Jane changed in Jane's room. 'This is my last decent dress, saved from the wreck,' Dorothy looked at it doubtfully. 'It's good silk but I'd

320

forgotten how old-fashioned it was — look at the sleeves!'

Jane had an inspiration. 'Why not wear it like that? With your hair the way my Mama used to do hers? Let me help.'

Dorothy began to feel easier, watching Jane braid and pin the tresses. 'This evening isn't to celebrate the wedding, is it? Matthew and Effie won't be there?'

'Heavens, no! Just the four of us. I'm not supposed to tell you — Ted wants to do that himself — he's been accepted for the engineering course at Birmingham University. Eighteen months but Archie says it'll take all of that to have the plans approved and the garage built. They'll bore you silly with it tonight. Pretend you haven't heard when Ted tells you, though.'

'Of course.'

Jane's mouth was full of hairpins and when Dorothy asked idly, 'Will Luke be there?' could only mutter indistinctly, 'No ... Newcastle.' A tremendously happy thought occurred: was Dorothy really interested in Luke rather than Archie? Jane's spirits soared. How marvellous — and if so, they'd be sisters-in-law. Well, sort of.

When it came to her choice for the evening, Katriona insisted on the new burgundy taffeta from Paris. 'It's only a quiet dinner dance,' Jane demurred but when Dorothy wailed, 'Ooh! Jane, how could you!' she was glad. If her friend was interested in Luke, might that not mean that one day, she and Archie Cavendish . . ?

In her bedroom, Charlotte and Miss Attewood were examining the hats brought back from Paris, admiring the craftsmanship. Charlotte had chosen to wear the black silk with the jaunty red bow for the wedding. 'A remarkable creation, audacious yet elegant. The epitome of your style if I may say so, Mrs Davie.'

'Thank you. One isn't supposed to try and eclipse the bride's mother of course. However . . .'

Miss Attewood assumed her professional manner. 'One did one's best, one tried to advise, but madam would insist on those *hideous* feathers being added to a perfectly *honest* straw! Oh, isn't this lovely!' She'd discovered amid the tissue, an apricot soufflé of net and ribbon. Charlotte looked at it with sad regret.

'When I decided on that, I still had hopes of remarrying.' Miss Attewood observed a respectful silence. 'Instead of which . . .' Charlotte reached out and stroked the veiling, 'Never mind, it's all in the past. You know — you and I gain much of our enjoyment out of hats.' As the idea came, Charlotte stared in the mirror at Miss Attewood's reflection, 'We both prefer working in that department to any of the others.'

Miss Attewood began to see the drift. 'We couldn't branch out in Darlington? Not to sell such as these . . ?' She fingered the jaunty bow. 'Our clientèle has not sufficient *courage.*'

'No, but in Harrogate ladies are elegant and fastidious.'

'Oh, yes they are! Oh, Mrs Davie, would it be possible?'

'I don't see why not, with my share of the proceeds. Would you be willing? As my assistant? It would be a small establishment.'

'Select.'

'Oh, very.' Charlotte immediately saw the plain stone frontage, the discreet window, above all the elegant continental lettering across the facade. '*Madame MacKie. Chapeaux.*'

Miss Attewood sighed with delight.

'Perfect.'

'Girls, we have a problem and wondered if you knew of a solution. When I go to Birmingham next week, Archie's going to need a new chauffeur.'

'I can manage the brake, even the gears,' Archie apologized. 'It's the oncoming vehicles.'

'He has this unfortunate habit of removing his glasses before he starts to drive.'

'I think it's an unconscious desire not to see any other cars but I admit it has created the odd difficulty,' Archie sighed.

322

'It certainly has,' Ted said with feeling. 'So he needs someone right away. Any ideas?'

They thought of the same person simultaneously. 'Thomas Allen?'

'Exactly.'

'Who?'

Jane giggled. 'He works in the stock-room. He's the one who blackened Matthew's eye last night.'

Ted grinned.

'Oh, him! Stout fellow. Can he drive?'

'Yes,' Dorothy assured him, 'And he's a perfect dear underneath.'

'Say no more,' Archie said solemnly and she blushed. Seeing it, Jane had a moment's unease.

'But would it be a permanent post?' Dorothy asked. 'He has a young lady as well as his mother to support.'

'Don't see why not.' Archie consulted Ted. 'We're going to need staff. A driver who could demonstrate new cars would be useful.'

'Absolutely.' Having solved the problem, Ted turned his attention to Dorothy. 'Is that a waltz, d'you think?'

'No, silly! It's a foxtrot.'

'Well, I expect we can waltz to it if we try. May I have the pleasure?'

On their own, Jane and Archie were tongue-tied. 'Splendid orchestra.'

'Rather!' He watched Ted and Dorothy, 'What a charming girl Miss Creswell is. In that dress with the flowers in her hair, she reminds me of a Victorian photograph. Whereas you, Miss McKie . . .' The look on Jane's face confused him; Archie had rehearsed the compliment but it tumbled out higgledy-piggledy.

'Peonies . . . in the garden at Gainsford . . . your dress . . . petals . . You know the sort of thing . . .' Blast! he thought. Jane blushed and said she thought she understood. Archie decided to tread on firmer ground.

'Has Matthew been told yet, about the Emporium?'

'No. Fortunately he's been kept busy, finding a house and furnishing it — paying out money in fact. That hurts Matthew more than anything. Uncle John bought out his

323

share of Armitages so that he'd have enough cash. Poor old Matthew ... he was hoping to use that as capital for future plans.'

'Marriage ... rather an expensive business,' Archie said diffidently. 'Chap should establish himself first.' He wondered if he could bring himself to explain a certain problem of his own.

'Once Matthew gets his share of the Emporium, that should help him get started.'

'Jolly decent of your uncle to insist on doing the same for Ted; our enterprise might have foundered if he hadn't.' It was the same diffident tone and Jane didn't notice the implication.

'Uncle's always been like that,' she said eagerly, 'He's a pretty selfless person, really. He's only waiting until Mama's decided what she wants to do before he breaks the news to Matthew.'

Archie knew the moment was past. He ached to hold Jane, yet he was desperately nervous.

'That beautiful gown looks remarkably like a dance dress, Miss McKie.'

'Yes it is, rather,' Jane agreed.

'Would you care to?'

'Yes, please.'

It wasn't as awkward as he'd feared because Jane was so light on her feet. She floated, dark eyes shining. 'I do enjoy dancing, don't you?'

'I prefer watching you.' Her cheeks were the colour of her dress. But would you rather be in Luke's arms, Archie wondered miserably. Stop it, stop it he scolded himself, haven't you been dreaming of this moment for years?

An hour passed without either of them being aware; each convinced they'd never been so happy, each too shy to admit it. When they returned, reluctantly, to the table, Ted had ordered champagne.

'Thank goodness! Dorothy and I were about to send out a search party. Here. We've one or two matters to celebrate tonight.'

'Such as your imminent departure to the Midlands, chum,' Archie raised his glass. 'To my non-combatant comrade in

324

arms, E. McKie, esquire. Stretcher-bearer *extraordinaire*!'

'To Ted!'

'Well, thanks awfully. Actually, I was going to drink to the partnership.' Ted raised his glass to Archie. 'To Cavendish and McKie.'

'I like the sound of that,' Archie agreed happily, 'but what about the ladies?'

'Oh, yes, the girls,' Ted was nonchalant. 'To the delightful Miss Creswell, who has improved beyond all recognition and to Jane, who I'm sure you'll agree old chap, is looking particularly handsome — here, I say!' His eyebrows went up. 'We've forgotten the happy couple. We ought to drink to them first!'

'Oh gosh, so we have!' Dorothy raised her glass. 'To Matthew and Effie —'

'Not forgetting Mrs Macgregor,' Archie interposed, at which Ted banged down his glass on the table and shouted, 'Hang on a minute!'

'What on earth is he up to now, can you see Dorothy?'

'He's talking to the violinist ... back he comes. Oh, my dear — no!'

Patrons of the Palais de Dance in Grange Road were a little startled when the four young things at the corner table joined in the chorus, helpless with laughter:

'And her mother came, too!'

Effie was tired. It had been a long day and as Matthew fumbled in the dark, she said wearily, 'Oh here, let me show you!' He moaned as he reached a climax and she shushed him gently because it was nearly over. 'Don't be too excited, Mattie. Mother might hear.'

He switched on the bedside light, taking her by surprise. She shielded her eyes, forced into a shocked giggle at the sight of his bruises. 'You do look a fright! Black and blue all over.' Effie dearly wanted to know why he'd been so badly beaten but was nervous; those cats'-eyes stared at her so critically.

Matthew examined his wife, sprawled in the sheets; the dark brown triangle — no gold there — the pallid face emphasized by the stiffly waved yellow hair. He'd

325

imagined his screen goddess, the heavy satin slipping from her shoulders and his face buried in her yielding, fragrant bosom. Effie had been eager enough but he was left with the sourest of tastes.

'You're no virgin! How many men have you had?' She twisted away from his gaze; this was what she'd dreaded all along.

'You want too much for your money,' she muttered defiantly.

'It *is* my money after all.' The eyes were bitter, ' "A mother's most precious possession"!'

'It was easy enough for you — how were we supposed to live? My father's been in prison since I was five!'

Oh God, thought Matthew then burst out indignantly, 'You could have worked!'

Effie shrugged thin shoulders. 'Where's the fun in that?' Her defiance faded, replaced by anxiety as she saw the look on his face. She'd seen that look on other men but this time the situation was dangerous. 'Forget about them, Mattie. I love you. There'll never be anyone else but you for ever and ever . . . cross my heart!' He made no move to touch her. Cold fear filled Effie's heart.

'Kiss me!' she whispered urgently, pulling him close. She exerted herself to please and when it was over this time, she murmured, 'We had to survive, Mattie, don't be angry with me. You didn't know any of them. None of it matters now we're married.'

Love-making was at an end.

CHAPTER TWENTY-TWO

New Beginnings

John walked through the empty building, checking the rooms, closing each door behind him. What a rabbit-warren it was. Home to how many at one time? Mary would have remembered.

In the dining-room, threadbare patches were evident now the furniture had gone. Men from the auction rooms had been scathing. 'It'll fall apart, Mr McKie. Best leave it where it is.' Someone else could consign the carpet to oblivion.

Summer sunlight shone on the outline where the sideboard had been and the square above where Mary's picture had hung: Abraham sacrificing the lamb. John was glad Jane had taken it. 'Aunt Mary embroidered so beautifully and you know I can't sew, Uncle.' He could gaze at it in the evenings in the house they'd rented in St John's Crescent. John had chosen that because of its proximity to William Cullen and Dorothy Creswell; he and Jane would be glad of the company of old friends and it would be home for Luke and Ted for as long as they needed one.

Charlotte had claimed two gilt Salon chairs she'd stored in an attic for her new *boutique*. John chuckled. Charlotte, who hadn't a word of French, now 'Madame McKie'. All the same, she'd been canny about those chairs.

'When the Salon was torn down, I couldn't bear to let them all go. I kept thinking they might come in useful. They're so stylish!' She took his arm as she said, 'I remember Davie telling me the Salon was all your idea. As elegant as Versailles.'

When John emptied his desk he found the two receipts for the crystal chandelier; the first when he'd purchased it and the second when he'd sold it last year. For double the price. Quality, even if Matthew didn't believe in it.

Matthew. The only one who'd fought every step of the way to prevent the sale going through. The scene was still vivid in John's memory.

'Why wasn't I consulted?' It had been a shout, not a question. John had begun to explain but Matthew didn't want to hear. 'You want to destroy me, that's why you're doing this? You're jealous because I'm more ambitious than you ever were!' That brought anger. John's voice rang out.

'Your parents, Mary and I, Mr and Mrs Armitage — we began the Emporium. Mr Hart, Miss Attewood, Bertha, Katriona, Mrs Beal were among those who built it up. They were proud to be a part of it. Loyalty, Matthew, it's something that can't be bought —'

'You paid enough for it in the end,' Matthew sneered. 'The size of their pensions — you're the laughing stock of Darlington.'

John's gaze didn't waver. In the same quiet voice he said, 'I doubt it, not among my friends. They understood as you never did, what the Emporium stood for.'

'I wanted to expand it into a chain of stores!'

'No, you wanted to use our goodwill for your own purposes. I will not allow you to drag our good name down. You will have the same as the others down to the last penny. What you do with it is up to you. Your standards are not those of McKie Brothers, Matthew. You must make your own way, on your own terms.'

'It's spite, nothing but spite. You've always hated me!'

'I loved your father. I think he would understand.'

Hammering jarred John's senses, bringing him back to the present. All the fittings were to go, all the fine mahogany apprentices had polished once a week over the years. The newcomers told John gently how much more modern it would be once the conversion was finished. They'd taken on former employees who would begin in the re-opened departments on Monday: not just fashion this time but every aspect of home furnishing as well.

Matthew wouldn't be there. He'd pretended he didn't care but both he and John knew the reason. However modern, the new owners had a high regard for old-fashioned honesty and the taint of past deeds clung to Matthew yet.

John looked down on the shop floor from the top of the staircase. Did anything remain? Some hint of what he and Davie had achieved? There was only dust. The air was thick with it.

He hurried past the wooden lift doors and into the yard. Across the yard, above the stables, he had a sudden vision of a face at the window staring at stars which shone like bits of candle flame.

'I'm glad you told them to take down the name.' Charlotte had come in from the colonnade and stood beside him.

'There was no point in leaving it.'

'No. Mrs Beal stopped me just now in the street. She's bored with retirement —'

'Already!'

'Despite your annuity, she's decided to let that back bedroom again.' When Charlotte smiled, her mouth trembled. 'Just one lodger, not two.'

'Who knows . . . he may turn out to have a brother.' John polished the pince-nez. 'Did you know Ted gave her that photograph of Blackie? He asked if he could have it.'

'That was kind . . . Poor Billy.' She saw John was on the verge of tears and made a deliberate effort to be brisk. 'I shan't forgive you for persuading Katriona to stay. I was relying on her to come with me.'

'She offered when she heard Jane and I were setting up house together. I'm sure you and Miss Attewood will find someone suitable in Harrogate. I think Katriona prefers to be near old friends.'

'I trust you don't intend to vegetate! Men of your age can go downhill very quickly when that happens.' Why did she always manage to rub him up the wrong way?

'Charlotte, this morning I hung up my plate as an accountant. A new office in a brand new building with a scandalously high rent. Two keen articled clerks to keep me on my toes and whose salaries I shall be responsible for. I would hardly describe that as "vegetating"? Don't make me out to be an old man, please! I was feeling quite spritely until you suggested it.' He wasn't of course, but for her sake he wouldn't let the sadness show.

'You've been very generous,' she said suddenly, 'I wish you'd kept more money for yourself.'

'My needs are modest,' John said simply. 'And the children must have their chance. We had help in our turn, remember.'

'Oh, I do!' Charlotte reached up and kissed him on the lips. 'Thank you for providing me with new horizons, John. I needed to escape from the old ones. Ah, here's my taxi.' She climbed inside quickly and didn't look at the Emporium once. All her life's happiness and sorrow was embedded in its walls. 'Look after Jane for me, and come and visit as often as you can.'

'I shall. Goodbye, Charlotte.'

John hid unashamedly until his own cab arrived. He closed the door and shut the yard gate for the last time. Mr Clough was waiting outside.

'We've took down the name but you can still see t'outline. D'you want us to paint it over?'

'No.' Surely it wouldn't take long to fade? John handed him the keys. 'St John's Crescent, driver.'

The surgery was only three doors away. Luke split his time between the two houses, staying with Dr Cullen when unofficially 'on call' and with John and Jane the rest of the time. Katriona was worried at first but realized she had no real need; these two were busy with the future; they'd put the past behind them.

If only Jane would learn how to encourage Archie Cavendish but that never seemed to happen, and it irritated Katriona. Instead Jane progressed diligently from typing pool to personal secretary and appeared very satisfied with life. William Cullen gave his verdict on Luke's intentions.

'I'm glad you've decided to strike out on your own, Luke. I didn't think so at first, of course; felt rather slighted to tell you the truth. But dammit, I delivered you into this world, Ada helped nurse you, it's high time we cut the umbilical.'

'This current research into pneumoconiosis fascinates me.'

330

The doctor grunted. 'Then the Durham coalfield should provide enough scope. One man I've heard of, difficult chap by reputation, he's looking for an assistant in a pit village practice. He's the company doctor for the coal-owners — delicate path to tread, that. It's early days yet but d'you want me to make further enquiries?'

It was several months later when Dorothy arrived breathless on their doorstep. 'Jane? Oh, good, you're home. I'm so excited, I can't wait a second longer. I ran all the way from the tram —'

'Dorothy, what is it? Uncle John's here, he's with Katriona.'

'Oh, splendid! I must tell him as well.' The blonde curls bobbed ahead as she hurried into the kitchen. 'Please. Do listen all of you. I have an important announcement — ahem! Mr and Mrs Allen have asked me to be godmother — and Ted's asked me to marry him! There, isn't it marvellous, aren't you pleased?'

Amid the welter of hugs and kisses, Jane was amazed. 'Marry Ted? I thought you didn't even like him?'

'Oh, pooh!' Dorothy laughed, 'That was me being a tease. Of course I *liked* him, you funny old thing. Mind you, I haven't accepted him yet. He proposed so badly I told him he'd have to keep practising. You see, there I was, explaining to Mr Cavendish that the spare parts of a missing cylinder head would be sent up by train when Ted calls out from underneath a new car — where he's inspecting a chassis — "Shall we get married because it looks like being a nice summer?"

'I was absolutely stunned! I said "What's that got to do with it?" and he slid out and said how silly I was. That if we were married we could attend Luke's graduation and then go on up to Scotland for our honeymoon — and Mr Cavendish said, "What a good idea. I hope you'll agree, Miss Creswell because Ted's concentration is shot to pieces nowadays", and I didn't say anything at all!' Dorothy stopped and beamed at them.

'Does that constitute an engagement?' John was bewildered.

331

'Oh, no.' She shook her head vigorously. 'It means he's *asked*, that's the important thing. And when he does it again properly, I shall accept.'

Katriona began to laugh, 'What if he doesn't, Miss? Ted might change his mind and ask someone else.'

'Then I shall skin him alive,' Dorothy announced. 'Actually, I think he might try again this evening because he wants us all to go and celebrate. That's why I ran all the way, so you can change into your best frock, Jane. Oh, yes — Mr and Mrs Allen are calling their baby Isobel, isn't that sweet?'

She saw Jane's face. 'You are *pleased*, dearest?'

'Confused . . . utterly and totally confused!'

'Oh, it'll be all right once Ted's gone down on bended knee. I shall accept then, quick as a flash!'

'But I thought you wanted to marry Luke?' Dorothy was incredulous.

'Don't be silly! He's the last person. If I threw a flat-iron at Luke he'd just stand there looking hurt. If I threw one at Ted, he'd fling it straight back and hit me on the head.' She spread her hands to indicate the difference. 'You do understand?'

'It wasn't just Luke, was it Jane?' Katriona was enjoying herself, 'it was Mr Cavendish as well?' Jane wanted to kill her.

'Of course not!'

'Archie Cavendish?' Dorothy was amazed, 'How could it possibly be him? He's madly in love with *you*.'

John declared the suspense would be too much, they must celebrate the non-engagement without him but by the time Ted and Dorothy arrived, matters had been resolved.

'He didn't give me roses, thank heaven,' Dorothy admitted, 'He gave me his new set of feeler gauges and told me I could chuck them in the river. That's when I realized Ted was serious. And he kept sounding the horn until I agreed. You know how fussy neighbours can be in the Crescent — so I did.'

'Did you go down on one knee?' Jane asked suspiciously.

'In my best suit? Have a heart!'

332

'But you will next time you propose, won't you dear?' Dorothy said sweetly, and Ted groaned.

Any anxieties Jane had about the evening proved unnecessary. Archie Cavendish told her she looked charming and promptly began discussing bank loans with John. Dorothy and Ted were engrossed; apart from listening to Ted's incoherent assurances that Dorothy was the loveliest and best of all women, very little was said that required Jane's attention.

At the finish, slightly put out, she discovered she'd agreed to be a bridesmaid and that was all.

'Wish me luck,' Dorothy said as they parted. 'We're planning to go and see Pa.'

'What about your mother?'

'Yes,' she sighed, 'that, too. Although when I rang the nursing home, Matron said she wasn't interested. All she worries about is the next spirit communication from Jack.'

The four of them travelled to Harrogate to visit Charlotte in Archie's new 'bus. Ted drove with Archie beside him. Jane could only stare at the back of the fair head and wonder what was going on inside.

The plain grey stone frontage with white painted woodwork and discreetly illuminated window was in a narrow street between the Valley Gardens and the Pump Room. All the shops were small, elegant and full of extremely desirable frippery. Peering at three hats, each mounted on a gilt stand against heavy folds of pale grey velvet, Jane was full of admiration. *Madame McKie's* was an exclusive world.

Mama had achieved it herself, with Miss Attewood's help, of course. As for the garage, there were already apprentice mechanics working under Ted's supervision, and Archie talked of expanding the premises to include a showroom. Matthew had two small shops, one in Darlington, the other in Stockton, even if both were pretty horrid.

And what have I done? thought Jane. It might sound tame, but I actually enjoy working for two elderly solicitors who remember father and treat me with great courtesy. Evenings spent with Uncle and Katriona are very pleasant and Dorothy and I go to the pictures whenever we feel like it. From now on, she'll want to be with Ted, of course. Has

333

the time come for a change? Perhaps, although I'm not sure what; I enjoy being a capable secretary. It's a sight easier than being a nurse!

Charlotte declared she found the engagement most satisfactory. 'Once he's married to you Dorothy, Ted will settle down, I feel sure.'

Miss Creswell agreed primly that he might. 'He can be a frightful handful, Mrs Davie. I expect his father was just the same?' Jane was astonished to see her mother blush.

Am I jealous of Dorothy? Yes, I am, she sighed, that's why I'm feeling so unsettled all of a sudden. Will I ever be as radiant as she is? Not unless Archie Cavendish asks me to marry him and as he obviously has no intention of doing so, I might as well cry for the moon! There's certainly nothing I can do to show him how I feel.

Jane hid her face against the cool glass in the window-seat above her mother's shop. Memories of the scene with Luke still returned to torment her occasionally. Never again would she risk letting her feelings rule her head even if it meant losing Archie. Let Dorothy tease how she would, Jane couldn't bear the hurt of rejection a second time. She tried to ignore her emotions and concentrate on the exquisite home her mother had fashioned for herself.

This small parlour was utterly feminine, a reflection of Charlotte's role at this new stage of her life. The scale of the room and its furniture meant that Ted looked large and ungainly. 'It needs eighteenth-century people drinking chocolate in knee breeches and ruffles,' thought Jane. 'Mama's settled for elegant widowhood and it suits her but if Ted gets through the visit without breaking an ornament, I shall be amazed.'

'Mr McKie and Luke are determined to bring Miss Shields down for the degree ceremony and Ted and I want her at our wedding, so dear Katriona has agreed to go all the way to Scotland to fetch her,' Dorothy explained happily. 'I'm dying to meet Miss Shields — she sounds absolutely *ferocious*!'

'You'll charm her, you're bound to,' Ted said fondly.

'We're taking her back to Scotland ourselves, with Luke, Uncle John, Katriona, Jane and Mr Cavendish.'

'What — all of you going on your honeymoon!'

'It'll be such fun,' Dorothy said eagerly, 'Ted's hiring an eight-seater tourer. There'll be plenty of room.'

'It's a Packard . . . Thirty-six cylinders . . .' Ted looked at his intended dreamily. 'What I've always wanted.'

Charlotte snorted. 'Dorothy, I should warn you the croft is small and primitive. You can't possibly stay there, not all eight of you!'

'It's only Luke and Mr McKie who'll be staying there, Mama Charlotte,' Archie soothed. 'The rest of us are booked into a hotel. Thought we might appreciate the odd jug of hot water, the occasional feather bed, that kind of thing.'

He smiled but Charlotte wasn't satisfied. 'I trust there will be no impropriety.'

'My wife and I will chaperone the party,' Ted grinned.

'Luke wants a holiday before he begins in his new practice, Mama. The rest of us are going to have plenty of exercise on the moors and fill our lungs with fresh air.'

'Luke and Mr McKie will be travellin' by train anyway,' Archie explained. 'Leaves more room in the Packard for Katriona and Miss Shields.'

Charlotte's brow uncreased. Morality would be observed if Katriona were there. 'Is it to be a white wedding?'

'We'd rather not, if you don't mind.'

'Bit put off by the last occasion,' Ted chipped in breezily. 'Matthew's wedding, rather an embarrassment all round, I thought.'

'Ted — behave!'

'Yes, Mama.' He grinned. 'You know, where the young 'un went wrong, he never took a proper gander at Mrs Macgregor. Only saw Effie. Big mistake! Want to know what your wife will look like at fifty? Put her mother under the microscope first.'

Dorothy's happiness slipped slightly. 'You haven't seen mine recently.'

Ted said kindly, 'We'll bring her round, you'll see. Got to persuade her to let go of Jack, then it'll be all right. After all, look what we've managed with your Pa.'

'What's that?' asked Charlotte.

'Simply the threat of grievous bodily harm and Mr Creswell decided to make amends immediately.' Ted was cheerful. 'I shall have a rich wife.'

'Not that rich,' Dorothy reproached. 'I told Pa I wanted to marry a six-foot-tall, former boxing champion who was waiting to see him in the outer office. Ted burst in like a bear, shook Pa's hand and crushed every bone. Pa agreed to reinstate my allowance. Actually, I think Ted reminded him of Jack in a way.' She blushed, 'Pa's offered to settle money on any babies we may have.'

'Expensive things.' Ted shook his head at the prospect.

'Shockin',' Archie agreed. 'Very damp. Need peggin' out five times a day. Exceedingly smelly on occasion.'

'That's enough, Mr Cavendish. Dorothy, I insist you choose a hat before you go. You too, Jane.'

'How kind! I don't know that I could afford . . .'

'As a gift, of course. Neither you nor Jane could pay my prices. Come along, Miss Attewood and I have found a charming blue bonnet —'

'Mrs Davie, could I ask an enormous favour? Could you possibly come to London to advise on my trousseau?' Which as Charlotte explained to Miss Attewood afterwards, proved what a delightfully intelligent girl Dorothy Creswell was.

Mrs Macgregor read the offending news item to Effie over breakfast.

'It's that flirt of a Creswell girl — it says her father used to manage a shipyard! She was sly. Didn't I always say she was sly? And Ted McKie only a mechanic? I'm surprised her father allows it. Have we had an invitation yet?'

'No. I don't suppose we'll get one anyway.' Effie sounded dreary. There were no ups and downs in her life nowadays and she pined for variety.

'Don't be stupid, we're entitled. Where's Matthew anyway?'

'In Manchester.'

'He's away too often. Oughtn't you to go with him, Effie? Look what he got up to when he went to Glasgow.'

'Oh, shut up, will you!'

'It's only natural I should be concerned, and see here . . .' Mrs Macgregor waved the newspaper, 'You insist on an invitation, hen. Stand up for our rights. We're family, even if they are a stuck-up bunch.'

The processions followed one another through the quadrangle, up the stone steps, down the length of the panelled hall; the procession of Deans of Faculties, the Vice-Chancellor's Procession followed by the guests of the Senate. Black gowns with vivid silk-lined hoods, Principal Officers, Chairmen of Boards of Studies and the Clerk of Convocation with his staff of office. Behind came scholars and fellows and, lastly, those who would remember the day to the end of their lives.

John listened intently to the Latin address as did Helen Shields. They obviously understood every word, Jane marvelled, even though Uncle's schooldays had been a long time ago. How Miss Shields must have drummed the lessons in!

The Vice-Chancellor charged those about to be honoured to add further laurels to their achievement. Helen and John nodded in agreement. This was only the beginning: a door that had been prized open at last. The roll-call began in alphabetical order with the sleek dark head half-way down the line;

'1st class Honours, Awarded a mark of distinction in surgery, Luke McKie.' Jane couldn't take her eyes off John, she'd never seen him so happy. And for Helen Shields, full of memories, the trumpets sounded on the other side.

'This is a splendid wedding breakfast,' Helen pronounced her verdict emphatically because of the wine. She wasn't surprised at being the guest of honour. From the peninsula to Darlington, in her eyes, was an expedition worthy of Scott. 'And a very pleasant ceremony. Everyone so pleased and happy . . . very pleasant.'

'We're honoured you came,' said Ted, 'Wouldn't have been a proper wedding without Miss Shields.'

'This has been the most satisfying week of my life. All I ask, Ted, is that I survive the return journey.'

'You will, ma'am,' Archie promised. 'Couldn't look Mr John McKie in the face, otherwise.' The word 'face' reminded Helen of something.

'There was a strange pair of women in the church. Very colourful. I don't seem to see them here?'

'Matthew's wife and her mother, perhaps?' Ted said easily. 'Invited them to the wedding. Afraid we didn't include them in the feast. Not enough buns.'

'Oh I don't think so, not Matthew's *wife*.' Helen shook her head doubtfully.

'Have some more cake?' said Dorothy.

As always, the one thought uppermost in Matthew's mind at the end of the day was that Mrs Macgregor would be there. He never rushed home; he worked late into the evenings, travelling, visiting suppliers. He'd once asked Effie to desert her mother but she had refused. 'I need her, she's stronger than I am. I hate her sometimes but who else have I got?'

Any suggestion that she attempt to make friends frightened her. Women, especially younger women, were the predators who might steal Matthew away. Effie admitted as much when Matthew pressed her.

As if I'd have the energy for that, he thought wearily. Anyway he still loved Effie, that hadn't changed. Under her guidance, their love-making could be wild and passionate — if only he could forget all those other faceless men who'd preceded him!

Nothing had gone the way he'd planned. He ignored John's advice and bought an expensive home. The bill for furnishing it had terrified him but Effie insisted every item was necessary. His remaining capital had been invested in two small shops but there was no 'chain', nor prospect of one. It took all his time and energy to keep track of disappearing shop assistants and goods for which customers constantly demanded refunds. It hadn't occurred to Matthew in the heady days of his dreams that cheapness could mean poor quality and that his two shops were in towns with flourishing markets dealing in the same level of trade.

Once, only once, he'd asked Effie to 'help out'. Left to her own devices with a till was the worst mistake of his life.

338

'It was only a few pounds!'

'That was our profit, Effie! I need that to pay for more stock.' She'd shrugged impatiently. 'You've got money in the bank. Use some of that for God's sake.' Effie was jealous of that bank account. Money was something you kept ready to hand and when it was gone, you simply asked for more.

'Home' was a new house with a garden that had been neat and spruce when they'd moved in.

'Effie and I adore flowers, don't we, hen?' But Mrs Macgregor had never had a garden before and thought flowers and shrubs managed things for themselves. Matthew groaned; the tangled jungle was always there, waiting to be tamed.

Perhaps today at least, both ladies would have enjoyed themselves . . .

'I'm back . . .' There was rarely a welcome. It didn't occur to Effie that Matthew might like to find a meal ready. She waited until he returned and, if she was tired, suggested it would be nicer to eat in a restaurant. Tonight food was forgotten; she was angry, goaded on by her mother. 'Hallo my darling . . . Was it a pleasant wedding?'

'Awful!'

'Very shabby.' Mrs Macgregor gave her verdict. 'The sly creature didn't even have a veil!'

'Why weren't we invited to the reception!' It was out. Matthew had avoided telling her as he tried to avoid everything nowadays, because there was bound to be a scene.

Suddenly he was too tired to care. If she'd been wary, Effie would have noticed the opaque quality of his blue eyes but she was in a petulant state, encouraged by Mrs Macgregor.

'Ted warned me Miss Shields would be there. Your mother would have drunk herself stupid with all that wine and as Helen Shields is renowned for speaking her mind . . .' Matthew shrugged, 'why should I permit the two of you to ruin Ted's day. He was decent enough to be my best man, it was the least I could do.' Suddenly he wanted to hurt Effie because of all the frustration. 'Personally, I've always rather admired Dorothy Creswell.' As he saw the instant fear, Matthew tried to soften the blow. 'What a pity you and she couldn't be friends. It's not too late, Effie,' he pleaded. 'Jane and Ted would be glad to make it up. Ted said as much when I went round to beg for that wretched invitation.'

Mrs Macgregor began to screech, her mouth twisted and ugly with smeared lip rouge and the spots of red on her cheeks livid against the leathery skin. In a pause when she'd literally run out of breath, Effie's tired voice could be heard: 'I'd like to make it up with Jane, Mattie ... I'm sick of listening to this sort of thing all day.' It had taken courage; her hands shook as she clasped them in her lap. Mrs Macgregor's mouth was slack from disbelief but Matthew felt the faintest stirrings of hope. Husband and wife looked at one another, all pretence stripped away.

'I'm glad you feel like that, Effie. I'll try and think of a way.'

'Do you know what would make me blissfully happy?' Mrs Edward McKie confided a little later that evening. Her husband's expression was a mixture of incredulity and dismay.

'Good God, Dorothy, how have I failed so abysmally?'

'Oh, dear, how tactless of me!'

'It was, rather.'

'Well come over to my side and let me kiss you better. There, how's that.'

'So-so. Not perfect by any means. Ah ... now ... Improving ... Yes, yes ... Oh, yes!' A little later still he asked, 'You were saying?'

'Ah, yes. My idea of a perfect present would be if Jane and Archie —'

'Dorothy, you have mentioned that a couple of times already. In fact if we make it any more obvious, you'll frighten poor Archie away for good. Best man and bridesmaid? Not forgetting the holiday.'

'Yes,' Dorothy was smug. 'It's a long way to Scotland and we'll be staying in all those lovely hotels, with candle-lit suppers! I shall bang their heads together if they're not engaged at the end of it.'

Luke parked his car at one end of the pit village main street and walked the full length of it. This was his chosen place of work; from today, he would dedicate his life to it.

Red House Row, pronounced 'Red'us'ra' by all who lived in it, was an eloquent name for endless ribbons of identical terraces punctuated by a chapel, church and public houses with one red brick building at the end of the main street, built for the manager of the co-operative store. The purpose of the village had been to contain as many pit workers as possible without an unnecessary penny being spent in the process. Luke could only admire the success of the coal-owner's intention.

The tiny dwellings were closely packed back-to-back, separated by narrow dark alleyways. Front doors opened onto the streets, back yards contained earth closet and coal store. The occupants' lives were governed by coal. Smoke poured out of chimneys built too close together, blotting out the sky when there wasn't sufficient wind to clear it away. From the time a man rose from his bed 'til the moment he climbed back into it, his whole life and that of his family centred round the pit.

The first time Luke had visited, it had poured with rain. In the sunshine, the place didn't look much better. Men and women passed as he sauntered along, glancing out of curiosity rather than greeting him. It was understandable; what reason could any stranger have for walking along these pavements?

Dr Mitchell's house had been built before Red'us'ra was created. Then there had been small farms and open countryside, a time when the existence of black gold beneath the soil was unknown. The house was stone-built, set halfway up a low hill that overlooked the village. From there, the lines of terraces made a depressing pattern. So much humanity crammed together with the huge winding gear dominating their skyline; those wheels and cables that lowered men under the earth and raised them again, their strength diminished infinitessimally, shift by shift, because of the dust they inhaled.

Beyond the village there were trees and undulating parkland, the edge of the coal-owner's property. He never visited, preferring London, but his manager and bailiff were in solidly built, middle-class four-bedroomed prosperity. Their houses faced the trees not the pit. Dr Mitchell had pointed this out to Luke on his previous visit.

It hadn't been an enjoyable interview. Several times, Luke had been provoked but had kept his temper. 'Difficult'? Dr Cullen didn't know the half of it, he thought. What was worse, he'd come here before his results were through and was feeling at his most vulnerable, a situation Dr Mitchell spotted immediately.

For his part, Harold Mitchell was feeling his years. He'd interviewed so many who'd come, full of glib assurances, and disappeared quickly. He was tired of being used by young men.

'So am I your first staging-post, Mr McKie?' There was more than a hint of a sneer.

'I'm afraid I don't understand.'

'Oh, I think you do.' Dr Mitchell had waved a hand at the small, battered surgery and view beyond. 'Surely you intend better than this — if your hopes regarding your degree are fulfilled?'

'I insist — I repeat what I said before — this is exactly the kind of practice I would like to join. I had hoped Dr Cullen's letter made that plain . . ?'

'Oh yes, the letter.' Dr Mitchell scrabbled among the mound on his desk. 'Rose is away at present,' he grumbled. 'She sees to things.' He abandoned his efforts. 'So tell me again what he said.' It was another dig; that Luke must know the contents. Luke fell into the trap and reddened. Dr Mitchell noticed with a small smile.

'He overpraised me, no doubt,' Luke muttered.

'No doubt at all. Part of the letter comes back to me now.'

It would, thought Luke angrily. 'The gist was that I'd worked out my reasons for wanting to be a doctor whilst I was a prisoner of war. Certain events at that time . . .'

The old man nodded. 'A fellow prisoner died, I think? A miner?'

'I believe he gave up hope. We talked of his former life. He told me of the fear men have, working in a pit; of their dread of lung disease in old age. He had no reason to want

342

to survive and I found that dreadful. I still do. I warn you, Dr Mitchell, if you refuse I shall simply apply in another coal-mining area. I'm not giving up.'

'Uh-huh. Well there's always a shortage of medical men in such places. Some have no-one at all. It's not a *glamorous* life.'

It was Luke's turn to smile. 'Dr Cullen used that word the first day I assisted him. In Potter's Yard.'

Harold Mitchell chuckled. 'You've been there, have you? I was a locum in Darlington once or twice in my younger days. So . . . you know what an overflowing earth closet smells like and how to spot typhoid? You'll need to be alert here if it's a hot summer. Sanitary improvements are not high on the list of priorities.'

'They should be.'

'Beware evangelism, Mr McKie . . .' The old doctor wagged a finger. 'It's a careful balance twixt servant and master in Red'us'ra.'

Luke drove the elderly car carefully up the hill. He'd been frugal with the purchase; Ted assured him it would last a couple of years even if the steering had a bit of 'play' in it. Luke parked outside the surgery gate and knocked at the front door.

The woman who opened it startled him. Dr Mitchell had referred to 'Rose', describing her as a widow. This was a young woman of about twenty-seven, tall and rather stately with pale sandy lashes framing light coloured eyes.

She held out her hand, composedly. 'I'm Rose Galbraith. You must be Dr McKie.'

Archie Cavendish had admired Jane McKie from the moment he saw her and now the depth of his love was deep and passionate; yet he could not express it. When affection first deepened, he'd been cautious. Not during a war Archie had thought, that wouldn't be fair on a woman. He hoped Jane would understand, not that he'd spoken since that too would have implied commitment.

343

So he'd waited, he'd defied his father over his career and now there was a problem. Insurmountable in Archie's eyes: he had no money.

Establishing the garage had taken more than he'd estimated. His father, furious at being defied yet again, had used his influence with weaker Trustees. Funds due to Archie had been withheld. Desperate though he was, Archie couldn't find a way to obtain them. The Trustees belonged to the age of pony and trap, the combustion engine was to be abhorred; they agreed with Archie's father that previous behaviour, as a Conchie, indicated mental instability.

But for Ted's stake in the enterprise, the business would have collapsed. As it was, Archie needed a loan if they were to expand — and a loan would take years to repay.

Jane had money, that was the irony. Archie knew that, and Ted still had half his capital intact but he would need that to provide for Dorothy. It went against Archie's code to ask any of the McKies for more help. Pound for pound, John McKie had said. That must be the way even if it meant debt but the bleak result was that Archie Cavendish could not support a wife.

The honeymoon expedition reached the peninsula and delivered Miss Shields and Katriona safely. Luke and Ted arrived and began the annual renovation of the croft. The two couples went for many walks over the moors, sometimes accompanied by John and Luke. It came about naturally that the newly-wedded pair strayed in one direction and the other two in another. Jane waited; Archie didn't declare himself.

'This holiday was a mistake,' Jane told herself. 'Archie Cavendish must think I'm throwing myself at him — how shaming!'

'I must tell her it's impossible,' Archie thought miserably. 'Jane's the most marvellous girl I've ever known but it just isn't fair!' Yet he put it off again and again for fear of losing her forever.

On their final day Jane suggested at breakfast that she would enjoy retracing one walk they'd all taken along the silvery-white sands of Sanna.

There had been a storm during the night and Dorothy stared at the rain-washed window panes. 'Would you mind if I stayed indoors, Jane? I think the wind might be a bit too bracing in the bay.'

'Me, too,' Ted said promptly. 'Want to check the arrangements for our party this evening. Totted up last night. Nearly twenty guests if all the Hamiltons come.'

'How splendid,' Dorothy was enchanted. 'Our first dinner party — and I don't have to do the cooking. I must stay in and help, though.'

'Yes, of course.' Jane looked tentatively at Archie, 'I suppose it might be wiser if we stay in as well?'

'Not a bit.'

They walked past the lovely inlet on the southern shore, through the village and began the gentle climb over the moor. Jane told him the legends she remembered, of Vikings and Celtic chieftains, and the names they'd left behind in the landscape.

The wind was stronger now. The lush softness was behind them as they gazed across at the blue Moidart hills. Despite all that instinct forbade, Archie took her hand. Jane smiled but her heart plummeted when she saw his face. What have I done? He doesn't love me! He can't if he can look at me like that!

It was essential to find a place where they could talk. They skirted the edge of Kentra and found a cleft in the rocks, lined with heather.

'Would you mind if we sit here?' Archie asked formally.

'Not a bit.' It was the wind that had made her eyes water of course. Angrily, Jane brushed away the moisture.

'Jane, I'm frightfully sorry ... I *can't* ask you to marry me.'

Shock made her say abruptly, 'Why on earth not?' It was a tone Charlotte might have used; it made Archie Cavendish straighten his back.

'Because I haven't any money,' he raised his voice, equally bitter.

'Good lord!' Jane stared at him. 'What have you done with it? Squandered it?'

'Hell, no! I've scarcely spent a sou on myself for the past two years —'

'All right, calm down!' She was alarmed. 'I'm awfully sorry I spoke like that — I'd always imagined you'd got pots of the stuff.'

'I have! Or rather I should have. I was entitled to the whole trust at twenty-five. Father's persuaded the other Trustees to withhold two-thirds of it.'

'But why?'

Archie was full of anger now. 'I went to see him again the day before Ted's wedding — I begged him to release the money!' Archie couldn't hold any of it back. 'It wasn't just for the garage — it was so that I could marry you!'

Jane appeared cool but she also saw the funny side to what, in her eyes, wasn't a problem at all.

'When I hand over my money to you, Archie, which of course I shall, I'll insist on being mentioned *before* the garage in any future conversations you may have.'

'I couldn't possibly accept it. Apart from the morality, it's your security against the future.'

'Oh, don't be so childish! What future? One without you? You want to marry me, you said? I presume that's because you care for me in some way? Perhaps it's the wind but I don't think I caught the word — love?'

'Of course I love you, I've been in love with you for years!'

'Well, I want to marry you, blast you Archie Cavendish! And I've waited long enough!' She ached to comfort him just as much as Archie desired to kiss her. He held himself, stiff and taut against her passionate whisper, 'I love you!'

But then: 'I'm sorry, Jane. Can't be done. It isn't fair to risk the only capital you have when I might drag you down.' The cold rejection was savage to her raw heart. All the pent-up emotion she'd been cherishing boiled over, 'Why, why, why?' she cried but Archie, equally distressed, refused to budge.

The wind blew harder, lifting the incoming waves and tearing at their clothes. John had been anxious to return before the deluge broke but when Luke began to talk

346

of Red House Row, he forgot to keep an eye on the weather.

'Oh, lord, look at those clouds. We're going to be soaked!'

'We might escape, if we hurry.' Bodies bent, they leaned into the wind as they half-walked, half-ran back along the curve of the bay. 'Look, I don't think those two have noticed. Shall I give them a shout?'

'I shouldn't! Archie Cavendish might not thank you for it.' Comprehension spread over Luke's face.

'You mean — he and Jane . . ?'

'I hope your powers of observation improve, for the sake of the patients.'

'Oh, I'm glad . . . very, very glad.'

'So am I, and relieved. I thought he'd never get round to it. Katriona wanted to choke it out of him months ago.'

'Come on, there's the first drop of rain!'

They were towelling themselves dry in the croft before John referred to it again. 'When Ted comes to collect us for the dinner party I think I might drop a hint? Should Archie spring the announcement tonight, we ought to be prepared with champagne.'

'Definitely! You can do your stuff as uncle of the bride-to-be.'

'You're not going to escape scot-free. I happen to know Miss Shields intends saying a few words to the assembled company. I warn you, she may refer to you as "Dr McKie" more than once.' Luke groaned. 'And you'll have to satisfy her insatiable curiosity over the practice.'

'Thank goodness Jane and Archie will provide a diversion,' he said with feeling.

Dorothy was extremely puzzled when she returned to their hotel room. Like John, she was confident tonight would be Jane's happiest. With her kind heart, Dorothy wanted to be the first to love, kiss and congratulate her friend.

Ted was waiting for her. She looked at him quizzically but he shook his head. 'No go, old thing.'

'Are you sure?'

347

'I asked Archie point-blank. He was dripping wet, literally. Formed his own puddle and was practically up to his knees. I said, "Ah-ha, I can tell you're in love otherwise why try and drown yourself." '

'Oh, very funny!' Dorothy scowled. 'Archie's terribly sensitive.'

'Well it didn't sound like it just now. He told me to go to hell.' His wife was discouraged. 'What about Jane?'

'Her clothes were wringing wet, too. I ran a hot bath for her and when Jane was in it and couldn't escape, I said "Are you and Archie engaged yet?" '

'And . . ?'

'And she threw the flannel at me and burst into tears.'

'I hate to disappoint you, old thing, but I don't think we should interfere further.'

'I *know* they're fond of one another!'

'Be that as it may — and some people have a funny way of showing it — I'd say those two have no immediate plans for matrimony. Come on, dry your eyes. I've got to fetch Uncle and Luke.'

'To Luke, who has made one or two dreams come true, and to his success as a doctor!'

'To Luke!'

'Speech!' Ted cried happily. 'Come on, don't just sit there . . on your feet, old man.' Luke rose and looked round the circle of expectant faces, so many Hamiltons and McKies linking him with the past.

'Not long ago, we were remembering Alex McKie with sorrow and affection. It was a time when some of us had come back to the place we love, to renew our bodies and spirits. On that occasion, we gave thanks for a life well spent . . . tonight, I give thanks for a future. It is John McKie who has enabled me to have that future and I thank him with all my heart . . . Yet it occurs to me that there is another whom we should both honour for it is she who has enabled so many here to achieve their dreams. Ladies and gentlemen, I ask you to remember what this lady has done for generations of children on the peninsula, to make their hopes and aspirations a reality. I give you Miss Helen Shields.'

'Oh my!

'Mistress Shields!'

'Jolly well said, Luke,' Ted chuckled quietly. 'You've rendered her speechless! All the same, old boy, I think you should take her into a quiet corner and tell her all the gory details about your new life.'

'What's to be done about Jane?' whispered Luke. 'It's a brave front but I'm worried it might crack.'

'She's all right now. She's collared Uncle John and they're looking very serious, so let 'em get on with it. Archie's down in the mouth but I'll lend him my manly shoulder to cry on. Dorothy and Katriona are seeing to the rest. Action stations!'

'Uncle John, I have a problem. Will you help me solve it?'

'If I can, my dear.'

'I'd like Archie to have my savings.'

The pince-nez came off quickly. 'Are you engaged?'

'No, we're not! Oh, I do wish people would stop asking.'

'I'm terribly sorry . . .'

'He tried to make me promise I wouldn't tell anyone but that's absolutely ridiculous. The fact is he can't ask me to marry him because he hasn't a sou until his father stops being difficult and he needs more money to expand.'

'My dear, that garage business is in its infancy. It will be some time yet before its success is assured. I'm worried enough that Ted and Dorothy might go under without adding your capital —'

'Uncle John, I believe in him and I've waited long enough. I want Archie to have my money and I shall drag him to the altar by the scruff of the neck if necessary.'

'I sincerely hope it won't come to that!'

'There's one more thing. I'm not going back with the rest of you, I'm going by train. I shall leave first thing in the morning. It'll be less embarrassing for Archie and I have things to do in Darlington.' The chin was at such a familiar angle, it made John quake.

'Very well, my dear.' He'd never argued with Charlotte.

349

'Now Luke . . . after such a compliment it seems churlish to ask more of you but I want to hear all about it!' Helen's eyes gleamed. 'You thought to deflect any questions? Dear me, how naive.' Luke smiled affectionately. They were having coffee beside the fire in the hotel sitting room with Hester Hamilton and her father. Luke stared into the flames and began to describe his new world.

'I shall be a company doctor in a pit village. You can see the village and the scars left by the mine workings from the surgery window. You can hear colliery trains, and the whistle for the change of shift. If the windows are open you can hear the winding gear but they're usually left shut, because of the grit.

'There's dust everywhere, in the air, on the window ledges. If you clean it away in the morning, by midday there's another layer. The women nearest the pit wash their curtains once a week, it's so bad. Children breath it from the day they're born, you can hear the effect when you sound out their lungs.

'Dr Mitchell has been there over twenty years. He's had four assistants, none of them have stayed. I shall.' It was said with conviction.

'Just the two of you?' asked Hester, 'You and the other doctor? Who does the cooking?'

'Mrs Galbraith. She's a niece by marriage, a nurse, and Dr Mitchell offered her a home when her husband was killed at Passchendaele. The house has two front rooms, one's the surgery and the patients come in through a side door and wait in the hall. The other is the living room — although not much used, according to Dr Mitchell. It's a busy practice. There's a dispensary next to the dining room and a kitchen of course.

'Upstairs there's a guest room which father can use when he visits. My bedroom looks out over the countryside at the back, for which I'm grateful.' Luke pulled out his pocket-book. 'I knew you'd want to know every detail, Miss Shields, so I wrote it all down: my room has brown curtains, greeny brown carpet, chair, table, bed, wardrobe, wash-stand and brass fender. How's that?'

'Most evocative, thank you Luke.'

'Well at least I remembered!'

'Have you met any of the patients?'

'About half a dozen. I was only there during one period of surgery. I spent most of the day settling in.' And becoming acquainted with Mrs Galbraith, thought Helen Shields.

In his room under the hotel eaves, Archie Cavendish watched dawn break in a calm sky. He hadn't slept. He'd relived every moment of yesterday and the whispered, 'I love you!' The echo, the memory of the hurt in Jane's eyes haunted him. Throughout the fear and pain of France he'd dreamed of hearing her say those words. Yet how could he have acted differently? To take her in his arms would have been to deceive her.

Jane's generous offer made him clench his fists against an unjust fate. There was no way in which he could accept her fortune because there was no likelihood of obtaining what was rightly his. It wasn't in Archie's nature to act dishonourably but his sore heart ached that he'd had to refuse her love.

Idly he watched the station taxi draw up and luggage taken out. The figure that followed made his aching heart lurch again. Jane was leaving; the only woman on earth, but he had to let her go.

At breakfast, Dorothy was dismayed. 'By herself? On a train?'

'At her own request,' John said firmly. 'Jane has made the journey alone before, you need not be concerned.'

'But why?'

'To spare Mr Cavendish embarrassment.'

Dorothy was totally perplexed. 'What on earth are they up to . . . Have you any idea? Ted said he'd never known Archie so depressed but neither of them will say why!'

John had been sworn to secrecy. 'I think we must wait and see. However dreadful the suspense,' he added, seeing her expression, 'Possess your soul with patience, Dorothy.'

'I can't,' she moaned, 'I haven't got that sort of soul!'

351

CHAPTER TWENTY-THREE

Tenacity of Purpose

'There is a person to see you, sir.' The butler offered the card on his salver. The master of Gainsford took it, read it and tossed it back disdainfully.

'What on earth does she want? Is she a Salvationist?'

'She is not wearing the uniform, sir. She said it was a private matter.'

'Tell the mistress to deal with it.'

'She particularly asked for you, Mr Cavendish. Quite definite about it. A respectable-looking person, sir. Youngish.' The butler had noted the fiery determination and didn't fancy trying to show Miss McKie the door before she'd achieved her objective. 'I do not think she requires much of your time, sir.'

A languid hand indicated that Mr Cavendish could bear to part with five minutes of it and Jane was admitted.

Waiting in the huge hall, she'd felt oppressed. It was much larger than Archie's vague description had led her to expect. Once she'd overcome her nervousness and began to look about more keenly, Jane found one impression recurring: 'It's like a mausoleum ... Empty ... yet full of objects. No sign of people living here, that's why. And so cold!' She shivered and promptly gave herself a mental shake. This was no way to begin: she had to be brave as a lion today. The butler emerged and walked slowly across the echoing vastness.

'Mr Cavendish will see you now, madam. If you would be so kind as to follow.'

Mr Cavendish made the mistake of not rising from his chair. He was accustomed to forming an opinion of a person's status and adjusting his behaviour accordingly. In his estimation, this was not a gentlewoman who had called. Indeed, how could it be, without a chaperone? This was a person from the middle-class who had no business interrupting his empty, profitless day.

In all probability she would invite him to add his name to a subscription list for some worthy cause. Acidity began to ferment. Females had no right to demand a private interview for such a purpose. Mr Cavendish had no intention of subscribing to any charity — which was hardly surprising since he never did — but how dare this woman encroach on his privacy!

Jane's first clear impression of Archie's father as he leaned forward in the chair, was of a mottled bitter face. His rudeness stiffened her resolve.

'Madam?'

She waited icily for the door to close behind the butler. Mr Cavendish noticed and was furious. 'I have very little time to spare, madam!' It was on a rising note because she continued to regard him steadily but didn't speak. 'It is not my custom moreover to admit strangers without an appointment.' Mr Cavendish moved unexpectedly quickly over to the fireplace and seized the bell-pull.

Jane spoke. 'How do you do. My name is Miss McKie. I am come here on family business.'

'I have no family.'

She stared. 'I am addressing Mr Thomas Cavendish? I asked your butler when I arrived —'

'Of course you are!'

'Then you have a son, Mr Cavendish.'

The bitter face hardened. So that was it. 'What's he done now? Got the housemaid into trouble, is that it? Is that why you are here? Want money do you? Get out! My son is a coward. I threw him out!' Mr Cavendish was so triumphant, spittle flecked Jane's costume.

She'd come here to plead on Archie's behalf but the implication was abominable.

'Your son — whom I intend to marry, Mr Cavendish — is one of the two bravest men I know. The other is my brother and neither are cowards — what an atrocious insult! When Archie's arm was blown off —' Mr Cavendish opened his mouth and Jane raised her voice; she was absolutely determined he should hear '— your son was trying to reach a man on the wire. Archie crawled out of the shell-hole up to where the man had been but could only find half the body. He was so bemused, with his remaining hand he tried to untangle the corpse but it disintegrated. That's what he was doing when the Welshman rescued him. I know because Archie had nightmares when he stayed with us, and yelled with fear thinking he was back there on the wire, with bits of flesh coming away in his hand! That in my opinion, is not cowardice.'

Only then did Jane notice Mr Cavendish was tugging frantically at the bell-pull. 'If you still think it was, Mr Cavendish, and if you believe all the terrible things done to Ted and Archie because they refused to kill didn't prove how brave they were, may I suggest it's because you never left these shores? Your generation were the ones who talked about Glorious War and stayed at home.'

Mr Cavendish panted with rage in an attempt to silence her. 'I shall never admit Archibald to this house. Never! We have a long tradition in this family, Service and Honour, but how could you possibly understand that? You are not in the same mold!' Jane heard the door open behind her and guessed she was about to be thrown out.

'Why are you trying to stop Archie succeeding?' she demanded furiously. 'People need cars and garages, not guns and killing each other. Archie's using the money he's inherited wisely; he employs people.' She'd given Mr Cavendish the opportunity he wanted.

'Had he been a true gentleman, Archibald would have known that his place was here employing people as servants, not acting as a tradesman in some "garage"! Get rid of her!' Jane turned. By the door she saw not only the butler but a silent grey-haired woman who stared at her. Was this Archie's mother? Jane spoke out harshly.

'All that stuff about family tradition is absolute piffle! Like the silly emptiness of "Honour and Glory". That was blown to pieces on the wire and thank God for it. Archie and Ted survived but millions didn't because of hypocrisy. You're nothing but a dinosaur, Mr Cavendish: extinct, but not yet aware of the fact. Good afternoon.' She swept forward so swiftly, the butler had to step aside and came at a fumbling run to catch up with her across the hall.

Quivering with pain and fury, Jane tugged the heavy front door and held it open. Fresh air! That's what this place needed, a hurricane of fresh air to blow it into oblivion.

Thomas Allen was standing by the car door and Jane sank into the passenger seat thankfully.

'Back to St John's Crescent, Miss?'

'Yes, please. Before they set the dogs on me!' Thomas Allen took hold of the starting handle and winked.

'Hounds, miss. That's what they're called in a place like this.' Jane giggled hysterically. All the same, she thought, I've cooked Archie's goose properly this time. He'll have to accept my money and swallow his wretched pride!

At the end of Luke's first surgery, one abiding impression remained. 'Everyone coughs in Red'us'ra, Mrs Galbraith. I can hear them out in the waiting room, they're always coughing.'

'It's usually the men because of the coal dust, Dr McKie. The women only cough if they smoke. Not many in this village can afford to do that,' she concluded.

'That's interesting. Does that mean. . . ?' Luke paused because his taste-buds had become more involved than his powers of deduction. 'I say, this is very good.'

'Thank you.' Rose Galbraith continued to eat calmly. 'It's called liver and onions, Dr McKie. We have it about once a fortnight.'

'Yes, I know what it is!' Luke couldn't decide whether she treated him as a half-wit on purpose. 'Mrs Beal used to cook it at home but she didn't add the extra tasty bits.'

'My husband was stationed in India. I learned how to use spices there.'

'He was a regular soldier?'

'Officer.'

'I beg your pardon. How very interesting ... to be stationed out east?' Mrs Galbraith made no reply. As a widow and her uncle's house-keeper, a succession of young doctors had tried to probe the impassive demeanour; to each she exhibited the same detachment. Like his predecessors, Luke was piqued. During his period as house-man, nurses had responded in a much more friendly way to his overtures. Rose Galbraith was now regarding him with apparent curiosity.

'Is that your normal appetite, Dr McKie? If so I'll increase the size of the helpings.'

Luke flushed. 'Since the prison camp ...'

'I understand. Do you have any other symptoms?' He was irritated and wished he hadn't told her; most women were sympathetic. 'I ask simply for information, Dr McKie,' Rose continued. 'One of Dr Mitchell's previous assistants, older than you of course, had a delicate stomach. Naturally one had to adjust various ingredients in cookery —'

'I have no other symptoms, thank you Mrs Galbraith. I must perhaps apologize for the size of my appetite?'

'Oh, please don't do that.' Rose smiled and the sun emerged — 'I'm delighted not to have some finicky old man to cater for' — and disappeared.

Jane was anxious when she requested an interview on a private matter. The two solicitors were so correct in their behaviour, it seemed discourteous to bring a personal problem to their attention. 'May I ask a theoretical question, Mr Bolt?'

'Yes .. ?' Worried eyes peered more closely. From experience, questions rarely fell into that category.

'Can articles of a Trust be altered after they've been put into effect?'

'Ah-hah ...' A happy vista unwound in Mr Bolt's mind's eye, of legal highways and byways down which one could wander *ad infinitum* at one pound and ten shillings per hour.

Jane said hurriedly, 'It's a friend of mine. He hasn't any money because his father's nobbled — persuaded —

the Trustees not to hand over two-thirds of his grandfather's Trust Fund. Now his father says Archie can have the rest of the money provided he signs an undertaking.'

'Ye–es. . . ?'

Jane cleared her throat. 'An undertaking not to marry me.'

'Oh, my! Oh, dear . . . What an interesting question you've raised, Miss McKie. Perhaps the best thing would be for your friend . . ?'

'Mr Archibald Cavendish.'

'For Mr Cavendish to make an appointment and bring copies of his Trust and any relevant correspondence.'

'Thank you very much, Mr Bolt. Could you please let me have the bill because Archie . . .'

'With pleasure, Miss McKie.'

'Uncle John?'

'Mmm . . .'

'Have you transferred all my money into Archie's name yet?'

John replied evasively, 'These things take a little time, Jane. I am investigating another possibility, first.'

She was impatient. 'He needs it as soon as possible, you know. The thing is, could you keep about a hundred pounds back? I may need it for legal costs.'

The *Evening Gazette* slipped from between John's fingers. 'Jane! What have you been up to now?'

As yet Archie knew nothing of Jane's further scheming. He was still recovering from the repercussions of her visit to Gainsford but the secret of his new poverty couldn't be hidden any longer, much to his shame. Full of embarrassment, he finally admitted his predicament to Ted.

'Why on earth didn't you tell me before? That's what partners are for, old lad.'

'I'm sorry,' Archie mumbled.

'Is that why you and Jane haven't seen one another lately? And now you say she's created havoc with your esteemed parent?' Ted grinned. 'Sounds as if my sister takes after Mama more than I realized. What exactly has

357

she been and gone and done?' When Archie told him, Ted howled with laughter.

'It's not funny! I felt such a fool —'

'Oh, don't be such a prig! Of course it's funny — it's a hoot! Oh lord, I wish I'd been there. I must ask Thomas if he managed to hear any of it —' There was a tap at the office door and Dorothy stuck her head round.

'Archie — can you see someone sent round by Mr McKie? His name's Hopkins and he says he's come on business.'

John McKie acted faster than he'd ever done before. He hadn't wasted time explaining his scheme to Archie; Hopkins could do that for himself. He had to protect the interests of his niece. He asked Messrs Bolt and Wilkinson, employers of Miss Jane McKie, for an appointment at their earliest convenience. He arrived five minutes early, was shown into an old-fashioned room by a junior clerk and was surprised to find both gentlemen waiting for him and looking extremely pleased with themselves.

'It was my colleague who thought of it, Mr McKie.' Mr Bolt looked complacent.

'But you added the touches of finesse, Charlie.' Mr Wilkinson tried to conceal his pleasure.

'Perhaps we had better explain?'

'Please do.'

'We have been given permission by both parties to do so, Mr McKie. When Mr Cavendish approached us we examined his documents carefully and discovered his father had acted improperly. The original intention was clearly stated. Mr Archibald Cavendish had every right to expect his inheritance to be paid in full on his twenty-fifth birthday. However, one has to consider the bullying nature of Mr Thomas Cavendish, his autocratic manner in his dealings with fellow trustees — some of whom depend on him for employment — to understand the essence of the problem.'

'My niece has made me cognizant of the events which occurred.'

'Ah . . .' said Mr Bolt.

'Yes, indeed,' agreed Mr Wilkinson. He shook his head. 'We shall be sorry to lose her.'

'Oh, lord — why? What's happened?' John looked from one to the other in dismay.

'Why, sir, nothing. Miss McKie has given absolute satisfaction from the first day she came. Eh, Charlie?'

'Charming girl. Competent, quick — accurate. Can't tell you how sorry we'll be.'

'We never employ married women, Mr McKie. Prefer them to stay at home and look after their husbands.'

'And you think. . . ?'

'Miss McKie was good enough to indicate her intentions regarding Mr Cavendish,' said Wilkinson. 'I would say he's as good as — nobbled!' Both gentlemen laughed hugely at the joke. 'Now, as to Charlie's scheme —'

'No, George. You must take some of the credit. But let us allow Mr McKie to form his own opinion.'

A drawer was opened and a file pushed across the desk top as though it contained the highest secrets of the realm.

'You may read what is inside, Mr McKie.'

It was a letter addressed to the editor of the *Northern Echo*. It had been written and rewritten, it had been polished and begun all over again. Its length had been pondered upon and then revised until in its brevity and style, it was a jewel.

When he'd finished reading it, John took off his pince-nez and a slow smile stole over his face until it reached from ear to ear when it exploded into wild laughter. 'But if this is published, Mr Cavendish will be exposed to public humiliation! Of course, it should be — it must be — providing every word is true.' Native caution regained the upper hand in John McKie.

'We intend, sir, that Thomas Cavendish of Gainsford, Esq. Justice of the Peace, Lord of the Manor of Gainsford, tyrant, humbug and, in this instance, damn great bully! —' George Wilkinson crowed at Charlie Holt's indiscretion, '— *believe* that it will be published. Fortunately the editor of the *Echo* is a personal friend. We were at varisity together. We both contributed to *Isis*. . .' Charlie Holt sighed. 'His articles were accepted. Mine were not.'

'This . . .' John tapped it, 'is worthy of — *The Times*!'

'Oh, my dear sir, it's not for genuine publication! It's to frighten the man into proper behaviour. And of course, we shall have to pay for a few copies *containing* the letter to be printed. That too has been arranged. And we have spoken privately to the Cavendish family's solicitors, revealing not only that we are aware Mr Archibald has been wrongly treated, but that we are *intending* to go public on the matter. They are as nervous. . . ?' Mr Holt looked at Mr Wilkinson for inspiration.

'As nervous as we were on Armistice night, Charlie. We let off a firework and it fell into the stationery cupboard,' he explained. 'Now the purpose behind this stratagem, threatening the worst type of humiliation to a man of Thomas Cavendish's disposition, is obviously —'

' "Withholding his rightful inheritance from his son Archibald, so grievously wounded in the service of his country, threatening the lifetime's happiness of a beloved daughter of Darlington —" '

'Mr McKie has read the letter, George. Is obviously to make Mr Cavendish *believe* it really is about to happen. His solicitor will have alerted him to our threat. Once the editor of the *Northern Echo* telephones Mr Cavendish to warn him that his newspaper will be on the streets within hours containing a terrible accusation —'

'And a messenger arrives at his door with an early edition of the following morning's paper for his inspection —'

'Mr Cavendish will be given the choice of exposure and fighting the accusations through the courts, or signing the undertaking which we have already prepared, the contents of which the Cavendish solicitors accept is correct, for Mr Archibald Cavendish's trust to be released unconditionally forthwith.' Charlie Holt and George Wilkinson sat back with the air of men whose task has been well done.

'So there we are,' said Mr Wilkinson. 'At least, we hope we are. Oh, we have had such fun thinking this one up, haven't we Charlie.'

'Such a welcome change from Torts and Malfeasances —'

'Not 'alf.'

It had become an established habit that Miss McKie and Mrs Edward McKie spent their Thursday evenings together because that was the occasion when Mrs McKie's husband visited his 'other woman'.

'It took ages for me to discover who it was. Ted can be so deliciously provoking.' Mr McKie's wife settled herself full-length on the sofa, completely unperturbed. 'They sit and talk for hours about Billy and Blackie. Ted says there aren't many who remember Billy now and he thinks it does Mrs Beal good to have a bit of a weep now and then.'

'I didn't know who it was Ted visited,' Jane admitted. 'There are some things one doesn't enquire into too closely.'

'One does when one is married,' Dorothy assured her, 'One keeps an absolutely eagle eye. Kindly remember that, Jane, when you and Archie —'

'No!' Jane blushed scarlet. 'Not again!'

'Oh, for heavens' sake, how much longer? I want to wear my blue outfit and in another month I shan't be able to get into the skirt. Archie will be comfortably off now Mr Hopkins wants to put money in as well. What a Godsend that he was one of your uncle's clients — all the dear man wants is to invest money in a garage and treat himself to a car occasionally. My dear, he's simply potty about engines. Ted took a disgraceful advantage of him. I was simply appalled. Would you like more tea?'

'Don't move. I'll pour.'

'Thank you. Anyway, after Mr Hopkins had practically pushed a cheque into Archie's hand, Ted asked if he'd like to see under one or two bonnets — and there he was when I found him, underneath a car, covered in oil! He was so pathetically grateful when Ted said he could tighten one or two bits with a spanner. When are you seeing Archie again?'

'Tomorrow.' Jane blushed.

'And about time,' Dorothy said severely. 'Goodness knows why the two of you have taken so long.'

'Archie was a bit shaken by my visit to his father, not to mention the business over the trust fund. There've been a lot of ruffled feathers to smooth at Gainsford. And after Scotland ... we both needed time to recover, Dorothy.'

361

Her friend did a quick calculation. 'Banns take three weeks don't they? My dear, you must positively dash round to the vicar — I might just make it if I shift the hook and eye.'

The following evening Katriona was waiting in the hall when Jane came downstairs. 'Let me have a look?'

'I refuse to wear anything special!'

'That's all right. That dress always suited you. He's in there with your uncle — and if you do anything daft tonight to upset things . . .'

Jane burst into the parlour to escape. 'Hello, Archie.'

'Good evening, Jane. I say, I do like your new dress.'

'Thanks.' Tiny white lies were permissible between husband and wife, Dorothy had assured her.

'Shall we go? I've got a cab outside.'

It was a quiet restaurant outside Darlington. Archie had taken her there once, several months before. 'I thought we might be a bit more private. Not many people we know come here.'

'Yes. Archie, we haven't been able to discuss what happened since all this began . . . I wanted to apologize for upsetting your father that day.'

'Why? You probably didn't take much notice of the butler in the excitement but according to him, it was a famous victory. Father had apoplexy after you'd gone and that newspaper business almost finished him entirely.'

'I'm awfully glad you've got your Trust money but I regret my part in your quarrel. I think you still hoped for a reconciliation with your father; I've made that impossible.'

Archie thought about this carefully. 'I'm not sure you're right, Jane. Mr Holt hit the nail on the head; you've got to give bullies a taste of the same medicine. I've always tried to be placatory and that hasn't worked. Father's terrified of you, that's obvious. When I went over to thank him, he couldn't stop talking about you. No-one has ever spoken to him like that before. Once you're my —' but Archie stopped, just in time. 'I think it possible I might be invited to Gainsford again,' he finished lamely.

'Good.' Jane gazed deeply into her glass of sherry.

362

'Dorothy's told you the other good news?'

'About Mr Hopkins, yes. Will you be able to build the showroom now?'

'I hope so. Provided Ted's latest plan is accepted. He and Thomas Allen have been measuring turning circles until they're dizzy, trying to decide the right shape and size . . . The thing is, Jane, are you still in love with Luke?'

He'd thrown her properly this time. Jane went bright red.

'Because if you are, I shall find a way of pulling out of the garage and handing over to Ted entirely. I'm only a figurehead — can't even drive.' Archie waggled his artificial hand disconsolately. 'As my father pointed out, I'm an incompetent tradesman. You deserve better.'

She sat so silent and still, he held his breath. When she spoke, it was a whisper. 'I'm not in love with Luke. I thought I was once . . . it was a long time ago. The dark eyes were big with concern. 'Are you sure, Archie? There's been so much thunder and lightning, everyone pushing and jostling us to become engaged . . . Have you honestly had long enough to consider?'

Archie Cavendish's heart did a strange leap and his breathing became constricted. 'Bless you . . . I've thought about you ever since I met you! In France, in the hospital . . . every morning, every night. In Scotland, England — I'll even go to Ireland and Wales and think about you, if you like. I love you, Jane. I absolutely worship the ground you cover so lightly. You've slain all my dragons — let me make an honest woman of you in return. Please, my beautiful, darling girl . . . say you will?'

Jane looked at the dear face, the wise eyes, shy and half-hidden behind the glasses as he waited for her answer, and knew what it was to be gloriously, unbelievably happy.

'Yes, please, Archie.'

CHAPTER TWENTY-FOUR

The Way Forward

The wind whipped grit into their eyes. Luke could taste the dust on his tongue. Rose Galbraith walked beside him. It had been Dr Mitchell's idea that she should accompany him on visits to those patients he hadn't yet met. That and the fact, discussed privately between them, that Luke's youth might be a problem.

'They're used to a fossil poking them about. The women especially start being coy and imagining things when it's a young man asking rude questions.'

Rose gave a quiet smile; from within her shell she had noticed Luke's good looks and thought those might be more of a problem than his age. 'Dr McKie's only fascinated if patients have something very interesting wrong with them. You should see how gentle and thorough he was with Mr Bates. After we'd visited yesterday, the doctor was really upset because he couldn't do more for him.'

'Aye, well, he must learn to accept we're not infallible. It wasn't dying miners I meant. I want to be sure he doesn't behave tenderly with any of our female patients. He's young and far too keen for his own good, Rose, so we'll keep an eye on him for a few more weeks.'

Today it was a house close to the pit. Father and mother watched while Luke coaxed the first of the children onto his knee. They all had measles but he wanted to test the child's eyes. She was feverish and restless, wanting to rub them because of the pain. Luke moved his silver pencil from side to side as he petted her. 'See this, Gwenny . . . keep watching while I move it. Where am I pointing it now?'

Rose Galbraith waited patiently. When the examination was finished and Luke conferred with the mother, she began to talk to the miner. They were interrupted by his paroxism of coughing. His wife broke off to fetch a glass of water. From the way she supported him, it was obvious these attacks were common. Luke took out his stethoscope again. 'Would you object if I examined you?' Before they left Luke, as usual, asked the mother where she kept the washing soda in relation to the tub. Rose now knew the reason behind the constant question, for when she'd asked, he told her of the scalding in Potter's Yard.

Out on the street once more, she listened to his passionate concern for the miner. 'All the classic symptoms yet he might be young enough for treatment. I was reading of a most interesting development —'

'Doctor! Dr McKie!' The shout came from a vehicle parked across the street. The woman passenger waved again.

Rose Galbraith was amused. 'That's the royal summons. You'd better obey, doctor.' She watched the exchange.

When he returned Luke was extremely cheerful. 'That was the pit manager's wife, Mrs Perkins.'

'Dr McKie, I know. There are only three cars in this village. I think I can guess what Mrs Perkins was after and it wasn't medicine.'

'It was a perfectly civil invitation to dine!' Luke wished Mrs Galbraith wouldn't continue to treat him like an idiot.

'Which you accepted?'

'Naturally. One surely expects some social intercourse —'

'I wasn't criticizing, doctor. Please. I simply want to point out to you that Mr and Mrs Perkins have a couple of nubile daughters and Dr Mitchell's previous assistants have been much in demand. I trust you'll have a pleasant evening but I would advise caution. Mr Perkins' word is law in Red'us'ra.' Which was the reason for Luke's delight; he was eager to launch his campaign.

Unfortunately he threw discretion to the winds across Mrs Perkins' dinner table. The pit manager regarded him with extreme disfavour.

'Are you trying to tell me my job, doctor?'

365

'Not at all, sir.'

Belatedly, Luke realized his zeal had got out of hand. The fair Misses Perkins were glazed with boredom, their smiles transfixed after hearing so much about diseased tissue. Beside Luke's plate, trails of salt and pepper indicated the branches of the bronchial tree. Mrs Perkins had given up attempting to divert him. Now all she wanted was for Luke to go, but her husband was determined to teach him about the facts of life first.

'Let me tell you, Dr McKie. All this talk of yearly tests and biopsies and blood sampling — that's totally unnecessary —'

'I can assure you —'

'And I can assure *you*, doctor that *I* decide what medical examinations will be carried out here. How did that miner's wife pay you yesterday for attending her children? Did you notice or were you too occupied with Joe's lungs?'

'I believe Mrs Galbraith collected tokens —'

'Tickets, doctor. Company tickets at sixpence each, issued by me to employees to pay for their medical expenses — your salary in fact!' Mr Perkins was working himself up into a fine bout of temper. 'How many tickets would a biopsy cost, doctor? Who would subsidize all the blood samples?'

It was rhetorical but Luke didn't pause to think. 'That aspect has been considered and already some most interesting facts have emerged —'

'I'll bet they have! Especially if you medical folk have anything to do with it — *the cost of coal to this country is a disgrace!*' Even Luke had the sense to keep quiet now.

He listened to the rambling diatribe about workers who held the country to ransom and coal-owners who could barely keep their heads above water. Luke thought of the thousands of acres of parkland and held his tongue. He was told with great energy that miners' wives didn't know when they were well off and remembered the fight against dirt. He heard of arrogant men who expected company benefits when they were malingering and sickly. Above all he was told of the wickedness when miners demanded an increased hourly rate as well as a cut in the shift so that the pit manager didn't know which way to turn. Mr Perkins had to

366

refill his glass before he could be quit of despair over this.

Luke nodded and murmured astonishment as each new fact was held up for inspection. He'd been a complete fool. He'd done all those things he'd been warned against, he'd set his cause back years. He might even have lost his position. His only remedy was to eat humble pie; every damn slice of it.

'Mr Perkins, what you've told me has been a revelation. You were right, sir. I had no idea of all the intricacies of operating a pit. It was arrogant to offer suggestions about health care. I admit it, and apologize. May I make a request? Would it be possible to visit the mine?'

Mr Perkins was still suspicious, 'What for? To seek out more cases of pneumoconiosis?'

'I want to see all the latest machinery you've been describing. How much did you say it cost again?'

Luke marvelled until his face ached. He begged the Misses Perkins to play the piano, he asked Mrs Perkins for the recipe for egg custard because he was sure his uncle's housekeeper had never heard of such a thing — which greatly surprised his hostess. Very late, when he had some hope that his job might be secure, Luke crawled home to bed. Dr Mitchell had left a note on the hall-stand.

'Severe toothache. Please deal with any calls.'

There were two, and one was a confinement; the anxious husband knocked at the surgery door just as Luke was buttoning his pyjamas.

'Good morning, Dr McKie. Did you have an enjoyable evening?' Rose Galbraith, serene and morning-fresh, the sandy fair hair piled high in its distinctive coronet of braids, examined the haggard face critically. 'You look a little pale.' She put down a large plate of bacon and eggs.

'I take it my dismissal wasn't among the morning post?'

'Unless I missed seeing it, no, doctor. There's only the one envelope, beside your plate.'

Luke glanced and saw it was from Jane. He pushed the congealing mass aside. 'I'm awfully sorry, Mrs Galbraith . . . I was up all night, delivering the Rook baby among other things.'

367

'Did you remember to fill in the certificate before you went to bed?'

'No I did not! Dammit, I only got back about an hour ago. Thank goodness I'm not taking surgery this morning.'

The fair wide brow creased. 'But Dr McKie, Dr Mitchell's not here. He's gone to visit the dentist in Whitley Bay.'

'Where?!'

'It's an old school-friend. He's always gone to him. He probably won't be back until this evening. Shall I get the certificate book and you can fill it in now? Before surgery begins. There are only eight patients waiting so far.'

Half-way through the morning she brought him strong coffee. At lunch-time she told him how she'd managed to accost Mrs Perkins outside the butchers.

'I said you'd told me what an enjoyable evening you'd had, that Mr Perkins had given you an invaluable insight into mining and that you'd never met anyone who could play as well as Winifred. She's the younger daughter, by the way. It's safer to admire her.' Luke gaped. 'From the way you spoke at breakfast, something had to be done, doctor. But I'd be obliged if you'd think twice in future.'

The criticism was mild; Luke acknowledged he deserved far worse. 'Mrs Galbraith, may you receive your reward in paradise!'

'I'm too busy to wait that long, doctor. I plan to turn out the dispensary tomorrow and you can give me a hand.'

It was another six months before Jane and Archie were married; Jane claimed she was too happy to rush. She and Archie had the rest of their lives ahead of them and she wanted to savour each day as it came. She was also wise enough to listen to John's advice: let Archie have a little more time to establish himself in business. Ted consoled Dorothy with a new outfit and a few encouraging words.

'We'll sit next to the front. If the heir arrives during the ceremony, the vicar can nip across and do what's necessary.'

'I shall look a frump. I'm so enormous already.'

'You'll look like a great big ripe juicy peach, my love.' There was a pleasant interlude in the conversation. 'I think Jane's right,' Ted said when he resumed. 'Archie's got too much on his plate at present. Once the new showroom's under way, I can supervise that and he can disappear on his honeymoon without too much worry.'

'Jane asked me to help make out a guest-list. Do you think I should put down Matthew and Effie?'

'That's up to Jane,' Ted protested, 'You and I dodged the issue by having a quiet ceremony. This time, Mama's really got the bit between her teeth.'

'What about — Archie's father?'

'That's Archie's problem, old thing. If I were you . . .'

'I know,' Dorothy sighed. 'Don't interfere. I wonder who Luke will bring?'

'Why should he bring anyone?'

'Because he must have made some friends by now. I shall write Mr Luke McKie plus partner on his invitation card.'

'Perhaps he'll bring that new pup of his. It's a ripping little dog, Dorothy. I saw it when I went over to see to his car. One of his grateful patients gave Luke first choice of the litter.'

Jane asked if she could learn to drive because it seemed the most practical thing to do. Archie was secretly pleased. 'The combustion engine and I have a working relationship, my darling. I sell 'em and someone else drives 'em. Rum, perhaps but there it is. Even when I had both hands, I never enjoyed driving.'

'You're awfully kind . . .' Jane looked at the spanking new coupé with shining eyes. 'Is that really for me?'

'Provided I'm in the passenger seat. How does Thomas rate your expertise?'

'He thinks I'm capable.'

'Shall we put it to the test?'

They found a place beside a stream where John McKie had once declared his love to Mary and hundreds of other lovers had done the same. It was a spot where to be at peace and in ecstasy at the same time was only natural. After they'd kissed and kissed and were content, Jane stretched out and listened to the bird-song. Archie gazed at her in deep satisfaction. The thick hair had escaped from confinement as usual, the large dark eyes had a dreamy expression. Her thoughts were far away but he wasn't hurt. It was a sprite he was marrying, an airy spirit that flew off in various directions before coming back to him. How such a tender creature had managed to bring his father to heel was a mystery.

'Penny for them?' It was Jane who asked.

'Oh, I was wondering about the now famous visit to Gainsford.'

'What about it?'

'How you came to behave the way you did, actually,' He was diffident, not wanting to upset her but Jane smirked.

'Part of me's inherited from Mother, of course.'

'Well if it's all the same to you, Jane . . . I quite like your mother, admire her enormously *et cetera*, but your father sounded more of a tender-hearted sort of chap.'

Jane rolled over, supporting her chin on her hands. 'How on earth did you manage to be decent, considering your parents?'

Archie opened his eyes wide in myopic astonishment. 'D'you know, I've no idea. Mother used to be nice I think, before father squashed her into nothingness. I wonder if the butler did it, if you see what I mean? I wouldn't blame her a bit if that was the way of things, he's the only decent bloke at Gainsford.'

Jane began to laugh and laugh. 'Supposing it were true,' she gasped, 'and you've come into all that money . . . and your father, who insists you're only a tradesman not a gentleman . . . supposing he was right!'

'Well for God's sake don't tell a soul,' Archie begged. 'Otherwise we'd end up penniless after all. Come here, wench. I haven't been kissed for at least five minutes.'

When they paused for breath this time Jane said a little solemnly, 'I was wondering about the future. What it has in store for us?'

'I'm rather glad I didn't know what was coming the day war was declared. Don't think I'd have bothered to get up that morning if I had.'

'What do you hope for, Archie, seriously?'

'D'you mean — success? Things like that?' He gave it his usual careful thought. 'I'm not frightfully ambitious I'm afraid. If Ted and I make a go of the garage, that'll see me happy enough. Maybe we could open another one later on but if you wanted some dashing entrepreneur, you've picked the wrong chap, Jane.'

'What about Gainsford?'

'Sell it,' Archie said with feeling. 'Invest the proceeds in any young 'uns we may have by then, for their future.' Jane squeezed his hand. 'If I can make you happy, my sweetheart, that's what I want the most.' He hugged her gently. 'What about you?'

'It's strange, I used to dream of doing so many things. We all did. Now Luke's in a very humble practice and thoroughly committed. Ted? Well, Uncle always had ambitions for him to run the store with Matthew but Ted's far happier working with you. As for me, I'm blissfully content. I shall miss the office . . . I'll need to find something else to do. I don't fancy being idle, Archie. I've never sat at home twiddling my thumbs.'

'Feel like doing a bit more driving?'

'I love it here!'

'It's those idle moments you're worried about. I want to show you something.'

Back in the car, Archie unfolded a list of directions and a map. 'Don't peep,' he ordered, 'Keep your eyes on the road or you'll make me nervous. Turn left at the next crossroads.'

It was an old stone farmhouse set on a knoll with a small stream where the land flattened out into the dale. There were trees behind, planted years ago as protection against the prevailing wind. Outbuildings framed the yard and included an extensive stable block. In front of the house was a small garden edged by a low dry-stone wall with a green-painted gate.

Jane pulled up obediently and Archie got out. 'You can drive the car into the yard if you like.'

'Why, are we calling on someone?'

He was checking his watch. 'Not exactly. How far from Darlington, would you say?'

'Coming direct, about twenty minutes. Probably less.'

'Come on.'

The house was uninhabited. Jane wasn't entirely surprised when she saw Archie had a key. 'It's too large, my love.'

'Ssh. Just follow me round for a minute and don't say anything.'

It was empty but there was no forlorn air about the house. Jane followed Archie from room to room, admiring the thick walls and the wide vast views of moorland and dale. There was nothing grand; the ceilings were low but each room was a comfortable size apart from the huge kitchen.

Jane saw the way the house had developed, it had doubled in size when a second half had been added on yet the whole had a harmony that felt right. Archie led her across the yard, through each of the outbuildings. When he'd finished he asked, 'What's your first impression — forget about the size — just the general idea of the place?'

'It's perfect; snug and comfortable ... there must have been someone who liked flowers once — you can see how the garden's laid out. It's interesting the way it's like two halves of an apple, joined together. But there's simply too much of it Archie.'

'Do you think Katriona would like the kitchen?'

Jane shook her head. 'No, no. It's far too large for us and we couldn't ask Katriona to leave Uncle John. What we should be looking for is a small place to rent, like Ted and Dorothy have.'

'Which half would you prefer? I'd like the side that looks out on the hills.' Jane stared at him. 'Divide it up,' Archie said helpfully. 'Ted's bringing Dorothy out tomorrow if the two of you agree. Neither of us wants to go on renting places, sheer waste of money and you can't put your feet up on the mantelpiece. We'd be quite separate here, each have our own half. Separate entrances, etc,' Archie insisted, 'but we could be matey when we felt like it. I thought your uncle could live there.' He pointed to the stable block. 'Make a very desirable res. that would, once Mr Clough's put his thinking-cap on. Got the idea from the Emporium ... Wanted us to have a bit of space but have chums on hand as well. Ted needs his own workshop with all his ideas, he could use the old dairy for that.' Archie's voice

372

began to falter. 'Perhaps you'd rather be private in a little house in town?'

'Oh, Archie!' Jane's eyes were beginning to shine again.

'Kept thinking how it was for me at Gainsford, on my own. Frightened of the dark. No kid would be frightened here, especially if there were lots of 'em about.'

'Not too many,' she said sternly.

It was late when the child knocked at the surgery door and asked for Luke. He and Dr Mitchell were enjoying a rare quiet half hour when Rose interrupted. 'It's Mr Bates' son, Dr McKie. His father's bad again.'

'I'll get my coat.'

Dr Mitchell was thoughtful. 'About a quarter of one lung left?'

'About that,' Luke agreed. 'It's his spirit, and his devoted wife that's kept him going.' He took down the lead and fastened it to the dog's collar. The pup whined because he'd settled to sleep. 'Come on, got to comfort the children tonight, Patch.'

When he'd gone, Rose said quietly. 'The doctor promised Mr Bates he'd stay with him.'

Harold Mitchell knocked out his pipe. 'That's work for the minister in my opinion but if McKie chooses to do it, I shan't stop him.'

'The man's afraid,' said Rose. 'He's not a believer, I heard him tell Dr McKie. I think the doctor wants him to die with dignity, not to show fear in front of his wife; pride's about all Mr Bates has left.'

She couldn't sleep. Eventually Rose pulled open her curtains and stared at the darkened village. It was the time of night when everyone slept. Another hour before lamps were lit and the next shift emerged into the early dawn.

The Bates' house was too far away for her to see whether a light was on. On an impulse, Rose dressed, pulled on her coat and scarf and slipped outside.

The night wind was keen as she hurried along. She'd lived in the village for over four years, hating it at first. Her natural reticence had driven her deeper into the loneliness

373

of widowhood, that and the fact that none in Red'us'ra had known her husband so could not talk of him. She'd hugged sad memories and had closed her eyes to any small tentative gestures of friendship. Tonight, something inside Rose changed; she wanted to give back, be a part of a community again. It was still too soon to think Luke McKie might be part of the reason.

She went in the back way knowing the door would be unlocked. The Bates' two children were sitting quietly, cuddling the pup. He was alert but Rose bent and shushed him.

She unpacked the few bits of food she'd brought and wondered if she should venture upstairs. The door to the stairway opened. Mrs Bates stood with tears running down her face.

'Doctor told me I'd best come away . . . Fred won't give up while I'm there. It makes you that desperate to see him struggle.'

'Sit down. I'll make us some tea.'

The woman watched Rose go about the task quietly. 'Fred doesn't want me to know he's feared. I did but I couldn't say aught, it would only upset him. He likes to pretend he's still got his strength . . . that he'll mend . . .' The tears were flowing strongly now, 'He were that bonny once.'

'I know.'

In the room above, Luke held the hand that had so little strength left. 'Your wife's gone for a bit of rest, Mr Bates.'

The eyes had understanding in them. With a great effort, the miner asked, 'What's date, lad . . .' Luke thought tiredly.

'The third, I think. Wednesday, the third of May.'

The face against the pillows had a shadow of a grimace. 'Me birthday . . . I'm fifty-four . . .' He clutched at Luke with all his strength as death overcame him.

They trudged back silently. There were glimmers in some upstairs windows in the village. When they reached the surgery, Luke couldn't bring himself to enter. 'I'll leave you here, Mrs Galbraith. Just take the dog for a bit of a walk up the hill.'

'I'll come with you.'

The sky had lightened enough to see the stone path. They passed the small patches of allotments, the last of the pigeon lofts and went more slowly up the final rise. At the top, the wind whipped Luke's hair into his eyes. He looked up bitterly at the red-streaked sky. 'Each man that dies before his time is one more failure.'

Rose repeated Harold Mitchell's words. 'You're not infallible, Dr McKie.'

'Don't try and discourage me! It's not god-like qualities I'm after, all I want is to give men their chance at life. People like Frank deserve to see their children grow, it's not much to ask . . . and if I can't give them that, Rose . . .' She was silent, unable to console him. 'I know I've wasted time, alienating people . . . I must try harder and win back their respect.'

Rose remembered the tests, carried out without anyone else's knowledge and paid for by Luke. How long before the money or his idealism ran out?

'Will it take time to find a cure?' she asked a little timidly.

'Years probably before we know enough. There's work being done. Perhaps in my lifetime, maybe not.'

And what would his span be? Her husband's had been cut short at twenty-five, a year younger than Luke. Rose Galbraith pulled her scarf tight against the wind and offered a silent prayer that Luke would be given time to succeed.

'Go gently,' she told him. 'People will listen, eventually.'

He turned abruptly and caught her compassionate gaze. Before Rose could withdraw, he said awkwardly, 'I can't manage on my own.'

It was too raw and she automatically distanced herself. 'Shall we go back, doctor?' But the rebuff wasn't entirely convincing. Despite the wind Luke heard the hesitancy in her voice and was glad.

Jane walked up the overgrown path with trepidation. 'Hallo, Effie. May I come in?'

The unseen Mrs Macgregor called through a half-open door, 'Who is it, Effie? Tell them to go away, we're eating.'

Jane smiled nervously. 'It's my lunch hour, too, I can't stay long.'

'Mother's at home.'

It was a warning, not an explanation. Jane inclined her head. It had been too much to hope that Mrs Macgregor might be out. Anyway, hadn't she come expressly to deliver a message to the woman?

Effie led the way into what she referred to as 'the lounge'. Mrs Macgregor looked up from her leg of chicken. Grease shone on her chin.

'What's she doing here?'

'It's the invitation to my wedding. I wanted to deliver it personally.' Jane held out the envelope to Effie.

'What about the reception?' her mother cried shrilly, 'You're another who's marrying someone rich — I saw it in the paper. We're not respectable enough to go to the reception when McKies marry rich people!'

'Archie and I would be very pleased if you could come to both parts of the ceremony.' Jane's little joke was again addressed solely to Effie.

'My daughter hasn't anything smart enough to wear,' Mrs Macgregor sneered. 'Matthew's too stingy with his money.'

'How is Matthew?' Jane asked tactfully.

'All right. Away as usual.' Lack-lustre, Effie opened the envelope and took out the card.

'Mama will be very pleased to see him. We all will. Please come, Effie,' Jane said quietly. 'It'll make my day to have the family there.' There was a small emphasis on the word 'family'. Effie finished reading and stared, eyebrows raised. By way of answer, Jane nodded imperceptibly. She steeled herself to be unpleasant but Mrs Macgregor hadn't finished.

'No doubt your young man is taking you to live in some grand house with servants?'

'Who, Archie? Heavens, no. Dorothy and I are going to share an old farmhouse but it's certainly not grand. We spent last week at the auctions rooms, furnishing it. As soon as it's ready we'll invite everyone to see it —'

'Second-hand furniture! My daughter wouldn't put up with that.'

'Archie and Ted need their money for the garage,' Jane retorted, 'but it's an awfully nice old place. Sort of homey and lived-in. Perhaps you'll come one day?' She rose, and

376

delivered her bullet. 'I'm afraid we haven't included you among our guests, Mrs Macgregor, that is what I came to explain. The invitation is for Effie and Matthew. Ted, Uncle John and I felt that despite our best efforts, you've shown nothing but ill-will toward our family and Archie and I are determined to have a happy day.'

Effie looked at Jane helplessly as Mrs Macgregor stared, open-mouthed. If only there were a way to whisk Effie out of reach of the inevitable storm. Instead Jane said briskly, 'I'm afraid I have to get back,' and felt a coward for doing so. 'Please give my love to Matthew,' she added.

The spiteful whisper followed her into the hall. 'Marrying someone maimed!'

'Hire a charabanc . . .'

'To take all those children who've come top of their class in any subject for a day out at Redcar and Saltburn,' Luke explained again.

'Yes, I heard you the first time, but why?' Dr Mitchell sat back in his chair. 'Who shall pay for it?'

'I shall. I have a cousin who can arrange it. I shall demand preferential rates, naturally.'

'That doesn't answer my original question.'

'If the children of Red'us'ra grasp the fact that there will be rewards for academic achievement, it may encourage them to try harder. The schoolmaster agrees.'

Harold Mitchell looked at him narrowly. 'Are you about to upset another apple-cart?'

'Oh, no. I've learned my lesson,' Luke said coolly, 'I've invited Perkins to bid the expedition farewell — for the benefit of a newspaper photographer. He accepted and no doubt he'll take the credit for the whole idea. Next year, I shall invite him to perform the same ceremony again on condition the company contributes to the costs. By then he won't be able to refuse but on this first occasion I shall pay.'

'And the idea behind your scheme, doctor?'

Luke looked at Rose steadily. 'I'm sure you've already worked that one out, Mrs Galbraith. It's a principle I came across in Scotland. It is that if you convince children of the value of education by opening up new horizons, they

377

will eventually want to escape the drudgery of their present existence.'

Harold Mitchell began to smile. 'And you've persuaded Perkins . . . ?'

'To give the whole idea his blessing.'

'Whatever next!'

'A clinic,' Luke told him calmly. 'But that will take longer, I fear. No matter. I have the time and gradually I'm learning to be patient.' He no longer looked at Harold Mitchell but at Rose as she began to clear the dishes. Luke shook the crumbs from the table-cloth and folded it. 'I shall be seeing Ted on Saturday at my cousin's wedding . . . would you care to accompany me, Mrs Galbraith? I'm sure there are many details about the excursion I shall overlook. And it promises to be a very enjoyable occasion . . .'

His transparent ploy annoyed her. 'No thank you.' The door snapped shut.

'Patience . . .' Dr Mitchell reminded him blandly. 'And there is another thing you should learn, Dr McKie. It's that women have to be led gently to the water.' Seeing Luke's embarrassment, his attitude softened. 'Rose was very much in love with Richard . . . Go easy. I know she thinks highly of what you've achieved so far in Red'us'ra. She's talked of it privately. In her reserved way, Rose is equally anxious to do what she can. You'll find you have much in common, given time. But don't be in too much of a rush, my boy. The ghosts are with us yet.'

'Oh, bother!' Dorothy said loudly and Dr Cullen was immediately alert.

'What is it?'

'Luke's come on his own.'

'Why shouldn't he? Are you all right?'

Dorothy saw the look on his face. 'Don't worry, it's not the heir. Although I will admit he is jiggling about with all this excitement. Luke should have a female acquaintance by now and when I helped Jane with the invitations, I wrote "plus friend". He can't go on being a monk, it's not healthy.'

'Mrs Ted —'

'I know! Don't be impatient and *don't* interfere,' Dorothy sighed then brightened immediately, 'I can't wait to see mama-in-law's hat. She wouldn't let me sneak the tiniest peep — absolutely maddening!'

'Here come Katriona and Mrs Beal . . . beaming from ear to ear. I didn't realize St Cuthbert's would be so full today. Who are that jolly-looking pair?'

'Mr Bolt and Mr Wilkinson. Jane used to work for them. Oh, lord, Mrs Macgregor's defied the ban!' Dorothy exclaimed, 'and look at the way she's pushing the ushers aside, dragging Effie behind her . . . She's not going to plonk herself on the front pew!'

'She's been shown very firmly into the one behind. And Matthew's jammed himself in between her and the aisle, thank goodness. Let's hope she's not drunk.' William Cullen shook his head.

'If she gate-crashes the reception, she will be. Ooh, Dr Cullen — Oh, my!' But again he relaxed when he saw where Dorothy stared. Charlotte McKie, mother of the bride, bowing to right and left and leaning on Ted's arm, made her way up the nave. Ted grinned at the effect she was having on the congregation. As he passed by Dorothy, he winked. She sighed again.

'Absolutely — *sensational.*'

Dr Cullen recognized what he thought of as feathers and felt. 'Rather dashing . . . like a chevalier. Hope it doesn't eclipse Jane.'

'No.' Dorothy was emphatic, 'Nothing could do that. I've seen her. She's sparkling like the sun, moon and stars, all put together.'

'D'you know, my dear, I once thought of asking Mrs Davie to marry me . . .'

Dorothy stared, round-eyed and instantly sentimental. 'Oh, Dr Cullen, I do wish you had! What stopped you?'

'The fear that she might accept.'

Ahead of them, Ted joined an extremely pale-looking Archie.

'Action stations, chum; she's on her way, positively ablaze with happiness.' The familiar chords began and they all rose.

Jane was simply dressed and the mass of hair was bound in flowers that reflected the pink in her cheeks. It was the sheer joy that flowed from her that none would ever forget. Her dark eyes shone as she saw Archie, waiting so eagerly to claim her; there was no shyness in his bride but an honest loving heart open for all to see. 'I've come home,' Jane thought, 'this man is mine and I am his. Please dear God, let me make him happy!'

CHAPTER TWENTY-FIVE

Son and Heir

'— name this child . . .' Standing between Luke and Archie, Jane listened to Dorothy's choice.

'Adelaid Charlotte,' Luke announced. The minister dipped his fingers and made the sign of the cross.

'Adelaide . . . Charlotte . . . I baptize thee . . .'

Charlotte had only been slightly disappointed when she was told. Ted explained apologetically, 'I once mentioned how sad great-aunt had been that there was no-one to carry her name forward, so Dorothy decided to make amends.'

'I understand, dear. I think I'm rather pleased. I know Jane wants to use "Mary" when her turn comes. It's fitting that it should be so.' Charlotte was adjusting her perspective to that of being unique.

It was the day before the christening; they were in the huge farmhouse kitchen, watching Dorothy and Jane taking turns rocking the perambulator outside as they enjoyed the late sunshine. Katriona regarded the idyllic scene sardonically.

'I'll say one thing, Ted. It's a grand pair of names for a son and heir.'

'Next time round,' he promised. 'If I can stand the strain. How much longer?' Katriona looked at the clock.

'About fifteen minutes provided the charabanc doesn't break down.'

'What, with Thomas Allen in charge? Nonsense.'

'Is he coming to live here, have you and Archie decided?' Charlotte asked.

'Over there . . .' Ted nodded at the last of the outbuildings. 'Mr Clough starts work next week. It's a grand little family: two kids plus Mrs Allen and Thomas's mother. They should just about fit in. Little Isobel will be company for Addie. And when the time comes, Thomas and I plan to build cars to our own design in the old dairy. We can try 'em out in the paddock.'

John wandered in from the main road. 'No sign of them yet. D'you think it'll rain?'

'If it does, we move the tables in here out of the yard and the kids can let off steam in the barn.'

'If that happens, I shall go to the sitting room, dear.' Becoming a grandmother had altered Charlotte's behaviour. Her hat for the christening had been noticeably more subdued than the one worn at Jane's wedding three months earlier; it had not, however, changed her views on children. 'Dorothy will probably need a refuge, too.'

'Oh, she likes kiddies, the more the merrier,' Ted began tactlessly. 'Hallo? That's not them ... sounds more like a car.' He strode out into the yard and they heard him say, 'Oh, lord! Fancy that lot deciding to come today of all days?'

They heard Mrs Macgregor's grating cry, 'Jane said we were welcome any time.'

'Delighted to see you all,' Ted said blandly. 'How are you, Effie?'

She moved swiftly to where he stood, 'I'm awfully sorry but *she* insisted on being included. We tried to shake her off, Matthew especially, but you know how difficult it can be. Mother was determined to see where Jane and Dorothy lived.'

'Actually, me dear, I think your inquisitive parent is going to get more than she bargained for today,' Ted chuckled. 'Luke's due any moment with one or two young friends. While we're waiting for him, come and meet the latest member of the family.'

Jane ran across the grass. 'Effie, I'm so glad to see you.'

Dorothy lifted the baby out of the pram. 'Here, do take her. She adores being cuddled.'

'Like her mama,' Archie teased.

382

Mrs Macgregor was still extricating herself from Matthew's car when a horn sounded. The charabanc swept into the yard and twenty Red'us'ra children, in a frenzy after their first day at the seaside, exploded out of it in one great turbulent wave.

'Not a tot, Uncle. Fill it up to the brim and give Archie the same, he's still shaking.'

'Weren't they heavenly,' Dorothy chirped, 'And so gentle with the baby — she was horribly spoiled this afternoon.'

'The one who gets my sympathy is Patch,' Archie said. 'Twenty little beggars all wanting to play with him and feed him biscuits. No wonder he was hiding under the stairs — I'd have had a nervous breakdown.'

'How often is Dr Luke planning to bring charabancs here?' Katriona asked grimly, 'for I shall be joining the wee dog myself next time.'

'No you won't, Kat,' Ted grinned. 'You wouldn't have wanted to miss Mrs Macgregor's reaction for the world. I thought she was going to have a fit. Those kids had her twigged the minute they spotted her.'

'The one that imitated her accent,' Jane began to giggle.

'And her walk in those high heels.'

'It was most unfortunate,' Charlotte attempted to be firm then gave way and laughed helplessly, 'the shock on that woman's face when she realized what they were up to. . . !'

They were recovering and wiping their eyes when Dorothy said happily, 'We'll be able to meet Luke's new lady-friend properly tomorrow. I invited her to the christening. She was a bit reluctant but I persuaded her.'

'Who?' asked John, astonished.

'Mrs Galbraith who was helping Luke with the children. He's absolutely head over heels you know.'

John stared at her in amazement. 'How on earth d'you know that?'

'Instinct,' Dorothy said firmly, 'and I'll bet you two shillings.'

In her room overlooking the moor, Rose Galbraith stared unseeing at the view. Dorothy McKie had coaxed so charmingly but Rose was afraid. To attend the christening meant committing herself; she wasn't yet ready for that. On the ride home, Luke hadn't spoken of it; he was learning when to hold his tongue.

There were familiar routine sounds below as patients slipped in and out of the surgery entrance, bidding Dr Mitchell good night. In a moment or two, she would have to go down and make supper. That was when she'd give Luke her decision, whether to accompany him, or stay here in safety as her uncle's housekeeper.

Rose stood very still, silhouetted against the curtain. As Luke walked up the path, having delivered the last of the children he saw her, cameo-like, against the darkness behind. Daily, the longing in him grew, to take this beautiful, frozen woman and warm her back to life, yet he did nothing. It had to be her decision.

'Ah ... steak and kidney.' Dr Mitchell helped himself lavishly to potatoes. 'How was the outing? I trust you returned with approximately the same number of children?' He looked from one to the other but it was Rose who spoke.

'It went very well ... and I've had another invitation, Uncle. I'd like to accept if you can manage without me tomorrow.'

In church John stood beside Charlotte and listened to the words of the blessing. In front of him the group round the font waited with bowed heads, Ted's bright red hair towering above the rest.

Dorothy nursed the first of the next generation, Addie, whose fair tufts looked as if they'd rival her mother's own eventually. Jane and Archie were close enough to hold hands and Luke had moved, to be nearer Rose Galbraith. His dark head was on a level with her thick coronet of plaits.

I wonder, thought John.

Behind him, he heard Cullen's rumble, 'It's been a good year, John. Best so far, I'd say.'

Charlotte whispered over her shoulder. 'There's more to come.'

HB 11 U